The Saga of the Volsungs
and other stories

Viking Legendary Sagas Vol. I

Translated by Gavin Chappell

Thor's Stone Press

Translation and introductions copyright © 2013, 2014
Gavin Chappell.

Previous versions of these sagas have been published
separately as Kindle e-books.

ISBN: 150017579X
ISBN-13: 978-1500175795

CONTENTS

INTRODUCTION

The legendary sagas, or *Fornaldarsögur*, are a branch of medieval Icelandic literature, a subgenre of the sagas themselves, lengthy narratives that bear a superficial similarity to modern novels; the legendary sagas concern themselves with legendary times predating the settlement on Iceland in the tenth century AD. While fantastic episodes are not unknown in sagas outside this bracket, such as *Grettis Saga*, and they abound in the Sagas of the Knights, (retellings of continental chivalric romances), the legendary sagas are the closest to the pagan world of Norse mythology, and also include parallels with poems such as the Old English *Beowulf* and the Middle High German *Nibelungenlied*. Although the term *Fornaldarsögur* was coined by Carl Christian Rafn in the nineteenth century, the distinction between realistic stories and 'lying sagas' was already drawn in medieval times, famously by the Norwegian king Sverri in *King Sverri's Saga*, where the eponymous king comments on Hrölfr of Skälmarnes' story of Hröngvidr the Viking and Oläfr Lidsmanna King and the howe-breaking of Thräinn the Berserk, all references to the saga of Hrömundr Gripsson, which will be included in a later volume of Viking Legendary Sagas.

This saga, and the immense Latin historical/legendary work of Saxo Grammaticus, *Gesta Danorum (History of the Danes)*, contain evidence that many of the sagas collected by Árni Magnússon (13 November 1663 – 7 January

1730) existed in oral forms or in manuscripts that did not survive into modern times. As we have them, however, most of the sagas contained in this volume date from the fourteenth or fifteenth century. For this reason, and due to aesthetic considerations, it was traditional for scholars to dismiss the *Fornaldarsögur* as late and inferior works in comparison with the great literature of the Sagas of the Icelanders, much of which dates to the twelfth and thirteenth centuries.

In more recent times, however, much interest has been taken in the Viking Legendary Sagas, due to their links with the pagan and mythological past. Works such as *The Saga of the Volsungs* and *The Saga or Hervor and Heidrek* (both contained in this volume) can be shown to have links with earlier Germanic poetry, while *The Saga of Hrolf Kraki and His Champions* shares many characters with Beowulf. Other sagas, containing mighty heroes and monstrous villains, excitement and adventure, have failed to excite academics, but at various points from the seventeenth century have proved the most popular, inspiring everyone from Wagner to George Lucas. It would be fair to say that the modern genre of fantasy literature, from the days of William Morris, JRR Tolkien and Poul Anderson to the present day, owes more than a little to these stories of warriors and wizardry.

This book and the following two volumes (in production at the time of writing) are based on the seminal work of Carl Christian Rafn (January 16, 1795 – October 20, 1864), who first collected them in the same order and published them in 1829-30 under the name *Fornaldarsögur Norðurlanda*, 'ancient sagas of the Northlands'.

THE SAGA OF THE VOLSUNGS

The Saga of the Volsungs was written in thirteenth century Iceland, part of a vast collection of prose stories known as the sagas. In itself, it is the product of hundreds of years of oral storytelling, and the same stories appear in the poems of the *Elder Edda*, another work of medieval Iceland, and also in the medieval Austrian epic poem, the Nibelungenlied, although here the central character is known as Sifrid rather than Sigurd. Characters in the saga are also alluded to in the Old English poem Beowulf and they appear in Viking Age sculpture both from Scandinavia itself and also the British Isles.

The saga tells the story of a legendary family known as the Volsungs, descended from the Norse god Odin, covering several generations, up until Sigurd, who slew Fafnir the Dragon and took the creature's cursed treasure, resulting not only in his own death but that of everyone to possess it after him.

It is believed by historians that some events and characters in the saga originate in events of the fifth century AD, near the beginning of which the Burgundian kingdom centred on Worms was destroyed by Hunnish attackers. The character of Gunnar seems to be based on the historical Burgundian king Gundicarius, while Atli is Attila the Hun himself. Other characters may also have historical counterparts; Jormunrek, who appears briefly at the end, is partly based on the fourth century AD Gothic king Ermanaric, although in other stories he owes more to Odoacer, who ruled fifth century Italy after the abdication of the last Western Roman Emperor, Romulus Augustulus. It has been suggested that Sigurd and Brynhild recall the Frankish king Sigebert and his Visigothic wife Brunnhilda. Other theories link Sigurd and the Rhinegold with the first century AD Germanic warrior Arminius, who defeated the Romans at the Battle of the Teutoberger Wald. Other elements of the story, however, belong entirely to the realms of mythology and legend: the frequent appearances of the Norse god Odin in his guise as a one-eyed old man, and the presence of dwarfs, werewolves, witches and dragons.

The story, in its various versions, became popular once more in the nineteenth century. It has inspired, directly or indirectly, writers such as William Morris and JRR Tolkien, filmmakers Fritz Lang and George Lucas, and composers and musicians from Richard Wagner, (whose *Ring Cycle* is the best known modern adaptation of the story), to Zodiac Mindwarp and the Love Reaction.

Chapter One

Here we begin by speaking of a man named Sigi who was called the son of Odin. A second man is named in the story, called Skadi. He was sturdy and strong, but Sigi was more important and of nobler blood as men considered it at that time. Skadi had a slave who now enters the story. He was called Bredi. He knew well the work that he did. In skill and also in achievements, he was held to be as good as men thought more worthy, or better than some.

It is said that one time Sigi went hunting, and with him went the slave, and they hunted throughout the day up until the evening. But when they compared their catch, they saw that Bredi had caught many more animals than Sigi, and Sigi liked this very little and said that he was surprised that a slave shall outdo him in hunting. He ran at him and killed him, and then he buried his corpse in a snowdrift. He went home in the evening and said that Bredi had ridden away from him into the wood, - 'and he was soon out of my sight, and I know nothing more of him.' Skadi doubted Sigi's story and thought that it was a lie and that Sigi had killed the slave, so he sent men to look for Bredi, and the end of their searching was that they found him in the snowdrift, and Skadi said that men should call such drifts Bredi's Drift from now on, and people did so, and afterwards everyone used that name for any snowdrift as big. Then it was clear that Sigi had killed the slave and murdered him. Then they call him a wolf in holy places[1], and now he could not stay at home with his father. Then Odin accompanied him from the country, such a long way that it was incredible, and he did not rest until he came to some ships. Then

---

[1] An outlaw.

Sigi went raiding with men his father gave him before they parted, and he was successful in his warfaring. It came about that at last he won land and a kingdom. And then he married a noble woman, and he was a mighty and great king, and ruled Hunland, and was the greatest of warriors. He had a son by his wife, whose name was Rerir. Rerir grew up with his father and soon became tall and handsome.

Chapter Two

Sigi lived into his old age. He had many who envied him, so that at last those who he believed the most trustworthy turned against him, his wife's brothers. They attacked him when he least expected and he had few men with him, and they succeeded, and Sigi fell in that encounter, with all his retinue. His son, Rerir, was not in this fight, and he got a great gang of friends and noblemen, and seized both land and kingdom that had been ruled by his father Sigi. And when he thought the feet stood firm under him in his rule, he remembered his feud with his mother's brothers who killed his father, and the king now collected a large army and went against the brothers, and it seemed that what they had done before meant he could little trust their kinship, and so he followed this reasoning, until he had killed all of his father's killers, though it was dreadful by all accounts. Then he acquired lands and state and property. He was mightier than his father.

Rerir got great booty, and a wife who he thought suited him, and they were together very long as well, but they had no heir and no child. They both thought that bad and they prayed to the gods with great fervour that they might have a child. It is said that Frigg heard their prayers and she told Odin what they asked. He was not without resources and he called a wish-maiden, the daughter of Hrimnir the giant, and put in her hand an apple and asked her to take it to the king. She took the apple, drew on her crow-cloak and flew till she came to where the king was sitting on a mound. She dropped the apple on the king's knees. He took this apple and thought he knew that it would help. He went home from the cairn, to his men, and came to the queen, and she ate that apple.

It is said that the queen soon found out that she was with child, but for a long time she could not give birth. Then it came that Rerir should go to the wars, as is the custom of kings to keep peace in their own country. In this journey it came to pass that Rerir took sick and died, intending to return to Odin, which seemed desirable to many at that time. It stayed the same in the case of the Queen's illness, that she might not give birth to her child, and this went on for six winters, she remained sick. Then she learnt that she would not live long, and she asked that they would cut the child from her, and so it was done as she asked. It was a boy, and he was big when he was born, which was to be expected. It is said that the boy kissed his mother before she died. A name was given him and he was called Volsung. He was king of Hunland after his father. From early on he was big and strong and full of courage in manly activities. He became the greatest warrior and achieved victory in every battle which he had when raiding. Then when he was quite mature in age, Hrimnir sent him Ljod, his daughter, who took the apple to Rerir, Volsung's father, as the story said earlier. Then he was married to her, and they were together a long time as well, and there was great love between them. They had ten sons and one daughter.

Their oldest son was named Sigmund; Signy was their daughter. These two were twins, and they were in every way chief of all King Volsung's children, and mighty, as were all his children, which has been remembered for a long time and it has been highly spoken, how the Volsungs were powerful, overbearing men and surpassed most people, as is told in the sagas, both in cunning and prowess and all great deeds. It is said that King Volsung built a fine hall in such a manner that an oak stood high in the hall, and the boughs of the tree stood out over the roof with beautiful blossoms, but the trunk was down in the hall, and they called it Bairnstock.

Chapter Three

Siggeir was another king. He ruled Gautland. He was a mighty king and had a great retinue. He went to King Volsung and asked for Signy as his wife. The king responded well to this request, and so did his sons. She herself was unwilling to do this, but she asked her father to make the decision as he did in other things concerning her. The king accepted advice to marry her off, and she was betrothed to King Siggeir. The arrangements for the wedding feast were that King Siggeir was to come to King Volsung and the king prepared the feast to his best ability. When this feast was ready, the people who King Volsung had invited came on the named day and also King Siggeir, who had many honourable men with him. It is said that large fires were lit along the whole length of the hall, and the tree stood in the middle of the hall, as was mentioned earlier.

It is said that when the people were sitting by the fires in the evening, a man came into the hall. He had never been seen before by anyone present. He wore a spotted cloak, was barefoot and had linen breeches joined up tight to his legs. He wore a hood on his head and held a sword in his hand as he went to the Bairnstock. He was very big and seemed to be old and he was one-eyed. He brandished the sword, and plunged it into the trunk so that it sank in up to the hilt. No one greeted this man. Then he began speaking and said, 'He who pulls this sword from the tree shall receive it from me as a gift, and he shall prove to himself that he never bore a better sword in his hand than this.' After that the old man went out of the hall, and no one knew who he was or where he went. Then they stood up and no one wanted to be last to pull out the sword. They thought that he who was the first to reach it would have the best of it. Then they went to do this with the noblest men first, followed by the rest, one after the other. No one managed to pull it out, because there was no way they could budge it when they tugged at it. Then Sigmund, son of King Volsung, came and took the sword and pulled it out of the trunk, and it came loose before him. This weapon seemed so good to everyone that no one thought he had ever seen such a good sword, and Siggeir offered three times its weight in gold for it. Sigmund said, 'You could have taken this sword from where it was no less than I, if it had been your honour to do so, but you shall never have it now that it is in my hand, even if you offer for it all the gold that you have.' King Siggeir was angry at these words, and thought this reply scornful. But because he was a wary, double-dealing man, he acted as if he was not perturbed by this matter, but that same night he considered how he could pay Sigmund back, which happened later.

Chapter Four

It is said that Siggeir went to bed with Signy that night. The next day the weather was fine. King

Siggeir said that he would go home and not wait for the wind to rise or the sea to become impassable. It is not said that King Volsung or his sons discouraged him, because they saw that he would not settle for anything but to leave the feast. Then Signy said to her father: 'I do not wish to go away with Siggeir, and nor does my heart smile at him, and I know from my foresight and from our kin-fetch [2] that this wedding will cause us great evil, if it is not quickly undone.' 'Do not say this, daughter,' he said, 'because it will be a great shame for both him and us to break this promise without reason, and we could not trust him or his friendship if the wedding were broken off, and he would pay us back with evil, however he could, and the only honourable course is for us to honour our side of the bargain.' Then King Siggeir prepared to return home. And before they went from the feast, he asked King Volsung to visit him in Gautland in three months' time and bring all of his sons with him and as large a following with him as he wanted, and was fitting for his honour. King Siggeir wanted to pay them back for the shortcomings of the feast, and he would not remain more than one night, but it was not the custom of people to act thus. King Volsung promised to come on the established day. Then the in-laws parted, and King Siggeir went home with his wife.

Chapter Five

Then the story tells that King Volsung and his sons left at the appointed time for Gautland at the request of King Siggeir, and sailed away in three ships all well-appointed, had a good voyage and brought their ships to Gautland when it was late in the evening. On that same evening Signy, daughter

___

[2] The guardian spirit of the Volsung people.

of King Volsung, came and called her father and her brothers aside, and told them what King Siggeir intended, that he had gathered an invincible army - 'and means to betray you. Now I ask you,' she said, 'that you go back to your country and get as many men as you can and then come here and avenge yourselves, and do not go to your defeat, since you will surely fall to his deceptions if you do not take advantage of this trick, which I advise you. ' Then King Volsung said: 'All the nations speak of the word that I spoke unborn, the oath I made that I would neither flee fire nor iron, and I have yet to do so, and shall I alter that in old age? Nor shall the maidens mock my sons at play, saying that they were afraid of death, for a man died only once and no one can escape death at the time allotted. It is my advice that we do not flee, and rather that we do the work of our hands as is manliest. I have fought a hundred times, and I have sometimes had more men, sometimes fewer, but I have always had victory, and it shall not be heard that I fled or asked for peace.'

Then Signy wept sorely for him and asked if she might not return to King Siggeir. King Volsung said, 'You shall surely go home to your husband and remain with him, however it goes with us.' Then Signy went home, but they stayed there that night. And in the morning, as soon as it was day, King Volsung told all his men to rise and go ashore and prepare to fight. They went ashore fully armed, and they did not have to wait long before King Siggeir came there with all his army, and there was the hardest battle between them, and the King encouraged his men to fight the hardest, and it is said that King Volsung and his sons went through King Siggeir's men eight times that day and hewed on either hand. But when they would do so again,

King Volsung fell in the midst of battle and his entire force with him except his ten sons, because the odds against them were greater than they could withstand. Then his sons were taken and put in chains and led away.

Signy heard that her father had been killed, and her brothers had been taken and sentenced to death. Then she took King Siggeir aside. Signy said: 'I ask that you do not kill my brothers quickly but let them be put in the stocks, and the saying comes to me: sweet to the eye while seen, and so I ask longer life for them no more, because I think that I will not get my wish.' Then Siggeir answered. 'Surely you are mad and witless when you ask for more evil for your brothers than they are given, but I shall grant you this, for it seems better to me that they endure worse suffering and have more pain before death.'

Then he let it be so done as she asked, and he took a great beam and fitted it on the feet of the ten brothers somewhere in the woods, and they sat there all day until night. But at midnight as they sat in the stocks, a she-wolf came out of the forest. She was both strong and evil-looking. The first thing she did was to bite one of them to death. Then she ate him whole. After that, she went away. But in the morning Signy sent a man whom she believed trustworthy to her brothers, to see how matters stood. When he came back, he said that one of them was dead. She felt sorely that they should all go, yet she could not aid them.

It is soon told. Nine nights the same she-wolf came at midnight and bit one of them to death, until everyone was dead, except Sigmund. And now, before the tenth night came, Signy sent her trusted servant to Sigmund, her brother, and gave him honey, and said that he must smear it on Sigmund's face and put some in his mouth. Then he went to Sigmund, and did as she had said and went home. The night after it was the same, the she-wolf came as was her habit, and she meant to bite him to death as she had done his brothers. But now she sniffed the scent of him who was honey-smeared and she licked his face with her tongue and then thrust her tongue into his mouth. He was not afraid and he bit the she-wolf's tongue. She started back and pulled herself away hard and drove her feet against the stocks so that she broke everything apart, but he held on so tight that the tongue tore out of the she-wolf's mouth, and that was her death. But it is said by some that the same she-wolf was King Siggeir's mother, and she turned herself into this likeness by trollcraft and sorcery.

Chapter Six

Sigmund was set free because the stocks were broken, and then he went to live in the forest. Signy still sent to know how matters were, whether or not Sigmund lived. When her men arrived, he explained the entire incident and how it had gone with him and the she-wolf. They went home and told Signy what had befallen. Then she went there and met with her brother, and they decided that he should make an earth-house in the woods, and so it went on for a while with Signy hiding him, and providing him with what he needed. But King Siggeir thought that all the Volsungs were dead.

King Siggeir had two sons by his wife, and it is said that when the eldest was ten years old, Signy sent him to Sigmund that he should give his help, if Sigmund wanted to avenge his father. The boy went to the forest, and late in the evening he came to

Sigmund's earth-house. Sigmund welcomed him fittingly, and said that he could make the bread, 'but I will gather firewood,' - and put in his hand a flour bag, but he went himself to seek firewood, and when he came back, the child had done nothing about bread making. Sigmund asked if the bread was ready. He said: 'I dared not take the flour bag, because there was something alive in the flour.' Sigmund thought that this boy would not do well at that he wanted him to do. When the siblings met, Sigmund said that he was no closer to the aid of a man although the boy was with him. Signy said: 'Take him and kill him. Why should he live longer?' And so he did.

Then the winter drew on. And a year later, Signy sent her younger son to meet Sigmund, and to make a long story short, things went as they had done before, and he killed the boy at the grim counsel of Signy.

Chapter Seven

It is said that once upon a time, when Signy sat in her chamber, there came to her a witch very skilled in magic. Signy spoke to her: 'I would like to do this,' she said, 'We should exchange shapes.' So the witch woman said, 'You shall decide.' And now she did it through her trickery, they changed appearances, and the witch woman settled in Signy's place by her advice and went to bed with the king in the evening, and he did not realise that it was not Signy beside him. Then the tale says of Signy that she went to the earth-house of her brother, and begged that he provide a room for the night, 'because I have got lost in the woods out there, and I do not know where I am going.' He said that she should stay there, and he would not refuse her protection, one woman, and he knew that she would not pay him back so badly as to reveal where he was. Then she went to his home, and sat down to eat. He looked often at her, who seemed a beautiful and comely woman. But when they were full, he said to her that he wanted them to share a bed for the night, and she did not refuse, and he lay with her for three nights. After that, she went home and found the witch woman and asked that they swap back appearances, and so she did.

And as time went by, Signy had a child. The boy was called Sinfjotli. When he grew up, he was tall and strong and handsome, and very similar in appearance to Volsung, and he was not even ten years old before she sent him to Sigmund's earth-house. She had tested the previous sons before she sent them to Sigmund by sewing gloves on their hands through flesh and skin. They endured this poorly and cried about it. And she did this to Sinfjotli. He did not react. She flayed off the robe so that the skin came off with the sleeves. She said the pain would be enough for him. He said: 'Volsung would think this hurt little.' And now the boy came to Sigmund. Sigmund asked him to knead flour, but he would get them firewood, and he handed him a bag. Then he went to the wood. When he came back, he had finished his baking. Sigmund asked if he had found anything in the flour. 'It is my thought,' he said, 'that there was something alive in the flour when I first began to knead, but I have kneaded it all together.' Sigmund laughed and said, 'You will not eat this bread this evening, for you have kneaded in with it the most venomous serpent.' Sigmund was so mighty a man that he could eat poison so that it did not harm him, but although Sinfjotli could stand poison on his skin, he might not

13

eat it or drink it.

Chapter Eight

It is now said that Sinfjotli seemed too young to Sigmund to take revenge with him, and that he needed practice with hardship, so then they went around the woods in summer and killed people for gold. Sigmund thought he was very akin to the Volsungs, although he believed that he was the son of King Siggeir, and that he had his father's evil but the Volsungs' daring, and he could not be much of a relative (to Siggeir) because he often reminded Sigmund of his sorrows and frequently egged him on to kill Siggeir the king. Then one time when they went to the wood to gain gold, they found a house and two people with thick gold rings sleeping in it. They had been spellbound skinchangers, because wolf-coats hung up over them in the house. Each tenth day they could get out of the skins. They were kings' sons. Sigmund and Sinfjotli put on skins and could not get out of they, and they followed the nature which had been there before, and howled like wolves. They both understood their howling.

Then they lay out in the forest, and each went their own way. They made a pact with each other that they should not stop if seven men were against them, but if they met more he who was first be set upon should give a wolf howl. 'Let us part not from this,' said Sigmund, 'because you are young and daring. They will think it good to hunt you.' Then they went their own ways. And when they were apart, Sigmund found seven men and gave a wolf howl. And when Sinfjotli heard this, he went there and killed everyone. They parted again. And when Sinfjotli had not long gone through the forest, he found eleven men, and he fought against them, and it went so that he killed them all. He was weary, and badly wounded, and he went under an oak to rest there. He waited long for Sigmund, and then both were together for a while. He said to Sigmund, 'You call for help to slay seven men, and I am a child in age beside you, and I did not ask for your help killing eleven men.' Sigmund ran at him so hard that he staggered and fell. Sigmund bit his throat. On that day they could not get out of their wolf-coats. Sigmund then laid him on his back and took him home to the hall, and he sat with him, and said that the trolls could take the wolf-coats. On one day Sigmund saw two weasels. One bit the other in the throat, and ran to the forest and took a leaf and put it on the wound, and the weasel sprang up unwounded. Sigmund went out and saw a raven flying with a blade of the herb and it gave it to him. He put it on Sinfjotli's wound, and he sprang up whole, as if he had never been wounded. After that they went to the earth-house and stayed there until they could get out of the wolf-coats. Then they took them and burned them and prayed that they should be no further harm. And in that disguise they did many famous deeds in the kingdom of King Siggeir. And when Sinfjotli was full grown, Sigmund thought he had tried him fully.

Little time passed before Sigmund decided to seek his revenge, if it was possible. And then they went away from the earth-house one day and came to Siggeir's royal town late in the evening and then went into the porch of the hall, inside which were tuns of ale, and they hide there. The queen learnt where they were, and wanted to see them. And when they met, they took counsel, and they sought to avenge their father that night. Signy and the king had two children of young age. They played with gold and slid it across the floor of the hall, rushing along. And one gold ring rolled farther out of the house, to where Sigmund was, but the boy ran out looking for the ring. Then he saw where two tall grim-looking men sitting wearing white helmets and mailcoats. Then he ran into the hall for his father and told him what he had seen. Then the king suspected that there would be treachery against him. Signy heard what they said. She stood up, took both children and went out of the hall and said to Sigmund and Sinfjotli that they should know that they had betrayed them, - 'and I advise you both to kill them.' Sigmund said, 'I will not kill your children, even if they have betrayed me.' But Sinfjotli did not hold back and drew his sword and slew the two children and flung their bodies into the hall to King Siggeir. The king stood up and called on men to take the men who had hidden in the porch all evening. Then the men run outside and would handle them, but they defended themselves well and valiantly, and he who was closest to them long remembered the worst of it. And at last they were overborne by men and taken prisoner, then bound and put in chains and they sat there all that night.

Then the king pondered to himself the slowest death he could give them. And when morning came, the king had made a large barrow of stones and turf. But when the barrow was built, he put a flat stone in the middle of the mound, so that one side of it pointed up, the other down. It was so great that it split the barrow in two so that none could pass it. Then he told them to take Sigmund and Sinfjotli into the barrow and put them on either side of the stone, since it seemed to him that it would be worse that both could hear each other but could not go to the other. And when they were covering the mound with turves, Signy came and she carried straw in her arms, and she threw it into the barrow to Sinfjotli and told the slaves not to speak of this to the king. They agreed, and then closed the barrow. And when night fell, Sinfjotli said to Sigmund, 'I do not think we will lack food for a while. The queen threw bacon into the barrow and wrapped the outside around with straw.' And again he took hold of the meat and found that in it was thrust the sword of Sigmund, and because it was dark in the barrow he recognised it by its hilt, and told Sigmund. They both celebrate. Then Sinfjotli drove the sword point into the stone, and pulled it hard. The sword bit into the stone. Sigmund took the sword and now they sawed the stone between them, and did not stop until it was done, as is sung:

> '*Sinfjotli sawed,*
>
> *And Sigmund sawed,*
>
> *In two with strength*
>
> *The stone was cut.*'

And then they were both loose in the barrow and they cut through stones and iron, and so got out of the barrow. Then they went back to the hall. All men were sleeping. They carried wood to the hall and set fire to it, but those who were inside woke up with the smoke, and realised that the hall was alight. The king asked who had lit this fire. 'Here I am with my sister's son,' said Sigmund, 'and we think that this lets you know that not all the Volsungs are dead.' He asked his sister to go out and receive good things and great honour from him, and reparation for her grief. She said: 'Now you know whether I have remembered King Siggeir killing King Volsung. I

17

killed our children, who I felt worthless to avenge him, and I went into the woods to you in a witch's shape, and Sinfjotli is our son. So he is keen; he is the son of both a son and a daughter of King Volsung. I have done this so that King Siggeir will be killed. All I have done was so that I would get revenge, and I too will not live long. I shall now die happily with King Siggeir though I married him unwillingly.' She kissed Sigmund, her brother, and Sinfjotli, and went into the fire, and bade them farewell. Then she died with King Siggeir and all his retinue.

The kinsmen gathered men and ships, and Sigmund sailed to his father's land and chased out of the country the king who had set himself in the place of King Volsung. Sigmund became a mighty and famous king, wise and great in counsel. He had a wife named Borghild. They had two sons. One was named Helgi, the other Hamund. But when Helgi was born, Norns [3] came and spoke over him, and said that he should be the most famous of all kings. Sigmund had returned from battle, and he went to his son with a leek, and gave him the name Helgi and gave him Hringstead and Sunfell and a sharp-shearing sword as name-fastening gifts, and blessed him, and said he would become famous like all Volsungs. Helgi became high-minded and well-liked, and surpassed all other men in every skill. It is said that he went to the wars when he was fifteen years old. Helgi was the king over the army, but Sinfjotli

[3] The goddesses of fate. The *Prose Edda* says they are three women, Urd, Verdandi and Skuld, but it goes on to quote Fafnir the Dragon, as does this saga later on, explaining that they are many and varied, including gods, elves, and 'daughters of Dvalin' i.e. dwarfs.

was with him, and they shared command.

Chapter Nine

It is said that Helgi encountered the king named Hunding in war. He was a mighty king and ruled many men and countries. They entered battle with each other, and Helgi went powerfully, and the fight ended with him achieving victory, but King Hunding fell with a great part of his army. Then Helgi seemed to have grown greatly in reputation because he had killed so powerful a king. The sons of Hunding gathered a huge army to avenge their father on Helgi. It was a hard battle, and Helgi went through the brothers' troop and up to their banner and killed Alf and Eyjolf, Hervard and Hagbard of Hunding's sons, and got there a renowned victory.

And when Helgi went from the battle, he met in the forest many women fair and worthy to look upon. They rode in noble array. One excelled the rest. Helgi asked her for her name. She called herself Sigrun and said that she was the daughter of King Hogni. Helgi said: 'Come home with us, and be welcome.' Then the king's daughter said, 'Other work lies before us than to drink with you.' Helgi answers, 'What is that, king's daughter?' She said: 'King Hogni has promised me to Hodbrodd son of King Granmar, but I have promised him that I would marry him no more than I would marry a young crow. Yet this will go ahead, unless you stop him and go to meet him with an army and take me away, because I would live with no king but with you.' 'Be merry, king's daughter,' he said. 'First we shall try our prowess, before you are married to him, and we shall see who of us prevails, and on this I pledge my life.'

After that Helgi sent men with generous gifts of treasure to summon his men and he gathered all his people at Raudabjorg. Helgi waited until a great company came to him from Hedinsey, and then his great fleet came from Norvasund with fair and large vessels. King Helgi called to the captain of the ships, who was named Leif, and asked if he had counted his army. But he said, 'I can count the ships that are already out of Norvasund, sire. There are twelve thousand men, and half as many again in the other troop.' Then King Helgi ordered that they should turn into a fjord called Varinsfjord, and so they did. Then the storm grew strong and so great was the sea that when the waves beat on the boards it was like cliffs striking together. Helgi asked them not to be afraid and not to take in sail, but rather to hoist each one high. But they did not sink before they come into land. Then Sigrun, daughter of King Hogni, came down to the strand with a great force and directed them into a good haven called Gnipalund.

This news reached the nation, and Hodbrodd, brother of the king, came down to the coast from Svarinshaug, which he ruled. He called on them and asked who led the great force. Sinfjotli stood up and on his head he had a helmet bright as a glass and armour white as snow, a spear in his hand and a banner of renown and gold-rimmed shield before him. He knew well how to speak with kings. 'Tell them, when you have fed your pigs and dogs, and when you have seen your wife, that the Volsungs have come here, and you will find King Helgi here in the army if Hodbrodd wants to see him, and his entertainment is to fight and find fame while you are kissing slave-girls by the fire.' Granmar [4] said, 'In no

---

[4] Previously said to be the father of Hodbrodd; now

way do you know how to say seemly things, and we must speak of matters remembered from the past when you tell lies of lords and rulers. There is more likelihood that you fed on wolf-meat long in the woods and that you killed your brothers, and it is incredible that you dare to lead an army of good men when you have sucked the blood of cold carcases.' Sinfjotli answered: 'You do not clearly remember now that you were once a witch on Varinsey and you said would have a man, and you chose me to take that position. Then you were a Valkyrie in Asgard, and everyone would fight for your sake, and I fathered nine wolf whelps on you in Laganess, and I was the father of all of them.' Granmar said: 'Much can you lie. I think that you can be father of no one, since you were castrated by the daughters of the giant of Thrasness, and you are the step-son of King Siggeir, and you lay in the wilderness with wolves, unlucky was your hand. You killed your brother and made an evil name for yourself.' Sinfjotli answered: 'Do you remember when you were the mare of the horse Grani, and I rode you at full speed on Bravellir? Then you were the goatherd of Golnir the giant.' Granmar said: 'I would prefer to feed the birds with your carcass than bicker with you anymore.' Then King Helgi, 'It would be better and manlier for you both to fight, but these things are a shame to hear, and though Granmar's sons are not my friends, they are hard men.' Granmar then rode away to meet King Hodbrodd at a place named Sunfell. Their horses were called Sveipud and Sveggjud. They met at the gate and told him news of war. King Hodbrodd was in armour and had a helmet on his head. He asked who was there, - 'But why are you so angry?' Granmar said: 'Here come

---

apparently his brother.

the Volsungs and they have twelve thousand men off the coast and seven thousand on the island called Sok, but their greatest number, however, is at the place called Grindur, and now I think that Helgi will fight.' The king said, 'Send the message throughout our realm and go against them. Let no one sit at home who wants to fight. Send word to the sons of Hring and King Hogni and Alf the Old. They are great fighters.' They met at Ulfstein, and there was a fierce battle. Helgi charges through their ranks. There was great loss of life. They saw a large group of shield-maidens who were like flames to look at. Princess Sigrun was there. King Helgi attacked King Hodbrodd who fell before him. Then Sigrun said: 'My thanks for this great deed. We shall now share the land. It is a lucky day for me, and for this you'll get honour and renown; you have killed so great a king.' King Helgi succeeded to the kingdom and stayed there for a long time and married Sigrun and became a famous and renowned king, and he is no longer in this story.

Chapter Ten

The Volsungs went home then and they had gained fame by their achievements. Sinfjotli went to war again. He saw a beautiful woman and desired to marry her. The woman was being wooed by the brother of that Borghild who had married King Sigmund. They settled this matter in battle, and Sinfjotli killed that grim king. He harried wide and fought many battles, and always had the victory. He made himself famous and renowned above other men and came home in the autumn with many ships and much treasure. He told his father his news, and the king told the queen. She asked Sinfjotli to leave the country and said that she did not want to see him. Sigmund said he would not let him go, and offered recompense with gold and much treasure, even though he had not previously paid wergild for any man, but he said there was nothing to be gained by arguing with women. She could not get her way. She said, 'You shall have your way, sire; that is fitting.' Then she prepared the funeral for her brother with the advice of the king. This feast had the best of food and she invited many great men. Borghild served the men their drink. She presented Sinfjotli with a great drinking horn. She said, 'Drink now, step-son.' He took it and looked at the horn and said, 'The drink is befouled.' Sigmund said, 'Give it to me.' He drank. The Queen said: 'Why should other people drink beer for you?' She came a second time with the horn, 'Drink now,' and taunted him with many words. He took the horn and said, 'The drink is mixed with treachery.' Sigmund said, 'Give it to me.' The third time she came and told him to drink if he had the heart of a Volsung. Sinfjotli took the horn and said, 'Poison is in the drink.' Sigmund spoke. 'Let your moustache filter it, son,' he said. By then the king was very drunk, and that is why he said this. Sinfjotli drank and instantly fell down. Sigmund rose and his sorrow was almost the death of him, and he took the body in his arms and went into the forest, and finally came to a fjord. There he saw a man in a small boat. The man asked if he would accept passage across the bay. He assented. The vessel was so small that it would not take them all, and first the corpse was shipped, but Sigmund walked beside the fjord. And then the ship and with it the man vanished in front of Sigmund's eyes. And after that Sigmund returned home and banished the queen, and soon after she died. King Sigmund continued to rule his domain and he is thought to have been the greatest warrior and king in ancient times.

Chapter Eleven

Eylimi was another king, and he was powerful and famous. His daughter was named Hjordis, the fairest and wisest of women. And Sigmund heard that she was his match if no one else was. Sigmund visited Eylimi. He prepared a great banquet to greet him, on the condition that he had not come for war. Then messages went between them that he was come in friendship, not war. That feast was prepared with the best food, and with many people attending. Sigmund was given a marketplace and other provisions for his journey. Now he went to the feast, and both kings shared one hall. Also present was King Lyngvi, son of King Hunding, who also wanted to be Eylimi's son-in-law. He did not think they could both succeed on the same errand and he thought that war would be the recourse of the one who did not succeed. Then he said to his daughter: 'You are a wise woman, but I have said that you shall choose your husband. So choose between the two kings, and I will accept your judgement.' She said: 'This matter seems difficult to me, but I prefer the king who is most famous, and that is King Sigmund, although he is very old.' She was given to him, and King Lyngvi went away. Sigmund was married to Hjordis. Each day they feasted better and with greater enthusiasm.

After that King Sigmund went home to Hunland and his father-in-law Eylimi came with him and then he tended his kingdom. But King Lyngvi and his brothers gathered an army against him, and they went against Sigmund because they had always received the worst deal in previous negotiations, and this was worst of all. They wished now to bring down a Volsung warrior; they went to Hunland and sent Sigmund the message that they would not sneak up him, but they seemed to know that he would not escape. King Sigmund said he would go to the battle. He gathered an army, but he sent Hjordis to the wood with a handmaid, and much wealth went with them. She stayed there while they fought. The Vikings rushed from their ships with an unconquerable army. Eylimi and King Sigmund set up their banners, and trumpets were blown. King Sigmund now let sound the horn which his father had owned, and he urged his men on. Sigmund had a much smaller force. Now there was a fierce battle, and although Sigmund was old he fought hard and was always at the vanguard of his people. Neither shield nor armour withstood him, and again and again that day he went through the force of his enemies, and no one could see how things would go between them. Many spears and arrows were in the air. And his Norns spared him so that he was not wounded, but none could count how many man fell before him. He had both his arms bloody to the shoulders. And the fight had been going for some time when a man appeared in the battle, wearing a hood and a blue cloak. He had one eye and a spear in his hand. This man came against King Sigmund and lifted his spear before him, and when King Sigmund struck hard, the sword broke into two pieces. The tide of battle turned, Sigmund's luck disappeared completely, and many of his men fell. The king did not try to protect himself and he urged on his men. Then it was just as they say, one may not succeed against many. King Sigmund fell in this battle at the head of his war band, and with him Eylimi, his father-in-law, and the greater part of his forces.

Chapter Twelve

Then King Lyngvi sought the king's town and

he planned to take the king's daughter, but in this he failed; he got neither wife nor treasure. He travelled over the land and placed his own people in the kingdom. Then he thought had killed the entire house of the Volsungs and so he would not need to fear them in future. That night after the battle Hjordis went among the slain and she came to where King Sigmund was, and asked if he could be healed. But he said: 'Many men live when there is little hope, but my luck is gone, so I will not be healed. Odin does not want me to fight with my sword, it is broken now. I fought battles while he liked it.' She said: 'I would lack nothing if you were healed and avenged my father.' The king said, 'Another is meant to do that. You are carrying a son and you will bring him up well and carefully, and the boy will be renowned and the foremost of our house. Guard well the broken sword. From it can be made a good sword whose name will be Gram, and our son will bear it and do many great deeds which will never be forgotten, and his name will last while the world stands. I am content with this, but my wounds weary me and I will now visit our kinsmen who went before me.' Hjordis sat over him until he died, and then day broke. She saw that many ships had arrived on the shore. She said to her maid: 'We shall change clothes, and you will be called by my name, and say you are a king's daughter.' And they did so. The Vikings saw the great slaughter and the women going to the woods, and understood that great things had happened, and they leapt from the ship. But this force was led by Alf, son of King Hjalprek of Denmark. He had sailed along the coast with his army; now they came to the battlefield because they saw much slaughter. The king commanded them now to look for the women, and so they did. He asked who they were, but they could not be told apart. The maid answered for them, and told of the fall of King Sigmund and Eylimi and many other great men, and also who had done this. The king asked if they knew where the king's treasure was hidden. The maid said, 'It is most likely that we should know,' and she took them to the treasury. And they found great wealth, so that they thought they had not seen so much together in one place or more valuable things; they carried it to the ships of King Alf. Hjordis followed the king and so did the maid. He went home to his kingdom, but he made it known that those kings had been killed, the most famous of folk. The king sat at the helm, but the women were on the first bench of the ship. He talked with them and listened closely to them.

The king returned to his kingdom with much treasure. Alf was the most able of men. And when they had been home a short while, the queen asked Alf, her son, 'Why does the more beautiful woman have fewer rings and worse clothing? It seems to me that she is nobler who you have made less of.' He said, 'I have suspected that she does not have the manner of a serving maid, and she knew well how to greet noble men when we first met, and here I shall put this to the test.' When they were drinking, the king sat and talked with the women and said, 'How do you know it is daybreak, when the dark lightens, if you cannot see the stars?' She said: 'This is how I know it; in my youth I was accustomed to drink much before dawn, and when I stopped it, I still woke up at the same time, and this is my sign.' The king smiled at her and said, 'That was a bad habit for a king's daughter.' He found Hjordis and asked her the same. She answered him, 'My father gave me a gold ring that cools on my finger at dawn. That is my sign.' The king replies, 'Gold was common if slaves wore it. You have hidden from me long enough, and if you had said this I would have treated you as if we were children of the same king, and I will still treat you with honour, for you shall be my wife, and I will pay your dowry when you have a child.' She answered and told all the truth about her situation. She was now held in great honour and she seemed the worthiest of women.

Chapter Thirteen

It is said that Hjordis bore a boy, and the boy was brought before King Hjalprek. The king was glad when he saw the boy's piercing eyes, and he said no one would be his like or equal, and the boy was sprinkled with water and named Sigurd. Everyone said of him that none was his match in conduct and growth. He was raised by King Hjalprek with great love. And when renowned men and kings are mentioned in the sagas, Sigurd is foremost for strength and ability, effort and bravery. He had had more of these qualities than every other man in the northern world. Sigurd grew up with Hjalprek, and everyone loved him. Hjalprek betrothed Hjordis to King Alf and paid her dowry.

Regin was the name of Sigurd's foster-father and he was the son of Hreidmarr. He taught him sports, chess, and runes, to speak many tongues as was the custom of king's sons, and many other things. One day, when they were both together, Regin asked Sigurd if he knew how much treasure his father had had, or who was guarding it. Sigurd said that the kings watched over it. Regin said, 'Do you trust them completely?' Sigurd answered: 'It is fitting that they guard it as long as it suits us, because they can watch over it better than I.' Another time Regin came to speak with Sigurd, and said: 'It is strange that you want to be the groom of kings or treated as a beggar.' Sigurd said: 'It is not true, because they consult with me about everything. I can have whatever I want.' Regin said, 'Ask him to give you a horse.' Sigurd said, 'It will be done as soon as I want.' Sigurd met the kings. Then the kings said to Sigurd: 'What do you want of us?' Sigurd said: 'I will accept a horse for my entertainment.' The king said, 'Choose yourself a horse, and anything else that you would have of ours.' The next day Sigurd went to the forest and met an old man with a long beard. Who he was was unknown. He asked where Sigurd was going. He replied: 'I am choosing horses. Advise me about this.' He said, 'Let's go and drive them to the river Busiltjorn.' They drove the horses out into the deep river, and all swam to land except one horse. Sigurd took him. He was a grey, young in age, big and handsome. No one had ever mounted him. The bearded man said: 'This horse is descended from Sleipnir, and he must be carefully raised, because he will become a better horse.' The man disappeared. Sigurd called the horse Grani, and it was the best of horses. It was Odin he had met. Again Regin said to Sigurd, 'You do not own enough treasure. I wish that you did not run around like a village lad, but I can tell you where there is much wealth, and it is more likely that in seeking it you will acquire honour and respect.' Sigurd asked where it was and who kept it. Regin answered, 'He is called Fafnir, and he lies not far away. The place is called Gnita Heath. And when you get there, you will say that you have never seen more treasure and gold in one place, and you will not need more, even if you become the oldest and most famed friend of kings.' Sigurd said, 'Though I'm young, I know the nature of this serpent, and I have heard that no one dares to go against him because of his size and evil.' Regin answered, 'It is not so. He is no bigger than other grass snakes, and much more is made of it than is deserved, and so it would have seemed to your fathers. And if you are of the Volsung race, then you do not have their spirit, which is considered foremost in every form of distinction.' Sigurd said: 'It may be that I do not have much of their valour or skill, but there is no need to taunt me since I'm not much more than a child. But why do you urge this so much?' Regin said, 'There is a story behind it, and I will tell you.' Sigurd said, 'Let me hear it.'

Chapter Fourteen

'This is the beginning of my story. Hreidmarr was my father, a great and wealthy man. One of his sons was named Fafnir, another was Otr and I was the third, and I was the least accomplished and honoured. I worked with iron and with silver and gold, and I could make something useful from everything. Otr, my brother, had another craft and nature. He was a great fisherman, better than other men, and he went in the shape of an otter by day and was always in the river and carried fish in his mouth. He brought his catch to his father, and he was thus a great help. He was like an otter in many ways; he came home late and ate with his eyes shut, because he could not bear to see his food diminish. Fafnir was the tallest and fiercest of the sons and he wanted to call everything his own.

'There was a dwarf named Andvari,' said Regin. 'He was always in the waterfall called Andvari's Force and he got his food in the shape of a pike, because there were many fish in the falls. Otr, my brother, was always in the waterfall and he carried the fish in his mouth and put them on land one after the other. Odin, Loki, Hoenir were travelling when they came to Andvari's Force. Otr had caught a salmon and he ate half-dozing on the riverbank. Loki took a stone, and flung it at the otter, killing him. The Aesir thought they had had great luck in their fishing and they skinned the otter. That evening they came to Hreidmarr's dwelling, and showed him their catch. Then we seized them by the arms and told them what was the fine, and the wergild, that they should fill the otter skin with gold and cover the outside with red gold. Then they sent Loki to get gold. He went to Ran and got her net, then went to Andvari and cast the net for the pike, but he leapt into the net. Then Loki said:

> *'Who is the fish*
>
> *That runs through the flood,*
>
> *And cannot save himself from peril?*
>
> *Ransom your head*
>
> *From Hel* [5]
>
> *And find me the fire of the water.'*

> *'Andvari is my name,*
>
> *Oin was my father,*
>
> *I have gone over many falls.*
>
> *An evil Norn*
>
> *Ordained in early days,*

---

[5] The goddess of death.

31

That in water I must wade.'

Loki saw the gold that Andvari owned. When he had handed over the gold, he kept back one ring, but Loki took it from him. The dwarf went into his rock, and said that the ring would be the death of everyone who owned it, and so would all the gold. The Æsir delivered the gold to Hreidmarr's dwelling and stuffed the otter skin and set it on its feet. Then the gods had to pile up the gold and cover the outside. When that was done, Hreidmarr went out and he saw a single whisker, and told them to cover it. Then Odin took the ring from his hand, Andvari's Bequest, and covered the hair with it. Then Loki said:

'Gold is now your payment,

And you have payment

For my head.

For your son

Bliss is not created,

It is death for both of you.'

'Then Fafnir killed his father,' said Regin, 'murdered him, and I got none of the treasure. He became so bad-natured that he lay out and allowed none to benefit from the treasure but him, and then he turned into the worst of serpents and now lies upon the treasure. Then I went to the king, and I became his smith. But this is my story of how I lost my father and my brother's wergild. Gold is now called 'otter's ransom' and is spoken of as such.' Sigurd answered: 'Much have you lost, and your kin have been very evil. Now make a sword with your skill, so its equal does not exist and I can work great deeds if I am brave enough, and if you want it that I shall kill this great grim dragon.' Regin said, 'I shall do that with confidence, and you will be able to kill Fafnir with this sword.'

Chapter Fifteen

Regin made a sword, and gave it to Sigurd. He took the sword and said: 'This is your forging, Regin,' and he struck the anvil with it, and broke his sword. He threw the sword down, and told him to forge better. Regin made another sword for Sigurd. He looked at it. 'You will like this one too, but you are a hard man for forging.' Sigurd tried the sword and broke it like last time. Then he said to Regin: 'You are like your kindred, untrustworthy.' He went to his mother. She greeted him well and they spoke and drank. Sigurd said: 'Have I heard correctly that King Sigmund gave you the sword Gram in two pieces?' She said: 'It is true, that.' Sigurd said, 'Give me it, I would have it.' She said he looked likely to win fame and gave him the sword.

Sigurd met with Regin and told him to make a good sword with these pieces. Regin was angry and went to his workshop with the broken sword and he thought Sigurd was very demanding about its forging. Regin now made a sword. And when he brought it out of the forge, it seemed to the apprentices that fire burned from the edges. Then he told Sigurd to take the sword, and said he did not know how to make a sword, if this one failed. Sigurd hewed at the anvil and cut it down to its base, and it did not break or crack. He praised the sword greatly, and went to the river with a lock of wool and threw it upstream, and the lock cut in half when it drifted into his sword. Sigurd went home happy. Regin said:

'You must fulfil your vow now that I have made the sword, and see Fafnir.' Sigurd said, 'I will fulfil it and yet I have another duty; I must avenge my father.'

Sigurd was more beloved by all people the older he was, and every mother's son loved him well.

Chapter Sixteen

Gripir was the name of a man who was the brother of Sigurd's mother. Soon after his sword was made, he went to meet him, because Gripir could see the future and knew the fate of men. Sigurd asked Gripir how his life would go. He was silent for a long time, however, but finally to Sigurd's fervent pleas he told him all his future, exactly as it went afterwards. And when Gripir had said these things as he had asked, he rode home. And soon after that he met Regin. He said, 'Kill Fafnir, as you promised.' Sigurd said, 'I shall, and yet before that, I will avenge King Sigmund and the other relatives of ours who fell in that battle.'

Chapter Seventeen

Sigurd met the kings, and he said to them: 'I have been here for a while, and I am indebted to you for your affection and great honour. Now I wish to leave the land and find Hunding's sons, and I want them to know that not all the Volsungs are dead. I would have your support.' The kings said they would provide everything that he requested.

He now had a great fleet and everything was most carefully arranged, ships and arms, so that his journey would be more magnificent than any before. Sigurd commanded the dragonship, which was biggest and the most splendid. The sails were very

good quality and glorious to see. Then they sailed
with a good wind. And when a few days were passed,
bad weather came and a storm, and the sea churned
like foaming blood. Sigurd did not order the sails to
be reefed, though they tore, but instead ordered
them set higher than before. When they sailed by a
craggy headland, a man called out to the ship and
asked who commanded the fleet. He was told that
the chief was Sigurd Sigmund's son, now the most
famous of young men. The man answered,
'Everyone says one thing about him, that no king's
son is his equal. Would you lower sails on a little
boat and take me with you?' They asked him his
name. He answered:

> 'Hnikar they hailed me,
>
> When I gladdened Hugin,
>
> Young Volsung,
>
> When I had conquered.
>
> Now you may address
>
> The old man of the rock
>
> As Feng or Fjolnir.
>
> I will accept passage.'

They sailed landward and took the man
aboard their ship. Then the wind subsided, and they
sailed until they came ashore in the kingdom of
Hunding's sons. Then Fjolnir vanished. They
unleashed fire and iron, killing people, and burning
and destroying the settlements as they went. A great
multitude fled before them to King Lyngvi and told
him that an army had arrived in the land and it went

with more ferocity than ever before, saying that Hunding's sons had not been farsighted when they had said they need not be afraid of the Volsungs, - 'since now Sigurd the son of Sigmund leads the army.' King Lyngvi sent the summons to war throughout his entire kingdom. He refused to run away, and called all his men to his house, he would provide the force; and now he went with his brothers against Sigurd with a great army. There was the hardest of battles between them. You might see there many spears and arrows aloft, axes swung violently, shields split and mailcoats hewn, helmets slashed, heads split and many men fallen to the ground. And when the battle had been going a very long time, Sigurd advanced past the standards with the sword Gram in his hand. He hewed down both men and horses and went through the ranks and had both arms bloody to the shoulder, and he jumped ahead of the crowd where he went, and neither helmet nor armour withstood him, and no one thought he had ever seen such a man before. This battle lasted for a long time with great casualties and fierce encounters. It happened there, as seldom happens when the local army fights, that they could not advance. So many men fell among the forces of Hunding's sons that no one knew their number. And Sigurd was at the forefront of his forces. Then the sons of King Hunding came to meet him. Sigurd smote King Lyngvi and split his helmet and head and armoured body, and then he cut his brother Hjorvard into two pieces, and then he killed all the sons of Hunding who were still living, and most of their retainers.

Sigurd now returned home with victory and great wealth and glory which he had got on that journey. Feasts were now made ready for him at home in the kingdom. And when Sigurd had been home a short while, Regin came to speak with him, and said: 'Now you will want to strike the helmet from Fafnir, as you promised, because now you have avenged your father and other relatives.' Sigurd said, 'I will fulfil that which I have promised, and it has not escaped my memory.'

Chapter Eighteen

Then Sigurd and Regin rode to the heath on the track that Fafnir was accustomed to crawl when he went to the water, and it is said that the cliff was thirty fathoms high at the spot where he drank. Sigurd said: 'Regin, you said that the dragon was no more than a grass snake, but his tracks seem over-large to me.' Regin said, 'Dig a pit and settle there. And when the serpent crawls to the water, stab him in the heart and so bring about his death. Moreover, you will get great renown.' Sigurd said: 'What will happen if I get in the way of the dragon's blood?' Regin said, 'No one can give you advice if you are afraid of everything. You are not like your relatives in courage.'

Then Sigurd rode to the heath, but Regin ran away very scared. Sigurd made a pit. When he was at this work, an old man with a long beard came to him and asked what he was doing there. He explains. Then the old man said, 'This is madness. Dig more pits and let the blood run into them, but you sit in one place and stab the serpent in the heart.' Then the man disappeared. Sigurd dug pits as he was told. And when the serpent crawled out to the water, there was a great earthquake so that the whole ground nearby shook. He blew poison across the path before him, but Sigurd was neither afraid nor worried by the noise. And when the serpent crawled

37

over the pit, Sigurd thrust the sword under his left shoulder, so that it sank in up to the hilt. Then Sigurd got up from the pit and pulled out the sword, and his arms were covered in blood up to the shoulders. And when the big serpent felt his death wound, he thrashed his head and tail so that all was destroyed before it. But when Fafnir knew his death-wound, he asked: 'Who are you, and who is your father, and what is your father's house, that you are so bold to dare bear weapons against me?' Sigurd said, 'My family is unknown to men. My name is Noble Beast, and I have no father or mother, and I have travelled alone.' Fafnir said: 'If you have no father or mother, from what wonder were you born? And though you will not tell me your name on my dying day, you know that you are lying now.' He said, 'My name is Sigurd, but my father was Sigmund.' Fafnir said: 'Who egged you on to do this deed, and why were you so easily persuaded? Had you not heard that all people are afraid of me and of my helm of awe? Sharp-eyed boy, you had a keen father.' Sigurd said, 'A hard mind encouraged me to do this, and I was supported by a strong hand and a sharp sword that it is now known to you, and few are tough in their old age when they are cowardly in childhood.' Fafnir said: 'I know if you grew up with your kindred that you would know how to fight when angry, but this is much stranger, that a captive prisoner should have dared to fight me, since very few captives are valiant in the fight.' Sigurd said: 'You taunt me that I was taken away from my kinsfolk? But even if I was taken in war, yet I was not bound, and you found that I was free.' Fafnir said: 'You take all I say as if it is said with malice. But this gold which was mine will be your death.' Sigurd answered: 'Everyone wants to have treasure until that one day, but at that time each shall die.' Fafnir said: 'You hardly want to take my advice, but you will drown if you go across the sea unwarily. Remain on land until it is calm.' Sigurd said, 'Tell me, Fafnir, if you are knowledgeable: who are the Norns who separate sons from mothers?' Fafnir said: 'They are many and varied, some are of the gods, some are of the elves, and some are the daughters of Dvalin.' Sigurd said: 'What is the island called where Surt and the Aesir will mingle their blood?' Fafnir said: 'It is called Oskapt.' And again Fafnir said, 'Regin, my brother, caused my death, and it gladdens me that he will also cause your death, and it will go as he wishes.' Still Fafnir said, 'I have carried the helm of awe since I lay upon the heritage of my brother, and so I blew poison all round me in all directions and no one dared to come near me, and I was afraid of no weapons, and I never found so many men before me that I did not think myself much stronger, and all were afraid of me.' Sigurd said: 'The helm of awe you speak of grants few victory, because everyone who finds himself in company with others will find in the end that no one is the boldest.' Fafnir answered: 'I advise you to take your horse and ride away as quickly as possible, because it often happens that he who gets a mortal wound avenges himself.' Sigurd said: 'This is your advice, but I will do otherwise. I will ride to your lair and take all the gold that your kinsmen had.' Fafnir said, 'You'll ride there, and you will find so much gold that it will be enough for all your days, but that same gold will be your death, as it will be the death of all who own it.' Sigurd stood up and said, 'I will ride home, even if I lost this treasure, if I knew that I would never die, and each valiant man wants to have treasure until that day. Yet you, Fafnir, will lie in your death throes until Hel has you.' And then Fafnir died.

Chapter Nineteen

After that Regin came to Sigurd, and said, 'Greetings, sir, you have won a great victory. You have killed Fafnir, and no one was so bold that they dared to sit on his path, and this glorious deed will be remembered while the world stands.' Now Regin stood and looked down at the ground a long time. And after this, he said with great feeling: 'You have killed my brother, and I am hardly innocent of this work.' Then Sigurd took his sword, Gram, wiped it on the grass and said to Regin: 'You ran far away when I did this job and I tested this sharp sword with my hand and my strength. I fought with the serpent while you lay in a heather bush, and did not know where the sky or the ground was.' Regin said, 'This serpent would have been lying long in its lair if you had not used the sword that I made you with my hands, and without it you would not have done it or anyone else.' Sigurd said, 'When men come to fight, the man would do better to have a strong heart than a sharp sword.' Then Regin said to Sigurd with great sorrow, 'You killed my brother, and I am hardly innocent of this work.' Sigurd cut the heart from the serpent with the sword named Ridill. Then Regin drank the blood of Fafnir and said: 'Grant me one request, a small thing for you. Go to the fire with the heart and roast it and give it to me to eat.' Sigurd went and roasted it on a spit. And when the juices came bubbling out, he touched it with his finger and felt to see if it was roasted. Then he put his finger to his mouth. And when the heart blood of the serpent touched his tongue, he could understand bird voices. He heard nuthatches speaking in the bushes nearby. 'There Sigurd sits and roasts Fafnir's heart. He should eat it himself. Then he would be wiser than any man.' Another said: 'There lies Regin, plotting to betray one who trusts him.' Then the third, 'He should cut off his head, and then he could have the great store of gold.' Then the fourth, 'He would be wise if he followed your advice, and then rode to Fafnir's den and took the hoard of gold that is there, and then rode up to Hindfell, where Brynhild sleeps, and he will find great wisdom there, and he would be wise if he took your advice, and considered his needs. I suspect there is a wolf when I see its ears.' Then the fifth, 'He is not as wise as I believe, if he spares Regin after killing his brother.' Then the sixth, 'It would be wise if he killed him and took the treasure.' Sigurd said: 'No, it will not be my fate that Regin is my bane, and instead both brothers shall go one way.' He brandished his sword Gram and cut off Regin's head.

And after this he ate some parts of the serpent's heart, but some he kept, then he ran to his horse and rode along the path of Fafnir and came to his lair, and he found that it was open, and all the doors were of iron, and so were all the fastenings and all the posts in the house were iron, and they were sunk in the ground. Sigurd found a hoard of gold and the sword Hrotti, and he took the helm of awe and a golden mailcoat and many treasures. He found so much gold there that he thought it looked like two or three horses would be needed to carry it. He took all the gold and carries it in two large chests, and then he took the reins of the horse Grani. His steed would not move, and whipping did not work. Sigurd now found out what the horse wanted; he leapt up behind and put to him his spurs, and the horse ran as if it had no burden.

Chapter Twenty

Sigurd now rode a long way until he came up to Hindfell, and he headed south on the way to the land of the Franks. On the mountain he saw a great light, as if fire burned, and it shone up to the sky. But when he came and stood there he saw a rampart of shields with a standard above. Sigurd went into the shield-rampart and saw a man lying there, surrounded by all the weapons of war. He took the helmet from the man's head and saw that it was a woman. She wore a mailcoat, and it was so tight that it had grown into her flesh. Then he cut through the neck opening and down through the armour and out through both sleeves, and it cut as if it was cloth. Sigurd said she had had a long sleep. She asked who was so strong he could cut through her mailcoat - 'and break my sleep, or has Sigurd Sigmundsson come here, who has the helmet of Fafnir and carries his bane in his hand?' Then Sigurd said: 'He who has done this work is of Volsung family, and I have heard that you are a rich king's daughter, and the same has been told us about your beauty and wisdom, and I will test that.' Brynhild said that once two kings had fought. One was named Helm-Gunnar. He was old, and the greatest warrior, and Odin had promised him victory. The other was Agnar or Audabrodir. 'I struck down Helm-Gunnar in battle, but in revenge Odin stabbed me with a sleep thorn and he said I would never have victory and he also said I must marry. And in return I vowed that I would marry no one who might know fear.' Sigurd said, 'Teach me the ways of great things.' She said: 'You know them better than I, but I will gladly teach you if there is anything that I know that will please you also, of runes, or other matters that concern all things, and we shall both drink together, and the gods give us both a good day that you will gain profit and fame from my wisdom and you will later remember what we talk of.' Brynhild filled a jar and brought it to Sigurd, and said:

'Beer I give you,

Battlefield's ruler,

Mixed with strength

And much glory;

Full of holy poetry

And healing runes,

Good spells

And pleasing speech.

Victory runes shall you know,

If you want to be wise;

Cut them on the swordhilt,

The centre ridge of the blade

And parts of the sword

And twice name Tyr.

Sea runes shall you make,

If you want to protect

Your sail steeds on the sound.

On the prow shall they be cut

And the steerboard;

And burn them on the oar.

No steep breaker will fall,

And you will find peace from the sea.

Speech runes shall you know,

If you want no redemption

In hate words for harm done.

Wind them about,

Weave them,

Tie them all together

At the Thing

When all shall

Go to the full court.

Ale runes shall you know,

If you want no man's wife

To abuse your good faith, if you trust them.

On the horn shall you engrave them,

And on the back of the hand,

And mark the rune 'Need' on your nail.

For the goblet make a blessing,

And beware misfortune

And throw a leek into the drink.

Then I know that

You will never get

Poison blended drink.

Help runes shall you learn,

If you would grant protection

And bring the child from the woman.

Grave them on the palm

And take her hand in yours

And beg the goddesses to succeed.

Limb runes shall you know,

If you want to be a doctor

And know how see to wounds.

On bark should they be cut,

And the needles of trees

Whose boughs lean to the east.

Mind runes shall you learn

If you want to be

Wiser than other men.

They were solved,

They were cut,

They were heeded by Hropt.

On the shields were they carved,

That stand before the shining god;

In the ear of Arvak

And on the head of Alsvinn,

And on the wheel that stands

Under Hrungnir's chariot;

On Sleipnir's reins

And the sleigh's shackles,

On bear's paw

And Bragi's tongue,

On wolf paw,

And eagle's beak,

On the bloody wings

And the bridge's end,

The soothing palm

And the healing step,

On glass and on gold

And on good silver,

In wine and in ale

And on the Vala's seat,

On the flesh of man,

The tip of Gaupnir

And the ogress' chest;

On the Norn's nail

And the beak of an owl.

All that were carved on

Were carved off,

Mixed with holy mead,

And sent many ways.

Some are with the elves,

Some with the Aesir

And the venerable Vanir.

Some are with men.

There are cure runes

And help runes

And all ale runes

And unmatched great runes,

For all to use, unspoiled

And uncorrupted,

To bring good luck.

Enjoy them, if you have learnt them,

Until the death of the gods.

Now shall you choose,

As a choice is offered,

Maple shaft of sharp weapons.

Speech or silence,

You must think for yourself.

All words are already decided.'

Sigurd said:

'I shall not flee, although

You know I am death-fated.

I was not conceived to be a coward.

I want to have all

Your loving advice

As long as I live.'

Chapter Twenty One

Sigurd said, 'There never was a wiser woman than you in the world, and I wish to hear more wise counsel.' She said: 'It is right to do your will and give you advice because you are wise to ask for it.' Then she said, 'Be good to your kin and take little revenge for their annoyances and treat them with patience, and you will have long-lasting praise. Do not do evil things, either to take a maid's love or that of a man's wife. Evil often comes from that. Have a merciful disposition with foolish men at great gatherings. They often speak worse than they know, and if you are called a coward, they may think that you are truly named such. Kill him another day and pay him for his spite. If you go down a path where evil spirits dwell, be wary. Do not take shelter near the path though you are benighted, because evil spirits who confound humans often live there. Do not allow beautiful women to tempt you if you see them at banquets, so that you lose sleep or distress your mind. Do not seduce them with kisses or other affection. If you hear foolish words from drunken men, do not argue with those who are drunk on wine and have lost their wits. Such matters will be great grief or death for many men. It's better to fight your enemies than be burned in your house. Swear no false oath, for cruel vengeance follows the breaking of a truce. Do the right thing by dead men, whether they are dead from sickness, or drowned, or killed by weapons. Prepare the dead bodies carefully. Do not trust them whose father or brother or other kinsman you have killed, even if he is young. Often a young son is like a wolf. Beware the wiles of your friends. I see your future poorly, but it would be better if you avoid the hatred of your in-laws.' Sigurd said: 'Nobody is wiser than you, and I swear that I will marry you, and you are to my liking.' She said, 'I would prefer to marry you of all men.' And they confirmed this with vows.

Chapter Twenty Two

Then Sigurd rode away. His shield was ornamented and plated in red gold and emblazoned with a dragon. It was dark brown above, bright red below, and his helmet and saddle and surcoat were also marked in this way. He had a gold mailcoat, and all his weapons were ornamented with gold. And a dragon was marked on all his weapons so that when he was seen, he would be recognised, wherever he went, by all those who had heard that he had killed the great dragon who the Varangians [6] called Fafnir. And all his weapons were ornamented with gold and brown in colour because he was far superior to other men in all manners and courtesy, and near enough in everything that everyone shares. And when major

---

[6] Usually used to refer to the Norse guards of the Byzantine Emperor; in this case, it seems to mean Scandinavians in general.

champions and renowned chiefs are considered, he will always be reckoned the chief, and his name is known in all tongues north of the Sea of the Greeks, and so it shall be while the world stands. His hair was brown in colour and his big locks were fair to see. His beard was thick and close, and of the same colour. He was high-nosed and large boned and had a broad face. His eyes flashed, so very few dared look at him beneath his brows. His shoulders were so broad that it looked like two men were in view. His body was well proportioned in height and size and he was handsome in every way. It is a token of his height that when he belted on the sword Gram, which was seven spans long, and waded through a field of full grown rye, he grazed upstanding grain with the tip of his sword. And his strength surpassed his height. He could use sword and spear well and could cast a javelin, hold a shield, bend a bow or ride a horse, and he studied a variety of courtesies in his youth. He was a wise man, and he could predict future things. He also understood bird speech. And because of all this, few things came to him as a surprise. He could speak eloquently and at length, so that no matter what he decided to speak of, everyone agreed that no course was feasible except to do what he said even before he had finished speaking. And it was his pleasure to support his men and test himself in great deeds and take treasure from his enemies and give it to his friends. He did not lack courage, and he never became frightened.

Chapter Twenty Three

Sigurd rode on until he came to a great estate. A great chief called Heimir ruled there. He was married to the sister of Brynhild, who was named Bench-Hild, because she had stayed home and learnt needlework and other womanly crafts, while

Brynhild wore helmet and mailcoat, and went to battle; she was therefore called Brynhild[7] . Heimir and Bench-Hild had a son named Alsvid, the most courteous of men. Men were playing sports outside. And when they saw a man riding up to the farm, they left the game and went to admire him, because they had not seen his like; they met him and greeted him well. Alsvid invited him to stay and take whatever he wanted. He accepted. They prepared to serve him nobly. Four men carried the gold from the horse; the fifth took care of him. Many good treasures and rare gifts were seen. It was thought great entertainment to see mailcoats and helmets and big rings and wonderfully big gold cups and all kinds of weapons of war. Sigurd stayed there for a long time in great honour. News of his famous achievements had now spread through all countries, how he had killed a terrible dragon. They enjoyed themselves, and each was loyal to the other. As their entertainment they prepared their weapons, made arrow shafts and hunted with hawks.

Chapter Twenty Four

Then Brynhild came back home, Heimir was her foster father[8] . She sat in a bower with her maidens. She was more skilful than other women. She sewed her tapestry with gold and embroidered it with the wonders that Sigurd had achieved, killing the serpent and taking the treasure, and the death of Regin.

And one day it is said that Sigurd rode to the

---

[7] Byrnie-Hild = a byrnie being a shirt of chainmail.

[8] Children of the nobility spent their childhood being fostered by other noblemen. Budli is Brynhild's father; Heimir, who is her brother-in-law, is also her foster-father.

woods with dogs and hawks and many people. When he came home, his hawk flew to a high tower and sat at one window. Sigurd went after his hawk. Then he saw a lovely woman, and realised that Brynhild was there. He considered her beauty and what she did worthy of all. He came into the hall, and would not join men's games. Then Alsvid said 'Why are you so quiet? This change is worrying your friends. Why can you not be happy? Your hawks are moping, and so is your steed Grani, and it will be long before this is made better.' Sigurd said, 'Good friend, hear what I think. My hawk flew to a tower, and when I retrieved it, I saw a beautiful woman. She sat alone with a golden tapestry and embroidered there my deeds.' Alsvid answered: 'You have seen Brynhild Budli's daughter, a noble woman.' Sigurd said, 'That must be true. What time did she come here?' Alsvid said: 'It was a short time between her arrival and yours.' Sigurd said: 'I learned this a few days ago: this woman seemed to me the best in the world.' Alsvid said, 'Such a great man should give no heed to one woman. It is bad to mourn for what a man never has.' 'I shall meet her,' said Sigurd, 'and give her gold and gain love and mutual affection.' Alsvid answered, 'Of old she has let no man sit with her or given him beer to drink. She wants to fight wars and win fame.' Sigurd said, 'I do not know whether she will answer me or not or if she will let me sit by her.'

A day later, Sigurd went to the chamber. But Alsvid stood outdoors by the bower and made arrow shafts. Sigurd said, 'Greetings, lady, and how are you?' She said, 'I am well. My kin and friends live, but it is unknown what fortune men carry to the end of their days.' He sits with her. Then four women went there with large goblets of gold, and with good wine, and stood before them. Then Brynhild said,

'This seat is granted to few, except when my father comes.' He said, 'Now give it to them whoever I please.' The room was hung with rich tapestries and cloth covered the floor. Sigurd said: 'Now it is come to pass, as you promised me.' She answered, 'You shall be welcome here.' Then she got up and with her the four maidens, and brought him a gold cup and told him to drink. He gave her a cup in return and took her hand and sat her down with him. He put his arms round her neck and kissed her, and said: 'No woman more beautiful than you has been born.' Brynhild said: 'It is good advice that you should not trust any woman, because they often break their vows.' He said, 'It would be the best of endings for us that we might enjoy each other.' Brynhild answered: 'It is not ordained that we should live together. I am a shield maiden, and I wear a helmet and ride with warrior kings, and support my warriors, and I am not opposed to fighting.' Sigurd said, 'Then our lives will be the most fruitful if we live together, and if not then our grief will be harder than a sharp weapon.' Brynhild answers, 'I must examine the troop of warriors, but you'll marry Gudrun Gjuki's daughter.' Sigurd said, 'A king's daughter will not seduce me, and I am not in two minds about this, and I swear by the gods that I shall have you as wife or no one otherwise.' She said likewise. Sigurd thanked her for these words and gave her a gold ring, and they plighted their troth again, and he went away to his men, and he was with them for a while, greatly prospering.

Chapter Twenty Five

There was a king named Gjuki. He ruled a kingdom south of the Rhine. He had three sons, named as follows: Gunnar, Hogni and Guttorm. Gudrun was the name of his daughter. She was the most famous of maidens. They outdid the children of other kings in all abilities, beauty and height. They were always at war, and did many a great deed. Gjuki had married Grimhild, who was skilled in magic. Another king was named Budli. He was more powerful than Gjuki and yet both were powerful. Atli was the brother of Brynhild[9]. He was a fierce man, tall and dark, and yet lordly and the greatest warrior. Grimhild was a fierce, grim-minded woman. The realm of the Gjukungs flourished and mostly because of his children, who outdid most others.

One day Gudrun told her maidens that she could not be happy. A woman asked her what it was that troubled her. She said, 'I have bad dreams so I am sorrowful in my heart. Explain the dream, since you ask of it.' She said, 'Tell me and do not be sorry, because one usually dreams before bad weather.' Gudrun said, 'This is not about the weather. I dreamed that I had a beautiful hawk on my hand. His feathers were of a golden colour.' She said: 'Many people have heard of your beauty, wisdom and courtesy. A son of a king will ask you for your hand.' Gudrun answered, 'I cared for nothing better than this hawk, and I would have lost all my treasure rather than him.' The woman replied, 'He who you marry will be well-bred, and you will love him dearly.' Gudrun said, 'It troubles me that I do not know who he is, so we will visit Brynhild. She will know.'

They adorned themselves with gold and fair clothes and went with their maidens until they came to the hall of Brynhild. The house was ornamented with gold and stood on a rock. And when their procession was seen, Brynhild was informed that

---

[9] And therefore the son of Budli.

many women drove to the town in golden chariots. 'It will be Gjuki's daughter, Gudrun,' she said. 'I dreamed about her last night, and we will walk out to meet her. More beautiful women will not visit us at home.' They went out to meet them, and welcomed them warmly. They went with them into a beautiful hall. The hall was adorned with silver and highly ornamented. Cloths were spread under their feet, and all served them. They had a variety of games. Gudrun was quiet. Brynhild said, 'Why can you not be happy? Do not do that, amuse us all and talk about great kings and their great deeds.' 'Let's do it,' she said. 'Who do you think were the greatest of kings?' Brynhild answered, 'The sons of Hamund, Haki and Hagbard[10] . They achieved many famous deeds in warfare.' Gudrun said, 'They were renowned yet Sigar took their sister, and burned another inside her house, and they were slow to avenge. But why do you not mention my brothers who now seem the foremost of men?' Brynhild said: 'It's well, but they are still not very experienced, and I know one who is greater than them, and it is Sigurd, son of King Sigmund. When he was a child, he killed the sons of King Hunding and avenged his father and Eylimi, his mother's father.' Gudrun said: 'What is the evidence of that? Was he already born when his father fell?' Brynhild said: 'His mother went to the battlefield and found King Sigmund wounded and offered to bind his wounds, but he said he was too old to fight, but told her to be comforted because she would bear a famous son, and it was the prophecy of a wise man. And after the death of King Sigmund she went to King Alf, and Sigurd was born there in great honour, and he did

[10] The story of Hagbard and Haki is to be found in Saxo Grammaticus' *Gesta Danorum*.

many deeds every day, and he is the most excellent man in the world.' Gudrun said, 'You have learned about him because of love. Yet I came here to tell you my dreams, I receive great grief from them.' Brynhild answered: 'Do not let this trouble you. Stay with your kinsmen, all of them will cheer you.' 'I dreamt,' said Gudrun, 'that we walked from the bower, many together, and we saw a large stag. He was far larger than other animals. His hair was of gold. We all wanted to take the animal, but I alone was able. The stag seemed better than all things. Then you shot the animal right before me. It was so great sorrow to me that I could hardly bear it. Then you gave me a wolf cub. It spattered me with the blood of my brothers.' Brynhild answers, 'I will tell you what will happen afterwards: Sigurd, whom I chose for my man, will come to you. Grimhild gives him bewitched mead, which will bring us all great sorrow. You will marry him and swiftly lose him. Then you'll marry King Atli. You will lose your brothers, and you will kill Atli.' Gudrun said, 'It is overwhelming sorrow to me to know that.' And they returned home to King Gjuki.

Chapter Twenty Six

Sigurd now rode away with that hoard of gold. They parted in friendship. He rode Grani with all his armour and load until he came to the hall of King Gjuki. He rode into the city, and one of the king's men saw that and said: 'I think one of the gods comes here. This man is all fitted out with gold. His horse is much bigger than other horses, and topped with fine weaponry. He is far above other men, and he carries himself over most men.' The king went out with his court and spoke to the man and asked: 'Who are you who ride into the city, which no one else dared do without leave of my sons?' He said,

'My name is Sigurd, and I am the son of King Sigmund.' King Gjuki said, 'Please come here with us, and receive everything that you wish.' He went into the hall, and everyone was short beside him, and they all waited on him, and he was held in great honour. They all rode together; Sigurd and Gunnar and Hogni, and Sigurd excelled them in all their skills, though all before him were great men. It was clear to Grimhild how much Sigurd loved Brynhild and how often he spoke of her. She thought to herself that it would be luckier if he settled there and married the daughter of King Gjuki, and she saw that no one was equal with him, and how important his support was, and he had much treasure, much more than men had known before. The king treated him as he did his sons, but they respected him more than themselves.

One evening as they sat drinking, the queen rose and went to Sigurd, saluted him, and said: 'It is a joy that you live here with us, and we will give all good things to you. Take this horn and drink.' He took it and drank. She said, 'King Gjuki shall be your father, and I your mother, your brothers Gunnar and Hogni and everyone who swears the oath, and then your equal will not be found.' Sigurd took it well, and because of that drink he forgot Brynhild. He stayed there for a while. And one day Grimhild went to King Gjuki and put her arms around his neck and said: 'The greatest warrior who has ever been found in the world has come here. His support would be of great use. Give him your daughter and much treasure and such power that he wants, and he will find pleasure here.' The king said, 'Rarely do men offer their daughters, but it is a greater honour to offer her to him than to have others propose.' And one evening Gudrun served the drink. Sigurd saw that she was a beautiful woman, and the most courteous in everything.

Sigurd was there two and a half years, so that they sat with fame and friendship, and one day the kings spoke together. King Gjuki said: 'Much good you have done us, Sigurd, and you have greatly strengthened our realm.' Gunnar said, 'We want to do everything to ensure that you stay here a long time, we have offered both status and our sister, and no other will get them, even if he asked.' Sigurd said, 'I thank you for your honour, and I accept it.' They swore an oath of brotherhood as if they were sons of the same family. An excellent feast was prepared and it lasted several days. Sigurd then married Gudrun. There were all kinds of joy and merriment, and each successive day was even better. They travelled in many countries, did many famous deeds, and killed many king's sons. No men achieved as much as they did now and they went home with much booty.

Sigurd gave Gudrun to eat of Fafnir's heart, and then she was much grimmer than before and wiser. Their son was named Sigmund. And one day Grimhild went to Gunnar, her son, and said: 'You flourish in all matters except for one thing, you are wifeless. Ask for Brynhild's hand. That would be the best match, and Sigurd will ride with you.' Gunnar answered, 'Yes, she is beautiful, and I am not unwilling,' and now he told his father and brothers, and Sigurd, and all encouraged him.

Chapter Twenty Seven

They now prepared magnificently for the journey, and they rode across mountains and valleys to King Budli where they submitted a proposal of marriage. He accepted it happily, unless she refused, and he said she was so proud that she would marry only the person she wished to. They ride to Hlymdale. Heimir greeted them warmly. Then Gunnar spoke of his errand. Heimir said Brynhild's choice of husband was what she would choose; he said her hall was close and he believed that the one she would marry was the one who rode through the wavering fire that burned about her hall. They found the hall and the fire and saw a fortress roofed with gold, and the fire burned outside it. Gunnar rode Goti, and Hogni Holkvi. Gunnar rode his horse towards the fire, but he retreated. Sigurd said, 'Why do you retreat, Gunnar?' He said, 'The horse does not want to run at the grim fire,' and he asked Sigurd to lend him Grani. 'I shall,' he said. Gunnar now rode at the fire, but Grani would not go. Then Gunnar could not cross this grim fire. They switched shapes as Grimhild taught Sigurd and Gunnar. Then Sigurd rode and he had Gram in his hand and he bound gold spurs on his feet. Grani leapt over the fire when he felt the spurs. Then there was a great din, the fire began to grow, the ground began to tremble. Flame stood against the sky. None had dared do this before, and it was as if he rode into the dark. Then the fire subsided, but he got down off his horse and went into the hall. So it is sung:

'*Fire was stirring,*

The ground trembled

And high flame

Towered to the sky.

Few there dared

Of the king's men

To ride to the fire

Or leap across it.

Sigurd pricked Grani

With his sword.

Fire extinguished

Before the prince,

Flame of all subsided

Before the praise-eager.

The glittering harness,

Regin had owned.'

And when Sigurd crossed over the fire he found a fair dwelling, and Brynhild sat there. She asked him who this man was. But he called himself Gunnar Gjukisson. - 'And you are meant for my wife by consent of your foster-father, as long as I ride your wavering flame, and if you agree.' 'I do not clearly know how I should respond to this,' she said. Sigurd stood upright on the floor and leaned on his swordhilt and spoke to Brynhild, 'In return I will pay you a large settlement in gold and good gifts.' She answered soberly from her seat like a swan on a wave and she had a sword in her hand and a helmet on her head and was in armour. 'Gunnar,' she said, 'do not speak of such matters to me unless you surpass everyone, and will kill those others who have asked for me if you have the courage. I was in battle with the king of Gardariki, and our weapons were

stained with human blood, and I yearn yet for this.'
He said: 'You have done many great things, but
remember your vow that if the fire was crossed you
would go with the man who did this.' She now saw
how true his answer was and marked the significance
of his words, and stood up and greeted him well.
Here he stayed for three nights, and they slept in one
bed. He took the sword Gram and laid it unsheathed
between them. She asked why he did this. He said
that it was fated that he would make his wedding to
his wife in this way, otherwise he would die. He took
from her the ring Andvari's Bequest, which he gave
her previously, and gave her another ring from
Fafnir's heritage. After that he rode away through
that same fire to his companions, and they switched
back shapes, and rode to Hlymdale and said how it
had gone.

On the same day Brynhild went home to her
foster father, and told him in confidence that a king
had come to her - 'through my wavering flame and
he said he came to marry with me and called himself
Gunnar. But I said that Sigurd alone would do that
when I swore my oath on the mountain, and he is
my first husband.' Heimir said that things would
have to stay as they were. Brynhild said: 'My
daughter by Sigurd, Aslaug, shall be brought up here
with you.' The kings went home now, but Brynhild
went to her father. Grimhild greeted them warmly
and thanked Sigurd for his aid. Arrangements were
made for the banquet. There was a great multitude.
King Budli came there with his daughter and Atli, his
son, and this feast lasted for days. And when the
festivities ended, Sigurd remembered all his oaths to
Brynhild although he kept quiet. Brynhild and
Gunnar sat together at the merriment and drank
good wine.

Chapter Twenty Eight

One day, when they went to the river Rhine to wash, Brynhild waded deeper into the water. Gudrun asked what this meant. Brynhild said: 'Why should I be your equal in this more than in other matters? I think that my father was greater than yours, my man has achieved many great deeds and he rode through burning fire, but your husband was the slave of King Hjalprek.' Gudrun answered in anger, 'You would be wiser if you were silent than to insult my husband. All people agree that no one has come into the world like him in all respects, and it is not fitting for you to insult him, for he is your first husband, and he slew Fafnir and rode through the wavering fire, though you thought him King Gunnar, and he lay with you and took the ring Andvari's Bequest off your hand, and now you can see it here yourself.' Brynhild now saw the ring and recognised it. Then she paled as if she was dead. Brynhild went home and spoke not a word that evening, and when Sigurd came to bed, Gudrun asked, 'Why is Brynhild so sad?' Sigurd said, 'I am not sure, but I believe we will know more clearly soon.' Gudrun said, 'Why does she not enjoy her wealth and happiness, and all men's praise, since she got the man she wanted?' Sigurd said, 'Where was she when she said this, when she claimed to have the best man or the one she would soonest marry?' Gudrun said, 'I will ask in the morning who she most wants to marry.' Sigurd answered, 'I will not let you, and you will regret it if you do that.'

But in the morning they sat in their chamber, and Brynhild was quiet. Then Gudrun said, 'Be merry Brynhild. Did our conversation trouble you? Or what prevents your happiness?' Brynhild answered: 'Evil alone led you to this, and you have a cruel heart.' 'Do not think that,' she said, 'and tell me instead.' Brynhild answered: 'Ask only what is better for you to know. That suits noble women. And it is easiest to be satisfied when all goes according to your wishes.' Gudrun said: 'It is early to boast, and this is somehow prophetic. Why are you goading me? I have done nothing to upset you.' Brynhild answered, 'You shall pay since you married Sigurd, and I cannot stand that you enjoy him and that great treasure.' Gudrun said, 'I did not know of your arrangement, and my father could well arrange for my marriage without asking you.' Brynhild answered, 'Our talk was not secret, and yet we had sworn oaths, and you knew that you betrayed me, and it shall be avenged.' Gudrun said, 'You are better married than you deserve, and your jealousy will not easily settle down in peace, and for that many will pay.' 'I would be happy,' said Brynhild, 'if you did not have the better man.' Gudrun said, 'You got a noble husband so that it is not certain who is the greater king, and you have plenty of wealth and power.' Brynhild answered: 'Sigurd fought Fafnir, and that is worth more than all the power of King Gunnar'- so it is said:

> *'Sigurd fought the serpent,*
>
> *And afterwards will*
>
> *Not be forgotten,*
>
> *While men live.*
>
> *But your brother*
>
> *Neither dared*
>
> *To ride across the fire*
>
> *Nor to leap across it.'*

Gudrun said: 'Grani would not leap the fire under King Gunnar, but he was not afraid to ride, and there is no need to scorn his own courage.' Brynhild answered: 'I will not hide the fact that I consider Grimhild badly.' Gudrun said, 'Do not blame her, since she treats you as a daughter.' Brynhild answered: 'She caused the beginning of all this misfortune that consumes us. She brought Sigurd the ruinous ale, so that he would not remember my name.' Gudrun said, 'You speak many false words, and this is a great lie.' Brynhild answered: 'Enjoy your Sigurd as if you have not betrayed me. You do not deserve to live together, and many matters will go for you as I foresee.' Gudrun answered, 'I will enjoy him more than you would want, and no one could say that he was too good to me even once.' Brynhild answered: 'I'll speak with you, and when you calm down, you will repent, and may we no longer bandy hateful words.' Gudrun said, 'You cast the first hateful words at me. Now you can pay me back for that, but cruelty is at the root of this.' 'Enough useless chatter,' said Brynhild. 'I was silent for a long time over the grief in my heart, but I only love your brother, now let us speak of other matters.' Gudrun said: 'Your thoughts see far beyond the present.' There was a great sorrow when they went to the river and she recognised the ring, from which came their argument.

Chapter Twenty Nine

After this discussion Brynhild lay in bed and the news reached Gunnar the king that she was sick. He went to her and asked what her problem was, but she said nothing and lay as if she was dead. As he continued his questions, she said, 'What did you do with the ring that I gave you? King Budli gave it me at our last parting when you sons of King Gjuki came to him and promised you would harry and burn unless you got me. Then he brought me to talk and asked who I would choose of those who were come, but I offered to defend the land and be chief of a third of the army. Then two options were available, that I should marry the man he wanted me to, or be without all his wealth and friendship, and he said that his friendship would be more profitable than his anger. So I debated with myself whether I was obliged to obey his will or to kill many men. I thought myself powerless to fight him, and I betrothed myself to he who rode the horse Grani with Fafnir's heritage and crossed my wavering flames and killed the men I chose should die. Now none dared to ride except Sigurd alone. He rode the fire because he lacked fear. He killed the serpent, and Regin, and the five kings, not like you, Gunnar, who blanched like a corpse. You are no king or warrior. And so I swore a vow at my father's home that I would love that man who is most nobly born but that is Sigurd. I am an oath-breaker now when I do not have him, and for this I will bring about your death. And I shall repay Grimhild with evil. I think no woman more cowardly or worse.' Gunnar answered, so that few could hear: 'You have spoken many false words, and you are a malicious woman, you blame the woman who is far beyond you, and was not as discontented as you are, nor did she torment dead men and she did not murder anyone, and she lives with praise.' Brynhild said: 'I have not had secret meetings or committed crimes, and my nature is different, and I would be willing to slay you.' Then she wanted to kill King Gunnar, but Hogni put her in chains. Gunnar said, 'I do not wish it that she live in chains.' She said, 'Do not concern yourself about that, because from this day you will never see me happy in your house or drink or play chess nor talk nor embroider with gold to make good clothes nor advise you.' She said that it was the greatest tragedy that she did not have Sigurd. She sat up and struck at her sewing so that it tore in pieces, and she asked that her bower door be opened, so people could hear her grief at long distances. Then there was much sorrow, and it was heard around town. Gudrun asked her handmaid why they were so sad and sorry – 'what is wrong with you, and why do you go about like crazy people, or what panic has you seized?' Then a woman of the court named Svafrlod said: 'This is a bad day. The hall is full of sorrow.' Then Gudrun said to her friend: 'Get up; we have had a long sleep. Wake Brynhild, go to do needlework and be happy.' 'That I will not do,' she said, 'to wake her or speak to her, and she has drunk no wine or mead many days, and she has incurred the wrath of the gods.' Then Gudrun said to Gunnar: 'Go to see her,' she said, 'and tell her that her sorrow saddens us.' Gunnar answered: 'It is forbidden that I meet her or share her treasure.' Still Gunnar went before her and tried in many ways to speak to her, and he did not get a response. He went away and met Hogni and told him to visit her. He said he was unwilling but went, however, and could get nothing out of her. And then Sigurd was found and asked to visit her. He said nothing, and so things went until the evening. And the day after, when he came home from hunting, he met Gudrun, and said: 'I have come to see that this horror is ill-omened, and Brynhild will die.' Gudrun answered, 'My lord, strangeness and wonder are linked with her. She has now slept seven days, so that no one dares to wake her.' Sigurd said, 'She does not sleep, she plots evil against us.' Then she spoke with tears: 'It is a great pity to foresee your death. Rather go and visit her and learn if she will settle down peacefully, give her gold and so appease her anger.' Sigurd went out and found the hall open. He thought her asleep and drew the bedclothes from her and said, 'Wake up, Brynhild, the sun shines all over town, and you have had enough sleep. Throw off your sorrow and take joy.' She said, 'What is this arrogance, that you come before me? No one has been worse to me in treachery.' Sigurd asked: 'Why do you not speak to the people? What troubles you?' Brynhild answered: 'I will tell you my anger.' Sigurd said: 'You are bewitched if you think I am cruel in my heart to you, when you received the one you chose as your man.' 'No,' she said, 'Gunnar did not ride through the fire, and he paid me no dowry in slain men. I wondered at the man who came into my hall, and I thought I recognised your eyes, and I could not clearly understand because a veil lay over my fate.' Sigurd said: 'I am not a nobler man than the sons of Gjuki. They killed the Danish kings and a great prince, the brother of King Budli.' Brynhild answered: 'Much evil I have to requite from them; do not remind me of my sorrow. You, Sigurd, slew the serpent and rode through fire for my sake, and no son of King Gjuki did that.' Sigurd answered, 'I was not your man, and you were not my wife, and a dowry was paid to you by a famous king.' Brynhild answered: 'I never looked at Gunnar so that my heart felt glad at him, and I hate him, though I hide it from others.' 'It is monstrous,' he said, 'that you do not love such a king, or what troubles you most? I think that his love for you would be worth more than wealth.' Brynhild answered: 'It is the worst of my sorrows that I cannot bring it about that a sharp sword is reddened in your blood.' Sigurd said, 'I am not afraid of it. It will be a short wait before I have a sharp sword sticking in my heart, and you could not ask for worse for yourself, because you will not live after me. From now on we have a few days of life.' Brynhild said, 'Your words do not result from little distress, you cheated me from everything dear, and I do not want to live.' Sigurd said, 'Live, and love King Gunnar and me, and I will give all my treasure that you do not die.' Brynhild answered: 'You do not you see my character clearly. You surpass all people, but you loathe no woman more than I.' Sigurd said: 'Another thing is true: I love you better than myself, though I was the object of treachery that cannot now be altered, because always, when I had my own mind, I mourned that you were not my wife. Yet I bore it as well as I could, since I lived in the king's hall, and I was happy that we were all together. It could be that what was prophesied will not come to pass, and it shall not be feared.' Brynhild answered, 'You have taken too long to tell me that my troubles cause you sorrow, but now I shall find no comfort.' Sigurd said: 'I very much wanted that we lie in one bed, and that you were my wife.' Brynhild answered, 'This is not to be said, and I will not have two kings in one house, and I would lose my life before I betray King Gunnar' - and she remembered now when they met on the mountain, and swore oaths - 'but everything is changed, and I do not want to live.' 'I could not remember your name,' said Sigurd, 'and I did not recognise you until you were married, and this is my greatest sorrow.' Then Brynhild said, 'I swore an oath that I should marry the man who rode my wavering flame, and I will keep that oath or die.' 'Rather than you die, I will marry you, and abandon Gudrun,' he said, but his sides swelled so that the rings of his armour snapped. 'I do not want you,' said Brynhild, 'or anyone else.' Sigurd went away. So says the Lay of Sigurd:

'Out went Sigurd

From their talk,

Worthy friend of Lofdi

And grieved,

So that the heaving breast

Of the battle-eager

Split from his sides,

That shirt woven of iron.'

And when Sigurd came into the hall, Gunnar asked if he knew what was afflicting her, or if she had her speech back. Sigurd said she could speak. And now Gunnar went to her a second time and asked what her sorrow meant or whether some remedy would cure it. 'I do not want to live,' said Brynhild, 'because Sigurd has deceived me, and no less you, when you let him come into my bed. Now I will not have two men in one house, and it shall be the bane of Sigurd or yours or mine, because he has told all that to Gudrun, and she despises me. '

Chapter Thirty

After that Brynhild went out and sat under the bower wall for some time and uttered many tragic laments, saying that all was hateful to her, both land and power, because she did not have Sigurd. And again Gunnar came to her. Then Brynhild said, 'You shall lose both power and wealth, life, and me, and I will go home to my kinsmen and sit in sorrow unless you kill Sigurd and his son. Do not raise a wolf cub.' Gunnar became very anxious and he thought he did not know what to do, he was oathbound to Sigurd, and various ideas played in his mind, however, it seemed the greatest disgrace if his wife would leave him. Gunnar said, 'Brynhild is more precious, and the most famous of all women, and I would sooner lose my life than her love,' and he called for Hogni his brother and said: 'I am faced with a hard choice,' and he said that he wanted to kill Sigurd, and that he had betrayed his trust, - 'and we will then have the gold and all the power.' Hogni said, 'It's not fitting that we break our oaths and breach the peace. We have had much aid from him. No kings are our equals as long as this Hunnish king lives, and we will never get such an in-law again, and think how good it would be if we should have such a brother-in-law and sister's sons, and I see how this trouble started. Brynhild has stirred it, and her advice leads us to great dishonour and destruction.' Gunnar said, 'This should be carried out, and I see how: we will egg on Guttorm our brother to do it. He's young and knows little and is not bound by oath.' Hogni said: 'That advice seems poor to me, and though the deed is done, we will pay for betraying such a man.' Gunnar said Sigurd shall die, - 'or I will die otherwise.' He asked Brynhild to stand up and be cheerful. She stood up and said, however, that Gunnar would not share the same bed as her until it had come to pass. Then the brothers consulted together. Gunnar said that this was a valid punishment for Sigurd having taken Brynhild's maidenhead, - 'and let us egg on Guttorm to do this work,' and called him to them, offering him gold and great power to do this. They took a serpent and wolf flesh and boiled them and gave him to eat, as the skald said:

> 'Some took a wood-fish,
>
> Some sliced wolf meat,

Some gave to Guttorm

Wolf's flesh

Mixed with beer,

And they worked many more

Acts of witchcraft.'

And with this food, and Grimhild's persuasions and all that, he became so violent and fierce that he would do this work. They promised him great honour in return. Sigurd did not anticipate this intrigue. He could not prevail against his fate or his death. Also he did not realise that he should expect betrayal from them.

Guttorm entered Sigurd's room in the morning as he lay in his bed. And when he looked at him, Guttorm dared not attack and disappeared out the back, and so it went a second time. Sigurd's eyes were so fierce that very few dared meet that gaze. And a third time he went in, and Sigurd was asleep. Guttorm drew his sword and stabbed Sigurd so that the sword went through into the mattresses under him. Sigurd woke from the wound, but Guttorm ran out through the door. Then Sigurd took the sword Gram and flung it after him, and it hit his back and cut him through his middle. His lower body fell one way, but his head and arms toppled back into the chamber. Gudrun was asleep in the arms of Sigurd, but she woke up to unspeakable grief. She was washed in his blood, and she cried tears of grief, so Sigurd rose on the bolster and spoke, 'Do not weep,' he said. 'Your brothers live to bring you pleasure, but our young son cannot keep an eye out for his foes, and they have provided badly for themselves.

They will not get such an in-law to ride in an army or such a sister's son, if he is allowed to grow up. And now it comes to pass as it was long foretold. I would not believe it, but none can endure his fate. Brynhild caused this, but she loved me more than any man, and I can swear that I never hurt Gunnar, and I respected our oaths, and I was not too great a friend of his wife. If I had known earlier that this would happen and I had been on my feet with my weapons, many of them would have lost their lives before I fell, and all the brothers would have been killed, and it have been would harder for them to kill me than to slay the wildest bison or boar.'

The king now lost his life and Gudrun let out a tormented sigh. Brynhild heard it and laughed when she heard her sob. Then Gunnar said, 'You do not laugh because you rejoice in your heart, or why have you lost your colour? You are monstrous and mighty, and most likely you are fated to die, and it would be fitting that you saw King Atli killed in front of you, and be forced to watch. Now we have to sit over our in-law who was killed by his brother.' She replied, 'No taunt that should be having killed enough, but King Atli is not be perturbed by your threats or anger, and he will live longer than you and have more power.' Hogni said, 'Now is come to pass that which Brynhild predicted, and we will not remedy this evil deed.' Gudrun said, 'My kinsmen have killed my husband. Now you will ride in the vanguard, and when you come to fight you will find that Sigurd is not to hand, and then you will see that Sigurd was your luck and strength, and if he had had a son like him, then you would be strengthened by his offspring and their kin.'

Chapter Thirty One

No one could understand why Brynhild laughed as she laughed as she asked for that which she lamented with tears. She said: 'It was my dream, Gunnar, that I had a cold bed, but you rode to your enemies. All your house will come to a bad end, you're oathbreakers, and you plotted his death; you mixed your blood together, you and Sigurd, you have forgotten this, and you have rewarded him with evil for all that he did for you when he caused you to be foremost. When he came to me he kept his oath, he laid between us a sharp-edged sword, tempered in poison. But early on you plotted to harm him, and me, when I was at home with my father, and I had all that I wanted, and I intended that none of you should be mine when you rode into the fortress with the three kings. Atli took me aside to talk and asked if I would marry the man who rode Grani. He did not look like you, and I betrothed myself to the son of King Sigmund, and no other, and matters shall go badly for you, even if I die.'

Then Gunnar stood up and put his arms around her neck and asked that she would live and accept compensation, and everyone else opposed her death. But she quickly pushed them away when they came to her, and she said that the man who discouraged her from what she intended would get nothing. Then Gunnar appealed to Hogni and begged his advice, and asked him to go and see if he could soften her temper, and said that now there was need enough on their hands to turn away her sorrow until time had passed. Hogni answered: 'No one should hinder her death because she has never benefited us or any man since she came here.' Then she asked for a great deal of gold and asked where everyone was who wanted to receive treasure. Then she took a sword, and thrust it under her arm and sank on to the mattresses and said: 'Let each one here now take gold, who would have it.' All were silent. Brynhild said, 'Accept the gold and enjoy it.' Then Brynhild said to Gunnar, 'Now I will tell you how things will go in a little time: soon you will make peace with Gudrun through the advice of Grimhild, skilled in magic. The daughter of Gudrun and Sigurd will be named Svanhild, and she will be the fairest of all women born. Gudrun will marry Atli against her wishes. You will want to marry Oddrun, but Atli will forbid this. Then you will have secret meetings, and she will love you. Atli will betray you and put you into a snake pit, and then Atli and his sons will be killed. Gudrun will kill them. Then a large wave will carry her to the fortress of King Jonak. She will have fine sons. Svanhild will be sent out of the country and married to King Jormunrek. She will be stung by Bikki's advice. And then your entire house will be gone, and Gudrun's sorrows are increased. Now I ask you, Gunnar, as a last request: make a great pyre on the level ground for all of us, me and Sigurd and those who were killed with him. Let there be tents reddened with human blood and burn the Hunnish king [11] with me on one hand, and my men on his other hand, two at his head, two at his feet, and two hawks. So it will be distributed equally. Lie a drawn sword in between us as before, when we entered one bed and vowed to become husband and wife. The door will not close at his heels if I follow him, and our funeral procession will not be unworthy, if five female slaves and eight servants that my father gave me are following him, and burn those who were

---

[11] i.e. Sigurd, whose forefathers ruled Hunland. A similar 'Viking funeral' features in the classic adventure novel *Beau Geste*.

killed by Sigurd there. And I would say more if I was not hurt, but now the wound hisses, and the scars are opened. However, I told the truth.'

Then Sigurd's corpse was prepared according to the old ways and they made a great pyre. And when it was kindled, the three winters' old son of Sigurd Fafnir's Bane's, whom Brynhild had ordered killed, was laid on top of his body, and Guttorm with him. And when the pyre was burning, Brynhild went out there and told her maids to take the gold that she would give them. And after this Brynhild died and she burned there with Sigurd, and so their lives ended.

Chapter Thirty Two

When they heard the news everyone said that that no one so great remained in the world and a man equal in all ways to Sigurd would never be born; his name would never be forgotten in the German tongue, and in the northern lands, as long as the world lasts. It is said that one day, when Gudrun sat in her chamber, she said, 'Better was the life that I had with Sigurd. He was better than all men as gold is better than iron or the leek is than other plants or the stag than other animals, until my brothers envied me of a man who surpassed all other men. They could not sleep until they killed him. Grani made much noise when he saw the wounds of his master. Then I spoke with him as a person, but his head drooped to the earth and he knew that Sigurd had fallen.'

Then Gudrun went away to the woods and heard on all sides the sound of predators and she thought it was better to die. She travelled until she came to the hall of King Half, and she sat there in

Denmark three and a half years with Thora Hakon's daughter and there was much celebration and eating. She wove a tapestry and depicted there many great deeds and fair games common at that time, swords and mailcoats, all a king's trappings, and the ships of King Sigmund sailing off the shore. And they embroidered a tapestry of the battle of Sigar and Siggeir, south at Funen. Such was their entertainment, and it comforted Gudrun a little in her sorrow.

Grimhild learnt where she was, and insisted on speaking to her sons and asked how they wanted to compensate Gudrun for her son and her man, saying that they were obliged to do so. Gunnar said he wished to give her gold and so recompense her for her grief. They summoned their friends and prepared their horses, helmets, shields, swords and mailcoats, and all kinds of armour. And this trip was outfitted splendidly, and no warrior who was great sat at home. Their horses were armoured, and each knight had either a gilded or burnished helmet. Grimhild decided to go with them and said their errand would be completed only if she did not sit at home. They had a total of five hundred men. They also had excellent men. There was Valdimar of Denmark and Eymod and Jarisleif. They went into the hall of King Half. There were Lombards, Franks and Saxons. They went in full armour and wore red fur cloaks, as is sung:

> 'Short mailshirts,
>
> Moulded helmets,
>
> Swords girded,
>
> And auburn hair cut short.'

They wanted to choose good gifts for their sister and they spoke well of her, but she trusted none of them. Then Grimhild brought her evil drink which she was forced to take, and she forgot her sorrow. The drink was mixed with the strength of the earth and sea, and the blood of her son, and inside the drinking horn were many runes, reddened with blood, as follows:

There were in the horn

Many runes,

Cut and reddened,

I could not conceive them:

The long heather-fish,

Of the Haddings' country,

Uncut ears of grain,

Beast's entrails.

In that beer were

Many evils mixed:

Herbs of all trees

And burned acorn,

Hearth's dew,

Sacrificed entrails,

Pig's liver boiled,

So claims were blunted.'

And after that, when all wanted the same, there was a great celebration. When Grimhild met Gudrun she said: 'Good luck, daughter, I'll give you gold and all manner of vessels that you will receive from your father's legacy, costly rings and bed hangings, Hunnish maidens who are most courteous, and then you will be compensated for your man. You shall wed King Atli the powerful. Then you will rule his wealth. Do not abandon your kin because of one man, but instead do as we ask.' Gudrun said, 'I will not marry King Atli, and joining the same race together like this will not enhance our honour.' Grimhild replied, 'You must not plan revenge now; you must live as if Sigurd and Sigmund were still alive.' Gudrun said, 'I do not forget him, he was the best of all men.' Grimhild said: 'You will marry this king. If not, you shall not marry at all.' Gudrun said, 'Do not offer me this king because only grief for our family will result from my marriage to him, and he will use your sons evilly, and thereafter will come fierce vengeance.' Grimhild became ill at her words and said: 'Do as we ask, and you will have great honour and our friendship, and those places named Vinbjorg and Valbjorg.' Her words were so strong that this could not be avoided. Gudrun said: 'This will happen then, but it is against my will, and it will not give much chance for enjoyment, but for mourning.' Then they mounted their horses, and their wives were placed in wagons, and they travelled seven days on horseback, another seven by ship and the third seven over land, until they came to a high hall. A great throng went to meet them, and an excellent feast was prepared, which had already been agreed upon, and it went with honour and great glory. And Atli drank the marriage toast to Gudrun at that feast. But her thoughts never laughed with him, and their marriage was with little affection.

Chapter Thirty Three

It is said that one night King Atli woke up out of sleep. He spoke to Gudrun, 'I dreamed,' he said, 'that you stabbed at me with a sword.' Gudrun interpreted the dream and said that to dream of iron indicated fire, - 'and your self-deception in thinking you're the foremost.' Atli said, 'Also I dreamed that two reeds grew up here, and I never wanted to harm them. Then they were torn up by the roots, and reddened with blood, and served on the table and offered to me to eat. Still I dreamed, that two hawks flew from my hand and had no prey to catch and went to Hel. It seemed to me their hearts were mixed with honey, and I thought I ate them. Then it seemed to me that beautiful whelps lay before me, and cried out loudly, and I ate their carcasses unwillingly.' Gudrun said, 'You do not have good dreams, but they will be fulfilled. Your sons are doomed to die, and many heavy things will come to us in time.' 'This I dreamed of yet,' he said, 'that I lay in bed and my death was appointed.'

This time drew near, and their life together was cold. King Atli wondered where Sigurd's hoard of gold could be, but only King Gunnar and his brother knew. Atli was a great king and mighty, wise, and he had a great retinue. Then he discussed with his men how it could be done. He knew that Gunnar and his folk owned much more treasure than anyone else; he decided to send messengers to the brothers and to invite them to a feast and honour them in many ways. The man who led them was named Vingi. The queen knew of the secret meeting and she thought there would be treachery to the brothers.

Gudrun scored runes and she took a gold ring and then tied a wolf's hair and she put this in the hands of the kings' messengers. Then they went as the King had ordered. And before they got ashore, Vingi saw the runes and changed them another way so that Gudrun seemed eager for them to see Atli. Then they came to the hall of King Gunnar, and they received them well and built big fires for them. And then they drank the finest drink with joy. Vingi said, 'King Atli sent me here, and he wishes that you would visit his home in great honour and accept great honour from him, helmets and shields, swords and armour, gold and good clothes, a war band and horses and a great domain, and that you both succeed him.' Then Gunnar turned his head and said to Hogni: 'What will we make of this offer? He invites us both to accept great power, but no king I know has as much gold as we do, since we have the gold that lay on Gnita Heath and we have large chambers of gold and the oldest of edged weapons and all kinds of armour. I know my horse and sword are the finest and oldest, and my gold is most precious.' Hogni said: 'I wonder at his offer, because he has rarely done such, and it seems madness to go to see him, and I wondered when I saw the treasure that King Atli sent us and I saw the wolf hair tied round a gold ring, and it may be that Gudrun thinks he has wolfish thoughts toward us and she did not want us to go, lest we perish.' Then Vingi showed him runes that he said Gudrun had sent.

Most of them went to sleep then, but some were drinking with several men. Then Hogni's wife, fairest of women, who was named Kostbera, went and looked at the runes. Gunnar's wife Glaumvor was noble and great. They served drinks. The kings became quite drunk. Vingi saw this and said, 'I cannot hide it that King Atli becomes too infirm and much too old to defend his country and his sons are too young and unready. Now he wants to give you power over the kingdom while they are so young, and he would be happy that you enjoyed it.' By then Gunnar was very drunk, but he was being offered great power, and he could not escape his fate, and now he said he would make the journey, and he told his brother. He said, 'Your word will stand, and I will follow you, but I am unwilling to make this journey.'

Chapter Thirty Four

And when they had drunk as much as they liked they went to sleep. Kostbera took a look at the runes and read the letters and saw what was cut there, but something else was underneath, and the runes were falsified. But by her wisdom she understood what they said. After that she went to bed with her husband. When they woke up, she said to Hogni, 'Are you going? It is ill-advised. Rather, go another time, and you are not skilled in reading runes if you think your sister asked you to come at this time. I interpreted runes, and I wondered how a woman so wise has cut them so wildly, but your death is indicated underneath, and there was a missing letter, or else someone else has falsified them. And now you will hear my dream: In my dream it seemed that a hard river rushed in here, and broke up the beams in the hall.' He replied, 'You often have premonitions of evil, and I have no mood to show hatred to others unless it is deserved. He will greet us well.' She said, 'You may try, but friendship is not behind the invitation. And again I dreamed that another river rushed in here with terrible uproar and broke up all the benches in the hall and broke your legs and your brothers', and it must mean something.' He said, 'What you thought was a river will be fields that will stretch out, and often when we walk in the field large husks cover our legs.' 'I dreamed,' she said, 'that your bedcovers were ablaze and fire leapt up from the hall.' He answered: 'I know clearly what it is: our clothes lie about neglected, and they are what will burn, what you thought were bedcovers.' 'I thought a bear came in here,' she said, 'and broke up the king's throne and shook his paws so that we were all scared, and took us all in his mouth so that we could do nothing, and it came as a great fear.' He said, 'What you thought a polar bear will be a great wind.' 'I thought an eagle came in here,' she said, 'and flew through the hall and spattered me with blood, and all of us, and this will bode evil, because I thought that it was the fetch of King Atli.' He said, 'Often we slaughter generously and kill a big bull for our entertainment, and it means oxen when you dream of eagles, and Atli means well to us.' And they ended their talk.

Chapter Thirty Five

It is told of Gunnar that there was a similar event, when they woke up. Glaumvor, Gunnar's wife, relates many of her dreams that seemed to predict treachery, but Gunnar reinterpreted them all. 'This was one of them,' she said, 'I thought that a bloody sword was carried here in the hall, and you were wounded, and wolves howled at both ends of the sword.' The king said: 'Small dogs will want to bite us; the barking of dogs is often shown by bloodied weapons.' She said: 'Again I thought women came in here, and they were sombre-looking, and they chose you as their husband. Perhaps they were your *dísir*.[12]' He said: 'Things become hard to interpret, and one cannot avoid one's destiny, but it

_____

[12] Goddesses of the family who appear before a death.

is not unlikely that I will be short-lived.' In the morning they got up and wanted to go, but others were against it. Then Gunnar said to a man named Fjornir, 'Get up and give us drink from the large goblets of good wine, because perhaps this will be our last feast. The old wolf will get our gold if we die, and the bear will not hesitate to bite with his battle-teeth.' The household led them out in tears. Hogni's son said, 'Go well and have good fortune.' The greater part of the war band remained behind them. Solar and Snævar went, sons of Hogni, and a great champion named Orkning. He was the brother of Bera. People followed them to the ships, and tried to persuade them against the journey, but they achieved nothing. Then Glaumvor spoke. 'Vingi,' she said, 'it is more likely that great unhappiness will arise from your coming, and important events will happen during your journey.' He answered, 'I swear that I do not lie, and may the high gallows and all the trolls take me if I lie in any word.' And he did not spare himself in these speeches. Bera said: 'Go well, and in good fortune.' Hogni answered: 'Be cheerful, whatever happens to us.' They parted to go to their own destinies. Then they rowed so hard and with such strength that the keel came off the ship as much as half. They hauled hard on the oars with big pulls, so that they broke handles and oar-pins. And when they came to land, they did not secure their ships. Then they rode their fine horses through dark woods for a while. They saw the royal town. There they heard a great noise and a clash of weapons and they saw a crowd of men and they made great preparations, and all the gates were full of men. They rode to the town, and the gate was shut. Hogni broke open the gate, and they rode into the city. Vingi said: 'It would be better that you had not done this. Now wait here while I find a gallows tree for you. I bade you courteously to come here but deceit lurked beneath. Now it will be a short time to wait before you will be hanged.' Hogni said: 'We shall never give way to you, and I hardly think that we'll shrink back where the men are fighting, and you will get nothing trying to scare us, and that will prove ill for you.' They flung him down and then beat him to death with their axe hafts.

Chapter Thirty Six

They rode to the king. King Atli appointed his war band for battle, and formations were deployed so that a courtyard lay in between them. 'We welcome you to us,' he said, 'now give me the hoard of gold that belongs to us, the treasure that Sigurd had, but now Gudrun owns.' Gunnar said, 'You will never get the treasure, and resolute men will meet you here before we give up our lives if you show us fight. It may be that, with little tightfistedness, you will provide a manful feast for the eagle and the wolf.' 'For a long time I held it in my mind,' he said, 'to take your lives, and to have the gold and reward you for your evil when you cheated your fine brother-in-law, and I will avenge him.' Hogni answered: 'It will not help that you have long plotted this deed, because you are not ready.'

Then the battle went hard, and at the outset was a shower of arrows. And now the news came to Gudrun. When she heard this, she drooped and threw off her cloak. After that, she went out and greeted those who had come, and kissed her brothers and showed them love, and that was their last greeting. Then she said, 'I thought I had found a way to stop you coming, but no one can withstand their fate.' Then she said, 'Will the man get nothing for seeking peace?' But all refused flatly. When she saw that the game was going against her brothers; she thought of a bold course; she put on armour and took a sword and fought beside her brothers and advanced like the bravest of men, and all tell this in the same way, that they had hardly seen a stronger defence. There was a great slaughter of men. However, the brothers' courage was greater than any others. The battle lasted a long while now, all afternoon. Gunnar and Hogni went through King Atli's ranks, and it is said that the entire field streamed with blood. Then the sons of Hogni pushed forward strongly. King Atli said, 'I have a great troop, and proud, great champions, but now many of us fall, and we have to repay you ill, nineteen of my heroes are killed, and eleven are the only ones left behind.' And there was a rest in the battle. Then King Atli said, 'We were four brothers, and I am now the only one remaining. I got a great marriage alliance, and I thought to promote my standing. I had a wife friendly and wise, generous and hard-minded, but I could not enjoy her wisdom because we rarely agreed. You have killed many of my kin, cheated me of my kingdom and the treasure, and brought about my sister's death, which grieves me the most.' Hogni said, 'Why do you say that? You broke the peace first. You took my kinswoman and starved her to death and killed her and took the treasure, and that was not royal conduct, and it seems laughable to me that you are recounting your grief and I would thank the gods that things go badly for you.'

Chapter Thirty Seven

King Atli urged his war band to make a fierce assault. They fought fiercely, and the Gjukungs pressed forward so hard that King Atli retreated into the hall, and then they fought inside, and it was a savage battle. The fight went with a great loss of people and it ended up so that everyone fell in the troop of the brothers, so that they were two, but before this many a man was sent to Hel with their weapons. Then King Gunnar attacked, and due to greater strength he was seized and put in chains. Then Hogni fought with great bravery and honour and killed twenty of King Atli's major champions. He flung many into the fire that was made in the hall. All were of one mind, that they had hardly ever seen such a man. But at last he was overborne and made prisoner. King Atli said, 'It is a great wonder how many people have fallen before this man. Now cut out his heart, and it will be his end.' Hogni said, 'Do as you like. I will heartily await what you wish to do, and you will understand that my heart is not afraid; I have endured hard ordeals before, and I was eager to endure suffering when I was unwounded. But now I am badly hurt, and you alone will decide our dispute.' Then an adviser of King Atli said: 'I have better advice: Take instead a thrall's heart, and spare Hogni. The slave is destined for death. As long as he has lived, he was wretched.' The slave heard, screamed, and ran to where he saw hope of shelter, and he said he had a bad deal from their hostility and he would pay. He greeted a bad day; he would die and leave his soft life and pig keeping. They grabbed him and drew their knives. He yelled out before he felt the point. Then Hogni spoke in the way customary for the strong when facing death: he interceded for the slave's life, and said he would not hear shrieking, he said that he was better at this game. The slave was freed and then given his life.

Then they were both placed in chains, Gunnar and Hogni. King Atli told King Gunnar that he should tell him the location of the gold if he would keep his life. He said, 'Sooner would I see the bloody heart of Hogni, my brother.' And now they seized the slave a second time and cut out his heart and brought it before King Gunnar. He said: 'The heart of Hjalli the cowardly can be seen here; it is different from the heart of Hogni the fearless, for it trembles now, and it did even more when it lay in his chest.' Then King Atli urged them to go after Hogni and cut out his heart. And he was so strong that he laughed while he suffered this torture, and everyone marvelled at his courage, and it has been remembered ever since. They showed the heart of Hogni to Gunnar. He answered, 'Here is the heart of Hogni the fearless and it is unlike that of Hjalli the cowardly, because now it stirs a little, but it stirred less when it lay in his breast. And so you, Atli, will lose your life, as we now lose ours. And now I alone know where the gold is and Hogni will not tell you. My mind wavered when we both lived, but now the decision is mine. The Rhine shall now have the gold until the Huns bear it on their arms.' King Atli said, 'Take the prisoner away.' And it was done. Gudrun summoned men to her and she met with Atli and said: 'Evil go with you, as you held your word to me and Gunnar.'

Then he placed King Gunnar in a snake pit. There were many serpents there, and his hands were bound tight. Gudrun sent him a harp, but he showed his skill by striking the harp with great art, plucking the strings with his toes and playing so well that few thought they had heard such strumming even with the fingers, and he continued to play skilfully until all the serpents were asleep except one great and evil-looking adder that crawled up to him and bit into his trunk until she struck his heart, and then he lost his life with great bravery.

Chapter Thirty Eight

King Atli now thought he had won great victory and he said so to Gudrun, even with a little mockery or even as if he boasted; 'Gudrun,' he said, 'now you have lost your brothers, and you brought it about yourself.' She said, 'You delight in describing this battle to me, but maybe you will repent when you try it, when a matter comes, and what you will inherit longest will be cruelty undying, and things will go ill for you as long as I live.' He said: 'We will now make our peace, and I will compensate you with gold and precious gifts for the way your brothers followed your wishes.' She said: 'For a long time I have not been easy to deal with, but I could tolerate matters while Hogni lived. You will never pay for my brothers so that I am satisfied, but often we women are forced to bow to your power. Now my kin are all dead, and now you alone will control me. I will accept my lot, and let us make a great feast, and I will honour my brothers and your kin.' Then she spoke gentle words to him, but she was still afflicted underneath. He was swayed and he believed that her words were sincere. Gudrun now prepared a funeral feast for her brothers and so did King Atli for his men, and that feast was turbulent.

Then Gudrun thought of her woes, and she waited for an opportunity to give the king great shame. And in the evening she took her sons to King Atli, when they played by their bedposts. The boys grew downcast and asked what they should do. She replied, 'Do not ask. You shall both be killed.' They said, 'Do with your children what you want. No one will stop you. But you will have shame for doing this.' Then she cut their throats. The king asked after them, where his sons were. Gudrun answers, 'I will tell you that and gladden your heart:

you gave me much grief when you killed my brothers. Now you shall hear my speech: you have lost your sons, and their skulls are now serving as cups, and you drank their blood mixed with wine. I took their hearts and roasted them on spits, but you ate them.' King Atli answered, 'You are cruel, because you killed your sons and gave me their flesh to eat, and little time is lost in between your evil acts.' Gudrun said, 'It is my desire to bring you great shame, and no punishment can be cruel enough for such a bad king.' The king said: 'Worse, you have done a deed without example, and such brutality shows a great lack of wisdom, and you deserve to be burned on a fire and beaten to death by stones, and you would have what you deserve for going on this way.' She said: 'You foretell this yourself, but I will receive another death.' They spoke with many words, breathing hatred.

Hogni had a son left behind named Niflung. The boy felt a great hatred towards King Atli, and he told Gudrun that he wanted to avenge his father. She took it well, and they planned it together. She said there would be much luck in it, if it could be done. In the evening, when the king had drunk, he went to sleep. When he was asleep, Gudrun went there with the son of Hogni. Gudrun took a sword, and thrust it into the chest of King Atli. Both she and the son of Hogni did the deed. King Atli woke at the wound and said, 'It will not do to bandage me or to provide cures, but who caused me this grim injury?' Gudrun said, 'I did this somewhat, but some of it was done by Hogni's son.' King Atli said, 'It was not honourable for you to do this, though there was some cause, and you were married at the advice of your kin, and I paid a dowry for you, thirty good horsemen and comely maidens and many others, and if you did not act with moderation unless you controlled the countries that King Budli had, and you often caused your mother-in-law to cry.' Gudrun said, 'You have said much that is false, and I do not care about that, and I was often uncomfortable in my mind, but you increased that much. There has often been great feuding in your house, and kin and friends often fought, and taunted one another, and it was a better life when I was with Sigurd. We killed kings and ruled their lands and gave quarter to those who wished, but the chiefs yielded to us, and we gave riches to whoever wanted. Then I lost Sigurd, and it was a small thing to bear the name of widow, but what I regret most is that I came to you, when previously I was married to the noblest of kings, and you never came out of a battle without being defeated.' King Atli answered, 'It is not true, but such tales improve neither your lot nor mine, because now I have been defeated. Act properly to me now and let my body be prepared fittingly.' She said, 'I will let you be nobly buried and make you an honourable coffin and wrap you in beautiful fabrics, thinking of your every need.'

After that, he died. She did as she had said. Then she set the hall on fire. And the retainers woke up with fear, and they would not tolerate the fire and hewed at each other and killed each other. There the life of King Atli and all his court was ended.

Gudrun would not live after these things, but her final day was not yet come. They say that the Volsungs and Gjukungs were the greatest, most fearless and powerful men, and so it is found in all the ancient poems. And now this war halted with these events.

Chapter Thirty Nine

Gudrun and Sigurd's daughter was named Svanhild. She was the fairest of women and she had keen eyes like her father, so that very few dared to return her gaze. She was more beautiful than other women just as the sun is more beautiful than other heavenly bodies.

Gudrun went to the sea and took stones in her arms and went into the sea and tried to kill herself. Then a large wave carried her out over the sea, and she crossed with their help and came at last to the fortress of King Jonak. He was a mighty king and had a great retinue. He married Gudrun. Their children were Hamdir and Sorli and Erp. Svanhild was raised there.

Chapter Forty

Jormunrek was another king. He was a mighty king at that time. His son was named Randver. The king insisted on speaking his son and said, 'You shall go on a mission to King Jonak with my counsellor named Bikki. There is a girl called Svanhild, the daughter of Sigurd Fafnir's Bane, who I know is the fairest maiden under the sun. I wish to marry her. I want you to ask for me.' He said: 'I am obliged, Lord, to go on your mission.' Then he prepared honourably for the journey. They went until they came to King Jonak and saw Svanhild, and they thought her beauty most worthy. Randver met with the king and said: 'Jormunrek wishes to offer you a marriage alliance. He has heard of Svanhild, and he wants her for his wife, and it is unlikely that she could be given to a more powerful man than he is.'

The king said that it was worthy advice and he was very famous. Gudrun said: 'Fortune is too fragile a thing to trust, that it does not break.' But with the exhortations of the king all that was considered, it was now agreed, and Svanhild went to the ship with an honourable entourage and sat on the quarterdeck with the king's son. Then Bikki said to Randver: 'It would be better that you married so beautiful a woman, but not that so old a man did.' He agreed with that idea and spoke to her with kindness and she did to him. They came home and went to see the king. Bikki said: 'It is important, sire, to know how matters stand, although it is hard to relate, but there has been intrigue against you and your son has got full love of Svanhild, and she is his mistress, and let this not go unpunished.' Previously he had given him much bad advice. However, this piece of his advice was his worst. The king listened to his many evil counsels. He could not calm his rage, and he said that Randver should be hanged on the gallows. When he was led to the gallows, he took a hawk and plucked all his feathers from him and said that they were to show this to his father. And when the king saw, he said: 'It can now be seen that he thinks that I am as stripped of honour as the hawk is of feathers' - and he commanded him to be removed from the gallows. Meanwhile Bikki had been busy, and he was dead. Still Bikki said: 'No one deserves worse than Svanhild. Let her die with shame.' The king answered: 'I accept your advice.' Afterwards she was bound in the fortress gate and horses were ridden over her. When she opened her eyes, horses dared not trample her. But when Bikki saw that, he had a skin bag pulled over her head[13] , and so it was done,

---

[13] This is comparable to similar scenes, i.e. in *Hrafnkel's Saga* where supernatural beings have to have their eyes covered

and then she died.

Chapter Forty One

Gudrun heard now of the execution of Svanhild and spoke to her sons. 'Why do you sit still and speak glad words when Jormunrek has killed your sister and had her shamefully trodden under horses' feet? You do not have temper like Gunnar or Hogni. They would avenge their kinswomen.' Hamdir answered, 'You hardly praised Gunnar and Hogni when they killed Sigurd and you were reddened with his blood, and your revenge for your brothers was evil, when you killed your sons, and we might better kill King Jormunrek together. Nor will we speak taunting words, as hard as we are egged on.' Laughing, Gudrun gave them drink from deep beakers. And after that she chose for them large mailcoats and other armour. Then Hamdir said: 'Here we shall part for the last time, and you'll hear news, and then you will hold a wake for us and Svanhild.'

After that they went. But Gudrun went to her chamber, her sorrow increased, and she said: 'Three men have I married, first Sigurd Fafnir's Bane, and he was betrayed, and that was for me the greatest grief. Then was I given to King Atli, but so cruel was my heart towards him that I killed our sons in my grief. I went into the sea, and with a wave it lifted me to land and I was given to the king. Then I gave

---

before they can be stoned to death. It seems that they are protected by the power of their eyes. In *Kormak's saga*, a magic sword must be kept hidden from the eyes of a berserk or else his evil eyes will blunt it. Berserks are commonly immune to edged weapons but, like Hamdir and Sorli, can be killed by stones or clubs.

Svanhild away from the country in marriage, with much treasure, and it is my saddest sorrow after Sigurd that she was trampled under horses' feet. And my grimmest woe is that Gunnar was put in a snake pit, but the hardest is that Hogni's heart was cut out of him, and it was better that Sigurd would welcome me and take me with him. Now no son or daughter sits here with me to console me. Remember now, Sigurd, what we spoke of when we shared a bed; that you would visit me out of Hel and wait for me.' And so ends her lament.

Chapter Forty Two

It is said of the sons of Gudrun that she had prepared their armour so that no iron bit it, and she asked them to cause no damage with stones or other large objects and said that they would be harmed if they did. And when they had gone on their way they met Erp, their brother, and asked how he would aid them. He said, 'As the hand helps the hand or the foot helps the foot.' It seemed to them that he would not help, so they killed him. They went on their way, and a little while later Hamdir reeled and put down his hand and said: 'Erp must have spoken truly. I would not have fallen if I had not braced myself with my hand.' A little later Sorli stumbled and stuck out his leg and regained balance and said: 'I would have fallen now, if I had not supported myself with my foot.' Then they said they had done evil to Erp, their brother. They went on until they came to King Jormunrek, and they went before him and attacked him. Hamdir cut off his hands, and Sorli hacked off his feet.

Then Hamdir said: 'Now his head would be off if Erp our brother lived, whom we slew on the way, and we have realised it too late,' which is sung:

'The head would now be off

If Erp lived,

Our battle-eager brother,

Whom we killed on our way.'

They had not followed their mother's wishes in this; they had used stones to wound. Then men attacked them, but they defended themselves well and valiantly, and slew many a man. Iron did not bite upon them. Then a man came, tall and ancient with one eye, and he said, 'You are not wise people, you should know how to kill these men.' The king said, 'Give us advice, if you can.' He said, 'You should stone them to death.' So it was done, and then stones flew at them from all sides, and so their lives ended.

THE SAGA OF RAGNAR SHAGGY-BREECHES AND HIS SONS

Written as a kind of sequel to *The Saga of the Volsungs*, and following directly on from the former in some manuscripts, *The Saga of Ragnar Shaggy-breeches* exists in an uneasy half-and-half world between legend and history. Although some characters in The Saga of the Volsungs are based on historical persons, its central hero, Sigurd the Dragonslayer, is a mythic superhuman. Ragnar Shaggy-breeches, however, and his ambitious sons, Ivar the Boneless and his brothers, are identifiable as historical figures – although Ragnar himself is as much of a dragonslayer as Sigurd, and his sons fight even stranger monsters. The link between Sigurd and Ragnar is a little tenuous, and entirely unhistorical; Aslaug, the daughter of Sigurd and Brynhild becomes Ragnar's second wife under bizarre circumstances.

Ivar himself appears in English history as a

Viking invader who killed various Anglo Saxon kings, including the St Edmund after whom Bury St Edmunds in Suffolk gets its name. In the saga, however, his transformed into a cunning trickster who uses a trick common to Germanic origin legends to become the founder of London. His father Ragnar is held to be based on a historical Viking leader who besieged Paris, while his murderer Ella is also historical – although there is no reason to believe they ever met, let alone that Ella consigned Ragnar to death in a snake pit. It is clear that the Christian Scandinavians of the High Middle Ages, the period during which the sagas achieved their written form, were ashamed of their heathen ancestors' excesses, and Ivar's character in particular receives a whitewash. In the end, he becomes a kind of saintly figure himself, whose uncorrupted body magically guards England from invasion until William the Conqueror disinters him.

The saga itself is something of a hotchpotch, with its anonymous author apparently drawing upon writers such as the Dane Saxo Grammaticus and the Norman Dudo of San Quentin, and it has never had the literary acclaim of *The Saga of the Volsungs*. Nevertheless, it has been adapted on several occasions in recent decades, being the basis for the 1958 film *The Vikings*, and more recently the *Vikings* TV series. Both of these adaptations have been criticised on grounds of historic accuracy, but when their source is taken into account, with its wild and unlikely legendary narrative, they seem very sober in comparison. To do the saga justice would require the talents of more idiosyncratic filmmakers; a Ray Harryhausen, if not a Terry Gilliam, would be required to adequately realise Sibilia, the giant troll-cow whose frenzied mooing drives her enemies insane...

Chapter One

In Hlymdale, Heimir heard what had happened, of the death of Sigurd and Brynhild[14]. And Aslaug, their daughter and Heimir's foster child, was three years old. Heimir knew then that there would be an attempt to murder the maiden and her family. So great was his mourning for Brynhild, his foster child, that he did not care about his kingdom or his possessions, but then, knowing he could not hide the maiden there, he had made a harp so big that he could fit Aslaug inside it, with many jewels and gold and silver, and he went away, travelling through many countries and eventually reaching the northern lands. So well-made was his harp that it could be taken apart and put together at the joints, and on the days when he came to a water-fall, and was nowhere near settlements, he took the harp apart and bathed the maiden, and he had a leek[15] that he gave to her to eat. And this was the nature of the leek; a man may live long by eating it, though he had no other food. And when the girl cried, he played his harp, and she fell silent, because Heimir was good at playing the tunes that were common in those days. He had many costly clothes with her in the harp, and much gold.

---

[14] This follows directly on from the end of *The Saga of the Volsungs*.

[15] Leeks are commonly ascribed wondrous powers in Norse and Germanic tradition.

And he went onwards until he came to Norway and reached a small farm, which was called Spangarheid, and a poor man named Aki lived there. He had a wife, and she was called Grima. There were no other people apart from them. That day the poor man had gone to the forest, but his wife was home, and she greeted Heimir and asked who he was. He said he was a beggar and asked the woman to provide lodgings for him. She said that not many came there and then she said could take him in with ease, if he thought he needed to stay. And it happened that he said that he thought that it would be most comfortable if a fire was lit for him and then he was escorted to the place where he would sleep. And when the woman had lit the fire, he set his harp on the seat with him, but the woman was quiet. Often her eyes went to the harp, because a thread from a costly robe hung out of it. When he warmed himself by the fire, she saw an expensive gold ring showing beneath his rags, because he was badly dressed. And when he had warmed himself as much as he thought he needed, he had supper. But after that he told the woman to show him to where he would sleep that night. Then the woman told him that he would be better outside than inside, - 'since my darling often gossips, when he comes home.' He let her decide, then went out with her. He took the harp and kept it with him. The woman walked out and went to a barn, and escorted him into it and said that he should stay there, and he might expect to enjoy his sleep. And now the old woman went away, and did other chores, while he himself slept.

The poor man came home when evening drew near, but his wife had done little that she needed to do, and he was weary when he came home, and hard to deal with, because everything that she should have done was not done. The poor man said that there must be a great difference in their happiness, when every day he worked more than he could, but she did not want to do the things that needed doing. 'Do not be angry, darling,' she said, 'because it may be that now, working briefly, you could insure that we are blessed forever.'

'What is this?' said the poor man.

The old woman said, 'A man came here asking for lodging, and I think that he has a lot of treasure with him, and he's sunk with age but must have been a warrior, and is now very weary, and I do not think I have ever seen his equal, and yet I think he is tired and sleepy.'

Then the poor man said, 'It seems to me unwise to betray one of the very few who have ever come here.'

She said: 'This is why you have long been a little man, because everything grows big in your eyes, and now there are two possibilities, that you kill him, or I'll take him as my husband, and we will chase you away. And I could tell you what he said to me early this evening, but you will think poorly about it. He spoke lustfully to me, and it is my plan to take him as my husband, and chase you away or kill you if you will not do as I want you to.'

And it is said that this poor man had an overbearing wife, and she nagged at him until he gave in, took his axe and whetted it until it was very sharp. When he was done, his wife took him to the place where Heimir slept, and he was snoring loudly. Then the old woman said to the poor man, that he should make his best attack, - 'and hasten away quickly, because you could not withstand your death if he gets his hands on you.'

She took the harp and went away with it. Then the poor man went to where Heimir slept. He struck him, and dealt him a great wound, and he dropped his axe. He ran away as fast as he could. Heimir woke after this injury, but he died from it. And it is said that so much noise rose from his death throes that the pillars of the house fell and the house itself collapsed and there was a great earthquake, and then his life ended.

The poor man went to where his wife was, and said then that he had killed him - 'though there was a while when I did not know how it would go, and this man was very strong, but I expect that he is now in Hel.'

His wife said that he should give thanks for the deed, - 'and I expect that we will have enough money now, and we will see if I have told the truth.'

Then they lit the fire, but the woman took up the harp and she wanted to open it but she had no option but had to break it, because she did not have the skill to do otherwise. And then she got the harp open, and there she saw a girl, and she thought she had not seen such a thing before. Also there was much treasure in the harp.

Then the poor man said, 'It will now happen as often it does, that evil will be given to those who betray he who trusts them. It seems to me that now we have a dependant.'

The woman said, 'This is not what I thought would happen, but no blame will result.' And then she asked the girl what family she came from. To this the young maiden said nothing because she had not learnt to speak.

'Now it is as I expected, our plan goes badly,' said the poor man. 'We are guilty of a great crime. How shall we provide for this child?'

'It is clear,' said Grima. 'She should be named Kraka, after my mother.'

Then the poor man said: 'How we shall provide for this child?'

The woman said, 'I have a good idea: we shall call her our daughter, and feed her.'

'Yet no one will believe it,' said the poor man. 'This child is much better-looking than us. Both of us are very ugly, and folk will think it unlikely that we will have such a child, as ugly as we both are.'

Then the old woman said, 'You don't know, but I know a few tricks we can use so that this does not seem surprising. I will shave her head and rub in tar, and other things when it is expected her hair shall grow back. Then she shall have a hood. She shall not be well dressed. We will look the same together. Perhaps, men will believe that I was beautiful when I was young. She will do all the worst work.' And the poor man and woman supposed that she could not speak because she never answered them. Then it was done as the old woman had said. So the girl grew up in dire poverty.

Chapter Two

There was an earl in Gautland named Herraud who was powerful and famous. He was married. His

daughter was named Thora, who was most beautiful
of all women and most courteous in all things which
may be better to have than to be without. Her
nickname was Town-Hart, because she stood out
from all women in fairness as a deer does from other
animals. The earl loved his daughter dearly. He built
her a bower a short way from the royal hall, and
surrounding the bower was a fence of wood. Every
day the Earl always sent his daughter something for
her entertainment, and he said that he would keep
this up. Then, it is said, one day he sent to her an
extremely beautiful little heather snake, and that
snake seemed good to her, and she put it in an ash
wood box and placed gold under it. It was a short
time before it grew bigger and so did the gold
underneath it. It came about that the snake could no
longer fit in the ash wood box, and then it coiled in a
ring around the ash wood box. And at last it
happened that it had no room in the bower, and the
gold grew under it as well as the snake itself. Then it
coiled outside the bower so that its head and tail
touched, and it became hard to cope with, and no
one dared to come to the bower because of the
snake, except he who brought it food, and it needed
an ox for every meal. It seemed to the Earl that great
harm would come from this, and he vowed that he
would give his daughter in marriage to any man who
could kill the snake, and the gold that lay beneath it
would be her dowry. The news became famous in
many countries, but no one dared to subdue this
huge snake.

Chapter Three

At that time Sigurd Hring ruled over
Denmark. He was a mighty king and is famous for
that war when he fought Harald Wartooth at
Bravellir and Harald fell before him, as everyone

knows in the northern parts of the world[16]. Sigurd had one son, named Ragnar. He was tall, handsome in appearance and intelligent, generous with his men, but fierce with his enemies. When he was old enough, he was given men and warships, and he became the greatest of warriors so that hardly anyone was his equal. He heard of what Earl Herraud had said; but he paid no attention, and acted as if he did not know about it. He had made clothes in a strange fashion, shaggy breeches[17] and a shaggy coat, and when they were made, then he had them boiled in pitch. Then he put them in safekeeping. One summer, he took his warriors to Gautland and anchored his ships in a hidden inlet a short distance from where the Earl ruled.

And when Ragnar had been there one night, he woke up early in the morning, rose and put on the same armour that was described before, put it on, took a great spear in his hand and went off the ship alone and when he came to the sand, he rolled himself in it. And before he went on his way, he took the spear nail out of his spear, and went from the ship to the gate of the Earl's farm and got there early in the day, when all men were asleep. Then he went towards the bower. And when he reached the wooden fence where the snake was, he attacked it, and thrust at it with his spear. And a second time he attacked. That thrust caught the snake's spine, and he twisted the spear quickly so that the spearhead came off its shaft, and so much noise was made by its death throes that all the bower shook. And then

---

[16] The so-called Bravic War is described in Saxo Grammaticus' *Gesta Danorum*. Another participant was Arrow-Odd, whose saga follows later.

[17] These are the origin of Ragnar's nickname.

Ragnar went away. A jet of blood hit him between his shoulders, but it did not hurt him, because the clothes that he had had made protected him. But those in the bower were awakened by the din and went outside.

Thora saw a man going away from the bower and asked him his name and whom he wanted to find. He stopped there and spoke this verse:

> *'I endangered my life,*
>
> *Beautiful dame;*
>
> *Fifteen years old,*
>
> *I defeated the earth fish.*
>
> *What misfortunes*
>
> *May come, I won't die,*
>
> *But I stabbed the heath-salmon*
>
> *Straight in the heart.'*

And then he went away, and spoke no more to her. The spearhead remained in the wound, but he had the shaft with him. When she heard this verse, she understood what he told her about his errand and also how old he was. And then she wondered to herself who he could be, and she did not know whether he was a human being or not, because it seemed that his stature was as great as it was said that monsters were when they were the age he was, and then she went back into the bower and fell asleep.

And when they came out in the morning,

people realised that the snake was dead, he was pierced through with a large spear and it remained in the wound. The Earl had it taken out, and it was so great that few could have wielded it was a weapon. Then the Earl considered what he had said about the man who killed the snake, and he thought that he did not know whether or not a human being had done this, and he discussed it with his friends and daughter, how he should search for him, and it seemed likely that he who had done this would afterwards seek the reward.

She advised him to summon a large gathering, - 'and say that all those men who do not want the wrath of the Earl and are able to attend the meeting to come, and if anyone who attends is the man who did this shall have the spear that fits with the spearhead.'

This seemed favourable to the Earl and then he called for a gathering. And when the day came for the gathering, the Earl came and many other chiefs. There was a great throng.

Chapter Four

It became known at Ragnar's ships that a gathering was planned. And Ragnar went from his ships with near enough his whole army to the gathering. And when they got there, they stood apart from other men, because Ragnar saw that a larger company had come there than was customary.

The Earl stood up and asked for silence and spoke; first he asked those men who had come to his summons to accept his thanks, and then he spoke of the incident that had occurred, starting from how he had spoken about what he had sworn concerning the man who slew the snake, then that - 'the snake is dead, and he left his spearhead in the wound, he who did this famous work. And if anyone who has come to this gathering is he who has the shaft from which the spearhead came and was carried away and so may prove his claim, then I shall do that which I have said, whether he is of greater or lesser rank.'

And when he ended his speech, he had the spearhead brought before everyone at the gathering, and told him who could take credit, or had the shaft that fitted the spearhead, to speak. Then it was done. No one was found who had the shaft until they reached Ragnar and showed him the spearhead. He said that it was his, and each fitted the other, shaft and spearhead. Then men thought that they knew that he must have done the snake to death, and because of this great deed he became famous in all the northern lands, and then he asked for Thora, the daughter of the Earl, and Herraud agreed to this happily, and then she was given to him in marriage, and they had a great feast with the best food in the kingdom. At this feast Ragnar was married. And when the feast ended, Ragnar went to his kingdom and ruled it and he loved Thora greatly. They had two sons, the eldest named Eirek, and the younger, Agnar. They were tall and handsome. They were much stronger than most other men who were around in those days. They played all kinds of sports.

It happened one time that Thora fell sick, and she died of this illness. Ragnar thought this so terrible that he refused to rule the kingdom and set other men to rule the country with his sons. Then he returned to his former lifestyle, and he went out raiding, and wherever he went, he won victory.

Chapter Five

That summer he sailed his ships to Norway, for he had many kinsmen and friends there and he wished to meet them. In the evening he sailed his ships into a little harbour, and there was a farm close by called Spangarheid, and they weighed anchor in the harbour that night. And when morning came, the cooks went ashore to bake bread.

They saw that a farm was close to them, and it seemed to them better to go to the house and do their work there. And when they came to this small farm, they met one person who they could speak to, and that was a woman, and they asked if she was the mistress and what was her name. She said that she was the mistress, - 'and my name you will not lack, my name is Grima, but who are you?'

They said they were servants of Ragnar Shaggy-breeches, and they wished to do their work, - 'and we want you to work with us.'

The old woman replied that her hands were very stiff. 'In the past I was able to do my work very well. But I have a daughter who can work with you, and she will come home soon. She is called Kraka. It has now come to pass that I can scarcely ever handle her.'

And Kraka had gone out with the cattle in the morning and she saw that many great ships had reached the land, and then she went and washed herself. But the woman had forbidden her to do that, since she did not want men to see her fairness, because she was the fairest of all women, and her hair was so long that it went down to the earth, and it was as fair as the fairest silk.

Kraka came home. The cooks had made a fire, and Kraka saw that men had arrived who she had not seen before. She looked at them and they at her. And then they asked Grima: 'Is this your daughter we see, this fair maiden?'

'It is not a lie,' Grima said, 'that's my daughter you see.'

'You two are surprisingly different,' they say, 'you are so ugly. But we have never seen so beautiful a girl, and no way does she have your looks, because you are utterly hideous.' Grima said, 'You can't see it in me now. My looks have altered from what they were.'

Then they discussed the girl working with them. She asked: 'What should I do?' They said they wanted her to knead the bread, and they would bake it afterwards. And then she began work, and she worked well. But they looked at her all the time so that they did not pay attention to their work and they burned the bread. And when they had finished their work, they went to the ships. And when they brought out their supplies, all said that they had never had anything so bad and the cooks deserved to be punished. And then Ragnar asked why they had cooked it like this.

They said that they had never seen a woman as beautiful so they did not pay attention to their work, and they thought that no one was more beautiful in the world. When they spoke so much of her fairness, Ragnar said that he thought that there could not be anyone as beautiful as Thora had been. They said she was no uglier. Then Ragnar said: 'Now I will send men who know well how to judge beauty. If it is as you say, then your carelessness will be forgiven, but if the woman is at all uglier than you say, you will take a great punishment on yourselves.'

And he sent his men to find this beautiful girl, but the headwind was so great that they could not go that day, and Ragnar spoke with his messengers, 'If the young maiden seems to you as beautiful as it is said, tell her to come to me, and I would see her, and I wish that she would be mine. I want her to be neither clad nor unclad, neither fed nor unfed, and what is more she must not be alone, however, no man must accompany her.'

Then they went until they came to the house, and they looked at Kraka closely and it seemed that they saw a woman so beautiful that they thought no other equally in beauty. And then they said the words of their master, Ragnar, and how she should be prepared. Kraka considered what the king had said, and how she was expected, but Grima thought it could not be done, and she said she knew that the king could not be wise.

Kraka said: 'Because he has spoken so, it can be done if we can understand what he was thinking. But surely I cannot go with you today, but I will come early in the morning to your ships.'

Then they went away and told Ragnar that she would come to meet them. And she stayed at home that night. But early in the morning Kraka told the poor man that she would go and talk to Ragnar. 'But I will be changing my dress somewhat; you have a trout-net and I will wrap it round me, but I'll let my hair hang down over it, and then I will not be bare. But I will taste of a leek, and that is little food, but it will be perceived that I have eaten. And I will have your dog go with me, and then I will not be all together alone, but no man will accompany me.'[18]

And when the old woman heard her intention, it seemed that she had great cunning. And when Kraka was finished, she went her way until she came to the ships, and she was fair to see because her hair was bright and looked like gold. And then Ragnar called to her and asked who she was and who she wished to find. She answered, and recited this verse:

'I dared not break your bidding,

When you bade me to come,

Ragnar, to meet with you,

Nor have I broken your mandate;

No man escorts me,

My skin is not bare;

Certainly I have a companion,

But I come entirely alone.'

Then he sent men to meet her and let them guide her to the ship. But she said she would not go unless assurance of peace was given to her and her companion. Then she was taken to the king's ship, and when she came to the foredeck, he reached out towards her, but the dog bit him on the hand. His men rushed to it, and hit the dog and tied a string bow at his neck, and this was his death, and no better did they hold the promise of peace. Then Ragnar set her on the deck with him and spoke to

---

[18] A similar motif appears in *The Peasant's Wise Daughter*, in Grimm's Fairy Tales.

her, and she answered him fittingly and he was pleased and happy with her. He recited this verse:

'Be sure, if she was

To the warden of the fatherland

Merciful towards me, the treasurable lady

Would take my hand.'

She said:

'Untarnished to my home -

If you want to honour our agreement,

Though the helmsman had pain -

Let me go hence.'

Chapter Six

Then he said that he liked her well and was sure that she should go with him. She said it might not be so. Then he said that he wanted her to remain there for a night on the ship. She said that it would not happen until he came home from the journey that he had intended, - 'and it may be that it will seem different to you.' Then Ragnar called the treasurer and told him to take the shirt that Thora had owned, which was all embroidered with gold, and bring it to him. Then Ragnar offered it to Kraka like this:

'Will you have this shirt,

Which Thora Hart had;

Cloth with silver marked?

The same well becomes you;

Hands that were white

Worked this garment;

She was dear, for the prince

Of heroes, until death.'

Kraka said in reply:

'I dare not have that shirt,

Which Thora Hart had,

Cloth marked with silver;

Better my wretched clothes;

I am called Kraka,

In coal-black clothes

Have I gone on stony paths

And by the sea, herded goats.'

'And I will certainly not take the shirt,' she said. 'I would not expect fine raiment as long as I am with the poor man. It may be that you would think me fairer if I were fairer clad, but I will now go home. But then you can send men after me, if this is still in your mind, and you want me to come with you.' Ragnar said that he would not change his mind, and she went home.

But they went as they had intended when they got wind, and he went about his errand, after the manner he had intended. When he returned, he came to the same harbour as he had been in before when Kraka came to him. And that same evening he sent messengers to tell her his words that she should ready herself to leave for good. But she said that she would not leave until the next morning. Kraka got up early and went to the bed of the poor man and woman and asked them whether they were awake. They said they were awake, and asked what she wanted. But she said that she was going away, and would no longer stay there. 'And I know that you slew Heimir, my foster-father, and I have no one to repay worse than both of you. But for this reason, I will not harm you both - because I have long been with you two, and now I will say that each day will be worse for you than the one before, but the last will be the worst, and now I will go.'

Then she walked all the way to the ships, and she was well received. They were given good weather. On the same evening, when men prepared for bed, Ragnar said that he wanted Kraka and him to sleep together. She said that it could not be so, - 'I want you to drink the wedding cup with me when you come into your kingdom, and this seems to me more respectful for me and you and our heirs, if we have any.'

He granted her wish, and they had a good journey. Then Ragnar came to his own country, and a lavish feast was prepared to greet him, and they drank a joyous ale for him and his wedding. And the first evening, when they were together in one bed, Ragnar wanted to make love to his wife, but she asked not to because she said that misfortune would be born out of it if she was not heeded. Ragnar said he would not believe it, and added that they were not far-sighted, the poor man and woman. He asked how long it would be. Whereupon she said:

'Three nights shall pass thus,

Separate at night, although

Living together in the same hall,

Not sacrificing to the gods;

Then we will avoid harm

To my son through this abstinence;

He who you're so eager to beget

Will have no bones.'

And despite this, Ragnar paid it no heed, and got his own way.

Chapter Seven

Time passed, and their marriage was good with much love. And Kraka knew she was pregnant and so it went until she gave birth to a boy, and the boy was sprinkled with water and he was given a name and was called Ivar. But the boy was boneless and there was gristle where the bone should be. But when he was young, he became so strong that none were his equal. He was the most handsome of men and so wise that none is known of who was wiser than he.

They were blessed with even more children. They named their second son Bjorn, the third Hvitserk, and the fourth Rognvald. These were great men, very valiant, and when they could learn all kinds of sports, they became skilled in them. And wherever they went, Ivar had himself carried on staves, because he could not walk, and he had advice for them whatever they did. Then Eirek and Agnar, the sons of Ragnar, became so great themselves that people seldom ever found their equals, and every summer they sailed in their ships and were distinguished for their harrying.

Then it happened one day that Ivar spoke to his brothers Hvitserk and Bjorn, asking how long they would sit at home rather than increasing their renown. They said that they would act according to his counsel as they did in other matters.

'Now I wish,' said Ivar, 'that we ask that ships and troops are given to us so that they are well manned, and then I wish that we gain treasure and glory, if it is possible.'

And when they had decided on this plan, they told Ragnar that they wanted him to get them ships and hardened troops accustomed to taking plunder and ready for anything. And he gave this to them, as they asked. And when this troop was prepared, they went out of the country.

But as they fought with men they got the upper hand and then they had both a great troop and much treasure. And then Ivar said that he wanted them to go on until they met a great, overwhelming force, and so try their skill. And then they asked where he knew to find such a force. And then he mentioned a place called Whitby, where sacrifices were made, - 'and many have sought to seize it, but have not been victorious,' and Ragnar had gone there and was forced to retreat having got nowhere.

'Is that troop so great,' they say, 'and so hardy, or are there other problems?'

Ivar said that there was a large company of troops and the shrine was powerful, and so all who had gone against it had been defeated. And then they said that he should advise whether they should take this course or not. But he said that he would rather find out which was greater, their hardiness or the sorcery of the people.

Chapter Eight

Then they headed for that place, and when they arrived in that country, they prepared to go ashore. And then it seemed to them necessary that some of them should watch over the ships. Rognvald, their brother, was so young that they thought him not to be ready for so great risk as they deemed it would be, and they had him guard the ships with some of the troops.

But after they went from the ships, Ivar said that the men of the city had two oxen, that were bullocks, and men turned and ran before them because they could not bear their bellowing and their trollishness.

Then Ivar said: 'Carry yourself as best you can even if you feel some fear, because nothing will harm you.'

Then they left with their troops. When they approached the city, they who lived in that place become aware of them, and then they released the cattle in whom they put great faith. And when the bullocks were loose, they charged forward ferociously and bellowed horribly. Then Ivar saw this, from where he was carried on a shield, and he asked for a bow to be brought, and so it was done. Then he shot at the evil bullocks, so that both were killed, and so he ended the battle that the man had most feared.

Then at the ships Rognvald began to speak and told his troops that those men that had such a pastime as his brothers had would be fortunate.

'And there is no reason why I should stay behind, but that they alone will have the glory. We will go ashore now.'

And then they did so. And when they come to the troops, Rognvald goes ferociously into battle, and it ended up that he fell. They reached the city, the brothers, and then began to fight again, and it ended up that the city people were forced out, and they fled. When they returned to the city, Bjorn recited this verse:

We fell bellowing,

Ours bit more than theirs

I may truly say,

Our swords, upon Gnipafirdi;

Each who wished to be,

Could be, before Whitby -

Nor let young men spare

Swords - a man's bane.'

And when they come back into the city, they took all the treasure, burnt every house in the town, and broke down all the wall. And then they sailed their ships away.

Chapter Nine

Eystein was the name of a king who ruled Sweden. He was married and had one daughter named Ingibjorg. She was the comeliest of all women and lovely to look upon. King Eystein was powerful and had many followers; he was spiteful and yet wise. He had settled at Uppsala. He was a great man for sacrifices, and there were so many sacrifices at Uppsala in that time that there were no more anywhere else in the northern lands.

They put great faith in a cow, and called her Sibilia. She received so many sacrifices that men could not withstand her roaring. And the king was accustomed, when faced by an overwhelming army, to send this cow before the troops, and such great devilish power followed her that his enemies became so maddened when they heard her that they fought among themselves and didn't care for their own well-being, and because men dared not fight against such overwhelming odds, Sweden remained unharried.

King Eystein was friendly with many people and leaders, and it is said that at that time there was a great friendship between Ragnar and Eystein, and it was their custom that on alternating summers each should prepare a feast for the other. Then it came about that Ragnar was to attend a banquet of King Eystein's. And when he came to Uppsala, he and his troop received a good reception.

And when they drank on the first evening, the king's daughter filled the cups for him and Ragnar. And Ragnar's men spoke among themselves about it, saying that it would not be otherwise but he would ask for the daughter of King Eystein, once he was no longer married to the poor man's daughter. Then it happened that one of his men pointed this out to him, and it ended up that he was promised her as his wife, although she would remain betrothed to him for some time.

But when the feast was ended, Ragnar went home, and it went well, and nothing is said about his journey until he was close to his city, and his way lay through the forest. They came to a clearing in the woods. Then Ragnar halted his troops and asked for quiet, and told all the men who had been with him in his journey to Sweden that no one should mention his intention to enter marriage with the daughter of King Eystein. Then he laid so strict a penalty on this, that whoever spoke of it should lose nothing short of his life. And when he had said what he wanted, he went back to the town.

And the people rejoiced when he came back, and they drank a joyous ale in his honour. When he came to his throne he has not sat long before Kraka came into the hall before Ragnar and sat on his knees and put her hands around his neck and asked: 'What news?'

But he said that he had nothing to speak of. And as the evening wore on, the men took to drinking, and then they went to sleep. When Ragnar and Kraka got into the same bed she asked him what had happened, but he said he had nothing to talk about. Then she wanted to talk further, but he claimed to be very sleepy and weary from travelling.

'Now I will tell you what has happened,' she said, 'if you will not tell me.'

He asked what it was.

'I call it news,' she said, 'if a woman is promised to a king, but it is, however, said by men that he already has another.'

'Who told you this?' Ragnar said.

'Your men shall keep life and limb, because none of your people told me this,' she said. 'You recall that three birds sat in the tree near you. They told me the news. I ask that you do not follow this course that you intend. Now I shall tell you that I am a king's daughter, and not a poor man's, my father was so famous a man that he still has not had his equal, and my mother was most beautiful and wisest of all women, and her name will be uplifted while the world stands.'

Then he asked her who her father was, if she were not the daughter of the poor man who lived at Spangarheid. She said that she was the daughter of Sigurd Fafnir's Bane and Brynhild Budli's daughter. 'It seems to me most unlikely that their daughter would be named Kraka or their child would grow up in the poverty that was at Spangarheid.'

She said, 'The story is this,' and then she told the story, how Sigurd and Brynhild met on the mountain, and how she was conceived. 'And when Brynhild gave birth, a name was given me, and I was called Aslaug.' And then she explained all that had passed until the time when she met the poor man.

Then Ragnar said, 'I am astounded by these crazy words about Aslaug which you speak.'

She said, 'You know that I am with child and it will be a boy that I have, but the boy will have a birthmark, so that it will seem as if a snake lies within the eye of the boy. If this comes about, I ask this, that you do not go to Sweden at the time that you would get the daughter of King Eystein. But if this fails to happen, go if you like. But I want the boy to be named after my father, if he has this glorious mark in his eye, as I think he will.'

Then that time came when she entered labour and gave birth to a boy. Then the serving women entered, took the boy and sprinkled him with water. Then she said that they should take him to Ragnar and let him see. And then it was done, this young man was born to the hall, and laid in the lap of Ragnar's cloak. And when he saw the boy, he was asked what he should be called. He recited:

'Sigurd, the boy will be called,

He will fight in combat,

Be much like the father

Of his mother, after whom he's called;

Thus will the most noted

Of Odin's race be named,

The snake-eyed,

Who will bring great slaughter.'

Then he took a ring off his hand and gave it to the boy as his name-fastening. And when he stretched out his hand with the gold, it touched the boy's back, and Ragnar thought it meant that he would hate gold. And then he recited a verse:

'Dear son of Brynhild's daughter

With gleaming brow-stones

Will be pleasing to heroes

And most faithful in heart;

Thus, he bears himself

Better, the sword's messenger,

Budli's heir, who detests

Immediately the red gold.'

And again he said:

'In no boy did I see,

Except one – Sigurd –

Bridles in brow-stones

Beard-slopes of the forehead;

This spirited hunter of beasts

By this sign is known,

Into his eyelids' arena

Has taken rings of the dark wood.'

Then he said that they should carry the boy out to the bower. And then it was ended, his going to Sweden. And then the lineage of Aslaug came out, so that each man knew that she was the daughter of Sigurd Fafnir's Bane and Brynhild Budli's daughter.

Chapter Ten

When the time had passed, the appointed day

came that Ragnar should go to Uppsala. He did not arrive and Eystein thought it was to his dishonour and his daughter's, and the friendship between the kings ended. And when Eirek and Agnar, the sons of Ragnar, heard this, they plotted between themselves to get a great troop, as many as they could gather, so they could harry Sweden. And they gathered a great troop, and prepared their ships, but it seemed very important to them that all went well when the ship was launched.

Then it happened that Agnar's ship shot off the rollers, and a man was in the way, and he got his death, but they called it the reddening of the rollers. This did not seem a good start but they would not let it delay their journey. And when their troops were prepared, they went with them to Sweden, and there, when they came soon to the kingdom of King Eystein, they went across it in war-array.

But the people of the country grew aware of them and went to Uppsala and told Eystein that an army was already in the land. But the king sent the war-arrow through his kingdom, and he gathered so many men together that it was a wonder. And the army went with him until he came to the woods, and they set up their camp, and he had the cow Sibilia, and very many were the sacrifices to her before she would go.

And when they were in the woods, King Eystein said, 'I have word,' he said, 'that the sons of Ragnar are in the fields in front of this wood, but it is said that they do not have one-third of our troops. Now we shall arrange our divisions for the fight, and a third of our troop shall meet them, and they are so hard to deal with that they will think that they have us in their hands and straight afterwards we shall come upon them with all our strength, and the cow shall go before the troop, and it seems to me that they shall not withstand her bellowing.'

And then it was so done. And when the brothers saw the troops of King Eystein, they thought their enemies were not overwhelming and it did not occur to them that there would be no more troops. And when this came soon after all the troops came out of the woods, and the cow was let loose, and she charged the troop and went fiercely, and caused so big a din that the warriors who heard it fought among themselves, except the two brothers who stood their ground. But the evil creature struck many men with her horns that day.

And if the sons of Ragnar were themselves powerful, they could not resist the overwhelming numbers of enemies and pagan witchcraft, and yet they faced it unflinchingly and acquitted themselves well and valiantly and with great renown. Eirek and Agnar were in the forefront of the battle that day, and often they went through the ranks of King Eystein. And then Agnar fell. Eirek saw that and then fought all most boldly and did not care whether he would depart or not. And then he was overborne by the great troop and captured. And then Eystein said that the battle should stop, and offered Eirek peace.

'And I will lay this offer before you,' he said, 'that I will give you my daughter.' Eirik said:

I don't want wergild for my brother

Or to buy your daughter with rings,

Eystein was responsible,

I hear, for Agnar's death;

No mother cries for me,

Hurry now to kill me,

And on a forest of spears,

High up, let me stand.'

Then he said that he wanted the men who had followed them to be spared and to go wherever they wanted. 'But I will have as many spears as can be taken up and have the spears thrust into the ground, and there I wish to be lifted up, and there I want to leave my life.' Then Eystein said that it would be done as he asked, if he chose that which went worse with them both. Then the spears were put up, and Eirik said a verse:

'I think no king's son,

As I know my fate to be,

Dying on so expensive a bed,

Breakfast for ravens.

Livid, those bloody ones,

Soon bellow over

Both brothers' bodies,

Though ill reward it be.'

And then he went to where the spears were set up, and took his ring and threw it to those who had followed him, and who were given peace, and sent it to Aslaug and recited:

'Carry my last utterance -

My eastward raids are over -

To the slender maid,

That she, Aslaug, may have my rings;

Let the best of mothers

Learn of my glorious death;

My gentle stepmother will hear

Word of her boy.'

And then he was heaved up on spears. He saw where the raven flew, and yet he said:

The seagull rejoices above the head

Of my now gory body,

Wound-hawk my eyes

Unseeing here wants;

I think if the raven strikes

My eyes from their sockets

Poorly rewarded is the wound-hawk

Which Ekkil often gave his fill.'

Then he yielded his life with great valour. But his men went home and did not stop until they reached where Ragnar resided. And then he was gone to the Kings. The sons of Ragnar, were not home from raiding. They stayed there three nights before they went to meet Aslaug. And when they came before Aslaug's throne, they greeted her honourably, and she received their greeting, and she had one linen handkerchief on her knee and had unloosed her hair which she was going to comb. Then she asked who they were, for she had not seen them before. He that had the words for them said that they had been comrades of Eirek and Agnar, sons of Ragnar. Then she recited a verse:

'What say you, king's friends?

Are the Swedes still in their country

Or otherwise,

Driven away?

I have heard that Danes went from the south,

But since then, know not,

And chiefs had reddening

Of the rollers.'

He recited in turn:

'We tell you, dame,

It is necessary, of the death -

Evil are the norns to your man -

Of the sons of Thora

I know no other tale as heavy

As this; now we come from hearing tell,

The eagle flies over the corpse of the slain.'

Then she asked how it had happened. And he recited the verse that Eirik had sung when he sent her the ring. Then they saw that she shed a tear, but it had the look of blood, and was as hard as a hailstone. No one saw her let a tear fall, neither before nor since. Then she said that she could not pursue vengeance until the others came home, Ragnar and his sons. 'You will stay here until then, but I shall not spare incitement for revenge, as if they were my sons.' Then they stayed there. And it happened that Ivar and the brothers came home before Ragnar, and they were not at home long before Aslaug went to find her sons, and Sigurd was then three years old. He went with his mother. And when she came to the hall, where the brothers were speaking, they greeted her fittingly, and each asked the other for news, and they spoke first of her son Rognvald's fall, and the events, and how it occurred. But that did not seem serious to her and she said:

> *My sons, leave me*
>
> *By myself to watch seagulls;*
>
> *You do not go*
>
> *Begging from house to house.*
>
> *Rognvald began the shield*
>
> *To redden in men's blood;*
>
> *He was the youngest of my*
>
> *Valiant sons to go to Odin.*

'I cannot see,' she said, 'that he could have

lived to become more famous.'

Then they asked what news she had. She said, 'The fall of Eirek and Agnar, your brothers, my step-sons, those men who I believe had the most courage. And it will not be strange if you do not endure this but greatly avenge it. And so I will aid you, and be of great support to you, so this will be more than commonly avenged.'

Then Ivar said that – 'it is certain that I will never go to Sweden eagerly to fight King Eystein and the witchcraft that is there.' She pressed him greatly, but Ivar spoke for all of them, and refused the journey. And then she recited a verse:

I don't reckon

That if you had all been killed,

A season would have passed without revenge

From your brothers; and I would rather

If Eirik had kept his life, and Agnar,

Although they were not born to me.'

'It is not certain,' said Ivar, 'whether the matter will stand differently if you recite one verse after another. Do you know for certain what strongholds lie before us?'

'I am not certain,' said she, 'or what may you say of the hindrances there might be?'

Ivar said that there is sorcery so great that no man had ever heard of anything like it. 'And the king is both powerful and malicious.'

'What is it that he believes in most when he sacrifices?'

He said, 'A huge cow called Sibilia. She is so very mighty that when men hear her bellowing his enemies will not stand, and it is hardly as if the fight is fought by men, but rather it may be believed that they face trolls at first before the king, and I will neither risk myself or my troops.'

She said: 'One thing you must consider is that you cannot both be called a great man and not work for it.' And when it seemed to her that things are beyond hope, she resolved to leave; she felt they did not value her words.

Sigurd Snake-eye spoke; 'I might tell you, mother,' he said, 'what I have in mind, but I might not affect their answers.'

'I want to hear it,' she said. Then he recited this verse:

'In three weeks,

If you grieve, mother,

We shall soon be ready,

War-preparations will be finished;

Eystein Beli shall not rule Uppsala,

Even if he offers much gold,

If our swords prove true.'

And when he had sung this verse, the brothers somewhat reconsidered their plans. And then Aslaug said, 'You say truly, my son, that you shall do my will. Yet I cannot see how we will achieve this if we are not fully supported by your brothers, but it might happen as best I think that this vengeance will be, and it seems to me that you proceed well, my son.' And then Bjorn said a verse:

> *'My heart holds courage*
>
> *In my hawk-keen breast,*
>
> *Though I do not boast of it,*
>
> *I am bold and hardy;*
>
> *You do not see in my eyes*
>
> *Worms or spiralling snakes,*
>
> *Yet my brothers gladdened me;*
>
> *I remember your stepsons.'*

And then Hvitserk said a verse:

> *'Before vowing, let's plan*
>
> *How revenge may be gained;*
>
> *Concoct some evil*
>
> *For the killer of Agnar;*
>
> *Heave hulls onto the billows,*
>
> *Hack the ice at the stern,*
>
> *See whose ship soonest*
>
> *Can set out to sea.'*

But Hvitserk said that the ice must be broken

because the frost was great, and their ships were in ice. And then Ivar began to speak and said that it had reached the point where he must take part, and then he recited a verse:

'You have courage a-plenty

And pluck as well,

But you need to be dogged,

And we want doughty men.

I'm borne before my warriors,

Although I'm boneless,

I have resentful hands,

Though little strength in either.'

'And the other one now,' said Ivar, 'we must put on such a mind as we can for gathering ships and warriors, because we must not hold back in this, if we are to gain victory.' Then Aslaug went away.

Chapter Eleven

Sigurd had a foster-father who gathered both ships and troops for his foster-son, so that they were all well prepared. And it was done so quickly that the troop which Sigurd would have was prepared after three nights passed; he also had five ships, all well-appointed. And when five nights passed, Hvitserk and Bjorn had fourteen ships prepared. Ivar had ten ships and Aslaug another ten, when seven nights were passed from the time when they had planned and declared their journey. Then they all spoke together, and told each other how many troops each had raised. And then Ivar said that he had sent knights overland. Aslaug said: 'If I knew for sure that this troop that is sent by land could be useful then it might be I will send a large force as well.'

'Do not delay,' said Ivar, 'we should go now with this troop we have gathered together.'

Then Aslaug said that she wanted to go with them, - 'and I know best what must be done to avenge the brothers.'

'It is certain,' said Ivar, 'that you will not come in our ships. It may be, if you wish it, that you will command the troop that goes by land.'

She agreed that it should be. Then she changed her name and she was then called Randalin. Then both troops departed, but before then Ivar said where they should meet. Then the troops had a good journey, and met in that place which was decided. And wherever they went in Sweden and the kingdom of King Eystein, they went in war-array, so that they burned all that stood before them, killing every man, and also they killed all that was living.

Chapter Twelve

Then it happened that some men escaped and met King Eystein and told him that a great army had come to the country, and so terrible was it to deal with that it would not leave anything unharmed, and it had destroyed everything that it had encountered, and no house stood. When King Eystein heard this news, he thinks he knows who these Vikings might be. And then he sent the war-arrow throughout his kingdom and summoned all his people who could provide troops and bear shields. 'We will have with us the cow Sibilia, who is a god, and let her charge before the troop, and it seems to me that it will go as before, that they will not withstand her roaring. I will egg on my troop to do their best, and so we will drive away the host of evil.'

And then it was done, that Sibilia was loosed. And then Ivar saw her, and heard the hideous roaring that came from her. He said that all the troops should make a great noise, both with weapons and war cries, so that they could hardly hear the voice of the evil animal that went against them. Ivar said to his bearers that they should carry him into the vanguard, so far as they could.

'And when you see the cow come towards us, throw me at her, and it shall go one way or another, that I shall give my life, or she shall get her death. Now take a tall tree and cut it in the form of a bow, along with arrows.'

And then the mighty bow and the great arrows which he had caused to be made was brought to him, but none considered them a weapon anyone could use. Ivar egged on every man to do their best. Then their troop went with great ferocity and noise, and Ivar was carried before their battle array. Such a great din began when Sibilia roared that they heard it as clearly as if they had stayed silent and stood still. That made it happen that their troop fought amongst themselves except the two brothers.

And when this wonder happened, the men who bore Ivar saw that he bent the bow as if he it was a weak elm branch, and it seemed as if he drew the arrow point back past his bow. Then they heard those strings twang louder than they had ever heard before. And then they saw that his arrows flew as swiftly as if he had shot the strongest crossbow and so it happened that the arrows hit each of Sibilia's eye.

And then she fell, but after that she went headlong, and her roaring was much worse than at first. And when she came upon them, he told them to throw him at her, and so he became as light as a small child, because they were not very near the cow when they cast him. And when he came down on the cow Sibilia, he became as heavy as a rock when he dropped on her, and every bone in her was broken, and she got her death.

Then he told his men to pick him up quickly. And then he was taken up, and then his voice was so ringing that it seemed to all the army as if he stood beside each man though he was far-off, and it became quiet as he gave his commands. And so he spoke to this end, that the fight that they had come for was soon ended, and no harm was down when their men briefly fought among themselves. Ivar egged them on to work much harm on the foe.

'And now it seems to me the most violent foe is gone, the cow is killed.'

Then both armies drew up on either side their troops and they clashed together, and fought so hard that all the Swedes said that they had never had their manhood so sorely tried. Then the brothers Hvitserk and Bjorn went so hard that no battle array stood before them. And then so many of King Eystein's troops fell that few still stood, but some fled.

So the battle ended, King Eystein fell, and the brothers won. And then they made peace with those who were left behind. And then Ivar said that he would not harry in that land because the land was then leaderless. 'And I want us to hold course until a more overwhelming resistance is before us.'

But Randalin went home with some troops.

Chapter Thirteen

Then they decided among themselves that they should harry the kingdoms of the south. Sigurd Snake-eye, Randalin's son, went with his brothers in every following raid. In these raids they fought against each city that was strong, and fought so that none defeated them.

And then they heard of one town that was both great and populous and hardy. And Ivar said that he wanted to go there. And what the city was called and who ruled it is also mentioned. The chief was called Vifil, from whose name the city was called Vifilsborg. Then they went in war-array and laid waste all the cities that they found until they came to Vifilsborg. The chief was not at home in his city, and many troops were with him. So they set up their tents on the plains that surrounded the city, and they were quiet that day when they came to the town and spoke to the men of the town. They asked them whether they would rather give up the city, in which case peace would be given to all men, or did they prefer to test their forces and hardiness, and then no men would receive quarter. But they responded swiftly, and said the city would never gain victory like that.

'And you will have to try us before that happens, and show us your valour and ardour.'

Then the night passed. And the day after they

attacked the city but could not prevail. They besieged the city for half a month and every day looked for ways they could take it, and they considered a variety of strategies. And it happened that after a long time they had no better chance of victory, and they decided to leave. And when the men of the city realised that they planned to leave, they went out on the rampart and spread valuable cloth over all the city walls and all the clothes that were fairest in town, and laid out the gold and treasure that was dearest in the city. And then one took to words with their troop and said, 'We thought that these men, the sons of Ragnar and their troops were hardy men, but we can say that they have not come closer to taking the city than others.'

Then after this they shouted at them and beat the shields, and egged them on as much as they could. And when Ivar heard this, he was so upset that he fell ill so that he could not stir, and they must wait until it would improve or killed him. He lies there all that day until the evening, and he spoke not a word. And then he spoke to the men who were with him, saying they should tell Bjorn, Hvitserk and Sigurd that he wanted to talk to them, and all the wisest men. And when they all came together in one place, the greatest lords in their troop, Ivar asked them if they had hatched any plot which would be more likely to succeed than those they had tried previously. But they all said that they did not have the ingenuity to hatch a plot that would succeed.

'It is now as it is often that your advice will be useful.'

Then Ivar said, 'I have one plan to mind that we have not tried. There is a great forest not far away, and now, when night has come, we will go out of our tents secretly to the forest, but we will leave our camp still standing, and when we get to the forest, each man shall bind branches to himself, and when it is done, we will attack the town on all sides, and strike fire with the wood, and there will be a great bonfire, and the city walls will lose their lime because of the fire, and then we shall carry up our war-slings and see how hardy they are.'

And then it was done, they went to the forest, and they were there as long as Ivar thought necessary. Then they went to the town following his plan, and when they struck fire with the wood so there was a blaze so great that the walls could not stand and they lost their lime, and they carried the war-slings to the town and broke a gap in the walls, and then a fight began. And when they stood equally opposed, the men of the city fell, some fled away, and some ended up running to their ships, then they killed every man in the city, and took away all the treasure, but burned the city before they went on their way.

Chapter Fourteen

Then they sailed until they came to the city named Luna. They had near enough sacked each city and each castle in all the kingdoms of the south, and they were so famous throughout the world that there was no little child who could not name them. Then they planned not to stop until they came to Rome, because people said the city was both great and populous and good and wealthy. And they did not know clearly how long a way it was there, and they had so great a troop that they could not feed them all. And when they were in the city of Luna they discussed the journey amongst themselves.

Then an old and cunning man came. They asked what kind of man he was, and he said that he was a poor beggar, and had travelled the land all his lifetime.

'You'll know much that we want to know to tell us.'

The old man replied, 'I do not think that there is anything concerning any country you wish to learn of that I cannot tell you.'

'We want you to tell us how long the path is from here to Rome.'

He said, 'I can tell you something to show that. Here you may see these iron shoes that I have on my feet, they are now ancient, and these others I have on my back are now worn out. But when I went from there, I tied on my feet these shoes that are broken, which I now have on my back, and they were both new, and I have been on the way ever since.'

When the old man said this, they thought that that they could not continue on the way they had intended to go to Rome. And then they turned with their army, and seized many cities, those that had never been captured earlier, and its proof is still seen today. [19]

Chapter Fifteen

The story says that Ragnar now sat at home in his kingdom, and he did not know where his sons

---

[19] This is a popular folktale, often used to explain the existence of topographical features, for example the Wrekin in Shropshire.

were, nor his wife Randalin. And he heard from his men, that no one could match his sons, and it seemed to him that no one would be as famous as they. Then he wondered what kind of fame he might gain, that would not be as long lived. He considered this and sent for his craftsmen and had them fell wood for two large ships, and men heard that these were two *knarrs* so large that no ships this big had ever been made in the northern lands, and thus he gathered much weaponry from his realm. And from that, people understood that he will be going out of the country on some raid. Many heard this in the countries nearby. And then the people and all the kings that ruled the countries feared that they might not be able to remain in their countries or realms. And then each of them set up watches in their countries, in case he should attack.

There was one day when Randalin asked Ragnar where he meant to go. He told her that he was going to England and would have no more than two merchant ships and as many men as they could transport.

Then Randalin said: 'This voyage that you plan seems to me inadvisable. I would advise you to take more ships and smaller ones.'

'There is no honour,' he said, 'if one conquers a land with many ships. But there is no tale that two ships have conquered such a country as England. And if I am defeated, it is better that I have taken few ships out of the country.'

Randalin answered: 'It seems to me no less expensive to build these ships, than if you had more longships for the journey. But you know that sailing to England is difficult, and if it so happens that your ships are lost, even if they come ashore, they're lost, if the army of the land comes, but it is better to hold course to ports in longships than merchant ships.

Then Ragnar recited this verse:

'No bold man may save Rhine amber,

If he wants warriors,

More dangerous for a wise chief

Than warriors are many rings;

Bad to defend the town-gate

With brand-red rings;

I know of quite a few warriors

Whose wealth lived after their death.'

Then he prepared his ships and gathered his men so that the *knarrs* are fully laden. Then many people discussed his plans. And again he recited a verse:

'What is it that the ring breaker

Hears roaring from the rocks,

That the sharer of hand-fire

Should forsake the difficult sea-serpents?

I, if the gods will it,

The giver of forearm layings,

Shall follow my plan

Without prevarication, Lady Bil.'

And when his ship was ready, and those troops who would follow him, and when a good wind looked likely to come, Ragnar said that he would go to the ships. When he was ready, she went with him to the ships. And before they parted, she said she would repay him for the shirt which he had given her. He asked how she would repay him. But she said:

'I sewed for you a shirt

Without any seams,

With glad heart woven

Out of greyed woollen hair;

Wounds will not bleed,

Nor edges bite you.

This holy shirt

Was hallowed by the gods.'

He said that he would accept that aid. But when they parted, it was clear that their separation went hard for her.

Then Ragnar steered their ships to England as he had intended. He got a sharp breeze, so that he wrecked both his merchant ships on England's shore, but all his troops reached the land, and brought their clothes and weapons with them. And when he came to the villages, cities and castles, he was victorious.

A king named Ella ruled England in those

days. He had heard news of Ragnar when he left his country. He had despatched men so he should learn when the army came to the country. Then these men went to King Ella and told him news of war. Then he sent a message throughout his kingdom, telling every man who could bear a shield or ride a horse, and who dared to fight, to come to him, and he gathered a great army that was a wonder to see.

King Ella and his men prepared for battle. Then King Ella spoke with his troop, 'If we are victorious in this battle and you know who it is Ragnar that has come against you then you shall not carry weapons against him, because he has sons who will never leave us be if he fell.'

Ragnar prepared for battle, and he had that cloak that Randalin had given him at parting, and in his hand that spear with which he defeated the snake which lay around the bower of Thora and no one else dared to face, but he had no protection except a helmet. And when they met, they fought.

Ragnar had a much smaller troop. The battle had not been going long before much of Ragnar's troop fell. But where he went, the army fled before him, and he went through the ranks that day, and there, he cut and struck at shields, armour or helmets, and his blows were so great that there was none who could withstand him, because none who cut or shot at him with weapons could harm him and he never received a wound, but he killed a large number of King Ella's followers. But the end of that battle was when all the troops of Ragnar fell, and he was overborne with shields and captured. Then, he was asked who he was, but he held his peace and said nothing.

Then King Ella said, 'This man will face a greater trial if he will not tell us who he is. I will throw him into a snake pit and let him sit there very long, and if he says anything from which we know that he is Ragnar, he shall be taken out with all haste.'

Then he was led from there, and he sat there very long, and no snakes bit him. Then they said, 'This man is very strong, no weapons bit him today, and now no snakes hurt him.' Then King Ella decreed that he would be stripped of the clothes that he was wearing, and they did so, and snakes clung to all sides of him.

Then Ragnar said, 'The piglets would grunt now, if they knew what the old boar suffered.'

And although he said this, they did not know for sure that it was Ragnar rather than another king. Then he recited this verse:

Battles had I -

They were thought brave,

Many folk did I

Harm, - fifty and one;

I did not think snakes

Would slay me;

Often things occur

That one least expects.'

And then he said:

'The piglets would grunt,

If they knew the boar-pig's state,

The injuries done to me;

They dig into my flesh

And stab at me harshly,

They have sucked me, these snakes;

Soon my body will

Die among beasts.'

Then he lost his life, and he was taken from out of there. But King Ella thought he knew that it was Ragnar who has lost his life. Then he thought to himself, how he could become certain of this and how he could keep his kingdom or know how Ragnar's sons would react when they heard. He decided on a course of action, prepared a ship and chose the person who was both wise and hardy to carry out the plan, and then he got men, so that this ship was well manned, and said that he wanted them to send a message to Ivar and his brothers and told them to speak of the fall of their father. But the voyage seemed most unpromising, so that few wanted to go.

The king said: 'And you must watch closely how each of the brothers reacts to the news. Sail away then, when you are given good weather.'

He had prepared this journey so that they wanted for nothing. And then they went, and they had a good journey. The sons of Ragnar had been raiding the kingdoms of the south. They turned their course to the northern lands, and decided to visit the kingdom Ragnar ruled. But they knew nothing of his war, how it had turned out, although they were very curious about how it had gone. Then they travelled across the south of the country. But everywhere, when men heard of the brothers coming, they abandoned their cities and took their treasure away and fled, so that they scarcely ever found provisions for their troops. One morning, Bjorn Ironside woke up and recited:

'Flying every morning,

Over these farms,

Luckless, of hunger

The heath-falcon will die;

Over the sands he should go,

South, where we tap wounds;

From the dead it flows,

The dew from the great blows.'

And then he said:

'It was first that we went,

Frey's game to hold,

When we had few warriors

In the Roman realm;

Since I let - for greybeards;

Over the slain growls the eagle;

For murder and slaughter -

My sword will be drawn.'

Chapter Sixteen

Then they voyaged on so that they came to Denmark before the messengers of King Ella did, and then they sat quietly with their troops. But the messengers came with their forces to the city where the sons of Ragnar were being given a banquet, and walked into the hall when they were drinking, and went up before the throne where Ivar was lying.

Sigurd Snake-eye and Hvitserk sat at chess, Bjorn Ironside was carving a spear-shaft on the hall floor. And when the messengers of King Ella came before Ivar, they greeted him respectfully. He accepted their greeting and asked where they were from and what news they brought. And he that was their chief said that they were Englishmen and that King Ella had sent them there with the news of the fall of Ragnar, their father.

Hvitserk and Sigurd let fall their chess-pieces and listened closely to the news. Bjorn stood on the hall floor and leaned on his spear shaft. Ivar asked them closely about what every event of his death had been. They told how everything had gone from when he came to England, and until he gave up his life. And when this story was over, he said this: 'The piglets would grunt' - Bjorn squeezed his spear shaft, so strongly, that his handprint was seen on it afterwards. When the messengers finished that story, Bjorn shook the spear apart, so that it broke in two pieces. Hvitserk held the chess piece he had moved, and he squeezed it so hard that blood jumped from each nail. Sigurd Snake-eye had been holding a knife and paring his nails when these things were being said, and listened so closely to what had happened, he did not realise until the knife was in the bone, and he did not flinch at that. Ivar asked how everything had happened, but his colour was sometimes red, sometimes blue, but he would suddenly turn pale, and he was so swollen that his skin was mortified from the wrath that was in his breast.

Then Hvitserk took to speech, and he said that it would be a speedy revenge if they were to slay the messengers of King Ella.

Ivar said: 'This will not be. They shall go in peace, wherever they want, and if there is anything that they lack, they should tell me, and I will get it them.'

And now that they had completed their errand, they went back out of the hall and to their ships. And when they got a good wind, they put out to sea, and voyaged well, until they reached King Ella, and told him how each of the brothers responded to this news.

When King Ella heard this, he said: 'It is to be expected that will we must fear Ivar, or none otherwise, because of what you say of him, and thoughts of vengeance do not run deep in them, and we will manage to hold our realm against them.'

Then he had watchmen sent throughout all his kingdom so that no army could surprise him.

When the messengers of King Ella had gone away, the brothers joined in discussing how they must avenge Ragnar, their father. Then Ivar said: 'I will have no part in this and I will not gather troops, because it went for Ragnar as I had foreseen. He prepared his action badly from the start. He had no complaint against King Ella, and it often happens that if a man stubbornly plan to act unfairly, he is brought down dishonourably. I will accept wergild from King Ella, if he will give it to me.'

But when his brothers heard this, they become very angry and told him that they would never be so cowardly, even if he wanted to be. 'Many would say that we rest our hands on our knees wrongly, if we are not to avenge his killing, but we have gone around the world in war-array and killed many innocent people. And it will not happen, but every seaworthy vessel in the realm shall be readied. The most skilled troops shall be gathered, so every man who may carry a shield against King Ella shall go.'

But Ivar said that he would leave behind all those ships he commanded - 'except one, which I will be on myself.'

And when it was known that Ivar would not take any part in the struggle and they would get much fewer men, they went nevertheless. And when they came to England, the king was soon aware, and he had the trumpets sounded, and he called all men who will follow him to himself. And when he had so many troops that no man could count them, he went against the brothers. When they met, Ivar was not in the battle. And when the fighting ended, the sons of Ragnar fled, and King Ella had won. When the king was pursuing the army, Ivar said that he would not return to their land, - 'and I will find out whether King Ella will do me any honour or not, and it seems to me better to accept wergild from him than to go against him again as we have now done.'

151

Hvitserk said that he would not deal with him but he could go about this as he wanted, - 'But never should we take payment for our father.'

Ivar said that he would part from them, and told them to rule the realm which they held all together, - 'but you will send me my belongings when I ask for them.'

When he had finished, he bade them farewell. He turned away to go to King Ella. And when he came to him, he greeted the king honourably and spoke to him: 'I have come to meet you, and I will speak to you, and accept such wergild that you would prepare for me. And now I see that I have nothing beside you, and it seems to me better to accept such wergild as you would give me rather than lose my people to you or myself.'

Then King Ella answered, 'It is said by some people that is not possible to trust you, and they believe that you speak most fair when you think false, and it will be difficult to fight you or your brothers.'

'I will ask little of you, if you will grant it. I shall swear in this way, that I shall never be against you.'

Then the king asked what wergild he wanted. 'I want,' said Ivar, 'you to give me as much of your country as an ox hide will cover[20], but the boundary shall be outside that, and I will not ask more from you, and I will think that you wish me little honour,

---

[20] A similar request is made by invading Saxons in Geoffrey of Monmouth's *History of the Kings of Britain*, and again by Saxons in Germany in Widukind's *History of the Saxons*.

if you will not do that.'

'I am not sure,' said the king, 'whether it will be to our harm if you have this much of my country, but I will give you this if you will swear not to fight against me, and I will not fear your brothers if you are faithful to me.'

Chapter Seventeen

Then they discussed these things and Ivar swore an oath to him that he should not strike against him and not plot to harm him, but he would have as much of England that an ox hide will cover, the largest he could get. Then Ivar took the hide of an old bull, and then he had it softened, and he had it stretched three times. Then he had it cut into strips as narrow as could be, and then he had them split in half, between the hair and the flesh. And when this was done the thong was so long it was a wonder, and no one had thought it could be so. And then he had it put round a field, but it was so wide, that there was room enough for a big city, and there he had marked the foundation of a great city wall.

And then he gathered many craftsmen and had many houses built on the ground, and there he had made a great city, and it is called London Town[21]. It is the greatest of all cities and the most famous in the northern lands. And when he had founded this city, he had his belongings sent over. But he was so generous that he gave with two hands, and people thought so much of his wisdom that all went to him for his help with counsel and their problems. And so

---

[21] Compare with *The Yarn of Ragnar's Son* (below), in which York – to become the centre of the Norse kingdom of Jorvik – is founded under identical circumstances.

he judged all cases so each thought he had the best of it, and this made him popular, so that every man is his friend, and King Ella often came to him for advice, and he judged the cases so they need not come before the king. And when Ivar had so proceeded with his plan, so it seemed that he was guaranteed peace, he sent messengers to his brothers and asked them to send him as much gold and silver as he asked. But when the messengers came to meet the brothers, they told them their errand, and also how things had gone according to his plan, because men thought that they did not know what tricks he prepared. And so did the brothers thought that he did not have the same character as he was wont to. Then they sent such goods as he had asked for.

And when these reached Ivar, he gave all the goods to the strongest people in the country and so he stole troops out from under King Ella, and all pledged that they would sit quietly, even though he prepared a raid. And when Ivar had so stolen the troops from under the king, he sent messengers to his brothers to tell them that he wanted them to send a levy through all the lands that they ruled, and they should demand as many men as they could get. And when this message came to the brothers, they understood at once that then he thought it very promising that they would then win victory. They gathered troops throughout Denmark and Gautland and all the realms that they had power over, and uncountable numbers were gathered when the muster was finished. Then they sailed their ships to England through both night and day, and wanted as little warning of their coming as could be.

But word of war came to King Ella. Then he gathered his forces but got few men because Ivar had stolen a large force from under him. Then Ivar went to meet King Ella, and said that he wished to do what he had sworn. 'I cannot influence my brothers' actions, yet I can plan to find them and learn if they will stop their army, and do no more harm than they've already done.'

Then Ivar went to meet his brothers and strongly urged them that they should go forth as best they could and let the battle be soon, - 'the king has a much smaller troop.'

But they replied that he did not need to egg them on, and they had the same plans as before. Then Ivar went to King Ella and told him that they were much too eager and angry to hear his words.

'And when I wanted peace between you, they shouted me down. Now I will fulfil my oath that I will not fight against you, and will remain quiet, and my troop as well, but the fight with you will go as it may.'

Then King Ella saw the troops of the brothers, and they went with so much haste that it was a wonder.

Ivar said: 'It is now, King Ella, that you should rally your troop, but I do think that they will give you a hard fight for some time.'

But when their troops met, there was a great battle, and they went fiercely, the sons of Ragnar, through the ranks of King Ella, and they were so fervent that their only thoughts at the time were how to cause the most harm, and the battle was both long and hard. And the end was that King Ella and his troops fled, but he was captured.

And Ivar was nearby then, and he said that

they should hasten his passing. 'Now is the time,' he said, 'to remember, the death he inflicted on our father. Now a man who is skilled in woodcarving shall carve an eagle on his back[22] so precisely that the eagle shall redden with his blood.'

And the man, when he was summoned to the task, did as Ivar told him, and King Ella was in great pain before the task was ended. Then he gave up his life, and it seemed to them that they had now avenged their father, Ragnar. Ivar said that he wanted to give them the realm that they held all together, but he said he will rule England.

Chapter Eighteen

After that Hvitserk and Bjorn returned to their kingdom with Sigurd, but Ivar stayed behind in England. From then on they kept their troop together and harried many countries. But Randalin, their mother, became an old woman. And Hvitserk, her son, raided on his own in the east, and met such overwhelming odds against him he could not lift his shield against them, and he was captured. But he chose the manner of his death, that a pyre would be made of human heads, and there he was to burn, and so he gave up his life. And when Randalin heard this, she recited a verse:

'One son had I;

He who found

His death in the east

---

[22] In *The Saga of the Volsungs*, Sigurd carves a similar blood-eagle on the back of his own father's killer.

Hvitserk was his name,

Never eager to scarper

He was burnt on skulls

Hacked from the slain,

The prince sought his own death

Strong and doughty, before he fell.'

And again she said:

'The people's tree had

Himself destroyed,

With uncounted heads under him

Fingers of fire played his fate;

On what bed was it better

For a battle-striker to lie?

With fame the all-ruling

High chieftain chose to fall.

But from Sigurd Snake-eye a great family line has come. His daughter was called Ragnhild, the mother of Harald Fairhair, who was first sole ruler of the whole of Norway. But Ivar ruled England until the day of his death, when he became mortally ill. And when he was in his death-sickness, he said that he should be moved to where the land was most open to raids, and that he expected that anyone who would land there would not get the victory[23]. And when he died, they did as he said, and was then laid in a mound.

Many people say that when Harald Sigurdsson[24] came to England, he arrived where Ivar was buried, and he fell on that raid. And when William the Bastard[25] arrived in the country, he went to the mound and broke it open and saw Ivar unrotten. Then he make a great fire and had Ivar burned in it, and after that he fought across the country and had victory.

But from Bjorn Ironside descend many men. From him descends a great family: Thord, who lived at Hofda in Hofdastrond, a great chief.

When the sons of Ragnar were all dead, their troops who had followed them dispersed down many roads, and it seemed to all of them who had been with the sons of Ragnar that there was no worth in any other ruler. There were two men who travelled in many countries to see if they could find any ruler who it would not be dishonour to serve, but they did not travel together.

Chapter Nineteen

In one country it happened that a king had two sons, and he took sick and died, and his sons wanted to hold a funeral ale for him. To this feast they summoned all the people that had heard of it, to go there after three winters. Then this was heard of

---

[23] A similar story is told in the *Welsh Triads* of Vortimer, son of Vortigern, and also of Bran the Blessed, whose head was unearthed by King Arthur.

[24] Harald Hardrada.

[25] William the Conqueror.

in many countries. And over these three winters they prepared the banquet. And when that summer came when they would hold the funeral ale, and the hour appointed, there were so many people present that no one knew of another like it, it was so large, and many large halls were appointed and many tents pitched.

And when the first evening was far underway, a man came into the hall. This man was so big that there was none his equal, and they saw from his trappings that he had been with noble men. And when he came into the hall, he went before the brothers and greeted them and asked where they would have him sit. They liked him and they asked him to sit in the upper bench. He took up two places. And when he had sat down, he was served drink like the others, and no horn was so great that he might not drink it off in one draft, and everyone seemed to see that he was more important than all others.

It happened that another man came to the banquet. The man was even taller than the first. These men both had low-hanging hoods. And when this man came in before the throne of the young kings he greeted them courteously and asked them to direct him to a seat. They said that this man was to sit further in than the other, on the upper bench.

Then he went to his seat, and they took up so much room between them that five men had to rise for them. But he that came first drank the least. But the second man drank so quickly that he poured into himself nearly every horn, and no one found, however, that he got drunk, and rather he seemed to scorn his bench mates and turned his back on them. He who came first said that they should have a game together, - 'and I will go first.' He pushed the other with his hand and said:

> *'Speak of your great feats -*
>
> *School us, I ask you;*
>
> *Where saw you the blood filled ravens*
>
> *Shudder on the bough?*
>
> *Often have you been found*
>
> *Otherwise, in the high seat,*
>
> *Not gathering bloody carcasses*
>
> *In the valley for carrion birds.'*

Then it seemed to those sitting farther out that he was challenged by this verse, and he said in reply:

> *'Be quiet, you stay-at-home,*
>
> *You're happy with little,*
>
> *You've never achieved*
>
> *What I have done;*
>
> *You haven't fattened the sun-seeking bitch*
>
> *With sword-play's drink*
>
> *But yielded the horses*
>
> *Of the harbour; what ails you?'*

Then answered he who first arrived:

'Strong cheeks of sea horses

We let run on the surf,

While our bright mailcoats

Were spattered with blood;

The she-wolf feasted, the hunger

Of eagles was fulfilled

By the flow from men's reddened necks

When we took the flour of the fishes.'

And then he who came later said:

'I saw you seldom

When the swift

Wading horses reached

The brewing white field;

And with lack of courage

You evaded the crows, by the mast

When again we pointed

Our red prows to the land.'

And again he who came earlier said:

'It little befits us

To bicker about our deeds

Which are greater than the others',

Over ale at the bench,

You stood on the sword-stag

As the surf bore it through the bay,

But I sat in the berth

When the red prow reached harbour.'

Then he who came later said:

'We both followed Bjorn

In the din of brands,

We were tried fighters,

When we fought for Ragnar;

From the heroes' beaks,

In the Bulgars' land

I have the wound in my side.

Sit closer, neighbour.'

They recognised each other at last, and sat together there at the banquet.

Chapter Twenty

There was a man named Ogmundur, who was called Ogmundur the Dane. One time he took five ships and anchored off Samsey in Munarvag. Then it is said that the cooks went ashore to prepare food, while the rest went to the woods for amusement, and they found there an ancient tree-man, who was forty feet high, and moss grown, and yet they could still make him out, and they discussed together who might have sacrificed to this great deity.

And then spoke the tree-man:

'It was long before,

When the bairns

Of the sea-king wandered

On the way here,

On the roller's tongues

Across the bright trail of salt,

Since then, this place

I have protected.

The warriors set me here

Near the southern sea of salt;

The sons of Ragnar

Sacrificed to me

In the south of Samsey.

Asked for men's death,

They told this man

To stand by thorns,

Moss-swathed;

Now on my cheeks

Clouds weep, neither flesh

Nor clothing warms me.'

And these man were amazed and they told many others.

THE YARN OF RAGNAR'S SONS

In many ways, *The Yarn of Ragnar's Sons* is a shorter retelling of the previous saga, even including some of the same poetry, which was probably the basis for both works. However, there are some interesting differences: for example, Ivar the Boneless is connected with York rather than London, which is slightly closer to the historic reality, and while the Saga omits to mention the Vikings' martyrdom of St Edmund, the East Anglian king, it is included in the *Yarn* alongside the blood-eagling of King Ella, in a version apparently culled from an Anglo-Saxon source. Here a murderous "Yngvar" appears as a character distinct from Ivar the Boneless, in fact one of his sons (modern historians think they are identical). However, it is at Ivar's orders that St Edmund is tortured.

Chapter One

After the death of King Hring, his son Ragnar succeeded as king of Sweden and Denmark. Then many kings came to the kingdom and seized land. Since he was a young man, they thought him unfit for decision-making or governing the country. There was one earl in West Gautland who was called Herraud, a vassal of King Ragnar. He was the wisest of men and a great warrior. He had a daughter called Thora Town-Hart. She was the fairest of all women of whom the king had heard. The Earl, her father, had given her a little snake one morning. She kept it first in a box. But this snake became so big in time that it coiled around her bower and bit its own tail. It became so fierce that people dared not come near her bower except those who gave it food and served the earl's daughter, and it ate an ox a day. People were very scared, and they knew that it could do great harm, it was so big and fierce. The Earl made this solemn vow at the vowing-beaker that he would marry his daughter, Thora, to the man who killed that snake, or who dared to talk with her in the presence of the snake. And when King Ragnar heard this news, he went to West Gautland. When he was close to the earl's farm, he put on shaggy garments: trousers and coat, sleeves and hood. These clothes were treated with sand and tar, and he took in his hand a great spear, and was girded with a sword, and so he left his men and went alone to the earl's farm and Thora's bower. And as soon as the snake saw that there was a stranger there, it rose up and blew venom at him. But he thrust his shield at it and went bravely towards it, and stabbed it in the heart with the spear. Then he drew his sword and cut off the snake's head, and it went just as it is told in *The Saga of King Ragnar*; he married Thora Town-Hart. And then he went to war, and freed all his realm.

He had two sons with Thora. One was named Eirik, the other Agnar. And when they were a few years old, Thora took ill and died. Then Ragnar married Aslaug, whom some call Randalin, daughter of Sigurd Fafnir's Bane and Brynhild Budli's Daughter. They had four sons. Ivar the Boneless was the eldest, then Bjorn Ironside, then Hvitserk, and Sigurd: there was a mark in the latter's eye, as if a snake was coiled round the pupil, and he was named Sigurd Snake-eye.

Chapter Two

When the sons of Ragnar were fully grown, they fought in many countries. The brothers Eirik and Agnar were second in rank, while third rank went to Ivar and his younger brothers with him, and they made Ivar the leader because he was very wise. They conquered Zealand and Reidgotaland, Eygotaland and Oland and all the islands in the sea. Then Ivar and his younger brothers established themselves in Lejre in Zealand, but it was against the will of King Ragnar. His sons all went to the wars, because they would not be less than King Ragnar, their father. That did not please King Ragnar and his sons turned against him and took his provinces against his will. He put a man called Eystein Beli on the throne of Upper Sweden and asked him to hold the kingdom for him and guard it against his sons, if they claimed it. One summer, when King Ragnar had gone with his army to the east, Eirik and Agnar, his sons, came to Sweden and brought their ships into Lake Malaren. Then they sent to Eystein in Uppsala, telling him to come to them. And when they met, Eirik said that he wanted King Eystein to rule Sweden under the brothers, and said he wanted then to marry Borghild, his daughter, and said that then they would be able to hold the kingdom against King

Ragnar. Eystein said he must ask his chieftains, so with that they parted. And when King Eystein brought this up, all the chieftains were of one mind to defend the land from the sons of Ragnar, and they brought together an irresistible army, and King Eystein went against Ragnar's sons. When they met, there was a great battle, and the sons of Ragnar were overborne by greater numbers, and the troop of brothers fell so that few remained on their feet. Then Agnar fell, but Eirik was captured.

Eystein offered Eirik peace and as much of the wealth of Uppsala as he wished in wergild for Agnar his brother, and also his daughter, who he asked for before. Eirik wanted no wergild and did not want the king's daughter, and he said he did not want to live after such a defeat he had had, but this he said that he would accept that he chose for himself his death day. And since King Eystein could not get any settlement from Eirik, he agreed to it. Eirik asked them to hold him up on spear tips and lift him above all the slain. Then Eirik said:

> *'I don't want wergild for my brother*
>
> *Or to buy your daughter with rings,*
>
> *Eystein was responsible,*
>
> *I hear, for Agnar's death;*
>
> *No mother cries for me,*
>
> *Hurry now to kill me,*
>
> *And on a forest of spears,*
>
> *High up, let me stand.'*

And before he was lifted up on the spears, he saw a man riding hard. Then he said:

'Carry my last utterance -

My eastward raids are over -

To the slender maid,

That she, Aslaug, may have my rings;

Let the best of mothers

Learn of my glorious death;

My gentle stepmother will hear

Word of her boy.'

Now it was done, that Eirik was lifted on spear-points, and so he died up above the slain. And when this news reached Zealand and Aslaug, she went at once to see her sons and told them the news. Bjorn and Hvitserk played chess, and Sigurd stood at the front. Whereupon Aslaug said:

'I don't think

That if you had all died,

A season would have passed without revenge

From your brothers; and I would have preferred it

If Eirik had kept his life, and Agnar,

Though they were not born to me.'

Then said Sigurd Snake-eye:

In three weeks,

If you grieve, mother,

We shall soon be ready,

War-preparations will be finished;

Eystein Beli shall not rule Uppsala,

Even if he offers much gold,

If our swords prove true.'

Bjorn Ironside said:

My heart holds courage

In my hawk-keen breast,

Though I do not boast of it,

I am bold and hardy;

You do not see in my eyes

Worms or spiralling snakes,

Yet my brothers gladdened me;

I remember your stepsons.'

Hvitserk answered:

Before vowing, let's plan

How revenge may be gained;

Concoct some evil

For the killer of Agnar;

Heave hulls onto the billows,

Hack the ice at the stern,

See whose ship soonest

Can set out to sea.'

Then Ivar the Boneless said:

'You have courage a-plenty

And pluck as well,

But you need to be dogged,

And we want doughty men.

I'm borne before my warriors,

Although I'm boneless,

I have resentful hands,

Though little strength in either.'

After that, Ragnar's sons mustered an overwhelming army. When they were ready, they went with a fleet to Sweden, but Queen Aslaug rode with fifteen hundred knights over the land, and the army was well equipped. She wore armour herself, and commanded the army, and they called her Randalin, and they regrouped in Sweden and plundered and burned wherever they went. King Eystein heard of this, and raised an army against them, of every man of fighting age who was in his realm. When they met, there was a great battle, and Ragnar's sons achieved victory, but King Eystein fell, and this battle became very famous. King Ragnar, where he was raiding, heard of this and was very angry with his sons that they had taken revenge without waiting for him. When he came home to his kingdom, he told Aslaug that he should do deeds no less famous than those his sons have done.

'I've now almost won back all the empire that my ancestors ruled, except only England[26], and so I have had made two merchant ships at Lidum in Vestfold,' - because his kingdom went up to Dovrefell and Lindesnes.

Aslaug said: 'Many longships could you have made for the price of these merchant ships. Besides, you know that big ships are not good for going to England with the streams and shallows, and this is not a well thought out plan.'

But all the same King Ragnar went with these merchant ships west to England with five hundred men and both ships were wrecked in England, but he himself, and all his men, came safely ashore. He set to harrying wherever he went.

Chapter Three

At that time a king named Ella ruled Northumbria. When he learned that a host had come into his kingdom, he collected a large army and went to meet them with an overwhelming army, and there was there a great and hard battle. King Ragnar was wearing the silk jacket that Aslaug gave him at parting. But the opposing army was so big that nothing could withstand them, so near enough all of his people were killed, but he himself went four times through the ranks of King Ella, and iron did

---

[26] According to legend, Scandinavian kings such as Ivar Wide-grasp ruled an empire that included Northumbria in England.

not penetrate his silk shirt. Finally he was captured and put in a snake pit, but snakes would not come near him. King Ella saw in the day that no iron bit him, when they fought, and the snakes did not want to hurt him. So he had Ragnar stripped of the clothes that he was wearing that day, and then the snakes were hanging off him on all sides, and he left his life with great courage.

And when the sons of King Ragnar heard this news, they went west to England to fight with King Ella. But since Ivar would not fight, nor his men, and the enemy army was huge, they were defeated and fled to their ships, and leaving it at that went home to Denmark. But Ivar stayed in England and went to King Ella and asked to be compensated for his father. And since King Ella saw that Ivar would not fight against him with his brothers, he thought he truly wanted to make a settlement with him. Ivar asked the king to give him as much land as he cover with the biggest old bull hide, because he said that he cannot go home to his brothers if he has received nothing. Ella thought this must true, and so they held to these terms. Then Ivar took raw hide and had it stretched as much as possible. And then he sliced the hide into thing thongs, and then split the flesh-side from the hair-side. Then he hauled it round a flat field and marked out foundations. He built strong city walls, and that city is now called York[27]. He befriended people all over the country and most of all the leaders, and eventually all the chiefs pledged loyalty to him and his brothers. Then he sent word to his brothers and said it was more likely they would be able to avenge their father, if

---

[27] Although he did not found it, Ivar's historical counterpart was more closely connected with York than with London.

173

they brought an army to England. And when they heard that, they mustered their host and went to England. And when Ivar becomes aware of this, he went to King Ella and said that he would not hide from him such news, but said that he could not fight against his brothers, but he would go and talk to them and sue for peace. The king accepted this. Ivar went to meet his brothers and egged them on to avenge his father and then goes back to King Ella and said that they were so savage and mad that they wanted to fight regardless. The king thought that Ivar acted with the greatest faithfulness. Ella went against the brothers with his army. And when they came together, many king's thanes went over to Ivar. The king was outnumbered, so that the greater part of his forces fell, and he himself was captured. Ivar and his brothers then recalled how their father was tortured. So they carved an eagle on Ella's back and then cut all the ribs from his backbone with a sword, so that his lungs were pulled out. So says Sighvat the poet in *Knutsdrapa*:

> '*And in Ella's back*
>
> *Ivar, who reigned*
>
> *at York, had*
>
> *an eagle hacked.*'

After this battle Ivar made himself king over that part of England which his forbears had owned. He had two sons born to a mistress, the one named Yngvar, the other Husto. They tortured King Edmund on Ivar's orders, and then he took his kingdom. Ragnar's sons went to war in many countries: England and Frankland and Gaul and out in Lombardy. But it is said that this was the furthest they got, when they won the city named Luna. And at one time they were going to go to Rome and take it, and their raiding is famed through all the northern lands where the Danish tongue is spoken. And when they came back to Denmark and their kingdom, they shared with the countries among themselves. Bjorn Ironside got Uppsala and Sweden and all belonging to that, and it is said that Sigurd Snake-eye had Zealand and Scania and Halland and all Oslo Fjord and Agder to Lindesnes and a great part of the Uplands, but Hvitserk had Reidgotaland and Wendland. Sigurd Snake-eye married Blaeja, daughter of King Ella. Their son was Knut, who was called Horda-Knut, who succeeded his father in Zealand, Scania and Halland, but Oslo Fjord broke away from him. He had a son named Gorm. He was named after his foster father, Knut the Foundling. He held all the land of the sons of Ragnar while they were at war. Gorm Knutson was tall and strong and doughtiest in all things, but he was not as wise as his former kin had been.

Chapter Four

Gorm took the kingdom after his father. He married Thyri, who was called Denmark's Salvation, daughter of Klakk-Harald, who was king in Jutland. But Harald was dead, Gorm took those realms under him. King Gorm took his army all over Jutland and demoted all petty kings as far south as the Schlei, and so he took much of Wendland, and he had many battles with the Saxons, and he became a powerful king. He had two sons. The eldest was called Knut, and the younger Harald. Knut was the most handsome men ever seen. The king loved him above any other man, and so did all the people. He was called Darling of the Danes. Harald favoured his mother's side in his looks, and his mother loved him no less than Knut. Ivar the Boneless was king of England for a long time. He had no children, because of the way he was made, that he no lust or love, but he did not lack wisdom or cruelty, and he died of old age in England and was buried there. So all the sons of Ragnar were dead. After Ivar, Adalmund took the kingdom. He was the nephew of Saint Edmund, and he converted much of England to Christianity. He took tribute from Northumbria, because it was heathen. After him his son named Adalbert took the kingdom. He was a good king and lived into old age. Towards the end of his reign a Danish army came to England, and the leaders of this army were Knut and Harald, the sons of King Gorm. They conquered a great kingdom in Northumbria, which Ivar had ruled. King Adalbert marched against them, and they fought north of Cleveland, and many Danes fell. And a little later the Danes went up to Scarborough and fought there and won. Then they went south to York, and all the people accepted their rule, and they did not fear them. And one day, when the weather was hot, the men went swimming in the water. And as the king's sons were swimming between the ships, men ran down from the land and shot at them. Knut was dealt a mortal wound, and they took the body and carried it out to the ship. And when people heard this, they gathered their forces, so that the Danes could not get ashore because of the gathering of the population, and then they went back home to Denmark. King Gorm was in Jutland. And when he heard this news, he collapsed and died of sorrow exactly a day later. Then Harald, his son, took the kingdom after him. He was the first of his faith and to be baptised.

Chapter Five

Sigurd Snake-eye and Bjorn Ironside and Hvitserk had raided many parts of Frankland. Then Bjorn returned to his kingdom. After that Emperor Arnulf fought with his brother, and a hundred thousand Danes and Norsemen fell there. Sigurd Snake-eye also lost his life, and Gudrod was another king who fell there. He was the son of Olaf Hringsson, son of Ingjald, son of Ingi, son of Hring for whom Ringeriki is named. He was the son of Dag and Thora Mother-of-Warriors. They had nine sons, and from them came the Dagling family. Helgi the Sharp was the name of Gudrod's brother. He had escaped from the battle with Sigurd Snake-eye's standard, and his sword and shield. He went home to Denmark with his troop and found Aslaug Sigurd's mother, and told her the news. Whereupon Aslaug recited this verse:

'Hunters of the slain sit

In cities of men;

It is evil to be rejected

By a raven named Sigurd;

Vainly they wait now,

Too soon Odin gave

The hero to the Valkyries.'

But because Horda-Knut was young, Helgi long remained with Aslaug to defend the country. Sigurd and Blaeja had a daughter. She was Horda-Knut's twin. Aslaug gave her her own name and brought her up and fostered her. She married Helgi the Sharp. Their son was Sigurd Hart. He was the most handsome and tallest and strongest of men who had ever been seen. Gorm Knutson and Sigurd Hart were the same age. When Sigurd was twelve, he killed the berserk named Hildibrand in a duel, and then twelve men. After that Klakk-Harald gave him his daughter Ingibjorg. They had two children, Gudthorm and Ragnhild. Then Sigurd learnt that King Frodi, his father's brother, was dead. He went north to Norway and became king over Ringeriki, his legacy. There a long story about him, as he did many great deeds. But it is said of his passing, he rode out into the wilds, hunting, as was his wont, and there came against him Haki Hadaberserk with thirty fully armed men, and they fought with him. Sigurd fell, but he had already killed twelve people, but King Haki had lost his right hand and had three other wounds. After that, King Haki and his men rode to Ringeriki to Stein, Sigurd's farm, and took away his daughter Ragnhild, and his son, Gudthorm, and many goods as well, and took them with him to Hadeland. And soon after he had a great feast prepared, intending to celebrate his wedding, but it was delayed because his wounds were bad. Ragnhild was then fifteen years old, but Gudthorm fourteen years. Autumn passed and then winter until Yule that Haki suffered from his wounds. King Halfdan the Black was staying at his estate in Hedmark. He sent Harek Gand with a hundred men, and they crossed the ice on Lake Mjosa to Hadeland one night and came in the day to King Haki's town and seized all the entrances to the hall where the retainers were sleeping. And then they went to King Haki's bed bower and took Ragnhild and Gudthorm her brother, and all the treasure that was there, and carried it off with them. They burned the house and all the retainers inside and then left. King Haki got up and dressed himself and went after them for a while. And when he came to the ice, he turned his swordhilt downwards, and fell on his sword and got there his death and he is buried on the bank of the lake. King Halfdan saw them coming over the ice with a covered wagon and assumed that their mission had gone exactly as he wished. So he had sent a message to all the settlements and invited all the great men in Hedmark and held a great banquet that day. He married Ragnhild, and they were together for many years. Their son was King Harald Fairhair, who first became king of all Norway.

THE YARN OF NORNA-GEST

The events of *The Yarn of Norna-Gest* are interlaced with those of *The Saga of the Volsungs* and other heroic sagas, and provide an alternative viewpoint on the deeds of Sigurd and his fellow characters. The hero, the eponymous Norna-Gest, "Guest of the Norns", is introduced as a visitor to the Christian court of the violent evangeliser Olaf Trygvasson, (King of Norway from 995 to 1000), who converted much of Norway with fire and the proverbial sword at the end of the first millennium. This prosaic setting is the venue for Gest's storytelling, relating tales of pagan antiquity, including characters such as Sigurd and the Volsungs, Starkad the Old, and the Sons of Ragnar Lodbrok. Some of the events are also recounted in *The Saga of the Volsungs*, but others are not included there, particularly *Brynhild's Ride to Hel* (based on an Eddic poem), and Sigurd's fight with Starkad, where the two greatest heroes of Norse legend meet to fight a titanic battle, much like Frankenstein and the Wolfman, or Godzilla and King Kong. Like Oisin in the Irish Fianna stories, Norna-Gest is a man who has outlived his own pagan age, and his encounter with the Christian Olaf Trygvasson seals his previously-determined fate.

Chapter One

It is said that at one time, when King Olaf Trygvasson was staying in Trondheim, it so happened that as the day drew on a man came to him on and saluted him honourably. The king welcomed him and asked who he was, and he said he was named Gest. The king answered, 'You will be a guest here, whatever your name is.' Gest said: 'I said my name, sire, and I will gladly accept lodging, if possible.' The king told him that he was ready. But since the day was ending, the king did not talk to his guest, since he went straight to his evening song and then to eat and then to sleep and quiet.

And on the same night King Olaf Trygvasson was in his bed and reading his prayers, while everyone else in that room was sleeping. Then the king thought an elf or spirit had come into the house, even though all the doors were locked. He came to the bed of every man sleeping there, and finally he came to the bed of one man who was lying there by the door. Then the elf stopped, 'Surprisingly strong is the lock here for an empty house, and the king is not so wise about such matters as others say, for if he was wisest of all men, he would not sleep so soundly.' After that, he disappeared through the locked doors.

Early the next morning the king sent his servant to establish who had slept in that bed during the night; it turned out that the guest had lain there. The king summoned him and asked him whose son he was. And he answered, 'Thord was my father and he was called Thingbiter, Danish in descent. He lived on a farm in Denmark called Groening.' 'You are a good-looking man,' said the king. Gest was bold in speech and bigger than most men, strong, and somewhat advanced in age. He asked the king if he could stay there longer with his retinue. The king asked him if he was a Christian. Gest said he had been prime-signed, but not baptized. The king said that he could stay with his men, - 'but for a short time will you remain unbaptised with me.' The elf had spoken about the lock because Gest had crossed himself that evening like other men, but he was actually a heathen. The king said, 'Do you have any skills?' He said he could play the harp and tell stories that pleased people. The king said: 'King Svein does evil if he lets unbaptised people travel out of his realm among the lands.' Gest said: 'The Danish King is not at fault, since I went away from Denmark long before the Emperor Otto had Denmark burned and forced Harald Gormsson and Earl Hakon Earl-of-Sacrifices into accepting Christianity.' The king asked Gest about many things, and he explained them well and wisely. People say that this Gest came in the third year of King Olaf's reign. In that year there came to him men called Grim and they were sent from Gudmund of Glasir Plain. They brought the king two horns which Gudmund had given him. These were also called Grim. They also had an errand to the king, which will later be told. Now it is said, Gest stayed with King Olaf. He was placed at the far end of the visitors' seats. He was a good mannered man and conducted himself well. He was also well liked by most men and well thought of.

Chapter Two

Shortly before Yule, Ulf the Red came home, and his men with him. He had been away on the king's business in the summer, because he was assigned to guard the land around the Vik in expectation of an attack by the Danes. He was accustomed to be with King Olaf in the middle of winter. Ulf had brought the king many good treasures which he had got during summer, and one gold ring he had obtained, named Hnitud. It was welded together in seven places, and each piece had its own colour. The gold was much better than other rings. The ring had been given to Ulf by a landowner named Lodmund, but it had belonged to King Half before that, for whom Half's Champions are named, and we hear that they had seized this treasure from King Halfdan the Ylfing. But Lodmund asked Ulf that in return, he would guard his land with the aid of King Olaf. Ulf agreed to that. The king was now holding a rich Yule celebration and he sat in Trondheim. On the eighth day of Yule Ulf the Red gave the ring Hnitud to King Olaf. The king thanked him for the gift, and for all of the faithful services that he had always shown him. The ring was passed around the room where they were drinking, because there were no halls built at that time in Norway. Each man showed it to the other, and it seemed they had never seen such good gold as was in the ring. And at last he came to the guest bench and so to Gest, the stranger. He looked at the ring and handed it back with the hand in which he held his drinking horn before. He thought little of it, and did not say much about this treasure, but talked merrily as before with his companions. A room servant served drinks at the bench. He asked: 'Do you like the ring?' 'Quite well,' they said, 'except for the new arrival,

Gest. He does not, and we think that he may not appreciate it, because he does not notice such things.' The room servant went to the king and told him this in the same words that the visitors had used, how he paid little attention to this treasure when he had been shown such a prize. The king said, 'Gest yet knows a lot more than you suspect, and he shall come to me in the morning and tell me a story.' Now the other guests at the far end of the table were talking to each other. They asked the newly arrived guest if he had seen such a good ring or better. Gest said: 'Since you think it strange that I say so little, I will say that I have surely seen gold no worse, in fact, better.' Then the king's men laughed and said that this promised to be great entertainment, - 'and you will wager with us that you have seen the same quality of gold as this, so that you can prove it. We will wager four marks in current coin, and you your knife and belt, and the king will judge who is right.' Gest said: 'I shall neither be mocked by you, nor fail to hold to the wager that you offer, and be sure I will wager here, and wager as you have spoken, and the king will judge who is right.' They ended their speech. Gest took his harp and played well and long into the evening, so that everyone was delighted to hear it, and he played the Gunnarsslag[28] best. And finally he moved on to the ancient Gudrunesbrogd. They had never heard that before. And after that they slept through the night.

Chapter Three

The king rose early in the morning and

---

[28] This poem is lost, although Gunnar Pálsson (1714-1791) composed a new poem of the same name. It describes the sufferings of Gunnar in Atli's snake pit (See *The Saga of the Volsungs*, Chapter 37).

attended mass. And when it ended, he went to breakfast with his retinue. And when he sat on his throne, the guests came before the king and Gest with them, and they told him all about their discussion and the wager that they had made. The king said, 'I am not overjoyed by your wager, even though you are staking your own money. I suspect that drink had gone to your heads, and it seems to me that you would best forget it, all the more if Gest thinks so.' Gest said: 'I want the agreement to remain.' The king said, 'It seems to me, Gest, that my men have talked themselves into a corner with this issue more than you have, but that will soon be made clear.'

After that, they went away, and the men began drinking. And when the drinking tables were taken away, the king called Gest to him and spoke thus: 'Now you are obliged to bring out your gold, if you have any, so that I may judge your wager.' 'It shall be as you wish, sire,' said Gest. He opened the purse that he had with him, and took out a bag and then untied it and put something into the king's hand. The king saw that it was a piece of a saddle buckle, and that it was of very good gold. He asked them to bring the ring Hnitud. When this was done, the king compared the gold and the ring, and then said: 'It certainly seems to me that the better gold is that which Gest has shown us, and any man who sees it will think so.' Many men with him agreed. He judged the wager in Gest's favour. The guests thought they had made fools of themselves over this issue. Gest said: 'Take your money and keep it yourselves, because I do not need it, but don't lay bets with unfamiliar people, because you never know when you meet someone that they haven't seen and heard more than you. But I wish to thank you, sire, for your decision.' The king said, 'Now I would like you to tell us where you got the gold that you carry with you.' Gest said: 'I am reluctant to do so, because most people would think what I say unbelievable.' 'Let us hear it,' said the king, 'seeing that you have already promised us your story.' Gest said: 'If I tell you what has happened to this gold, then I expect that you will also wish to hear the other story.' 'I suspect,' said the king, 'that you are right.'

Chapter Four

'Then I will tell you how I went south to the land of the Franks. I wanted to learn about Sigurd Sigmund's son and discover if what I had heard of his beauty and courage were true. Nothing happened until I came to the land of the Franks and met King Hjalprek. He had a great retinue around himself. Sigurd was there, son of Sigmund Volsungsson and Hjordis Eylimi's daughter. Sigmund fell in battle with Hunding's sons, but Hjordís married Alf, son of King Hjalprek. Sigurd grew up with all the sons of King Sigmund. They were all men of strength and stature, Sinfjotli and Helgi, who killed King Hunding and was thus called Hundingsbane. The third was named Hamund. Sigurd outstripped all the brothers. It is widely known that Sigurd was the most noble of all kings and the best in ancient times. It was then that Regin, son of Hreidmarr, came to King Hjalprek's dwelling. He was the most cunning of men, a dwarf in stature, a wise man, but fierce and skilled in magic. Regin taught Sigurd many things and loved him. He spoke of his forefathers and wondrous events that had happened. And when I had been there only a little while, I became Sigurd's servant with many others. Everybody loved him, since he was both gentle and humble and gave treasure to us all.

Chapter Five

One day, we came to Regin's home, and Sigurd was well received. Then Regin said:

'Here comes visiting

The son of Sigmund,

A determined man,

To our dwelling,

He has much might,

But I am an old man,

Vanquished by the fangs

Of the voracious wolf.'

And again he said:

'But I must honour

The battle-bold warrior.

Now Yngvar's son

Has visited us.

This warrior must be

Most powerful under the sun,

Prominent in all lands

With his praise.'

Sigurd was always with Regin, and he told him much of Fafnir, who lay on Gnita Heath in the shape of a snake, and was extraordinarily big. Regin made a sword called Gram for Sigurd. It was so sharp-edged, when he thrust it into the river Rhine, and threw a lock of wool in the stream, it cut it in half. Then Sigurd split Regin's anvil with the sword. After that, Regin egged Sigurd on to kill Fafnir, his brother, and recited this verse:

> *'Loud Hunding's*
>
> *Sons will laugh,*
>
> *Who prevented*
>
> *Eylimi's old age,*
>
> *If I was lured*
>
> *Into looking for more*
>
> *Red-gold rings*
>
> *Then revenging my father.'*

After that Sigurd prepared for his journey and decided to harry the sons of Hunding, and King Hjalprek gave him many men and some warships. Joining Sigurd in his journey was Hamund, Hjalprek's brother, and the dwarf Regin. I was there, and they called me Norna-Gest. King Hjalprek was familiar to me when he was in Denmark with Sigmund Volsungsson. Then Sigmund was married to Borghild, but they separated when Borghild killed Sinfjotli, Sigmund's son, with poison. Then Sigmund went south to the land of the Franks and married Hjordis, Eylimi's daughter. Hunding's sons killed him, and Sigurd had both his father and his mother's father to avenge. Helgi Sigmund's son, who was called Hundingsbane, was the brother of Sigurd, who

afterwards was called Fafnir's Bane. Helgi, brother of
Sigurd, had slain King Hunding and his three sons,
Eyjolf, Hervard, and Hjorvard. Lyngvi escaped with
his two brothers, Alf and Heming. They were the
most famous people for all abilities, and Lyngvi
surpassed his brothers. They were very skilled in
magic. They had harried many kings and killed many
mighty men and burned many cities and did most of
their plundering in Spain and the land of the Franks.
But at that time no imperial power had come north
of the mountains. Hunding's sons had conquered the
realm that Sigurd had in the land of the Franks, and
there were very large forces there.

Chapter Six

Now I must tell how Sigurd prepared for
battle against Hunding's sons. He had a great and
well-armed force. Regin planned the strategies for
the troop. He had a sword called Ridill, which he had
forged. Sigurd asked Regin to lend him the sword.
He did so, and told him to kill Fafnir when he came
back from this voyage. Sigurd promised to do that.
Then we sailed south along the coast. Then we met a
big storm raised by sorcery, and recognized it as the
work of Hunding's sons. Then we sailed a little along
the coast. There we saw a man on a promontory that
went out from the sea cliffs. He was in a green cloak
and blue breeches, had high-buttoned shoes on his
feet and a spear in his hand. This man sang out to us
and said:

> *Who rides*
>
> *The horse of Raevil*
>
> *On the raging waves,*

The resounding ocean?

Are your sails

Sea-swollen?

Will the horse of the waves

Withstand the gale?'

Regin said in return:

'Here we come, with Sigurd,

Across the ocean.

A fair wind is given us

To blow us to our graves.

Higher than the ship's prow

The waves soon will break.

Our sea-steeds will sink.

Who asks of this?'

The man in the cloak said:

'Hnikar they hailed me,

When I gladdened Hugin,

Young Volsung,

When I had conquered.

Now you may address

The old man of the rock

As Feng or Fjolnir.

I will accept passage.'

Then we made for land, and the wind died down quickly, and Sigurd told the man to wade out to the ship. He did so. Then the wind fell, and a perfect breeze sprang up. The man sat at Sigurd's knee and was very affable. He asked if Sigurd would accept some advice. Sigurd said he would, that he supposed he could give a lot of advice if he wished people to benefit from it. Sigurd said to the cloaked man:

'Tell me this, Hnikar,

All that you know of both

The holy gods and of men:

Which are the best omens,

If one must fight,

When swords are sweeping?'

Hnikar said:

'Many omens are good,

If men know

When swords are sweeping.

A faithful companion

I consider the dark raven

To be for a warrior.

This is another omen,

If you go outside

And prepare for a journey:

And you see two

Valiant warriors

Standing on the path.

This is a third,

If you hear a wolf

Howl beneath the ash tree.

It means good luck

Bringing you helmeted warriors

If you are the first

To see such fighters

Men should not struggle if

On the skyline they see

The late shining

Sister of the moon.

They will have victory,

Who can see,

Speedy swordplay,

Or the troop arrayed.

It is great harm,

If your feet stumble,

On your way to the fight:

Guileful disir

Stand on both sides

And wish to see you wounded.

Combed and washed

Shall each appear

At morning meal,

Because it is uncertain

What will come after.

It is ill to fall before good fortune.'

And after that we sailed south along Holstein, and to the east of Friesland and there to land. When the news reached Hunding's sons of our expedition they gathered troops and soon they had large numbers. And when we met them there was hard fighting. Lyngvi was foremost of the brothers in all the charges. They all fought with courage. Sigurd charged so hard that everyone fled before him, since the sword Gram was likely to wound them, but Sigurd needed not worry about taunts of cowardice. When he met Lyngvi, they exchanged many blows and fought very bravely. There was a pause in the combat, with men watching this duel. It was a long while before either wounded other, because they were both so skilled in arms. Then the brothers of Lyngvi charged forward and killed many men, but some escaped. Then Hamund, brother of Sigurd, turned to meet them, and I with him. It became another encounter. And the encounter between Sigurd and Lyngvi ended with Sigurd taking him prisoner, and he was placed in fetters. But when Sigurd came to us we had a speedy change. Hunding's sons and all of their troops fell, as night came on. And when dawn came the next morning, Hnikar had disappeared and was never seen again. Men think that it had been Odin. They discussed what kind of death Lyngvi should have. Regin suggested that the blood-eagle should be carved on his back. Regin then took his sword from me and carved Lyngvi's back, so he cut the ribs from the spine, and drew out the lungs. So Lyngvi died with great bravery.

Then Regin:

'Now is the blood eagle

With a broad sword

Carved on the back

Of the killer of Sigmund.

Few were braver,

When the earth was bloodied;

The leader of hosts,

Made Hugin happy.'

There was a great deal of plunder. Sigurd's warriors took it all, for he would have none of it himself. There were many expensive clothes and weapons. Then Sigurd killed Fafnir and Regin as well, since he intended to betray him. Sigurd took Fafnir's gold, and rode away. He was then called Fafnir's Bane. After that, he rode up onto Hind Heath and there he met Brynhild, and so matters went as it is told in the story of Sigurd Fafnir's Bane.

Chapter Seven

Then Sigurd married Gudrun, Gjuki's daughter[29]. He was then for a time with the Gjukungs, his in-laws. I was with Sigurd north in Denmark. I was also with Sigurd when King Sigurd Hring[30] sent Gandalf's sons, his cousins, against the Gjukungs, Gunnar and Hogni, and demanded that they would give him tribute or suffer otherwise, but they wanted to defend their country. Then Gandalf's sons challenged the Gjukungs to a duel on the border and then they went back home. But the Gjukungs asked Sigurd Fafnir's Bane go to battle with him. He said it should be so. I was still with Sigurd. We still sailed northwards to Holstein and landed there at Jarnamodir. Not far from the harbour hazel poles[31] were set up, where the battle would be. Then we saw many ships sail from the north. Gandalf's sons commanded them. Both of them attacked. Sigurd Hring was not there because he had to defend his country, Sweden, for Kurlanders and Kvens were raiding it. By then Sigurd[32] was very old. After that the troops clashed, and a mighty battle ensued, with much loss of life.

---

[29] See *The Saga of the Volsungs,* Chapter 26.

[30] Legendary king of Sweden and father of Ragnar Lodbrok (See *The Saga of Ragnar Lodbrok*).

[31] A Viking custom especially linked with single combat, but also mentioned in *Egil Skallagrimsson's Saga* in the context of a battle.

[32] i.e. Sigurd Hring.

Gandalf's sons were brave in their advance, because they were both larger and stronger than the others.

In their troop was one man, tall and strong. This man killed men and horses, so that no one could resist him, because he was more like a giant than a man. Gunnar asked Sigurd to attack this rascal, because he said otherwise there would be no success. Sigurd now readied himself to go against the great man, and a few men came with him, but most were unwilling. 'We swiftly came upon this great man,' said Gest, 'and Sigurd asked him his name and where he came from. He said he was Starkad Storverksson[33] from north of Fenhring out in Norway. Sigurd said he had heard of him and rarely to his credit. 'Such people are not merciful to the unwelcome.' Starkad said, 'Who is that man who defames me so much with his words?' Sigurd identified himself. Starkad said, 'Are you the one they call Fafnir's Bane?' 'It is so,' he said. Then Starkad wanted to run away, but Sigurd turned and lifted up the sword Gram, and hit him on the jaw with the hilt, so that two teeth flew out. It was a maiming blow. Sigurd told the dog to get away from there. Starkad turned quickly away from there. But I took a tooth and I have it with me. It is now on a bell rope in Denmark and weighs seven ounces. People think it a curiosity to see it there. After Starkad ran away Gandalf's sons also fled. We took much booty, and then the king went home to his kingdom, and stayed there for a while.

---

[33] A doomed hero who, much like Norna-Gest, was blessed with three lifetimes but cursed to commit three terrible deeds during that time. See Saxo Grammaticus' *Gesta Danorum, Fragment of a Saga about Certain Early Kings in Denmark and Sweden* and *The Saga of King Gautrek*.

Chapter Eight

A little later we heard tell of the cruel murder Starkad had committed, killing King Ali in his bath. It happened one day that Sigurd Fafnir's Bane rode to a gathering, then he rode through a muddy pool, and the steed Grani leaped up so wildly that in two jumps his saddle-girth broke and the buckle fell down to the ground. But when I saw where it shone in the mud, I took it up, and brought it to Sigurd, but he gave it to me. It was that same gold you were looking at a short time ago. Sigurd then jumped off his horse, and I rubbed his horse down, and washed the mud off Grani, and I pulled a lock of hair from his tail to prove his great size.' Then Gest showed the lock, and it was seven ells long. King Olaf said: 'Your stories seem entertaining to me.' Now all men praised his stories and talent. The king said that he wanted him to tell them more about his adventures. So Gest told them many amusing things up until late evening. Then they went to sleep. On the morning after, the king called Gest and wanted to speak further with him. The king said: 'I cannot fully discern your age, and how it can be that you are a man old enough to have been present during these events. Will you tell another story, so that we become better acquainted with such matters?' Gest said: 'I thought before that you would want to hear another of my stories, if I told you about what happened to my treasure.' The king said, 'Certainly you shall tell me more.'

Chapter Nine

'It is still to be told,' said Gest, 'that I went north to Denmark, and settled down on my father's estate, since he had died shortly before. And soon after I heard of the death of Sigurd and the

Gjukungs, and it seemed to me that was momentous news.' The king said, 'What caused Sigurd's death?' Gest said: 'Most people say that Guttorm Gjukisson put his sword through him when he was sleeping in bed with Gudrun. But Germans say Sigurd was killed out in the woods. But the *Gudrunar-raetha* says that Sigurd and Gjuki's sons had ridden to the Thing[34] and then they killed him. But they all agree that they set on him when he was lying down and surprised, and they betrayed him terribly.' But one courtier asked: 'How did Brynhild act then?' Gest said: 'Brynhild killed seven slaves and five handmaidens, and thrust a sword through herself and ordered that she be taken with them to the pyre and burnt with the dead. And this was done, one pyre was built for Sigurd and another for Brynhild, and he was burnt first, then she was. She was riding a chariot, and it had a canopy of precious cloth, and purple, and it glittered with gold, and so she was burned.' Then they asked Gest whether Brynhild had sung after she was dead. He said it was true. They asked him to recite it, if he could. Then he said: 'As Brynhild was driven to the pyre on the road to Hel, she went past some cliffs. An ogress lived there. She was outside the cave entrance and wore a skin kirtle of black colour. She had in her hand a long piece of wood and said: 'This I will add to your burning, Brynhild, and it would be better that you were burned living for your crimes than that you died after causing the death of Sigurd Fafnir's Bane, a good man, and often was I friendly to him, and I shall recite a poem of you with words of vengeance, that will make you hated by all who hear what you have done.' After that Brynhild and the ogress chanted poetry. The ogress said:

---

[34] Viking parliament.

'You shall not

Pass through

The stone-doors

Of my courts.

Better honour for you

To stay with your sewing

Rather than to visit

My dreary hall.

Why do you

Come from Gaul,

Fickle-headed one,

To visit my house?

You have fed many wolves,

Given them the blood of men you slew.'

Then said Brynhild:

'Revile me no more,

Bride from the rock,

In earlier days

I went freebooting.

You will not be regarded

As superior in virtue,

Than I, wherever

Noble men know us.'

The ogress said:

'You are, Brynhild,

Budli's daughter,

In an ill hour

Born into the world.

You gave the sons

Of Gjuki to slaughter

Their noble house

Destroyed.'

Brynhild said:

'I will tell you a

True tale,

Lying one,

If you will listen,

How they made for me,

Those Gjukungs,

A loveless life

And oath breaking.

Deliver me from grief

Courageous king,

Eight sisters

Living under an oak.

I had twelve winters,

If you wish to know,

When I swore and oath

To the young king.

I caused an old

Ogress' brother

Hjalmgunnar,

To go to Hel.

I gave the victory

You Auda's young brother.

Then Odin was angry

For that reason

He ringed me with shields

Red and white

In Skatlaund.

Then he told him

To end my sleep

Who in no country

Knew any fear.

And he made blaze

Round my south-facing hall

To burn high

Howling fire dogs.

Told him then to ride over along

Then was brought to me

The bed of Fafnir.

The gold giver

Rode good Grani,

Where my foster-father

Ruled his hall.

Alone he seemed there

The Danish Viking

Prized best of all.

We slept happily in one bed,

As if he were born my brother.

Each of us could

Lie there

One hand over the other

For eight nights.

So reproached me

Gudrun Gjuki's daughter,

Because I slept

In Sigurd's arms.

Then I knew

What I wished not to,

That they betrayed me

In matchmaking.

In struggle will we,

For too long,

Men and women

Be born alive.

We shall witness the end of ages,

Sigurd and I, together.

Sink now, ogress.'

Then the ogress cried in a menacing voice and ran back into the rock.

Then said the king's retainers: 'This is entertaining, now tell us even more.

The king said, 'There is no need to tell more about things like these.'

The king said, 'Were you ever with Ragnar's sons?'

Gest said, 'I was with them a little while. I came to them when they fought south in the Alps and sacked Vifilsborg. Then everyone was scared of them, because they had victory wherever they went, and they were intending to go to Rome.

'It happened one day that a man came to King Bjorn Ironside, and greeted him. The king welcomed him and asked where he had come from. He said he had come from Rome in the south. The king asked, 'How far is it to there?' He said, 'Here you may see, King, the shoes that I have on my feet.' He took an iron shoe from his foot, and it was all thick above, but very worn beneath. 'It is a long way from here to Rome as you may see by my shoes, how badly they have suffered.' The king said, 'It is a surprisingly long way to go, and we will turn back and not fight against the Romans.' And so they did, going no farther, and everyone thought it strange that their forces turned so quickly and changed their temper at a single word, of that which they had before all been resolved[35]. Ragnar's sons came back north and plundered no farther south. The king said, 'It is clear that the holy men in Rome would not let them go there, and he must have been a spirit sent by God that so soon changed their plans in such a manner that they did not make mischief in the holiest place of Jesus Christ in Rome.'

---

[35] See note 19 in *The Saga of Ragnar Shaggy-Breeches*.

Chapter Ten

The king questioned Gest further: 'Where did you come to the king who you thought best?' Gest said: 'The most joy I felt with Sigurd and the Gjukungs. Yet Ragnar's sons allowed their men to live independently as they wanted. But with Eirek at Uppsala was the most happy. Harald Fairhair was more troublesome with his courtiers than all of the previous kings. I was also with Hlodver, king of Saxony[36], and there was I prime-signed, because I would not be permitted there otherwise, because they observed Christianity well there, and there it seemed to me to be the best place.' The king said, 'You can tell us much, if we wish to ask.' The king now asked many things of Gest. And Gest told him it all, and at last he said: 'Now I can tell you why I am called Norna-Gest.' The king said he wanted to hear that.

Chapter Eleven

'I was raised by my father in the place that is called Groening. My father was a man rich in money and he held costly celebrations in his house. Back then, seeresses travelled the land, who were called prophetesses and told people's fortunes. Men invited them to their homes, prepared banquets for them and gave them gifts at parting. My father did so too, and they came to him with a large company, and they were going to predict my fate. I lay in the cradle and they spoke about my future. Over me two candles burned. They spoke to me and told me I would become a lucky man, and greater than any of my ancestors or the sons of rulers in the country and

---

[36] A Hlodver, king of Saxony is mentioned in *The Saga of Sigurd the Silent* as a contemporary of King Arthur.

said that all should pass as has been my fate. The youngest Norn[37] thought she was too little valued than the other two, because they did not ask her for such prophecies and so were they more highly prized. There were also very ribald men there, who pushed her from her seat, so she fell to the ground. Because of this she became angry. She called out loudly and wrathfully and told them no longer to make such good prophecies about me - 'because I decree that he will not live longer than the candle, which is burning beside the boy, takes to burn.' After that the elder seeress took the candle and quenched it and told my mother to keep it and not to light it before the last day of my life. After that the prophetesses went away and dragged away the young Norn and so kept her away, and my father gave them good gifts at parting. Then when I was a full grown man, my mother gave me the candle to keep safe. Now I have it with me.' The king said, 'Why did you come to us?' Gest said: 'This came into my heart: I came to you hoping for some good fortune, because you have been highly praised to me by good and wise men.' The king said: 'Will you now take holy baptism?' Gest said: 'I will do what you advise.' Then it was done, and the king took him into his favour, and made him his retainer. Gest was a loyal man and followed the king's rules. He was also a favourite with the men.

---

[37] Although this name is given to the goddesses of fate, particularly in the *Prose Edda*, it is used here to describe a mortal fortune teller. A similar motif, of the angry fairy godmother, appears in Perrault's *The Sleeping Beauty in the Wood*, which also has parallels in *The Saga of the Volsungs*. Norna-Gest's life depending on the candle is reminiscent of the Greek story of Meleager.

Chapter Twelve

One day the king asked Gest: 'How long would you live now, if you could choose?' Gest said: 'A brief moment henceforth, if God willed it.' The king said, 'What will happen if you take your candle now?' Gest took the candle out of the frame of his harp. The king asked him to light it, and so it was done. And when the candle was lit, it burned quickly. The king asked Gest: 'How old a man are you?' Gest said: 'Now I am three hundred years old.' 'You are very old,' said the king. Gest lay down. He asked them to anoint him. The king had this performed. When it was done, there was little of the candle unburned. The men realised then that Gest had little time left. It was just as soon as the candle was completely burned that Gest died, and all thought his death remarkable. The king thought highly of his history, and he said that what he said about his life seemed true.

THE SAGA OF HERVOR AND HEIDREK

The Saga of Hervor and Heidrek is the story of the sword Tyrfing, which was forged by dwarves under duress, with as many curses as blessings. Like the Rhinegold in *The Saga of the Volsungs*, its tale is one of tragedy and bloodshed, as it falls into the hands of owner after owner, causing chaos and mayhem as it does so.

The saga is renowned for its sequences of mystical horror, including the first Hervor's visit to the grave of her father, the undead berserk Angantyr, in which she wins back the cursed sword after a long dialogue with his ghost. This was the inspiration for the Romantic poet Anna Seward, the 'Swan of Lichfield', who based *Herva, at the Tomb of Argantyr. A Runic Dialogue* upon it. Another writer who found inspiration in this saga, among many others, was JRR Tolkien, who used the Riddles of Gestumblindi as one of the models for his riddle game in *The Hobbit*. Also of interest in the saga are the echoes it contains of real history as well as mythology; the early history of the Goths, before they left their kingdom in what is now the Ukraine to cut a bloody swathe across the declining Roman Empire. The name Tyrfing has been connected with that of the Tervingi, an early Gothic dynasty mentioned by Roman writers, and 'Gryting' with the Greutungi, another Gothic clan. Some of the characters who appear in the later sequence are also mentioned in the Anglo Saxon poem *Widsith* (line 115).

It has not become as famous as *The Saga of the Volsungs*, although it has inspired art and literature in modern times, but it has more often been used as a quarry from which other writers have extracted material. An uneven work in many ways, it nevertheless contains a great deal of interest: dwarves, magic swords and curses, warrior maidens and the undead, giants and gods, riddles and fate, all culminating in an epic battle between Goths and Huns, after which the legendary story continues into recorded history as far as the later Viking Age, linking the glorious Goths of history with the Swedish kingdom, a tradition that in many ways was revived during Sweden's imperial expansion in the seventeenth century, when, like the Goths before them, possessed by the *furor teutonicus*, - almost as if Tyrfing had returned - they issued forth from the womb of nations to lay waste kingdoms and empires.

Chapter One

There was a king named Sigrlami who ruled Gardariki[38]. His daughter was Eyfura, most beautiful of all maidens. This king had got from the dwarfs a sword named Tyrfing that was the sharpest of all swords, and every time it was drawn, it shone like the sunlight of dawn. It could never be unsheathed unless it were a man's death, and it must always be sheathed covered in warm blood. But there was no living thing, neither man nor animal, that could live another day if they received a wound from it, whether big or small. Never did it fail to hit nor been parried before it sank into the ground, and the man who wielded it in battle would get the victory if he struck blow with it. This sword is famous in all sagas.

There was a man named Arngrim[39], a famous Viking. He travelled east to Gardariki and stayed for a while with King Sigrlami and became captain of his troops to guard both the land and the people of the land, because the king was now old. Then Arngrim became so great a lord that the king gave him his daughter in marriage, and he became the most powerful man in his kingdom. He gave him his sword Tyrfing. The king sat quietly, and nothing more is said of him.

Arngrim went with his wife, Eyfura, north to the land he had inherited and settled in the island named Bolm. They had twelve sons. The eldest and most famous was named Angantyr, the second Hjorvard, Hervard third, Hrani fourth and then the two Haddings; no more are mentioned. They were all berserks[40], such strong and mighty champions

---

[38] Russia.

[39] The same character appears in Saxo Grammaticus' *Gesta Danorum*. Book 5

[40] Members of a warrior cult, sacred to the god Odin, who entered battle in a state of frenzy and were said to be invulnerable to fire and iron. It was noted that after the

that never did they go to war as more than a dozen, and they never went to war without winning the victory. Because of this, they were famed in all countries, and there was no king who did not give them what they wanted to have.

Chapter Two

It had happened one Yule Eve, when men made vows at the *bragarfull*[41] according to custom. Then Arngrim's sons swore oaths. Hjorvard made a solemn vow that he would marry the daughter of Ingjald, king of Sweden, a girl famous in all countries for fairness and skill, or no wife otherwise.

That same spring, the twelve brothers set out and came to Uppsala and went before the royal table, where his daughter sat with him. Then Hjorvard told the king his errand and his pledge, and everyone who was inside listened. Hjorvard asked the king to say quickly what the result of his errand would be.

The king considered this matter. He knew how powerful the brothers before him were, and of what excellent lineage. At that moment a man named Hjalmar the Brave stepped before the king's board, and said to the king, 'Lord King, remember now how much honour I have given you since I came to this country, and how many battles I have fought to win countries for you, and I given my service to you have. Now I ask that I may increase my honour and that you give me in marriage your daughter, on whom my heart has always been set. It is more fitting that you grant my request rather than that of these

---

berserk fit left them they were weaker than usual.
[41] A drink from a particular cup or horn that involved the swearing of oaths.

berserks, who have done evil both in your kingdom and those of many other kings.'

Now the king thought of the future and it seemed a great problem, the two lords competing for his daughter. The king spoke, saying they are both so great men, and of good noble birth that he could not refuse either, and he told his daughter to choose which one she wants. She said that this was fair, and if her father wanted to marry her off, she would prefer a man she knew to be good to one of whom she had only hears stories of evil, like the sons of Arngrim.

Hjorvard challenged Hjalmar to a duel south on Samsey and cursed him as a nithing[42], if he married the lady before this duel was fought. Hjalmar said nothing would deter him. Arngrim's sons then went home and told their father how this errand had turned out, and Arngrim said he had never previously been afraid for them on their journeys.

Then they went to the earl Bjarmar, and he prepared a great feast for them. And then Angantyr wanted to marry the daughter of the Earl who was named Svava, and then was their wedding ale was drunk. And then Angantyr told the Earl of a dream: He thought the brothers were there on Samsey, and they found a lot of birds, and killed every one. Then they took another path on the island, and two eagles flew toward them, and he thought he attacked one, and they had a hard fight, and both sank down before the end. But the other eagle had fought his eleven brothers, and he thought the eagle was winning. The Earl said that the dream needed no

---

[42] An honourless man.

interpretation and the fall of mighty men was shown to him there.

Chapter Three

But when the brothers got home, they prepared themselves for the fight, and their father followed them to the ship, and gave Angantyr his sword Tyrfing. 'I think,' he said, 'that good weapons will now be needed.' He bade them farewell; after that, they parted. And when the brothers got to Samsey, they saw two ships in the haven named Munarvag. The ships were the kind called 'ashes'.

They thought that Hjalmar would have travelled in these ships, and with them Odd the Wanderer, who was called Arrow-Odd[43]. Then the sons of Arngrim drew their swords and bit their shields, and the berserk frenzy came upon them. They went out onto the ships, six to a ship. But there were such good men on board that all took their weapons, and no man fled from his place, and no one spoke a word of fear. But the berserks went up one side and back down the other [of the ships], and killed them all. Then they went ashore howling. Hjalmar and Odd had gone up onto the island to see if the berserks had turned up. When they came back out of the forest to their ships, then the berserks went out of the vessels with their weapons bloody and swords drawn, but the berserk frenzy had left off. But then they were weaker than before, like after some kinds of sicknesses. Odd then said:

---

[43] Arrow-Odd has his own saga, which comes later in this volume.

'I felt fear once,

When they bellowed,

Abandoning the longships

(And screaming out

Ascended the island)

Inglorious,

Twelve men together.'

Then Hjalmar said to Odd, 'Do you see now that all our men are fallen? It seems to me likely that tonight we will all be Odin's guests in Valhalla.' And other than in that one speech, Hjalmar never said a word of fear.

Odd said, 'This would be my advice, that we flee into the woods. The two of us will not be able to fight the twelve that have killed twelve of the most valiant in in Sweden.'

Then Hjalmar said: 'Let us never flee from our enemies, but rather withstand their weapons; I want to fight the berserks.'

Odd said, 'But I am not wishing to guest with Odin tonight, and these berserks will all be dead before the evening, but we two shall live.'

These words are proved in these verses; Hjalmar said:

'Mighty are the warriors

Leaving the warships,

Twelve men together

Inglorious;

I think this evening

I will be Odin's guest,

Two sworn brothers,

But the twelve will live.'

Odd said:

To what you ask will I

Provide an answer:

This evening they will

Be Odin's guests,

Twelve berserks,

We two shall live.'

Then Hjalmar saw that Angantyr had Tyrfing in hand, since it shone like the sunlight of dawn. Hjalmar said, 'Will you fight Angantyr alone or his eleven brothers?'

Odd said: 'I will fight Angantyr. He will strike mighty blows with Tyrfing, but I believe my shirt is better than your armour for protection.'

Hjalmar said: 'When have you come before me in battle? You want to fight Angantyr because you think it the harder battle. Now I am principal in this duel and this is not what I promised the Swedish princess, to let you or anyone else fight this duel for me, and I will fight Angantyr,' - and then he drew his sword and went against Angantyr, and each showed the other the way to Valhalla. Then Hjalmar and Angantyr fought, and wasted little time between each of the massive strokes they gave. Odd called out to the berserks and said:

'One shall fight one

Unless they're wastrels,

Strong fighters,

Unless their courage fail.'

Then Hjorvard came forward, and he had a savage fight with Odd. But Odd's silk shirt was so tough that no weapons could bite it, and he had a sword so good that it cut through armour as if it was cloth. And he gave Hjorvard only a few blows before the berserk fell dead. Then Hervard stepped forward and went the same way, then Hrani, then one after another, but Odd fought so hard that he killed all eleven brothers. From the grim game comes the tale that Hjalmar received sixteen wounds, but Angantyr fell dead. Odd went to where Hjalmar was, and said:

What concerns you, Hjalmar?

Your colour is pale.

Multiple wounds are

Wasting your strength;

Your helmet is hacked,

And the harness on your flank,

Now I deem you have seen

The end of your days.'

Hjalmar said:

I have sixteen wounds; my byrnie is split,

My sight is darkened, I cannot see.

Angantyr's blade entered my heart:

That sharp sword was steeped in poison.

And again he said:

Five were the farms I had for my own,

But never have I known joy of them;

Now I must lie with my life taken,

Wounded by the sword on Samsey.

In the hall, the huskarls drink mead,

At my father's, feted with treasures:

Much mead makes men drowsy,

But the spoor of swords keeps me on Samsey.

I went from the white-cloaked woman,

To Agnafit on the edge of the sea;

It is true what she told me there,

That I would never be near her again.

Slip the red-gold ring from my hand,

And bear it to young Ingibjorg;

Her sorrow will remain in her thoughts,

For I'll never be seen in Uppsala again.

I sailed away from the songs of women,

Eagerly voyaging eastwards with Soti;

Travelling fast after joining a horde,

Left at last my friends in the hall.

From the east the raven flies, abandons his bough,

After him the eagle flies as well:

I feed him with flesh for a final time,

Now he will guzzle my dripping gore.

After that Hjalmar died. Odd took this news home to Sweden, but the king's daughter would not live after him and killed herself. Angantyr and his brothers were laid in a howe on Samsey with all their weapons.

Chapter Four

Bjarmar's daughter was with child; she was a very fair maiden. She was sprinkled with water, and named Hervor. She was brought up with the Earl and was strong as a man, and as soon as she was able, she trained herself more with shot and shield and sword, than sewing or embroidery. She often did more harm than good, and when this was forbidden to her, she ran to the woods and killed men for their gold. And when the Earl heard of this robber, he went there with his troops and seized Hervor and brought her home with him, and she stayed at home for a while.

On one occasion, Hervor was standing outside near where some slaves were, and she treated them badly, as she did other people. Then one slave said: 'You, Hervor, wish to do harm, and evil is expected from you, and the Earl forbids everyone to tell you your paternity because he thinks it shameful for you to know that the worst slave lay with his daughter, and you are their child.'

Hervor was angry at these words and went immediately to the Earl and said:

'I know this;

No glory can I boast,

Although Frodmar knew

My mother's favour;

I thought my father

Was a fighter,

But now it is said

That he was a swineherd.'

The Earl said:

'A lie have you heard,

Of little substance,

Bold, among fighters,

Your father was thought;

Angantyr's dwelling,

Sprinkled with dirt,

Stands in Samsey

To the south.'

She said:

'Now it calls me,

Foster-father, craving

To find

My kinsfolk;

Wealth they must

Have enough;

I will receive that,

Unless I perish.

'I will quickly wrap my hair

With a linen veil,

Before I break away;

Much rests on it,

When tomorrow comes

Should be cut

Both my shirt and kirtle.'

Then Hervor spoke with her mother and said:

'Ready me now

With requisite care,

Trustworthy woman,

As you would your son;

Truth comes to me

In my sleep,

Joy I would have

Here next year.'

Then she made ready to depart alone and took a man's gear and weapons and went where some Vikings were, and spent time with them for a while and called herself Hervard. A little later, that Hervard became leader of that troop, and when they came to Samsey, Hervard suggested they go up onto the island and said that there would be wealth in the burial mound. But all the troop members spoke against this course and said that such evil creatures walked there by day that it was worse than in the day than the night was elsewhere. She got her way at last, so the anchor was cast, and Hervard got into a boat and rowed to the shore and landed in Munarvag at the time when the sun went down, and found a man who herded a flock.

He said:

'Who among living folk

Walks the island?

Go swiftly

To seek shelter.'

'I will not flee

To find shelter

Because I know

No islanders;

Tell me instead,

Before I turn away:

Where are the howes

Named after Hjorvard?'

He said:

'Do not ask me,

You are not astute,

Friend of Vikings,

You fare far astray;

We must go as fast

As our feet will take us;

Out in the open

Things are awful for men.'

She said:

'Shepherd, we'll not faint,

Nor fear such crackling,

Although all the island

Blazes with flame;

Such men as these

Are too small a matter

To make us quake,

Let us speak more.'

He said:

'Foolish it seems to me,

Who goes from here

A man alone

In the gloomy dark;

Fires are flickering,

Mounds are opening,

Burns field and bog,

Run faster!'

Even then he run back to his farm, and they parted. Now she saw on the island where barrow fires burned, and she went there, and she did not feel fear, though all the mounds were on her path. She went through these fires in the dark, till she came to the mound of the berserkers.

Whereupon she said;

Wake you, Angantyr,

Hervor wakes you,

Your sole daughter

Svava's child;

Give me from the grave

The sharp sword,

That for Sigrlami

The dwarfs smithed.

Hervard, Hjorvard,

Hrani, Angantyr,

I invoke you

From under the tree roots,

With helmet and byrnie,

Biting sword,

Harness and shield

And carved spear.

All to dust

Have the sons of Arngrim gone

Men of evil

Have turned in the earth,

Of the weans of Eyfura

If not a one

Will talk with me

In Munarvag.

Hervard, Hjorvard,

Hrani, Angantyr,

So be it for you all

Within your ribs

As if in maggoty mounds,

You mouldered away,

If you give not your sword

Smithed by Dvalin;

It's not right for ghosts

To carry rich weapons.'

Then Angantyr said:

'Hervor, daughter,

Why do you disturb me?

You go to your doom

Filled with darkness;

You are mad

And your mind is darkened

When with wandering wits,

You wake the dead.

Father or other kin

Did not bury me; they kept Tyrfing

Of the two survivors,

Only one

Wielded it at last.'

She said:

'What you say is not so,

May the god not let you

Rest whole in your mound,

If you do not have

Tyrfing with you, and you

Are reluctant

To give the heirloom

To your only child.'

Then the mound opened, and it was all ablaze
and flames covered it all. Then Angantyr said:

'Hell-Gate is risen,

The howes are opened,

All is in blazes

On the island's border;

Grim is it outside

To look about;

Hasten, if you may,

Maiden, to your ships.'

She said:

'Burn not so,

Blazes in the night,

So your balefires

Abash me;

The maiden will not tremble

She shall remain unmoved,

227

Though she sees a ghost

Standing in the grave door.'

Then Angantyr said:

'I tell you, Hervor –

Hear me still –

Lord's daughter,

What shall be done:

Concerning Tyrfing,

Believe what I tell you,

It shall be the collapse

Of all your kin.

You will bear a son,

Who in later days

Will have Tyrfing

And trust in his strength;

Who will as Heidrek

To his horde,

Be born strongest

Under the sun's tent.'

Whereupon Hervor:

'I thought you might be

Considered a man,

Before I came here

Seeking your halls;

Hauled from the grave.

Hater of hauberks,

Danger to shields

Hjalmar's destroyer.'

Then Angantyr said:

'Beneath my shoulders

Lies Hjalmar's bane,

Surrounding it,

Swathed with flame;

I know no girl

Striding the green earth,

Who'd dare, this sword,

To carry in her hand.'

Hervor said:

'I will wield it

And hold it in hand

The sharp blade,

If I could but have it;

I do not fear

Burning fire,

The flames lower,

As I look towards it.'

Then Angantyr said:

'Fool are you, Hervor,

In your heart's courage,

With open eyes

To enter the fire;

Rather I will bring you

This blade from the grave,

Young maiden,

I may not refuse you.'

Hervor said:

'You are successful,

Viking's son,

When you give me

A sword from the grave;

I deem it better, king,

Now, to keep it

Than if I had Norway

Under my hand.'

Angantyr said:

'You do not see it;

You're cursed in speech,

Woman of evil,

Trust what I say;

Believe what I tell you,

Concerning Tyrfing,

It shall be the collapse

Of all your kin.'

She said:

'I will go

To the wave's horses,

Chieftain's maid

Cheerful in mind;

Little do I care,

King's companion,

How my sons

Shall afterwards strive.'

He said:

'You shall own Tyrfing

And enjoy it for long,

I had hidden

Hjalmar's bane –

Don't touch the edges,

Both are envenomed,

It is doom to men,

Worse than disease.

Go well, daughter,

Readily would I deal you

Twelve men's lives,

If you could believe,

In strength and endurance,

All is good, that the sons of Arngrim

Left behind them.'

She said:

'Lie you all,

Lifeless in the grave,

I am called away,

Hence I will be quick;

I think now

I am between worlds,

When high the fires

Around me flame.'

Then she went to the fleet. And when it was light, she saw that the ships were gone; the Vikings had been scared by the noise and fire on the island. She got a passage from there, and nothing is told about her journey until she came to Glasir Plain[44] and King Gudmund. She was there for the winter, and was still known as Hervard[45].

Chapter Five

One day, Gudmund was playing chess. Most of his pieces had been taken so he asked if he might have advice from anyone present. Then Hervard rose and went to the board and it was not long before his fortune turned. Then a man got up and drew Tyrfing. Hervard saw it and took away the sword and killed him and went out. People wanted to run after him.

Then Gudmund said: 'Be still, for your revenge on this person will seem less than you think, because you do not know who he is; my guess is that this man is a woman, before you take his life.'

Hervor was a long time at war and became very victorious. And when she was weary of this, she went back to the Earl, her mother's father, and she went with the other girls and got used to sewing and embroidery. Hofund, son of Gudmund, heard of her

[44] A legendary land inhabited by fair giants, whose ruler was Gudmund. It appears in several legendary sagas.
[45] While posing as Hervard, Hervor is often spoken of as if she is a man.

and went and asked for Hervor's hand and it was agreed and he took her home. Hofund was one of the wisest men for wits and foresight, he was set as judge for all surrounding lands, whether that involved natives or foreigners, from whose name Hofund was called in each land, is a man who is a judge. They had two sons. One was named Angantyr, the other Heidrek. They were both tall and strong, wise and accomplished. Angantyr was like his father in temper and wished everyone well. Hofund loved him dearly, and so did all the people. And the more good things he did, Heidrek made even more evil. Hervor loved him dearly. Heidrek's foster father was named Gizur. And one time, Hofund made a feast to which he invited all the lords of his kingdom except Heidrek and Gizur. Heidrek took it badly and went up at once and said he would do them some harm. And when he came into the hall, Angantyr stood up and asked him to sit with him. Heidrek was not cheerful, and sat for a long time drinking in the evening. But when Angantyr, his brother, went came out, Heidrek talked with those who were closest to him, and he turned so his speech, that they were angry, and each found evil with another. Angantyr then came back and told them to be quiet. And again the second time, Angantyr was gone, then Heidrek reminded them what they had said, and it went so that one struck the other with a fist. Then came Angantyr and asked them to keep the peace until morning. Still a third occasion, Angantyr walked away, Heidrek asked the man who had received the blow whether he dared not avenge himself. So he then went his persuasions that the man ran up and killed his neighbour, and then Angantyr came in. But when Hofund became aware of this, he asked Heidrek to leave and do no more harm in that time.

Heidrek went out and Angantyr, his brother, and parted there in the courtyard. Then Heidrek had gone a little way from the house, he thought that he had done too little harm, then turned back to the hall and picked up a large stone and cast it in the direction where he heard some men talking in the darkness. He heard that the stone did not miss its mark, and went to it and found a dead man and recognised Angantyr his brother. Heidrek went into the hall before his father and told him this. Hofund said he must leave, and coming never in his sight and said it would be better that he was cut down or hanged. Then Queen Hervor and that Heidrek had done ill, but it would be a great revenge, if he should never return to the kingdom of his father and go away so empty-handed. But Hofund's word carried so much weight that it went that he was the judge, and none was so bold that dared to speak against him, or ask for peace for Heidrek. The queen asked Hofund to give him some advice at parting. Hofund said he would teach him little and said he thought that it would be of little use. 'But, since you asked this, my queen, I advise him first that he helps no man who has killed his lord. I advise him second, never to free a man who has committed murder; and third, that he will not allow his wife to visit her family often, though she begs him; that fourth, that he is not late abroad with his mistress; that fifth, he should not ride his best horse, if he is in a hurry; that sixth, he never foster a child of a noble man who is more powerful than himself. But more likely it seems to me that you will not make us of this.' Heidrek said that he had given this advice with evil intent, and said he was under no obligation to do so.

Heidrek then walked out of the hall. His mother stood up and went out with him and follows him out of the courtyard and said, 'Now you have done so for yourself, my son, that you will not be going back; I am limited in the way I can help you. A mark of gold is here and a sword, which I will give you, but it is called Tyrfing and belonged to Angantyr the berserk, your mother's father. No man is so ignorant that he has heard nothing of it. If you find yourself where men exchange blows, never let it leave your mind how Tyrfing often has been blessed with victory.' Now she wished him farewell, and they parted.

Chapter Six

But Heidrek after had gone only a little way, he met some men and one of them was bound. They asked each other for news, and Heidrek asked what this man, who was treated so, had done. They said that he had betrayed his lord. Heidrek asked if they would take gold for him, and they agreed. He gave them half a mark of gold, and they let him go. The man offered Heidrek his services, but he said, 'Why would you be more faithful to me, an unknown man, when you betrayed your lord? So get away from me.' A little later Heidrek met some more men and one of them was bound. He asks what this man had done wrong. They say he had murdered his comrade. He asked if they would take gold for him. They agreed. He gave them the other half a mark of gold. The man offered Heidrek his services, but he refused. Heidrek walked a long way and then came to the land called Reidgotaland. There ruled a king who was named Harald, who was very old, and had a great realm to manage. He had no son. But his rule was weakened, because some earls warred against him with an army. He had fought against them but always been defeated. But now they had made peace on the condition that the king paid them tribute every twelve months. Heidrek stopped there and stayed with him for the winter.

It so happened that one time that the king was brought many goods. Then Heidrek asked if this was the king's taxes. The king said that it was otherwise and added: 'I must pay this treasure as tribute.' Heidrek said that it was unseemly that the king who had ruled a great realm should pay tribute to these wicked earls, and it would be better to go to war against them. The king said that he had tried and been defeated. Heidrek said: 'It would best if I repay you for your good cheer by being the head man of this venture, and I was thinking that, if I had the men, I would not consider it a great matter to fight with men more noble than these are.' The king said, 'I will give you an army if you want to fight the earls, and this will make your fortune, if you are successful; but it is likely that you will pay dearly for your error if you deceive yourself.' After that the king gathered a large army, and it was made ready for the campaign. Heidrek was leader of the army, and they went against the earls, harrying and plundering when they came to their realm. But the earls went to meet them with a large army when they heard of this, and when they met, there was a great battle. Heidrek was in the vanguard, and he had Tyrfing in his right hand, and nothing withstood the sword, neither helmet nor armour, and he killed everyone he encountered. And then he ran out from the vanguard and hewed on either hand, and he went so far into the enemy army that he killed the two earls, and then some of the men fled, but the greater number were killed. Heidrek went across that realm and laid all the land under tribute to the king as it had been before, and he went home with matters thus, possessing immense wealth and great victory.

Harald had him received with great honour, and invited him to remain with him and own as many realms as he should request. Heidrek asked for the daughter of King Harald, who was named Helga, and she was married to him. Heidrek took command of half of Harald's kingdom. Heidrek had a son with his wife, who he named Angantyr. Harald had a son in his old age, but his name is not known.

Chapter Seven

At that time there was a great famine in Reidgotaland, so that it seemed that the land would be laid waste. Lots were cast by soothsayers and the sacrificial chip[46] thrown, but it was heard that there would never be plenty in Reidgotaland unless the boy who was the foremost in the country was sacrificed. Harald said that Heidrek's son was foremost, but Heidrek said that the son of Harald was foremost. But out of this no one could find a resolution until they resorted to the man whose decisions were always trusted, King Hofund. Heidrek was chosen as the leader of this expedition, and with him many other famous men. When Heidrek met his father, he was well received. He told all his errand to his father and waited for his judgment. But Hofund said that Heidrek's son was nobler than other men in the country. Heidrek said: 'It seems to me that you condemn my son to death, or what do you adjudge me for the loss of my son?' Then King Hofund said: 'You shall ask that every fourth man who is present at the sacrifice is put under your control, otherwise your son will not be sacrificed. Then there will be no need to tell you what you should do.'

---

[46] This refers to a form of divination used in heathen Scandinavia.

When Heidrek came home to Reidgotaland, a council was called. Heidrek took thus to speech: 'This was the judgement of King Hofund, my father, that my son is nobler than other men in this country, and he is chosen for sacrifice. But in return I will have jurisdiction over every fourth man who has come to this gathering and I wish you to grant me this.' They did so. Then the men joined his troop. After that, he gathered the troop together with a trumpet-blast and set up a standard, now he attacked the king, and there was a great battle, and in it fell Harald and many of his troop. Heidrek conquered the kingdom that had belonged to King Harald, and he was made king. Heidrek said now that instead of offering up his son he would give all that were slain, and he gave the slain to Odin. His wife was so angry after the death of her father, that she hung herself in the hall of the Disir[47].

One summer, King Heidrek took his army south to Hunland, and fought with the king on who was called Humli and got the victory and took his daughter named Sifka, and she was brought home with him. But after the second summer he sent her home, and she was with child, and she gave birth to a boy called Hlod and he was very handsome, and he was fostered by Humli, his mother's father.

Chapter Eight

One summer King Heidrek went with his army to Saxony. When the Saxon king heard that, he invited him to a feast, and told him to take from his land what he wanted, and King Heidrek accepted that. There he saw the Saxon king's daughter, fair and beautiful of face, and Heidrek asked for this

[47] A group of goddesses and female spirits.

maiden, and she was married to him. There was a double feast, and then he went home with his wife and took with her immense wealth. King Heidrek now became a great warrior and extended their realm greatly in many ways. His wife often asked to go to her father, and so he let her, and she took Angantyr, her step-son.

One summer Heidrek was out raiding when he came to Saxony, the kingdom of his wife's house. He moored his ships in some hidden bay and went ashore taking one man with him, and came at night to the town, and went to the bower that his wife was accustomed to sleep in, and the watchmen were not aware of their coming. He went into the bower and saw that a man slept with her and he had fair hair on his head. The man with the king said that he had taken revenge for less. He answered: 'I will not do it now.' The king took the boy Angantyr, who lay in another bed, and he cut a great lock of the hair from the man resting in the arms of his wife, and taking both the lock of hair and the boy, went to his ships. The next morning he sailed into the harbour, and all the people went up to meet him, and there was a feast prepared. Heidrek had a gathering called, and great news was told him, that Angantyr, his son, had died a sudden death. King Heidrek said, 'Show me the body.' The queen said that it would only worsen his grief. He was taken there. There was a cloth wrapped up and a dog inside. King Heidrek said, 'Ill has it gone for my son's shape, if he has become a dog.' Then the king led the boy into the gathering, and said that he had discovered great guile in the queen, and related the whole business, commanding there that all men be called to that gathering. And when almost everybody else had arrived, the king said: 'He of the golden curls had not yet arrived.' He was sought, and they found a man in the cookhouse with a band about his head. Many wondered why he was wanted at the gathering, a common slave. When he came to the meeting, then King Heidrek said, 'Here you may now see whom the king's daughter wants rather than me.' He now produced the lock and compared it with the man's hair, and it clearly matched. 'But you, O king,' said Heidrek, 'have always done us good, and your realm will remained in peace with us. But your daughter I will no longer keep.' Heidrek went home to his kingdom, with his son.

One summer King Heidrek sent men to Gardariki[48] with the errand of inviting the son of the king of Gardar home to be fostered and Heidrek now intended to break all the counsels of his father[49]. The messengers came and met the King of Gardar and told him their errand and message of friendship. The King of Gardar said there was no expectation that the man would get his son into his hands, when he was known for so many evil things. Then the queen spoke: 'Speak not so, my lord; you have heard how great a man he is, blessed with victory, and it is greater wisdom that you accept this honour, or else your kingdom will not stand in peace.' The king said, 'You will do much to bring this about.' Then the boy was handed over to the messengers, and they went home. King Heidrek received the boy fittingly and fostered him well and loved him dearly. Sifka, Humli's daughter, was a second time with the king, but it was decided that he should say nothing of her, that it should be kept secret.

---

[48] Russia, as above.
[49] See Chapter 5.

Chapter Nine

One summer the King of Gardar sent Heidrek word that he wished him to come eastward to be feasted and for a friendly meeting. Heidrek then gathered a great multitude, and the king's son with him and Sifka. Heidrek went east to Gardariki and attended an excellent banquet. One day of this feast the kings went to the forest, and many men with dogs and hawks. But when they had slipped the dogs from the leash, they went their separate ways through the trees. Then the two of them were together, foster father and foster son. King Heidrek said: 'Do as I say, foster son. There is a farm close by. Go there and hide yourself, and take this ring. Be ready to come home when I send for you.' The boy said he was unwilling about this business, but did, however, what the king asked. Heidrek came home that evening and was sad and sat a little while drinking. But when he got into bed, Sifka said, 'Why have you became depressed, sire, what is it, are you sick? Tell me.' The king said: 'It is a hard thing to speak of, because my life is in danger if it is not kept secret.' She said she would not give him away and caressed him and winsomely pursued an answer: Then he said to her, 'The king's son and I stood beside a tree. Then my foster son asked for an apple that grew high up on the tree. Then I drew Tyrfing, and I cut down the apple, and it was done before I remembered that it would be a man's death if the sword was drawn, but we two were alone. Then I killed the boy.' The day after, at the drinking, the queen of Gardar asked Sifka why Heidrek was so sad. She said, 'He had reason enough, he has killed your son and the king's,' followed by the whole story. The queen replied: 'It is terrible news, and we must not let it get out.' The queen went away from the hall in great sorrow. The king saw this and called Sifka to him, and said: 'What were you speaking of with the queen, that made her so upset?' 'Sire,' she said, 'there is much cause. Heidrek has slain your son, and more likely he did it wilfully, and he deserves to die.' The king of Gardar commanded that Heidrek be taken and chained, - 'and it is now that things have turned out as I thought.' But King Heidrek had become so popular that none would do this. Then two men stood up in the hall and said nothing would stop them, and they put shackles on him. But these were the men Heidrek had released from death[50]. Then Heidrek secretly sent men after the king's son. But the King of Gardar had his people gathered by a trumpet blast and told them that he would have Heidrek hanged on the gallows. And at that the king's son came running to his father and asked him not to do that terrible deed and slay the noblest of men, his foster father.

Heidrek was released, and at once he made ready to return home. Then the queen said, 'Lord, do not let Heidrek go away like this, without an end to this quarrelling. That will not benefit your domain. Instead offer him gold or silver.' The king did so, and had much money carried to King Heidrek, and said he would give it to him and keep his friendship. Heidrek said: 'I do not lack treasure.' The King of Gardar told the queen. She said, 'Offer him lands and goods, and many followers.' The king did so. King Heidrek said: 'I have many goods and men.' The king of Gardar told his queen this. She said, 'Offer him that which he will accept, but that's your daughter.' The king said: 'I did not think that it would come to this, but you shall prevail.' Then the

---

[50] In Chapter 6.

king of Gardar went to King Heidrek and said,
'Rather than we part in anger, I would like you to
take my daughter with as much honour as you
choose yourself.' Heidrek accepted this offer blithely,
and the King of Gardar's daughter went home with
him. Now King Heidrek returned, and then wanted
to get rid of Sifka and took his best horse, and it was
late in the evening. Now they come to a river. Then
she became too heavy for the horse, so that it then
collapsed, and the king went on his way. He had to
carry her across the river. Then there was nothing
else for it, but he threw her off his shoulders and
broke her backbone, and left her corpse drifting
away down the river. King Heidrek held a great feast
and married the daughter of the king of Gardar.
Their daughter was named Hervor. She was a
shieldmaiden and was brought up in England with
Earl Frodmar.

King Heidrek settled down in peace and he
became a great chief and a wise sage. King Heidrek
brought a large boar. It was as big as the strongest
full-grown bull, and so fair that every hair seemed to
be of gold. The king put one hand on the head of
the boar and the other on the bristles and swore that
even if a man done him great wrong, he still would
have a fair trial from his counsellors, the twelve who
tended the boar, unless he could pose riddles that
the king could not solve. King Heidrek now became
the most popular of men.

Chapter Ten

There was a man called Gestumblindi, a
powerful man and a great enemy of King Heidrek.
The king sent him word to come and make a
settlement with him, if he wanted to stay alive.
Gestumblindi was not a great sage, and because he

knew he was not the man to bandy words with the king, he knew, too, that it would go badly for him, because his crimes were serious enough, to face the judgement of the counsellors; he sacrificed to Odin for help, asked him to consider his case and promised him many gifts. One evening there came a knock at the door quite late, and Gestumblindi went to the door and saw a man there. He asked him his name, but he said he was called Gestumblindi, and said that they should change clothes, and so they did. Gestumblindi went away and concealed himself, but the stranger went in, and it seemed to everyone that it was Gestumblindi, and the night drew near.

The day after Gestumblindi went to the king, and he greeted the king properly. The king was silent. 'Sire,' he said, 'the reason I came here was because I wish to make peace with you.' Then the answered king: 'Will you suffer the judgment of my wise men?' He said: 'Is there no other way for me to redeem myself?' The king said, 'There are others, if you think you're able to propose riddles.' Gestumblindi said, 'I have little skill in that, but it will be hard the other way.' 'Really,' said the king, 'but will you suffer the judgment of my wise men?' 'This will I choose,' he said, 'to propose riddles.' 'That is right and suitable,' said the king.

Then Gestumblindi said:

'I want to have what I had of yore;

Guess what that was:

Wit-taker, word-beater

And word-lifter.

King Heidrek, consider my riddle.'

The king said, 'Your riddle is good, Gestumblindi, I have guessed it. Bring him beer. That mars many men's senses, and many are the more talkative when the beer goes, but soon the tongue gets tangled, so that no word comes out.'

Then Gestumblindi said:

'From home I fared, from home I was faring,

Saw I the way of ways;

There was a way under and a way over

And a way every way.

King Heidrek, consider my riddle.'

'Your riddle is good, Gestumblindi, I have guessed it. You went over a bridge crossing a river, and the river way was beneath you, but birds flew over you and on either side, and that was their way.'

Then Gestumblindi said:

'What is that drink I drank yesterday?

It was not wine or water,

Nor ale nor mead, nor any meat,

Yet thirstless I went thence.

King Heidrek, consider my riddle.'

'Your riddle is good, Gestumblindi, I have guessed it. As you lay in the shade, the dew had fallen on the grass, and so you cooled your lips and so quenched your thirst.'

Then Gestumblindi said:

Who is that rowdy one,

Who walked a hard road

And he has fared there before?

Very hard kisses

Come from his two mouths

And on gold alone goes he.

King Heidrek, consider my riddle.'

'Your riddle is good, Gestumblindi, I have guessed it. It is the hammer that is used in gold-smithing, it shrieks shrilly when it hits the hard anvil, and that is its path.'

Then Gestumblindi said:

What is that wonder

That I saw without,

Before Delling[51]'s doors?

Unliving twain

Without breath

Boiled a wound-leek.

King Heidrek, consider my riddle.'

---

[51] In the *Edda* Delling is the husband of Night and the father of Day. It has been suggested that he is god of dawn.

'Your riddle is good, Gestumblindi, I have guessed it. It is the smith's bellows and they have no wind unless they are blown, otherwise they are dead as any other smith's work, but with them you can forge a sword as with any others.'

Then Gestumblindi said:

What is that wonder that I saw without,

Before Delling's doors?

It had eight feet, and four eyes,

And its knees towered over its belly.

King Heidrek, consider my riddle.'

'That's a spider.'

Then Gestumblindi said:

What is that wonder

That I saw without,

Before Delling's doors?

Its head is turned

Towards hell,

But its feet face the sun.

King Heidrek, consider my riddle.'

'Your riddle is good, Gestumblindi, I have guessed it. It is the leek. Its head is stuck in the ground, but it forks as it grows up.'

Then Gestumblindi said:

What is that wonder that I saw without,

Before Delling's doors?

Harder than horn, blacker than raven,

Whiter than egg-white,

No weapon is sharper.

King Heidrek, consider my riddle.'

Heidrek said, 'Trifling now are your riddles, Gestumblindi, what need is there to spend longer at this? It is obsidian, and sunlight shines on it.'

Then Gestumblindi said:

'An ale cask two brides,

Pale-haired

Female slaves,

Carried to the storehouse;

No hand turned it,

Nor hammer hammered it,

But outside the islands

Its maker sat upright.

King Heidrek, consider my riddle.'

'You riddle is good, Gestumblindi, I have guessed it. Female swans go to their nest and lay eggs; eggshell is not made by hand or forged with a hammer, but the swan who fathered the eggs rears erect beyond the islands.'

Then Gestumblindi said:

'Who are the women

On the wild mountains,

Who beget woman by woman,

A maid begets a child by a maid,

Yet these girls know no men?

King Heidrek, consider my riddle.'

'Your riddle is good, Gestumblindi, I have guessed it. Two angelicas and a young angelica between them.'

Then Gestumblindi said:

'I saw pass

A corpse sitting on a corpse;

Blind upon the blind

Riding to the surf,

On a breathless steed was it borne.

King Heidrek, consider my riddle.'

'Your riddle is good, Gestumblindi, I have guessed it. You found a horse dead on an ice floe and on the dead horse a snake, and it all floated along the river.'

Then Gestumblindi said:

'Who are those thanes,

Riding to the assembly

All happy together;

Their peoples seeking

Across the countries

A place to settle?

King Heidrek, consider my riddle.'

'Your riddle is good, Gestumblindi, I have guessed it. It is Itrek and Andad as they sit at their chessboard.' [52]

Then Gestumblindi said:

'Who are the women

Fighting together

Before their weaponless king;

The dark guard him

For every day,

But forth the fairer go?

King Heidrek, consider my riddle.'

'Your riddle is good, Gestumblindi, I have guessed it. Chess. That is; the darker pieces defend

---

[52] Itrek and Andad have not been identified.

first, but the white attack.'

Then Gestumblindi said:

Who is the lonely one,

Who sleeps in the hearth pit?

Of stones alone is he made;

No father or mother

A person eager for brightness,

Where he will live his life?

King Heidrek, consider my riddle.'

'That is fire hidden in a fireplace, and struck with flint.'

Then Gestumblindi said:

Who is that tall one,

Passing across the earth,

Swallowing water and wood;

Fearing the wind,

But not men

And war on the sun waging?

King Heidrek, consider my riddle.'

'Your riddle is good, Gestumblindi, I have guessed it. That is fog, which draws near to the earth, so that nothing can be seen because of it, not even the sun, but it is gone when the wind blows.'

Then Gestumblindi said:

What is this animal

That kills men's flocks

With iron around its outside;

Horns has it eight,

But none on the head,

Many move at its side?

King Heidrek, consider my riddle.'

'That's the chess king.'

Then Gestumblindi said:

What is this animal,

Cover for the Danes,

With bloody back,

But protector of men,

It meets spears,

To some gives life,

In its hollow hand

A man holds his body?

King Heidrek, consider my riddle.'

'It is a shield. Often in battles it becomes drenched in blood but it protects well a man who is nimble with it.'

Then Gestumblindi said:

What are those gamesome ones

Who pass over the countries

Forever sought by their father,

A white shield

In the winter they carry,

But black in the summer?

King Heidrek, consider my riddle.'

'It is ptarmigan; they are white in winter, but black in summer.'

Then Gestumblindi said:

Who are the women

Who walk grieving,

Forever sought by their father;

To many people

Have they caused evil at a word,

And thus will they live their lives?

King Heidrek, consider my riddle.'

'The maids of Hler[53] are named so.'

---

[53] Hler is a sea giant; his maids are the waves. His name is remembered to this day in that of Laeso (Hler's island), in Denmark.

Then Gestumblindi said:

'Who are the maidens,

Walking many together

Forever sought by their father;

Their hair is pale

Their hoods are white,

Yet these girls know no men?'

'They are the waves[54] that are so named.'

Then Gestumblindi said:

'Who are the widows

Running all together,

Forever sought by their father;

Kind but seldom

To mankind

And they must the wind awake?

King Heidrek, consider my riddle.'

'It is Aegir's women[55], so the waves are called.'

Then Gestumblindi said:

'A goose grew big,

---

[54] Compare with previous footnote.
[55] Aegir is another name for Hler.

Yearned for young,

To build her home

She gathered timber;

Kept her safe

Swords that bit straw,

The booming drink-rock

Lay above her.'

'The duck had dwelt in her nest between an ox's jawbones, and the skull lay over it.'

Then Gestumblindi said:

'Who is that tall one

Who gives many counsels

And looks half into Hel;

Protector of men

And ground-striving,

If he has a well-trusted friend?

King Heidrek, consider my riddle.'

'Your riddle is good, Gestumblindi, I have guessed it. An anchor with a good rope: if its fluke is in the ground, then it protects you.'

Then Gestumblindi said:

'Who are those brides

Who walk in the reefs

And have gone along the fjord;

Hard bed have they,

White-hooded women

Unmoving in the calm and coolness.'

'They are the waves, their beds are reefs and stones, but they are hardly seen in calm weather.'

Then Gestumblindi said:

'I saw in summer

At sunset,

I looked upon a stirring house

Unhappy,

Men drank

Beer in silence,

But howling lay

The tuns of ale.

King Heidrek, consider my riddle.'

'Piglets sucking a sow, who squealed.'

Then Gestumblindi said:

'What strange sight

Was it I saw

Before Delling's door;

Ten its tongues,

Twenty eyes,

With forty feet

Fares that beast?

King Heidrek, consider my riddle.'

The king said, 'If you are the Gestumblindi I thought, you're wiser than I expected. But you speak of the sow outside in the yard.'

Then the king had the sow killed, and she had nine piglets, as Gestumblindi said. Now the king wondered who this man must be.

Then Gestumblindi said:

'Four hanging,

Four walk,

Two point the way,

Two fend off the dogs,

One dangles behind,

Always rather dirty.

King Heidrek, consider my riddle.'

'Your riddle is good, Gestumblindi, I have guessed it. That is a cow.'

Then Gestumblindi said:

'I sat on a sail,

I saw dead people

Carry bloody flesh

To wood bark.'

'So you sat on the wall and saw a falcon carry an eider duck to the crags.'

Then Gestumblindi said:

'Who are those twain who have ten feet,

Three eyes, and a single tail?

King Heidrek, consider my riddle.'

'It is then that Odin rode Sleipnir.'

Then Gestumblindi said:

'Then tell me at last,

If you are wisest of all kings:

What did Odin breathe

Into Baldur's ear,

Ere he was borne to the pyre?

King Heidrek said: 'That you alone know, evil beast.' And then Heidrek brandished Tyrfing and smote him, but Odin changed into a hawk and flew away. But the king struck after him and cut off his tail feathers, and that is why the hawk has always been short-tailed ever since. Odin said: 'For this, King Heidrek, that you have attacked me and wanted to kill me despite my innocence, your worst slaves shall be your death.' After that they separated.

Chapter Eleven

It is said that King Heidrek had some slaves who he had taken in the west while raiding. There were nine together. They were of noble lineage and disliked their captivity. It happened that one night when King Heidrek lay in his sleeping room, and had few men with him, the slaves took weapons, went to the king's room and killed the guard posted outside. Then they went and broke into the room and killed King Heidrek and all who were inside. They took the sword Tyrfing and all the belongings that were inside, and took them away with them, and no one knew who had done this or where they might seek revenge. Then Angantyr son of King Heidrek called a gathering, and at this meeting he was made king over all the kingdoms that King Heidrek had. In this meeting he swore a vow, he should never sit on the throne of his father until he had his revenge. Shortly after the gathering Angantyr went away alone and travelled around looking for these people. One evening he went down to the sea beside the river Grafa. There he saw three men in a fishing boat, and then he saw a man catch a fish and asked his companions to give him the bait knife to cut off the fish's head, but he said he could not spare it. The other said, 'Take the sword from under the headboard and pass it me,' and he took it, drew it and cut the head of the fish, and then he recited a verse:

The pike has paid

By Grafa's pools,

For Heidrek's murder

Under Harvad[56] Mountains.'

Angantyr recognised Tyrfing at once. He went away to the forest and stayed there till it was dark. These fishermen rowed to land and went to the tent which they had, and laid themselves down to rest. Near midnight Angantyr came there and pulled down the tent and killed all nine slaves, and took his sword Tyrfing, and that was the proof that he had avenged his father. Angantyr went home now. Then Angantyr had a great feast held on the banks of the Dnieper at the town named Arheimar in his father's memory. And these kings ruled the lands, as follows:

'In olden time Humli

Ruled over the Huns

Gizur the Gauts,

The Goths, Angantyr,

Waldar the Danes,

And Kjar the Welsh,

Alrek the valiant

Ruled the English people.'

Hlod, son of King Heidrek, was brought up with King Humli, his mother's father, and he was the most handsome and most gallant of men. But there

---

[56] This seems to refer to the Carpathians, and along with the mention of the Dnieper, may represent memories of the Gothic kingdom in the Ukraine.

was an old saying at the time that a man would be born with weapons or horses. This meant that it was said about those weapons that were made at the time when a man was born, and likewise with animals, sheep, oxen or horses, if they were born at the same time, and it was brought together in honour of men of noble birth, as is told concerning Hlod Heidreksson:

'Hlod was born

In Hunland

With sword and blade,

And hanging armour,

Helmet adorned with rings,

Sharp sword,

Well-broken horse

In the sacred wood.'

Now Hlod learnt of the death of his father, and also that Angantyr, his brother, had been made king over all that country which his father had ruled. Now King Humli and Hlod decided that he should claim his inheritance from Angantyr, his brother, firstly with pleasant words, as follows:

'Hlod rode from the east,

Heidrek's heir,

He came to the courtyard,

Where the Goths dwelt,

To Arheimar

His heritage to claim,

There drank Angantyr

Heidrek's funeral ale.'

Now Hlod came to Arheimar with a large
army, as follows:

A man he found outside

By the high hall,

Wandering late,

Then said:

'Hurry in, friend,

To the high hall,

Demand me Angantyr

That he talk with me.'

The man entered, went to the king's table,
saluted King Angantyr fittingly and then said:

'Here is come Hlod,

Heidrek's progeny,

Your brother,

Eager for battle;

Great is that young man,

263

Mounted on his horse,

Now he wants

To talk with you.'

But when the king heard this, he put his knife down on the board, stepped away from the table and threw over himself his armour and gripped his white shield in his hand, and the sword Tyrfing in his other hand. There was a great din in the hall, as follows:

'Noise in the courtyard,

As the king rose,

Each would hear

Hlod's greeting

And learn how Angantyr

Would answer.'

Then Angantyr said, 'You are welcome, Hlod, my brother. Come in and drink with us, and first let us drink mead for our father and peace between us and for the honour of all of us with all the dignity we possess.' Hlod said: 'We have come here for something other than feasting.' Then he said:

'I wish to have half of everything

That Heidrek had,

Tools and weapons,

Rare treasure,

Cow and calf,

Quern, or rasping handmill;

Slave and a slave girl

And their children.

The famous forest

Known as Murk Wood,

The holy grave

That stands in Gothland

The well-made stone,

Which stands by the Dnieper,

Half of the armour

That Heidrek had,

Lands and peoples,

And polished rings.'

Then Angantyr said, 'You cannot succeed to this country by law, and you intend to do wrong.' Then Angantyr said:

'Sooner, brother,

Shall the shields break

And cold spears

Clash together,

Many good men

Fall to the grass

Before I share half my inheritance

With Humli's grandson

Or Tyrfing

Split in two.'

And again Angantyr spoke:

'I will give you

Glittering spears,

Wealth and treasure

That will content you;

Twelve hundred men I give you,

Twelve hundred mares I give you,

Twelve hundred bondsmen I give you,

Who will bear shields.

I will give each group

Many gifts,

Better than anything

Now they own;

A girl I will give

To every man,

A necklace clasped

On each maiden's neck.

I will measure silver

For you as you sit there,

As you leave

I will pour down gold,

Rings shall roll

All round about you;

A third of the Gothic nation,

You shall govern.'

Chapter Twelve

Gizur Grytingalidi, foster-father of King Heidrek, was with King Angantyr and he was very old. When he heard Angantyr's words, he thought it too great an offer and then said:

'This is a lavish offer

For a slave girl's lad,

A slave girl's brat,

Though born to a king;

The bastard son

Sat on a mound[57]

While the highborn one

---

[57] This may refer to an ancient kingship ritual. i.e. Hlod challenged Angantyr's claim.

Divided his inheritance.'

Hlod was now very angry to be called child of a slave and a by-blow, if he accepted the invitation of his brother, and at once he went away with all his people. He came home to Hunland and King Humli, his uncle, and told him that Angantyr his brother would not share the inheritance equally. Humli now asked what had happened and he became very angry that Hlod, his grandson, was called the son of a slave, and said then:

We shall sit in the winter

And blessedly live,

Talk, and quaff

Costly wines;

Teach the Huns

To tend their weapons,

That they will boldly

Bring to war.'

And again he said:

Well for you, Hlod,

The army will be equipped

And bold-hearted

Shall we go to battle

With warriors twelve years old

And colts two-winters old,

So shall we muster

Our Hunnish men.'

That winter Humli and Hlod sat quietly. In the spring they gathered together an army so large that afterwards the Hun country had no fighting men left. Everyone joined up who was twelve years and older, and could carry weapons in warfare, and they took all horses two-winters and older. It became so great a multitude that the troops could be counted only in their thousands, by nothing but thousands. A chief was placed over each thousand, and a standard over each battle array, and five thousand in each battle array, with thirteen hundred in each, and in each four times forty men, and there were thirty three troops. When this army had gathered together, they rode on into the wood that is called Murk Wood, which was the border between Hunland and Gothland. When they came out of the wood, they were in a country of wide, densely inhabited areas and level plains, and among the fields stood a fair stronghold. Over it ruled Hervor[58], sister of King Angantyr, and Ormar, her foster-father; they were set to guard the land against the army of the Huns, and they had a great troop there.

Chapter Thirteen

One morning at sunrise Hervor stood above the castle gate. She saw a big dust cloud, the kind thrown up by horses' hooves, in the south towards

---

[58] Previously mentioned in Chapter 9, where it is said that she was fostered in England by Earl Frodmar. Not to be confused with her ancestor of the same name.

the forest, and it hid the sun for a long time. Then she saw a gleam of a yellowish colour beneath the dust cloud, of beautiful shields overlaid with gold, gold helmets and bright cuirasses. Then she saw that it was the horde of the Huns and there were large numbers of them. Hervor went down hurriedly and called and asked her trumpeter to blow the summons for her troop. And then Hervor said, 'Take your weapons and make arrangements for battle, but you, Ormar, ride against the Huns and offer them battle before the south gate of the stronghold.' Ormar said:

'Surely will I ride

And carry my warboard;

For the Gothic nation,

Give battle.'

Then Ormar rode out of the fort and towards the horde. He called and told them to ride to the fort - 'and outside the south gate of the stronghold I offer you battle, and wait for the others, those who came earlier.' Now Ormar rode back to the fort, and now Hervor was ready, and all the army. They rode out of the fort now with the army against the Huns, and a major battle began. But because the Huns had many more warriors, more people fell in Hervor's host, and at last Hervor fell and a great troop around her. But Ormar saw her fall, and he fled, and so did all who favoured life. Ormar rode day and night, as fast as he could, to meet King Angantyr at Arheimar. The Huns now took to harrying and burning the land around. And when Ormar reached King Angantyr, he said:

'From the south I have come

To cry this news:

On the borders, fires blaze

And Murk Wood burns,

All the Gothic nation is sprinkled

With men's gore.'

And again he said:

'Heidrek's daughter I know,

Your sister,

Fell to the ground;

The Huns have

Slain her

And many others

Of people of the land.

Lighter was she in war

Than in lover's speech

Or at the bridal feast

Or sitting on the bench.'

King Angantyr, when he heard this, drew back his lips, and was slow to speak, but he said this at last:

'Unbrotherly were you played with,

My excellent sister.'

And then he looked over the court, and it there was no great troop with him. He said then:

We were many,

When we drank mead,

Now would we have more,

When we have fewer.

I see no one

In my war band –

Though I begged him

And bought him with rings –

Who will ride

And carry a shield

And the horde

Of the Huns seek out.'

Old Gizur said:

'I do not want

Any reward,

I claim no coin

Of clinking gold;

But I will ride

And carry a shield,

And the Hun people

Present with the war-staff.'

It was the law of King Heidrek that if an army invaded by land and the king set out a hazelled field[59] and determined the time of battle, the raiders would not ravage the land before the battle was decided. Gizur equipped himself with good weapons of war and jumped on his horse, as if he was young. Then he said to the king:

'Where shall I the Huns

Invite to battle?'

Angantyr said:

'On Dylgja Dales

And the Dunheid,

Call all of them to fight

Beneath the Jossur fells;

Often Goths there

Have offered battle

With fair victory

Won fame.'

Now Gizur rode away to where he came to the horde of the Huns. He rode no closer than so

---

[59] A field fenced off with hazel rods. In *Egil Skallagrimsson's Saga* the battle of Vinheid is fought in this manner. More commonly, the custom was used in the case of single combat.

that he could talk to them. Then he called out in a great voice, and said:

'Daunted are your troops,

Doomed is your leader,

Banners are aloft,

Odin is angry.'

And again:

'On Dylgja Dales

And the Dunheid,

I call all of you to fight

Beneath the Jossur fells;

You are carcasses

On every steed,

Now Odin let the spear fly,

As I say.'

When Hlod had heard Gizur's words, he said:

'Grab you Gizur

Grytingalidi,

Angantyr's man

From Arheimar.'

King Humli said:

We should not

Shoot the messenger,

Wrongly treat

Lone riders.'

Gizur said, 'We are not afraid of Huns or your horn bows.' He spurred his horse and rode to meet King Angantyr and stood before him and saluted him. The king asked whether he had met the kings. Gizur said: 'I spoke with them, and I summoned them to the field of battle on Dunheid in Dylgja Dales.' Angantyr asked how large a troop the Huns had. Gizur said,

Huge is their horde:

They have six divisions

Of soldiers,

In the divisions

Five thousand platoons,

Every thousand

Thirteen hundred,

A hundred

By four times counted.'

Angantyr learnt of the Huns' army. Then he sent men in all directions and summoned every man to his house who could bear arms and fight for him. He went to Dunheid with his troop, and it was a sizeable army. The horde of the Huns came to meet him, and it was twice as big.

Chapter Fourteen

On the following day they began their battle, and fought all that day, and in the evening went to their camps. They fought this way for eight days, while the chiefs were still unwounded, and no one knew the number of the fallen. But both day and night men swarmed to Angantyr from all directions, and so it was that he had no fewer people than at the first. It became even fiercer a battle. The Huns were ferocious and saw their position, that life was certain only if they were victorious, and they could not beg quarter from the Goths. The Goths were defending their freedom and their fatherland from the Huns, and they remained firm, and egged each other on. As the day went, the Goths attacked so fiercely that the Huns gave way. And when Angantyr saw that, he went out from the shield wall, and into the first division, and he had Tyrfing in his hand and cut down both men and horses. The ranks parted before the Hun kings, and the brothers exchanged blows. Then Hlod fell and King Humli, and then the Huns fled, but the Goths killed them and so many fell that the rivers were choked and turned from their courses, and the valleys were filled with dead horses and men and blood. King Angantyr went to search among the slain, and found Hlod, his brother. Then he said:

> *I offered you, brother,*
>
> *Uncounted treasures,*
>
> *Wealth and cattle,*
>
> *That would have contented you;*

Now you have won neither

War's reward,

No golden rings

Or greater realm.'

And again:

'Cursed are we, brother,

I am your killer,

It will never be forgotten;

Ill is the doom of the norns.'

Chapter Fifteen

Angantyr was king in Reidgotaland for a long time. He was a great man and a great warrior, and from him sprang royal dynasties. His son was Heidrek Wolfcoat who was long king in Reidgotaland. He had a daughter named Hild. She was the mother of Halfdan the Valiant, father of Ivar Widegrasp. Ivar Widegrasp came with his army to Sweden, which is told of in the sagas of the kings[60], but King Ingjald the Ill-Advised feared his army and burned himself and all his retinue with him in his farm at Raening. Ivar Widegrasp laid under himself all of Sweden. He conquered Denmark and Kurland, Saxony and Estland and all realms east as far as Gardariki. In the west he ruled Saxony and that part of England that is called Northumbria. Ivar subjected to himself all Denmark, and then he set

---

[60] The best source for this story is Snorri Sturluson's *Ynglinga Saga*, the first saga in *Heimskringla*.

King Valdar over it and gave him Alfhild, his daughter. Their son was Harald Wartooth and Randver who was afterwards slain in England. But Valdar died in Denmark, and Randver took the Danish realm and became king. But Harald Wartooth took on the name of king of Gautland, and then laid under him all the countries mentioned above, that King Ivar Widegrasp had. King Randver married Asa the daughter of King Harald Redbeard from the north in Norway. Their son was Sigurd Hring. King Randver died suddenly, and Sigurd Hring took the kingdom of Denmark. He fought with King Harald Wartooth at Bravellir in eastern Gautland, where Harald fell, and a great number of men with him[61]. These battles are the most famous in ancient history and had the most casualties, along with that which Angantyr and his brother fought in Dunheid. King Sigurd Hring ruled the Danish realm until his death, and after him King Ragnar Lodbrok, his son.

The son of Harald Wartooth was named Eystein the Ill-Advised. He was in Sweden after his father and ruled until the sons of King Ragnar slew him, as it says in his history. The sons of King Ragnar conquered Sweden, but after the death of King Ragnar, Bjorn Ironside, his son, took Sweden, and Sigurd the Danish, Hvitserk the Eastern kingdom, and Ivar the Boneless England[62]. The sons of Bjorn Ironside were Eirik and Refil. Refil was a warrior king and sea-king, but King Eirik ruled in Sweden after his father and lived only a little while.

---

[61] This war is most fully covered in Saxo Grammaticus' *Gesta Danorum*, Book Eight.

[62] Ragnar's story and that of his sons is told in *The Saga Of Ragnar Shaggy-Breeches* and *The Yarn Of Ragnar's Sons*.

Then Eirik, son of Refil, succeeded; he was a great warrior and a powerful king. The sons of Eirik, son of Bjorn, were Aunund of Uppsala and King Bjorn. Then the brothers divided Sweden in those days and they took the kingdom after Eirik Refilsson. King Bjorn built the town called Haugi, he was called Bjorn of Haugi. With him was the poet Bragi[63]. Eirik was the son of King Onund, who succeeded his father at Uppsala, and he was a mighty king. In his days Harald Fairhair[64] arose in Norway, first of his line brought Norway under one king. Bjorn was the son of King Eirik at Uppsala, he succeeded his father and ruled for a long time. The sons of Bjorn were Eirik the Victory-Blessed and Olaf and they took the kingdom after their father, and ruled a long time. Olaf was the father of Styrbjorn the Strong. In those days Harald Fairhair died. Styrbjorn fought with King Eirik, his uncle, at the Fyris Wolds, and Styrbjorn fell there. Eirik then ruled in Sweden until his death. He married Sigrid the Haughty. Olaf was their son, the king was adopted in Sweden, after King Eirik. He was a child, and the Swedes carried him about, and so they called him Cloak-King, then Olaf the Swede. He was the king long and he was powerful. He was the first Christian king of the Swedes, and in his days Sweden became Christian. Aunund was the name of the son of King Olaf the Swede, who took the kingdom after him and died of a sickness. During his reign King Olaf fell at Stiklestad. Eymund was the second son of Olaf the Swede, and he took the kingdom after his brother. In his day the Swedes neglected Christianity. Eymund

---

[63] Bragi Boddason, inventor of skaldic poetry, possibly immortalised as the Norse god Bragi.

[64] With this ruler, the first king of all Norway, the saga begins to enter verifiable history.

was king for only a little time.

Chapter Sixteen

Steinkel was a mighty man in Sweden and of noble stock; his mother's name was Astrid, daughter of Njal son of Finn the Cross-Eyed from Halogaland, whose father was Rognvald the Old. Steinkel was first an earl in Sweden, but after the death of King Eymund the Swedes took him as king. Then the throne of Sweden passed from the ancestral line of ancient kings. Steinkel was a great chief. He married the daughter of King Eymund. He died of sickness in Sweden close to the time when King Harald fell in England[65]. Ingi was the son of Steinkel, who the Swedes took as king after Hakon. Ingi was king for a long time and he was popular, and a good Christian. He ended sacrifices in Sweden and commanded all people to become Christian, but the Swedes believed too strongly in the pagan gods and kept their ancient customs. King Ingi's wife was a woman named Maer. Her brother was named Svein. King Ingi loved no man so well, and he became the richest man in Sweden. The Swedes thought King Ingi was breaking the ancient laws, when he found fault with those things Steinkel had let be. At a certain gathering the Swedes had with King Ingi, they gave him two choices, either he would keep the old law or they would have a new king. Then King Ingi said he would not throw out the belief that was right. Then the Swedes cried out and flung stones at him and threw him out of the legal assembly. Svein, the king's kinsman, remained at the gathering. He told the Swedes he would make sacrifices for them if they would give him the kingdom. They all agreed; he was made king over all

---

[65] i.e. Harald Hardrada, who died at Stamford Bridge in 1066.

Sweden. Then a horse was led before the gathering and hacked apart and divided for eating, and the sacrificial tree was reddened with blood. Al the Swedes cast off Christianity, and began to sacrifice, and they drove away King Ingi, and he went to West Gautland. Sacrificer-Svein was king of Sweden for three winters.

King Ingi went with his bodyguard, and some followers but it was a small army. He rode east over Smaland and into eastern Gautland and so into Sweden. He rode both day and night, surprised Svein early in the morning. They entered the house and set it on fire and burned all the people who were with him. Thjof was the name of a landed man, who was burned there, and he had been in the following of Sacrificer-Svein. Sacrificer-Svein went out and was killed. So Ingi retook the kingdom of Sweden and brought them back to Christianity and ruled the realm until his death when he died of a sickness. Hallstein was the son of King Steinkel, and he was king with King Ingi, his brother. The sons of Hallstein were Philip and Ingi, who succeeded to the kingdom of Sweden after King Ingi the Old. Philip married Ingigerd, daughter of King Harald Sigurdsson, and was king but briefly.

THE SAGA OF KETIL TROUT

The Sagas of *Ketil Trout* and *Grim Hairy-cheek* are two of the Sagas of the Men of Hrafnista, stories written in medieval Iceland about the legendary Norwegian ancestors of contemporary families. Like the rest of the Legendary Sagas, they are fantastic in tone, featuring trolls and other monsters. *The Saga of Grim Hairy-cheek* is in many ways a sequel to *The Saga of Ketil Trout*, as Grim Hairy-cheek is the son of Ketil Trout. He receives his unattractive epithet in his father's saga when his mother Hrafnhild catches sight of a hairy Lapp while conceiving him with Ketil. Ketil Trout's own nickname derives from his modesty or naivety when referring to a dragon he slays.

Ketil Trout is of a common type of hero in Norse saga, and indeed in international folklore; the 'coalbiter' or male Cinderella, who lazes by the hearth rather than taking part in domestic tasks until spurred on to adventure and heroic deeds, from which he receives 'a name that will never die beneath the heavens.' The despair of his father, considered a fool by other people on Hrafnista (modern Ramsta in Norway), he proves himself on a series of expeditions into the North where he slays dragons and fights trolls. Along the way he meets and marries Hrafnhild, daughter of Bruni, brother of the Lapp king Gusir. He slays Gusir, Bruni's rival, and obtains the magical arrows Flaug, Hremsa and Fifa and Dragvendill 'best of swords.' With these accomplishments he goes on to prove himself a hero among his own people, but he is faithless in love, and bad blood exists between his people and those of his abandoned wife Hrafnhild.

Chapter One

Here begins the saga of Ketil Trout.

There was a man named Hallbjorn, nicknamed Halftroll, who was the son of Ulf the Fearless. He lived on the island of Hrafnista, which lies near Raumsdal. He was a powerful man and influential over the farmers north of there. He was married, and had a son named Ketil, who grew up to be a big and strong man, but not handsome. But as soon as Ketil was a few winters old, he lazed in the kitchen, and he seemed a laughing-stock to brave men for doing this. This was Ketil's custom; he lay by the fire with one hand propping up his head, while he lay the other before his knees and poked the fire. Hallbjorn told him not to do this, and said that then things would improve between them. Ketil said nothing. He went away for some time, and was gone for three nights. Then he came home and had a chair on his back. It was well built. He gave it to his mother and said he had rewarded her for her greater love rather than his father.

There was a time in the summer, a day with good weather, when Hallbjorn went to gather hay and it was at risk of being spoilt. Hallbjorn went then into the kitchen to Ketil and said: 'Now it would be best, son, for you to help gather hay today. All of us are needed in the hay-making season.' Ketil sprang up and went out. Hallbjorn fetched two oxen and one serving-woman for the work. Then Ketil carried hay into the homefield and went so briskly that in the end there were eight piles in the barn. And everyone thought enough had been done, when evening came, all the hay was gathered, and the oxen had died from exhaustion. Hallbjorn said then: 'Now it seems to me, son, that you should manage the farm, because you are now young and growing and healthy. But I have become old and stiff and am not as strong as I was.' Ketil said he did not wished this. Then Hallbjorn gave him a large axe that was very sharp and a wonderfully good weapon. He said: 'Now that you have that, son, I must ask you that you stay indoors as soon as the sun has set, and most of all, do not go north to the islands that lie away from inhabited areas.' Hallbjorn told his son Ketil many things.

There was a man named Bjorn who lived not far away. He had always found fault with Ketil and mocked him, calling him Ketil, the fool of Hrafnista. Bjorn often went to sea to fish. One day, when he was out rowing, Ketil took bait, a fishing-line and a hook, and went out to the fishing-grounds, where he sat fishing. Then Bjorn passed by, and when he saw Ketil, he laughed a great deal and mocked him harshly. Bjorn went out further than anyone else, as he was accustomed. He fished well, while Ketil caught one cod, of very mean quality, but no more. Meanwhile, Bjorn was piling up his catches and now he set off home, and left Ketil, laughing at him. Ketil said then: 'Now I will give my catch to you, and the first of you to catch it can keep it.' He grabbed the cod and through it at the ship. It hit Bjorn so hard that it dented his skull, and Bjorn fell overboard and never came up afterwards, then Ketil rowed to land. Hallbjorn had little to say about this.

One evening after sunset Ketil took his axe in his hand and went to the north of the island. However, he had not gone very far from inhabited areas when he saw a dragon fly out from a hill to the north. It had writhing coils and a tail like a snake, but wings like a dragon. Fire seemed to burn out of its eyes and mouth. Ketil thought he had never seen such a fish, or any other such being, and that he would rather defend himself against a multitude of men than face it. The dragon came at him, but Ketil defended himself well and mightily with his axe. It went that way for a long time before Ketil pierced a coil and then cut the dragon in half. It fell down dead. After that Ketil went home, and met his father out in the farmyard. Hallbjorn greeted his son well and asked if he had had any trouble with the evil spirits that were said to live to the north of the island. Ketil said: 'I know nothing about telling tales about watching the fishes swim, but it is true that I cut a trout in half in the middle, where he was looking for a spawner.' Hallbjorn said: 'You must think such small matters of little value, when you consider such a monster small fry. I will now lengthen your name and call you Ketil Trout.' Then they went to rest.

Now Ketil sat in the kitchen a great deal. Hallbjorn often went out fishing, and Ketil asked to come with him. He said Ketil should sit by the fire, not go out sea faring. But when Hallbjorn came to his ship, Ketil was already there, and then Hallbjorn did not know how to drive him back. Then Hallbjorn went over to the prow of the boat, but told Ketil to go over to the stern and push the boat into the water. Ketil did so, but it went nowhere. Hallbjorn said: 'You are unlike your kinsmen, and I think it will be a while before there is strength in you. Before I was old I was accustomed to push the boat out alone.' Ketil heaved then and pushed the boat forward so hard that Hallbjorn was knocked onto the shingle, but the boat did not stop until it headed out to sea. Hallbjorn said then: 'You do not let me benefit from being family, when you want to break every bone in my body. But I will now say that I expect you are sufficiently strong, because I wanted to test your strength, and I withstood you as hard as I could, but you pushed it out as hard as you could. I think you show promise.' Then they went to the fishing-camp. Hallbjorn went to the hut, but Ketil went out to sea. He amassed a great catch. Then he encountered two men who were very unfriendly. They wished him to give up his catch. But Ketil refused that and asked them their names. One said he was named Hæng, and the other Hrafn, and they were brothers. They attacked him, but Ketil swung his club, knocked Hæng overboard and killed him, while Hrafn fled. Ketil went back to the hut, and his father came to meet him and Hallbjorn asked if he had met any men during the day. Ketil said he had met two brothers, Hæng[66] and Hrafn. Hallbjorn said: 'How went your encounter? I know about them, for I have dealt with them. They are brave men, outlawed from the dwellings for their rowdiness.'

---

[66] 'Trout.'

Ketil said he had killed Hæng by knocking him overboard, but Hrafn fled. Hallbjorn said: 'Son, you are eager for big fish, and it seems your nickname suits you.' The next day they went home with their catch. Ketil was eleven winters old at that time, and matters with his father were improving.

Chapter Two

At that time there was a great famine in Halogaland, and many people got their living from the sea. Ketil said that he would go fishing and not be entirely useless. Hallbjorn offered to go with him. Ketil said it would be better if he travelled alone in his boat. 'That is crazy,' said Hallbjorn, 'You are very self-willed. However, I will tell you of three firths. One is named Naestifjord, the second Midfjord, and the third Vitadsgjafi, and it has been a long time since I left two of them, but back then there was a hut with a fire in each.'

That summer Ketil went to Midfjord, and there was a fire in the hearth of a hut. On the shore of the firth, Ketil found a great hut, and its inhabitant was not at home when Ketil entered. He found a large number of carcasses in a great pit dug down in the earth, and he pulled everything out of there and threw them about him here and there. He found the carcasses of whales and polar bears, seals and walruses and all kinds of animals, but at the bottom of each pit, he found salted man's flesh. He dragged all this out, and spoiled it.

But when dusk fell, he heard a great splashing of oars. He went down to the seashore. Then a man came to land. His name was Surt, and he was big and evil. As soon as the ship touched the shore, he stepped overboard, took hold of the ship, dragged it up to the boathouse, and he sank into the ground to his knees. In a deep voice he said: 'It has gone badly here, because all my possessions have been wrecked and it has gone worst with that which was best, as my man-corpses are ruined. Such a matter is worth suitable reward. Now it has not turned out well, that Hallbjorn, my friend, sits quietly at home, but Ketil Trout, the kitchen-fool, has come here, and it would not be too much trouble to give him his deserts. It would be a great shame to me if I didn't get the better of him, he who has grown up by the fire and been a coal-biter.'

He went to his hut, but Ketil hid behind the door with his axe raised. And when Surt entered the hut, he had to bend down to fit through the doorway, and he thrust through his head and shoulders. Then Ketil hewed through his neck with his axe. It sang loudly as it sliced off his head. The giant fell dead to the hut floor.

Then Ketil loaded his boat and went back home that autumn.

The next summer he went to Vitadsgjafi. Hallbjorn forbade this and said it would be better for him to drive the wagon home for the harvest. Ketil said it would not do if he was untried - 'And I will go,' he added.

'When you are there, you will think yourself haunted,' said Hallbjorn, 'but it is clear that you want to see my fireplaces and deem yourself my equal in everything.'

Ketil said he was right.

Afterwards he went north to Vitadsgjafi and

he found a hut where he stayed. He had no problem fishing, because he could catch fish with his bare hands in that firth. He stored his catch in the boathouse, and then went to sleep. But the next morning, when he woke, he found all his catch had been taken.

The next night Ketil stayed awake. He saw a giant enter the boathouse, and wrap up a great burden. Ketil attacked him and struck him to the shoulders with his axe, and his load fell down. The giant ran away, having taken a wound, so that Ketil lost his axe, which remained fast in the wound. The giant was named Kaldrani. He ran down to the head of the firth and into his cave, but Ketil pursued him. Trolls sat beside a fire and they laughed much, saying that Kaldrani had got what he deserved for his deeds. Kaldrani said the wound needed ointment not scolding. Then Ketil entered the cave and said that he was a physician, and said he would apply the ointment, and bind the wound. Then the trolls went farther into the cave. But Ketil took the axe out of the wound and struck the giant a deadly blow. After that he went home to his hut, loaded his boat and went home.

Afterwards, Hallbjorn welcomed him, and asked him if he had heard of anything happening. Ketil told him he had gone a long way. Then Hallbjorn said that he was looking dejected - 'and did you stay there in peace?' he asked.

'Yes,' said Ketil.

Chapter Three

That autumn, before Winter Nights, Ketil prepared his boat. Hallbjorn asked what he intended to do. Ketil said he expected to go on a fishing expedition. Hallbjorn said that he would do no such thing, - 'and you do this without my leave.' Not much later, Ketil departed. When he had gone as far north as a certain firth, a violent gale seized his boat and dragged it away to sea, and he could find no harbour. He was swept away to cliffs on Finnmark's coast, where he landed at a break in the cliffs. Then he camped and went to sleep. However, he awoke later when the ship began to shake. He stood up and saw a troll woman had taken hold of the prow and was shaking the ship. Ketil jumped into the boat, grabbed a butter chest, then cut the moorings, and sailed away. The most violent gale was blowing. Then a whale came and protected his ship from the wind, and it seemed to have human eyes, and then he was swept onto a reef. He swam away to a rock. Then there was nothing for it but to swim to land. After a rest, he swam to land and discovered a way up from the beach, and he found a farm. A man stood outside before the doors, chopping wood. He was named Bruni. He welcomed Ketil and recited a verse:

> *'You are welcome, Trout!*
>
> *Here you will receive shelter*
>
> *And all through the winter,*
>
> *Guest with me.*
>
> *I will pledge myself to you,*
>
> *Unless you refuse her,*
>
> *My daughter,*
>
> *Before the day comes.'*

Ketil said a verse:

'Here will I accept shelter!

I think the power

Of the Lapps' magic

Caused that terrible wind.

And throughout the day

I baled doing three men's work.

But the whale calmed the ocean.

I accept shelter in your house.'

Then they went inside. Two women were within. Bruni asked Ketil if he wanted to lie beside his daughter or alone. She was named Hrafnhild and was very big and strong. It is said that her face was an ell wide. Ketil said he would lie beside Hrafnhild. Afterwards they went and slept together, and Bruni spread an ox hide over them. Ketil asked why he was doing this. 'I have invited here some Lapps, friends of mine,' said Bruni, 'and I do not want them to see you. They shall now come for your butter chest.'

The Lapps came and they were not narrow-faced. They said: 'It is a great joy to have this butter.' Afterwards they went away, but Ketil remained there and entertained himself with Hrafnhild. He often went to the archery range and learned skills. Sometimes he went hunting with Bruni. In the winter, after Yule, Ketil wished to go, but Bruni said he could not because of the severe winter and bad weather, - 'and Gusir, king of the Lapps, lies out in the forest.'

In the spring, Bruni and Ketil prepared to go out. They went to the firth mouth. When they were about to part, Bruni said: 'Go the way I show you, and do not go into the forest.' He gave him some arrows, including one with a spiked head, and said that he should use them, if he needed them in hardship. Afterwards they parted, and Bruni went home. When he was alone Ketil said: 'Why shouldn't I go the shorter way when I do not fear Bruni, the bugbear?' Then he went into the forest, and he saw a great blizzard and a man coming after him in a wagon drawn by two reindeer. Ketil hailed him with a verse:

> *'You, get out of your wagon,*
>
> *Quiet with your reindeer;*
>
> *Out late in the evening,*
>
> *Tell me, how are you named?'*

He said:

> *'Gusir they call me,*
>
> *The honourable Lapps,*
>
> *I am the leader*
>
> *Of all that tribe.*
>
> *Who is this man,*
>
> *Who I meet here,*
>
> *Who creeps like a wolf of the woods?*
>
> *You will speak fearfully,*

If you go away

Three times to Thrumufirth,

I say that you are no hero.' They were before Ofara-Thrumu. Ketil replied with this verse:

'Trout I am named,

I come from Hrafnista,

Son of Hallbjorn.

Why do you skulk here, wretch?

Must I speak peaceful words

With a cowardly Lapp?

I would rather bend the bow

That Bruni gave me.'

Gusir thought that now he knew the identity of this Trout, and that he was very famous. Gusir said this verse:

'Who goes on snowshoes

At the beginning of the day,

Eager for battle,

Fierce in your heart?

We shall struggle

To redden our arrows

In the blood of each other,

Unless courage wavers.'

Ketil said:

'I'm called Trout

As half my name,

I will challenge you

From this day onwards.

I shall certainly prove,

Before we part,

That farmers' arrows

Are sharp-pointed.'

Gusir said:

'Defend yourself against

The bitter sword-clash,

Hold your shield before you,

I will shoot hard,

Soon I will

Kill you,

Unless you yield to me

All of your wealth.'

Ketil said:

'I will not yield

Any of my wealth

And I will never run

Away from you alone.

Before, I will hew

The shield over your breast,

And you will see

The darkness come.'

Gusir said:

'You will not enjoy gold

Or treasure,

In peace at home

With a whole heart.

Your death will come

Quickly to hand,

If we go out to play

The spear game.'

Ketil said:

'I shall not deal

Gold to Gusir,

And will not be first

To speak of peace.

It is much better

And more courageous

To die suddenly

Than creep away.'

Afterwards they bent their bows and put arrows to their strings and shot, and each arrow hit the head of the other and fell. By then Gusir had one arrow left. Then Ketil took out his spike-headed arrow. Then Gusir took out a shaft that looked warped to him, and stepped on it. Ketil said:

'Fey is now

Found the coward,

That he tramples under foot

The shaft that is bent.'

Then they shot at each other, and the arrows missed each other, and the spike-headed arrow entered Gusir's breast. There he took his death. Bruni had made Gusir's arrow look warped, because he was next in line to the throne should anything happen to Gusir, and he thought himself wronged by these dealings. Gusir had owned the sword named Dragvendill, best of all swords. Ketil took that from Gusir's corpse and the arrows Flaug, Hremsa and Fifa. Then Ketil went to Bruni and told him what had happened. Bruni said that the blow struck close to home because his brother was dead. Ketil said he had won on the kingdom for Bruni. Then he went with Bruni to the settled lands, and they parted with many friendly words.

Nothing is said of Ketil's journey before he came home to Hrafnista. He met a farmer and asked whose ships they were that had gone to the islands. The man said there had gone the guests who would drink the funeral ale for Ketil, if they heard nothing of him. Ketil went in his ship to the islands and entered the house, and the men grew joyful. Now the funeral ale turned became greeting ale to celebrate Ketil's return. He stayed home for three winters.

Then a ship came to the island, and in it was Hrafnhild Bruni's daughter, and Ketil's son, who was named Grim. Ketil welcomed them. Hallbjorn said: 'Why do you ask this troll to come here?' and he was very exasperated and annoyed at her coming. Hrafnhild said that neither of them would come to harm from her, - 'and I will go away immediately, but Grim, our son, called Hairy-cheek, shall stay.' He was called that because one of his cheeks was hairy, and he was born like that. Iron could not wound him on that spot.

Ketil asked Hrafnhild not be angry over this. She said they would see little of her anger. Afterwards she headed home and went north along the coast, but told Grim to stay there for three winters, and said that she would come for him then.

Chapter Four

There was a man named Bard, a good farmer, who had a beautiful daughter named Sigrid. She was thought to be the most eligible woman around. Hallbjorn said Ketil should ask for her as his wife and think no more of Hrafnhild. Ketil said to him that he had not thought of taking a wife, and he was always morose after his parting with Hrafnhild. Ketil

said he would go north along the coast, but
Hallbjorn said that he intended to visit Bard and ask
him about this matter, - 'and it is evil, that you
should love that troll.'

Afterwards Hallbjorn went to Bard. The
farmer said that Ketil had been on great and difficult
journeys and he should seek his wife himself.

'Do you think I lie?' said Hallbjorn.

The man said: 'I know that Ketil would come
here, if this was his idea, and I am not sure that I
should not refuse you my daughter.'

So they bargained together, and the time for
the wedding was appointed. Then Hallbjorn went
home. Ketil did not ask him for news of his journey.
Hallbjorn said that many people would be more
curious about their own marriage than Ketil. Ketil
paid no attention to that, but despite this, these plans
went forward, and they had a good marriage feast.
Ketil was not naked the first night, when they went
to bed. Sigrid had no problem with that, and they
resolved things between them quickly.

After this, Hallbjorn died, but Ketil took over
the management of the household, and many people
stayed with him. Ketil had a daughter by his wife,
and she was named Hrafnhild. After three winters
had passed, Hrafnhild Bruni's daughter came to meet
Ketil. He asked her to stay with him. But she said
that she would not remain there. 'You have now lost
all chance of us living together, through your
looseness of mind and faithlessness.' Then she went
to her ship very deep in thought and heavy in mind,
and it was clear that she felt strongly about parting
with Ketil. Grim stayed behind.

Ketil was now the most powerful men in the north, and people had great confidence in him. One summer, he went north to Finnmark to find Bruni and Hrafnhild. They went in a little ship, and weighed anchor beside one cliff, near several more. Ketil told Grim to look for water. He went and saw a troll by the river who forbade him from proceeding further, and would have seized him. Grim was afraid and he ran back, and told his father. Then Ketil went to meet the troll and said this verse:

What is this oddity,

Who stands by the mountain

And scowls above the fire?

Relations between us neighbours,

I think, will improve.

See, the sun is shining.'

The troll disappeared, but father and son went home.

One autumn, two Vikings came to Ketil's farm. One was named Hjalm, and the other Stafnglam. They had harried widely. They asked for sanctuary from Ketil, who granted them these terms, and they stayed with him in high honour over the winter. That winter, at Yule, Ketil swore that he should not give his daughter Hrafnhild in marriage without her consent. The Vikings wished him good luck in this.

One day Ali the Uppdale-Warrior came there. He was from an Upplander family, and he asked for Hrafnhild's hand. Ketil said he would not give her away without her consent, - 'but I might speak with her about it.'

Hrafnhild said she would not love Ali nor make a marriage settlement with him. Ketil told Ali that this was so, and Ali challenged Ketil to a duel. Ketil agreed. The brothers, Hjalm and Stafnglam, said they would fight for Ketil. But he told them to hold shields for him. However, when they came to the field of combat, Ali struck Ketil and the shields did not protect him, and the point of Ali's sword entered Ketil's forehead and ploughed down to his nose, and it bled much. Then Ketil said this verse:

> 'Hjalm and Stafnglam,
>
> Protect yourselves both,
>
> Give room for the old one
>
> To go ahead.
>
> Fly, war-serpents.
>
> Valiant is the Uppdale-Warrior.
>
> Ugly is the sword-play,
>
> The old man's beard is visible.
>
> Clattering skin-kirtle,
>
> Shaking iron shirt,
>
> Quivering ring-shirt.
>
> The wooer of the maiden is afraid.'

Then Ketil swung his sword at his head, but Ali brought up his shield. Then Ketil went for his feet and cut off both, and Ali fell there.

Chapter Five

A little later there was a great famine; the fish remained away from land, and the crops failed, but Ketil had many people at the farm. Sigrid said she thought they would need food if they were to stay there. Ketil said he wanted no taunts, and he went to his ship. The Vikings asked what he intended to do.

'I shall go fishing,' he said.

They said they would go with him, but he said that he was not at any risks, and he asked them to take care of his farm for a while.

Ketil came to the place named Skrofa. And as he reached the shore, he saw a troll-woman in a bearskin kirtle on a peninsula. She had just risen from the sea and was as black as pitch. She squinted at the sun. Ketil recited this verse:

'Who is that ogress,

On the far peninsula

Who sneers at me?

Under the rising sun,

I have never seen

A more loathly looking one.'

She said:

'I am called Forad,

I dwell far to the north

In Hrafnsey,

Detested by farmers,

Great is my bravery,

Whatever evil thing I do.'

And then she said:

'Many men

Have I sent to hell,

They came here to fish.

Who is it I see

The little man,

Who sails through the reefs?'

He spoke: 'Call me Trout,' he said. She said: 'It would be better to stay near your home in Hrafnista, rather than drag yourself alone to the outlying reefs.' Ketil recited this verse:

'Arrogant I thought,

Before I came here,

The jeering of

Monstrous ogresses.

I curse the lazy man,

I came here for the fishing.

I won't be deterred,

Despite what Forad says.

Need is my spur,

I will aid my neighbours.

I would not risk

Hunting seals on this isle,

If on my island

There were enough.'

She said:

'I will not refuse it,

Wandering man,

That you have a life

Longer than others,

If of our meeting

To fearless warriors,

Little boy, you speak;

But I see that your heart shakes.'

Ketil said:

'When I was a youngster

Often I went alone

Across the outer seas.

Many murk-riders

I met on my way

I am not afraid of an ogress' snorts.

You have a long face, foster-mother,

And a nose like an oar,

I'm not looking for a monstrous ogress.'

She came closer to him and said:

'I began my journey in Angri.

Then I went to Steigar.

The tinkling short-sword clattered.

Then I went to Karmoy.

I will set fires in Jadri

And kindled flames in Utstein.

Then I'll go east to the Elfr,

Before the daylight shines,

And romp with the bridesmaids

And marry an earl.'

This was all along the length of Norway. She asked: 'What shall you do now?'

'I will boil meat and make a meal,' he said. She said:

'I will come to your cooking-fire,

And stroke your body,

Until I grip you greedily.'

'This is now what I expect from her,' said Ketil. She moved up to him. Then Ketil recited this verse:

'My arrow is true,

And so is your strength,

The shaft will meet you,

Unless you wriggle away.'

She recited this verse:

'Flaug and Fifa

I think to be nothing,

And I am not afraid

Of Hremsa's bite.'

These were the names of Ketil's arrows. He put an arrow to the string and shot it at her. She turned into a whale and dived into the sea, but the arrow hit her under a fin. Then Ketil heard a great shriek.

Then he watched the giantess and said: 'It will go as fate shapes it; Forad will not marry that earl, now he'll find her bed undesirable.'

Afterwards Ketil caught some fish and loaded his boat

One night he was woken by a noise from the forest. He ran out and saw a troll-woman, whose hair fell to her shoulders.

Ketil said: 'What are you doing, foster-mother?'

She bridled at that and said: 'I am going to the meeting of the trolls. There comes Skelking, king of the trolls, from the north out of the Arctic, and Ofoti from Ofotansfirth and Thorgerd Horgatroll, and other great monsters from the northern lands. Do not delay me; you are nothing to me, you who killed Kaldrani.'

And then she hurried out to the shore and so to sea. There was nothing short of a witch ride in the island that night, and although Ketil was unharmed, he went back home and stayed there for some time.

Then Framar, king of the Vikings, came to Hrafnista. He was a devout heathen, and iron did not bite him. He ruled a kingdom in Hunaveld, in Gestrekaland. He made his sacrifices at Arhaug. No snow would stay on that mound. His son was called Bodmod, who had a great farm by Arhaug, and was a popular man, but everyone wished evil for Framar. Odin had decreed this for Framar, that iron did not bite him. Framar demanded Hrafnhild in marriage, and Ketil answered that she would choose her own man.

She said no to Framar, - 'If I would not accept Ali, then I will hardly choose to marry this troll.'

Ketil told Framar her answer. He was very angry, and he challenged Ketil to a duel at Arhaug on the first day of Yule, - 'and you are the worst of nithings, if you do not come.' Ketil said he would come. Hjalm and Stafnglam asked to go with him. Ketil said he would go alone.

A little before Yule Ketil was ferried down to Namdalen. He wore a fur-coat and had skis on his feet, and he went up through the valleys and then through the woods to Jamtaland, and then east over Skalkskog to Halsingjaland, then east over Eyskogamark, - this forest divided Gestrekaland and Halsingjaland; it was twenty *rasts*[67] long and three broad, and made for an evil journey.

There was a man named Thorir who lived by the forest. He offered Ketil his aid and said that evildoers lived in the forest: 'and the worst of them is named Soti. He is treacherous and strong.' Ketil said that he would be no problem. He went into the forest and came to Soti's hut. He was not at home. Ketil kindled the fire. Soti came home and he did not greet Ketil but set out food on his own.

Ketil sat by the fire and spoke: 'Are you afraid to share your food, Soti?' he asked.

Then Soti threw some hunks of meat at Ketil. When they had eaten their fill, Ketil lay down beside the fire and snored a great deal. Then Soti leapt up, but Ketil awoke and said: 'What are you doing up, Soti?'

He said: 'I am going to blow on the fire. It was nearly out.'

Ketil slept again. Then Soti ran up with a two-handed axe. Ketil sprang up and said: 'You must have much butchery to do,' said he. After that, Ketil sat up all night.

In the morning, he rose, and asked Soti to go

---

[67] A *rast* is the distance a man can travel in one hour.

with him to forest. When night fell, they lay down under an oak. Ketil fell asleep, or so Soti thought, because he snored loudly. Soti sprang up and struck at Ketil, so he tore off the hood of his cloak, but Ketil was not in the cloak. Ketil woke and decided to test Soti.

He ran up and said: 'Now shall we test our skills in wrestling.' Ketil pulled Soti down over a log, struck off his head, and afterwards went on his way.

On Yule Eve, he came to Arhaug, place of sacrifice for good harvests for Framar and the local people. There was a heavy fall of snow. Ketil went on to the barrow and sat in the cold wind waiting for the meeting. When men came to Bodmod's farm, he asked: 'When will Ketil come to Arhaug?'

Men said there was no hope of this.

Bodmod said: 'I think I see a man I can't make out. Learn who he is and invite him to my farm.'

They went to the barrow but did not find Ketil, so they told Bodmod. Bodmod said he would have gone up onto the barrow. He went straight there and up on top of the barrow, where he saw a great heap on the northern side. Bodmod recited this verse:

> *Where is this tall one*
>
> *Who sits on the barrow*
>
> *And faces the wind?*
>
> *A frost-hard man,*

I think you are afflicted,

That you seek no warmth.'

Ketil recited this verse:

'Ketil I am named,

I come from Hrafnista.

I was raised under that roof;

My heart is full of courage

I can stand up for myself,

Yet I would like to get lodgings.'

Bodmod said:

'You will now get up,

Leave this barrow

And seek safety in my hall.

You will have meals

For many days,

If you will accept my welcome.'

Ketil recited this verse:

'I will now get up

And leave the barrow,

As Bodmod bids me.

My own brother,

Even if he were beside me,

Could give me no better invitation.'

Bodmod took Ketil by the hand. When he stood up, Ketil's feet slipped on the barrow. Then Bodmod recited this verse:

'You've been challenged, foster-son,

To enter battle

And fight Framar for gain.

In his youth,

Odin gave him victory,

And I think he is accustomed to battle.'

Ketil grew angry at the name of Odin, because he did not believe in him, and he recited this verse:

'I have never

Sacrificed to Odin,

Though I have lived long.

I know already

That the noble head

Of my foe he will lose.'

Then Ketil went with Bodmod, and stayed with him that night and sat next to him. And in the morning, Bodmod offered to go with him or provide him with a second in the duel with Framar. Ketil did not agree with that. 'Then I will go with you,' said

Bodmod.

Ketil agreed to that, and they went to Arhaug. Framar came bellowing to the barrow, and found Bodmod and Ketil there with a crowd of men. Then Framar recited the laws of the duel. Bodmod held a shield for Ketil, but no one did for Framar.

Framar said: 'You are now my enemy and no longer my son.'

Bodmod said he had broken their kinship because of his witchcraft. Before they fought, an eagle flew out of the forest to Framar and tore off part of his clothes. Then Framar recited this verse:

> *'This eagle is evil,*
>
> *I don't fear the wound I took,*
>
> *He sinks in his grey claws*
>
> *And tears at my blood vessels.*
>
> *The storm-carver screamed*
>
> *What vision does he see coming?*
>
> *Often have I gladdened eagles,*
>
> *Been kind to the ravens.'*

Then the eagle came on so fast, he had to protect himself with his weapons. Then Framar recited this verse:

> *'Wave your wings,*
>
> *I will reply to you with weapons.*

You hover, wide-flyer,

As if you warn me of menace.

You are confused, battle-inciter,

We two shall have the victory.

Turn to assault Trout;

He shall die now.'

The one being challenged had to attack first.
Now Ketil struck Framar's shoulder. Framar stood
silently, but the sword did not cut him, though he
was knocked back, the blow was so great. Framar
struck at Ketil and hit his shield. Ketil hit Framar's
other shoulder, but again it did not cut.

Ketil recited this verse:

'You drag now, Dragvendill,

With the eagle's prey.

You've met with harmful witchcraft

So you may not bite.

Trout did not know this,

That venom-hardened edges

Would recoil from attacks

As if Odin blunted them.'

And then he added this verse:

'What is it, Dragvendill?

Why have you become so blunt?

Now I have struck at him,

But you are unwilling to bite.

You give way in this sword meeting.

At the clash of metal you yield.

Never before have you failed

When warriors swung at each other.'

Framar recited this verse:

'Now the old man's beard shakes,

The old weapon swerves.

His sword defies him.

The maiden's father is afraid.

Whet your bone-twigs,

So they will bite

On courageous men,

If you think that good.'

Ketil said:

'It is not necessary to stir us up,

Seldom do courageous fighters

Care to question

My sword-blows' keenness

Bite now, Dragvendill

Or else break!

Both of us are doomed,

If you hesitate a third time.'

And then Framar said:

'The father of the maiden isn't afraid,

While Dragvendill is whole.

I know that this is certain:

It won't hesitate a third time.'

Then Ketil took his sword in his hand and turned the other edge forward. Framar stood in silence, as the sword cut through his shoulders, and did not stop before reaching his hips, and then the wound gaped outwards. Then Framar recited this verse:

'Trout is bold,

Dragvendill is keen,

As if they were unsaid

It cut up Odin's words.

Balder's father has broken faith;

It is unsafe to trust him.

Your hands be blessed!

Now we must part.'

Then Framar died, but Bodmod left the duelling-place with Ketil. Then Bodmod said: 'Now if you think to give me a reward for my support, then I wish that you give me your daughter.'

Ketil took that well and said that Bodmod was a good comrade. After that, Ketil went home and he grew to be very famous for his great deeds. He gave Hrafnhild in marriage to Bodmod. Ketil ruled over Hrafnista while he lived, and Grim Hairy-cheek succeeded him. Grim's son was Arrow-Odd.

And this saga ends here.

THE SAGA OF GRIM HAIRY-CHEEK

Grim Hairy-cheek inherits his father's lands and weapons, but also, it seems, something of his lucklessness in love and propensity for cohabiting with trolls. His saga is rather shorter, and episodic in nature; its most memorable episode contains elements reminiscent of Arthurian romance (the Loathly Lady motif) and later Scandinavian folklore (similar trolls appear in *East of the Moon, West of the Sun*). Grim himself is the father of Odd the Traveller, or Arrow-Odd, whose much longer saga is a sequel to his own story.

Chapter One

It is said of Grim Hairy-cheek that he was both tall and strong, and the bravest of warriors. He was called Hairy-cheek because one of his cheeks was covered with dark hair, and he was born with this. Iron could not harm him there. Grim took over the estate in Hrafnista after Ketil Trout, his father. He became wealthy. And he alone ruled near enough everything throughout all Halogaland.

Harald was a powerful and famous lord in the Vik. He married Geirhild, daughter of King Solgi, son of King Hrolf Berg of the Uplands. Their daughter was Lofthaena. She was the fairest of women and well educated. Grim Hairy-cheek went there in a boat with eighteen man and asked for Lofthaena's hand. It was agreed, and he was to marry her in the autumn. But seven nights before the wedding Lofthaena vanished, and no one knew what had become of her. When Grim came to the wedding, he missed his love there, because his bride was away, but he thought, however, that her father was not responsible. There he sat for three nights, and they drank, but with little joy. Then he went home to Hrafnista. It had happened five years before that Lord Harald's wife had died, and a year later north in Finnmark he married Grimhild Josur's daughter and brought her home. Soon she seemed to spoil everything. She ill-treated Lofthaena, her stepdaughter, which later was proved. Grim was ill content with life when he heard nothing of Lofthaena, his wife-to-be.

It happened, as is often the case, that great famine came to Halogaland. Grim Hairy-cheek got ready to go home and went in his boat with three men. He sailed north to Finnmark and so eastwards to Gandvik. And when he came into the bay, he saw that there was plenty of fish. He beached his boat, then went to a shelter and lit a fire for himself. But when they had gone to sleep for the night, they woke up to find that the storm had come bringing with it a whiteout. So much bitter cold followed this weather

that everything froze, both outside and inside. In the
morning, when they were dressed, they went out to
the sea. Then they saw that the fish had gone
without a trace. They thought they could not get
prosper here now, but they could not sail away. Then
they went back to the hut and were there all day.
During the night Grim woke to hear laughter from
outside the shelter. He sprang up quickly and took
his axe and went out. He also had with him as always
the arrows Gusir's Gifts that Ketil Trout, his father,
had given him. When he came out, he saw two giant
women down by the boat, and they tugged at its
stem and stern and they were going to shake the boat
apart. Grim spoke and recited:

What name have these

lava dwellers,

who would do violence

to my vessel?

I have never

known two such

hideous lasses

in all my life.'

The one nearest to him said:

'Feima is my name,

I was born in the north,

Hrimnir's daughter

out on the high fell.

Here is my sister

the stronger one,

Kleima her name,
come to the sea.'

Grim said:

'You'll get nowhere
Thjazi's girls
worst of women.
Soon I will be angry.
Both of you shall I send,
before sunrise,
to be tasty titbits
for the wolves.'

Kleima said:

'This came first,
when our father
cast spells,
sent the waves here.
You men,
unless it's your fate,
whole from here
will never flee.'

Grim said:

'I promise you both
point and edge,
hot fire,

at the first.

Then they'll teach,

Hrimnir's sluts,

which is best,

point or paw.'

Grim took one of Gusir's Gifts and shot at the troll that was furthest away from him so that she got her death. Feima said, 'That went ill, sister Kleima.' She waded up to Grim. He swung at her with his axe, and hit her shoulder blade. She shouted out and ran along the beaches. Grim lost hold of his axe, because it was stuck in the wound. Grim ran after her, and neither could he catch her nor she evade him, until they came to some big cliffs. There he saw a cave in the cliff face. There was a narrow path to follow, but she ran as if she was on flat ground. And when she ran up into the rocks, the axe fell out of her wound. Grim picked it up, and he hooked the axe in one crevice while he stood in the other, and pulled himself up after with the handle, and so he came up to the cave. There he saw a fire burning bright, and two old trolls by the fire. There was a man and woman. They touched with the soles of their feet. They were both wearing short and crisp skin smocks. He couldn't avoid seeing what both of them had between their legs. He was Hrimnir, but she was named Hyrja. But when Feima entered the cave, they greeted her and asked where her sister Kleima was. She said: 'You won't guess this, she lies dead by the shore, and I have my death wound. And you lie down and here you are by the fire.' The giant said, 'It has not been a glorious deed to kill you both, one six years old, and the other seven. Who has done this?' Feima said: 'That evil man Grim Hairy-cheek has done this. He and his father are worse than other men for killing trolls and mountain dwellers. Although he has now done this, he will however never find Lofthaena, his wife. And I think it entertaining, that now they are so close to each other.' Hrimnir said: 'Grimhild, my sister, did that, and she has been given many skills.' Feima fainted from blood loss, and she fell down dead. Then Grim went into the cave and cut so hard at the man Hrimnir that he took off his head. Then the woman Hyrja sprang up and ran at him, and they wrestled hard and long, because she was the greatest troll, but Grim was a powerful man. But it turned out that he threw her over his hip so that she fell. Then he cut off her head and walked out, leaving her dead, then went to his hut.

Chapter Two

The next day after the weather was good. Then they went to the beach and saw where a whale had been stranded. They went there and butchered the whale. A little later Grim saw twelve men coming. They came quickly. Grim greeted them and asked their names. The leader said he was Hreidar the Rash, and asked why Grim would rob him of his possessions. Grim said he found the whale first. 'You do not know,' said Hreidar, 'that I own all that comes ashore?'

'That I didn't,' said Grim, 'but all the same, we split it equally.'

'No, I will not,' said Hreidar. 'You shall leave the whale or else we fight.'

'We'll do that,' said Grim, 'rather than lose a whole whale.' They set to and fought, and it was the hardest struggle. Hreidar and his men gave both big blows and were nimble with their weapons, and within a little time, both Grim's men fell. Then the fighting was hardest, but it ended that Hreidar fell and all his men. Grim fell as well, because of pain and shortness of breath. He lay there among the slain the beach and expected only death.

But he had not lain long when he saw a woman coming, if you could call her one. She was no taller than a seven year old girl, but so stout that Grim thought he would never be able to get his arms round her. She was long faced and hard faced, hook-nosed and hunched shouldered, dark and wobble-chinned, dirty faced and balding. Black was both her hair and her skin. She had a crisp skin smock that went no further than her buttocks at the back. Most unkissable he thought her to be, because a string of mucus hung in front of her mouth. She went over to where Grim lay, and said: 'The Halogalander chiefs do poorly now. Will you, Grim, accept your life from me?' Grim said: 'I'm hardly sure, you are so ugly. What is your name?' She said: 'My name is Geirrid Gandvikekkja. As you might believe, I have some power in this cove, so make yourself ready one way or another.' Grim said: 'It is an old saying that everyone wants to live, and I will chose to accept life from you.' She took him up under her skin smock and ran with him as if he was a baby and so hard that the wind filled it. She did not stop until they came to a cave in a large cliff, and when she let him down, she seemed to Grim as ugly as before. 'Now you've come here,' she said, 'I would like you to repay me, since I saved you and carried here, so kiss me now.'

'That is not what I will do,' said Grim, 'so fiend-like you seem to me now.'

'Then I will not help you,' said Geirrid, 'and it seems to me that you will soon be dead.'

'In that case, it must be,' said Grim, 'though I say it unwillingly.' He went to her and kissed her. He thought her not so bad to touch as she was hideous to see. It had reached evening. Geirrid made a bed and asked if Grim wanted to lie alone or with her. Grim said he would rather lie alone. She said that she wouldn't waste time healing him then. Grim saw that it would not help him, and then he said he would rather lie with her, if he those were his choices. He did so. First she bound all his wounds, and he did not feel either pain or burning. It seemed to him wonderful how gentle-fingered she was despite the ugly hands she seemed to have, because he thought them more like vulture's claws than human hands. And when they went to bed, Grim fell asleep. When he awoke, he saw a woman so beautiful lying in bed with him that he thought he had hardly ever seen anyone so attractive. He was amazed by how similar she was to Lofthaena, his wife-to-be. Lying on the floor he saw the evil trollwife-skin that Geirrid Gandvikekkja had. Little strength was left in this woman. He got up quickly and hauled the skin to the fire and burned it to ashes. Then he went to the woman and dripped water on her until she came round and said: 'Now both of us are well: I saved your life in the first place, but you saved me from this.'

'How did you come here, and anyway how did you end up this way?' said Grim. She said: 'A little after you went, when you had hardly gone from my father Harald in the Vik, Grimhild, my stepmother, met me, and said, 'Now I shall pay you back, Lofthaena, because you have shown me wilfulness and stubbornness since I came into the kingdom. Let me tell you that you will become the ugliest troll and disappear north to Gandvik and live there in and a side-cave right beside Frost, my brother, and both of you will quarrel endlessly, and may they have it worse who is least able to harden themselves. And you shall be hated by both trolls and humans. You shall, also,' she said, 'remain in this bondage all your life and never get out, unless a man from humanity grants you the three things that you request, and I know that no one will do that. This is the first thing, that you save his life, the second, to kiss you, and the third is that he will sleep in the same bed as you, who will go much worse than anyone.' Now you have done all these things to me, even though you were obliged to. I would like you to take me to the Vik and my father, and marry me there, as was intended.'

They went to Grim's hut, and there were now plenty of fish. Whales lay in each inlet. He loaded his boat, and when he was done he sailed from the land, and they were both in the boat, Grim and Lofthaena. He had the same luck as Ketil Trout, his father, and the other Hrafnista men; he set sail in calm weather, and a fair wind began to blow. Then he sailed home to Hrafnista, and people thought it was as if he had recovered from death.

Chapter Three

A little later Grim went south to Vik, and Lofthaena went with him. Grimhild ruled over nearly enough everything all by herself there. But when Grim came, he had Grimhild taken and a bag put over her head and had stoned to death, but not before he told Lord Harald how things had gone. He had his wedding with Lofthaena and went home to Hrafnista. But Lord Harald married for a third time to Thorgils Thorri's daughter.

Grim and Lofthaena had not long been together before they had a daughter who was named Brynhild. She grew up in Hrafnista and was the most beautiful of girls. Grim loved her dearly. When she was twelve years old, a man named Sorkvir asked for her and he was son of Svadi, Raudfeld's son, son of Bard, son of Thorkell Boundfeet. She did not want to go with him, and so Sorkvir challenged Grim to a duel. Grim agreed to it. Sorkvir was of Sogn stock on his mother's side, and there were farms he owned. The duel was set for half a month's time.

Asmund was a lord in Norway. He had the town called Berurjod. He was a married man and had a son named Ingjald. He was a brave man and spent much time with Grim Hairy-cheek, and they had a great friendship, but though Ingjald was older, Grim was much stronger. Ingjald married a wife called Dagny who was the daughter of that Asmund who is called Gnod-Asmund, the sister of Olaf Army-King. With her he had a son called Asmund, who afterward was foster brother of Odd the Wanderer, who was with Sigurd Hring at Bravellir; his other name is Arrow Odd.

At the agreed time Sorkvir came to the duel with eleven men. These were all berserks. Grim came and Ingjald and many Halogalander farmers with him. They went to the island, and Grim had the first attack. He had the sword Dragvendil which his father had owned. The name of the man who held the shield before Sorkvir was Throst. Grim cut so hard with the first blow, he split the shield at length, but the sword sliced Throst from his left shoulder and right through him to just above his right hip, and the sword cut into Sorkvir's thigh so it took away his two legs, one above the knee, the other below, and he fell down dead. Then Ingjald and the rest turned on the ten who were left behind, and did not stop until they were all killed. Whereupon Grim recited this verse:

'Here we have cut down
to the earth
bear of glory
twelve berserks.
Although Sorkvir
was said to be strongest
of those bullies,
and Throst another.'

And again he said:

'First I will
follow my father:
my daughter,
will not,
be promised unwilling
to any person
young pine of velvets,
while Grim is still living.'

Grim went home now after his duel, and Ingjald to Berurjod. A little later, his father died, and he took all the property and became a farmer, and the greatest giver of hospitality.

Chapter Four

A few years earlier Bodmod had died. The man had had a daughter with Hrafnhild, his wife, and her name was Thorny. Her son was Thorbjorn Whalebone, father of Ketil the Broad, father of Thorny who married Hergil Button-Arse. Hrafnhild went home to Hrafnista, to Grim, her brother.

Thorkell was the name of a famous man. He was Earl of Namdalen. He went to Hrafnista and asked for Hrafnhild's hand. She was married to him. Their son was Ketil Trout, who burned in their house Harek and Hraerek, Hildrid's sons, because they slandered Harald, his uncle. After that Ketil went to Iceland and took land between Thjorsa and Markarfljot and lived at Hof. His son was Hrafn, the first lawspeaker in Iceland. His second son was Helgi, father of Helga, who married Oddbjorn Ash-smith. The third was Storolf, father of Orm the Strong and Hrafnhild, who married Gunnar Baugusson. Their son was Hamund, father of Gunnar of Hlitharendi, their daughter Arngunn, who married Hroar Tungu-Godi. Their son was Hamund the Lame. Vedrorm son of Vemund the old was a powerful lord. He asked to marry Brynhild, daughter of Grim Hairy-cheek. She went with him. Their son was Audbjorn, the father of Vedrorm, who fled from the king to the east in Jamtaland, and cleared the forest to settle there. His son was Holmfast, but the sister of Vedrorm was named Brynhild; Grim, her son, was named after Grim Hairy-cheek. The kinsmen, Grim and Holmfast, went west, raiding, and killed in the Hebrides Earl Asbjorn Skerryblaze, and took as plunder Olof, his wife, and Arneid, his daughter, and Holmfast got her and gave her to Vedrorm, his kinsman, and she was a slave, until Ketil Thrym married her and brought her out to Iceland. The place named Arneidarstead in the East Fjords is named for her. Grim married Olof the daughter of Thord Waddler, who the Earl had married.

Grim went to Iceland and settled Grimsnes up to Svinavatn and lived in Ondverdunes for four years, then at Burfell. His son was Thorgils, whose wife was Helga, daughter of Gest Oddleifson. Their sons were Thorarin of Burfell and Jorund of Midengi. Grim fell to Hallkell brother of Ketilbjorn of Mossfell in a duel at the Hallkell Hills.

Grim Hairy-cheek lived at Hrafnista, as previously mentioned. Eventually he had a son with his wife, named Odd, who was fostered with Ingjald at Berurjod. He was called variously Arrow-Odd or Odd the Traveller. Grim was a great man himself. He was strong in body and daring and often camped alone. He died as an old man. And here ends the story of Grim Hairy-cheek. But next comes *The Saga of Arrow-Odd*, which is a great history.

THE SAGA OF ARROW-ODD

If Norse saga has an equivalent of the *Odyssey*, then it must be *The Saga of Arrow-Odd*, a lengthy tale of a man blessed or cursed (much like Norna-Gest) with an unusually long life, in which he wanders, at times aimlessly, across the world of Viking mythology. Although in that respect it resembles the *Odyssey*, the story of Odd also has parallels with that classical poem's prequel, the *Iliad*, in that its doomed protagonist also participates in the greatest conflict to trouble the legendary, prehistoric Scandinavian world, the Bravic War.

However, for reasons unknown, possibly artistic, the author of the longer saga that has come down to us misses out Odd's involvement in this terrible war, although it appears in Saxo Grammaticus' *Gest Danorum* and the *Fragment of a Saga of Some Kings of the North*. Presumably, the author thought it a little bit too much, what with three hundred years of adventuring across the northern world; the curse (or blessing) of an inevitable death (reminiscent of Oedipus' fate in Greek myth, although Odd does a far better job, though still tragically inevitable, of avoiding it); not to mention a long-running feud with an even more invulnerable enemy: Ogmund Tussock, half-man, half-wraith, created by the powers of evil to avenge Odd's early raid on the mysterious world of Bjarmaland.

It is a long and terrible voyage that intersects with several other sagas, some of them previously translated, such as *The Saga of Hervor and Heidrek*, others still to be produced. Along the way, Arrow-Odd, son of Grim Hairy-cheek, son of Ketil Trout, encounters many foes in the worlds of men – Ireland, Russia, Greece, and Syria – and elsewhere. He meets the giants of Norse myth and the monsters of the St Brendan saga, scorns the sorcery of his Scandinavian homeland, converts to Christianity in Aquitania (without agreeing to do more than pay lip service), and outlives his friends and foes (other than Ogmund) until he has little left to do other than meet his inevitable fate.

Chapter One

There was a man named Grim who was called Hairycheek. He was so called because when he was born, he had an odd quirk; when Ketil Trout, father of Grim, and Hrafnhild Bruni's daughter went to bed together, as has already been mentioned, her father spread a hide over them because he had invited some Lapps there, and during the night Hrafnhild looked out from under the hide and saw one Lapp who was exceedingly hairy. And it was then that Grim got his mark; people think that he was begotten at that moment. Grim lived at Hrafnista. He was a wealthy man and powerful throughout Halogaland and elsewhere. He was married, and Lofthaena was his wife. She was the daughter of Lord Harald from the Vik in the east.

One summer, after the death of Harald, his brother in law, Grim made a journey eastwards to the Vik where he had much property. When Lofthaena knew of this, she asked to go with him, but Grim said that it could not be, - 'because you are expecting.'

'I will not be happy,' she said, 'unless I go.' Grim loved her dearly, and he let things go her way. She was very good-looking and in everything she did she was the cleverest woman in Norway. They fitted themselves out lavishly.

Grim sailed with two ships out from Hrafnista eastwards to Vik. But when they came to the country named Berurjod, Lofthaena said that she wanted them to reef sails because she could feel her labour starting, and so it was done, the ships made for land. A man named Ingjald lived there. He was married and had a son with his wife, a handsome youth called Asmund. And when they came ashore, they sent to the farm to tell Ingjald that Grim had come to the country with his wife. Then Ingjald had horses hitched to a cart and went to them himself and offered them all the hospitality they needed, and whatever they would receive. Then they went home to the farm of Ingjald. Lofthaena was shown to the women's house, but Grim was led into the hall and set on the high-seat, and Ingjald thought nothing he could do too much to show respect to Grim's group. But Lofthaena's labour pangs grew until she was delivered of a young boy, and the women who took care of him had never seen such a fine child. Lofthaena looked at the boy and said, 'Carry him to his father. He should name the child,' and so it was done. The boy was sprinkled with water and given the name Odd. There they stayed three nights. Lofthaena told Grim that she was ready to go, and Grim told Ingjald that he wanted to leave.

'It occurs to me,' said Ingjald, 'that I would like to get a sign of your respect from you.'

'That's well deserved,' said Grim, 'so choose your own reward, because I have no lack of treasure to pay you.'

'I have enough treasure,' said Ingjald. 'Then you must accept something else,' said Grim. 'I offer to become your son's foster father,' said Ingjald. 'I do not know,' said Grim, 'how Lofthaena will take that.' But she replied: 'I suggest you accept it, because it's a good offer.'

Then they were led to their ships, but Odd stayed behind at Berurjod. They took up their journey again, so that they arrived eastwards in the Vik, and they stayed as long as they thought necessary. Then they prepared to sail away from there, and they had a good wind until they came to Berurjod. Grim told his men to reef sails. 'Why should we not go on with our voyage?' said Lofthaena. 'I thought,' said Grim, 'that you would like to see your son.'

'I looked at him,' she said, 'before we separated, and it seemed to me that he had little love in his eyes for Hrafnista men, and so we will go on our way,' she said.

Now Grim returned home to Hrafnista and settled on his estate, but Odd grew up at Berurjod with Asmund. Odd was good at all the accomplishments of the time. Asmund followed him in all respects. Odd was very good-looking and smarter than other men.

Odd and Asmund became sworn brothers. They practiced archery every day, or swimming. No one was equal to Odd in any accomplishments. Odd would not play games like other people. Asmund always followed him. In all things Ingjald preferred Odd to Asmund.

Odd had every skilful man he found make him arrows. He did not take good care of them, and they lay around in people's way on seats and benches. Many were hurt by them, when people came in after dark and sat down. This one thing was agreed, that it made Odd unpopular. Men told Ingjald that he should talk to Odd about this. Ingjald met with Odd one day. 'There is one thing,' said Ingjald, 'foster-son, that makes you unpopular.'

'What is that?' said Odd. 'You do not take care of your arrows like other people,' said Ingjald. 'I think you could blame me for it,' said Odd, 'if you had given me something to keep them in.'

'I shall get you,' said Ingjald, 'what you want.'

'I think,' said Odd, 'that you will not get it.'

'It will not be so,' said Ingjald. 'You have a black three-year-old goat,' said Odd. 'Have him killed and skinned whole with both horns and hoofs.' And it was done as Odd asked, and he was brought the skin-bag when it was ready. Then he gathered all his arrows into it, and did not stop until the skin-bag was full. He had much larger arrows, and more of them, than other people. He had a bow to match.

Odd wore a scarlet robe every day, and had an embroidered gold headband round his brow. He had his quiver with him wherever he went. Odd did not make sacrifices, because he believed in his might and main, and Asmund did as he did, but Ingjald was a great man for sacrifices. The sworn brothers, Odd and Asmund, often rowed out from the land together.

Chapter Two

There was a woman named Heid. She was a seeress and a witch and knew how to predict the future with her wisdom. She went to banquets and told people how the winter would go and their fortunes. She had with her fifteen young men and fifteen girls. She was at a banquet not far away from Ingjald. One morning Ingjald was up early. He went to where Odd and Asmund rested, and said: 'I will send you both from the house today,' he said. 'Where will we go?' said Odd. 'You shall invite here the seeress, because we have now prepared a feast,' said Ingjald. 'I will not do that,' said Odd, 'and you will fall out of my favour if she comes here.'

'You must go, Asmund,' said Ingjald, 'because I expect you to.'

'I will do something,' said Odd, 'that will seem to you no better than this seems to me now.'

Asmund went and invited the seeress there, and she promised to come and came up with her following, and Ingjald went to meet her with all his men and invited her into his house. They had prepared auguries to be carried out that night. And when people had enough to eat, they went to sleep, but the seeress went to her night-time ritual with her followers. Ingjald came to her in the morning and asked what had been the result of the auguries. 'I think,' she said, 'that I have learned all you wish to know.'

'Then everyone shall go to their seats,' said Ingjald, 'and hear your words.' Ingjald was the first man to go to her. 'It is well, Ingjald,' she said, 'that you have come here. I can tell you that you shall live here until old age with great dignity and respect, and this may be much welcomed by all your friends.' Then Ingjald went off, and Asmund came. 'It is well,' said Heid, 'that you have come here, Asmund, for your honour and dignity will go around the world. You will not wrestle with old age, but you will be thought a good fellow and a great warrior wherever you are.' Asmund went to his seat, and everybody else went to the spaewife, and she told each of them their fortunes, and they were all well satisfied with their lot. Then she predicted the winter, and many other things that no one knew before. Ingjald thanked her for her predictions. 'Has everyone come here, those who are within the court?' she said. 'I think now almost everyone,' said Ingjald. 'What lies on the bench over there?' said the seeress. 'A cloak is lying there,' said Ingjald. 'I think it stirs sometimes, when I look,' she said. Then he sat up, who was lying there, and he began to speak and said: 'That's right, you thought that this is a man, because it is a man, and what he wants is for you to be quiet at once and babble not about my future, because I do not believe what you say.' Odd had a rod in his hand and said: 'I will hit you on the nose with this, if you prophesy at all about my future.' She said, 'I will still speak, and you will hear.' Then poetry came to her lips:

'Awe me not,

Odd of Jaederen,

With that rod,

Although we row.

This story will hold true,

Said by the seeress.

She knows beforehand

All men's fate.

You will not swim

Wide firths,

Nor go a long way

Over lands and bays,

Though the water will well

And wash over you,

You will burn

Here, at Berurjod.

Venom-filled snake

Shall sting you

From the ancient

Skull of Faxi.

The adder will bite

From below your foot,

When you are terribly

Old, my lord.

'This is to say, Odd,' she said, 'You may find it good to know that you are destined to live much longer than others. You shall live to be three hundred years old, and go from land to land, and always seem the greatest there, where you go. Your reputation will go around the world, but travel as far as you may, you'll die here, in Berurjod. The horse that is standing in the stable, black-maned and grey, Faxi, his skull will be your death.'

'You make the worst prophecies of any old woman,' said Odd. He jumped up as she said this and brought the rod down on her nose so hard that blood dripped on the ground. 'Take my belongings,' said the seeress, 'and I will go away from here, because I have never been treated like this before, that I was beaten.'

'Do not do that,' said Ingjald, 'for there's recompense for every ill, and you will stay here for three nights and get good gifts.' She took the presents, but she went away from the feast.[68]

---

[68] Similar sequences occur in Perrault's *Sleeping Beauty* and *The Yarn of Norna-Gest*.

Chapter Three

After this Odd told Asmund to come with him. They took Faxi and bridled him and led him behind them until they came to a valley. Here they dug a deep pit, until Odd had a struggle to get out, and then they killed Faxi and dropped him down into the pit, and Odd and Asmund brought the biggest rocks they could carry and piled them on top of him and poured sand between every stone. They built a burial mound beneath which Faxi lay. When they had ended their work, Odd said: 'I think that I should say that trolls are involved if Faxi comes up, and I think I have now frustrated the fate that would be my death.'

They went home after that, and met Ingjald. 'I want a ship as a gift,' said Odd. 'Where will you go?' Ingjald said. 'I'll go, I think, from here,' said Odd, 'from Berurjod, and never come here as long as I live.'

'I do not want that,' said Ingjald, 'because then you would do what I think worst. What people do you want to have with you?'

'We two shall go, Asmund and I,' said Odd. 'I would like you to send Asmund back quickly,' said Ingjald. 'He shall not come back any more than I,' said Odd. 'This you do ill,' said Ingjald. 'I will do this, I think, that you will like worst, because you invited the seeress here, and you knew that I thought it the worst,' said Odd.

Now Odd and Asmund prepared to go and they went to Ingjald and bade him farewell and went to the ship and pushed it out; then they rowed away from the shore. 'Where will we go?' said Asmund. 'Is it not a good idea,' said Odd, 'to seek my kin in Hrafnista?' But when they came to some islands, Odd said, 'Hard work will our journey be if we have to row all the way north to Hrafnista; we will now know if I have any of our family luck. I am told that Ketil Trout hoisted his sail in calm weather. Now I shall try it and hoist the sails.' And when they were under sail they got a fair wind, so that they came to Hrafnista early in the day; they pulled up their boat on the beach and then went to the farm. Odd had no other weapon than the quiver of arrows he had on his back, and a bow in his hand. But when they came to the farm, a man stood outside and greeted them well, and then asked for their names. 'I'm not telling you,' said Odd. Odd then asked whether Grim was home. He said that he was at home. 'Then call him outside,' said Odd. The man went in and told Grim that two men had come, - 'and said that you should go out.'

'Why can they not come in?' Grim said, 'Ask them to enter.' Out he went and told them what had been said. 'You must go in a second time,' said Odd, 'and tell Grim that he must come out and meet us both.' He went and told Grim. 'What sort of men are these?' said Grim. 'These people are handsome and tall. One of them has an animal skin on his back.'

'What you say of these men means that the sworn brothers, Odd and Asmund, are come here.' Grim went out with all those who were inside, and welcomed Odd and Asmund. Grim invited them with him into the house, and they accepted.

And when they sat down, Odd asked after his relatives, Gudmund and Sigurd. Their kinship went so that Gudmund was brother of Odd, the son of Grim and Lofthaena, but Sigurd was the son of

Grim's sister. They were promising men. 'They are to the north of the island and they plan to sail to Bjarmaland,' said Grim. 'Then I will see them,' said Odd. 'Well, I wish,' said Grim, 'that you stay here in the winter.'

'I will go first,' said Odd, 'and see them.' And then Grim went with him till they came to the island in the north. They had anchored there in two ships. Then their kinsman Odd called them to come ashore. They gave him a warm welcome, and when they heard the news, Odd said, 'Where have you decided to go?'

'To Bjarmaland,' said Gudmund. 'Asmund and I would go with you,' said Odd. But Gudmund had heard word of this, and said: 'There is no way, kinsman Odd, that you can come with us this summer. We two are now already equipped for our voyage, and you can come with me next summer, wherever you want.'

'That is well said,' said Odd, 'but it seems to me I may get a ship next summer and have no need to be your passenger.'

'You're not coming on this voyage,' said Gudmund, and with that they parted.

Chapter Four

Now Odd accepted his father's invitation to stay, and Grim sat him next to him, with Asmund on Odd's other side, and Grim made every hospitality available. But Gudmund and Sigurd lay anchored off the island half a month, and they waited for a fair wind.

One night Gudmund was restless in his sleep,

and the men wondered if they should wake him. Sigurd said that he should dream his dream. Then Gudmund woke. 'What have you dreamed?' Sigurd said. 'I dreamed,' said Gudmund, 'that I thought I lay beside the island, but I saw that a polar bear lay in a ring around it, and its tail met with the head of the beast just above the ships, but it was the cruellest bear that I have ever seen, because its hair all stood on end, and it seemed to me then that it would throw itself at our ships and sink them both, when I awoke. Now you interpret the dream,' he said. 'I think,' said Sigurd, 'that there is little need to interpret it, because when you thought you saw this cruel bear with all its hairs turned forward, and you thought that it would sink the ship, I see clearly that it is the fetch of Odd, our kinsman, and he is angry with us. And this is why you thought the bear fierce towards us. This I can tell you that we will never get a fair wind to sail with us, unless he comes with us two.'

'He will now not join us even if we ask him,' said Gudmund. 'What shall we do, then?' Sigurd said. 'This I advise,' said Gudmund, 'that we go ashore, and invite him to come with us two.'

'What shall we do if he does not want to go?' said Sigurd. 'We shall give him one of our ships if he does not,' said Gudmund. They went ashore and found Odd and invited him to come with them. He said he would certainly not go. 'We will give you one of our ships, if you come with us,' said Gudmund. 'Then I shall go,' said Odd, 'and I am ready.'

Then Grim followed them to the ship. 'Here are some treasures that I shall give you, kinsman Odd,' said Grim. 'They are three arrows, and together they have a name, and are called Gusir's

Gifts.' He then gave the arrows to Odd. He examined them and said: 'These are the greatest of treasures.' They were gold feathered, and they flew of their own accord, and back again, and there was never any need of looking for them. 'Ketil Trout took these arrows from Gusir, king of the Lapps. They bite all that they are told to, because they are dwarfs' work.'

'I have received no gifts,' said Odd, 'that I think equally fair,' and he thanked his father, and they parted in friendship, and Odd clambered aboard the ship and said that they should sail away from the island, and they unfurled the sails on Odd's ship, and so did they on the other.

Now they got a good wind and they sailed north to Finnmark, where the wind dropped, and they made for a harbour and stayed there that night, and there was a number of Lappish huts up from the shore. In the morning the crew went ashore from Gudmund's ship and raided each hut and plundered the Lapp women. They were angry at this treatment and yelled a lot. The crew on Odd's ship talked with Odd about going ashore, but he would not allow it. Gudmund came back to the ship that evening. Odd said, 'You went ashore?'

'That I did,' he said, 'and I had marvellous entertainment making the Lapp women shriek. Will you go with me tomorrow?'

'I will not,' said Odd.

When they had stayed for three nights, they got a fair wind, and there is nothing said of them until they got to Bjarmaland. They brought their ships to the river called the Dvina. Islands are numerous in that river. They cast anchor off a headland that jutted away from the mainland. Ashore they saw that many men had come out of the forest and gathered all in one place. Odd said, 'What do you think those people doing ashore, Gudmund?'

'I do not know,' he said, 'but what do you think, kinsman Odd?'

'I think,' he said, 'that this must be a great sacrifice or a funeral ale. Now you guard the ships, Gudmund, but Asmund and I will go ashore.' When they came to the forest, they saw a large building. Night was falling. They went to the door and took a look and saw many things. People were sitting on both benches. They saw that by the door was a vat. It was so well lit that there was no shadow, except behind the vat. It sounded as if the people within were happy. 'Do you know anything of their tongue?' said Odd. 'Not any more than birds' chirruping,' said Asmund. 'Or do you think you understand any of it?'

'No more than you,' said Odd. 'But do you see that one man serving drinks to both benches? I have a suspicion that he knows how to speak the Norse tongue. Now I will go in,' said Odd, 'and take up position where I think it is most hopeful, but you must await me here for a while.'

He then went in and took up a place near the entrance, and waited until the servant walked past. Then the servant found himself grabbed by Odd's hands and Odd lifted him over his head, but he shouted and told the Bjarmians that trolls had taken him. Then they sprang up and made for him on one side, but Odd fought them off with the servant. And it ended up that Odd and Asmund took the servant outside, and they did not feel brave enough to come out after them.

They came down to the ships with the servant, and Odd sat him on the seat with him and questioned him, but he held his peace. 'There is no need for that,' said Odd, 'because I know that you know how to speak the Norse tongue.' Then the servant said, 'What do you want to ask me?' Odd said, 'How long have you been here?'

'A few years,' he said. 'What do you think of it?' said Odd. 'I have never been,' said the servant, 'in a worse place than this.'

'What would you say,' said Odd, 'we could do that the Bjarmians would hate worst?'

'That's a good question,' he said. 'A mound stands on the riverbanks. It is made of two parts, silver and earth. Silver is placed there for each person who goes from the world, and so, when he came into the world, as much earth. The Bjarmians will think it the worst thing you can do if you go to the mound and bear away the silver.'

Odd called to Gudmund and Sigurd, and said. 'Your crew shall go to the mound following the servant's directions.' Then they prepared to go ashore, but Odd remained behind to guard the ships. The servant stayed with him.

Chapter Five

Then they went on till they came to the mound, and they gathered bags of treasure, because there was much silver. When they were ready, they went to the ships. Odd asked how it had gone, and they were cheerful and said there was no lack of loot. 'Now you shall,' said Odd, 'take the servant and watch him closely, because his eyes keep turning to the land as if he thought it not so bad with the Bjarmians as he let us think.' Odd went to the mound, but Gudmund and Sigurd guarded the ships. They sat and sifted the earth for silver, and the servant sat in between them, but then they saw him run up into the country, and they saw him no more.

It is said of Odd that he came to the mound. Odd said: 'Now we will gather bags ourselves, each after his own strength, so that our trip is not wasted.' It was dawn when they came away from the mound. They went until the sun had risen. Odd then halted. 'Why have you stopped?' said Asmund. 'I see a large crowd coming down from the forest,' said Odd. 'What shall we do now?' said Asmund. Then they all saw the crowd. 'This this does not look very good,' said Odd, 'for my quiver is back in the ship. Now I will go off into the forest and cut myself a club with this axe that I have in my hand, but you must go on to the headland that juts out into the river.' And so they did. When he came back, he had a big club in his hand. 'What do you think,' said Asmund, 'caused this crowd?'

'I think,' said Odd, 'that the servant escaped Gudmund and he has carried a warning of us to the Bjarmians, because I think that he thought being here was not as bad as he said. Now we must spread out in an array across the headland.'

Then the crowd hurried towards them, and Odd recognised the servant in the forefront. Odd called to him and said, 'Why did you lead us astray?' The servant said, 'I wished to learn what you liked best.'

'Where did you go?' said Odd. 'Inland,' he said, 'to tell the Bjarmians about you.'

'How do they like this business?' said Odd. 'I spoke up for you so well,' he said, 'that they will now do business with you.'

'That we will do gladly,' said Odd, 'when we get on board our ships.'

'It seems the Bjarmians think the least they could do is complete the business now.'

'What shall we trade?' said Odd. 'They want to trade weapons and give you silver for iron.' 'We do not buy it,' said Odd. 'Then let us fight,' said the servant. 'It's up to you,' said Odd.

Then Odd told his band that they should throw into the river any corpses that fell from the enemy troop, - 'because they will immediately use their magic against us, if they reach of any of those who are dead.' After that the fight began, and Odd went through the ranks, wherever he came to them, and cut down the Bjarmians as if they were saplings, and it was both a hard fight and long. But in the end the Permians fled and Odd chased the fugitives and then turned back and examined his troop, and few had fallen, but the majority of the slain were people of the land. 'Now we can do business,' said Odd. 'Let us now collect silver weapons in heaps.' And so they did, and then went to their ships. When they got there, the ships were all gone. Then Odd seemed short of friends. 'What shall we now do?' said Asmund. 'There are two ways to see it,' said Odd. 'Either they have taken the ships round the other side of the islands, or they have betrayed us worse than we expected.'

'That cannot be,' said Asmund. 'I will try to find out,' said Odd.

He went to the wood and kindled a fire up in a big tree. It caught light so that the flame stood at ear height. Then they saw that ships were coming to land. There was a joyful meeting between the kinsmen, and they sailed away with the loot, and nothing is said of their journey until they came to Finnmark and into that same harbour as they had been earlier.

When night began, they woke to hear a great crash up in the air, like they had never heard before. Odd asked Sigurd and Gudmund if they had heard tell of this before anywhere. And when they were discussing these things, there was another crash, and that noise was not less than the first. Then came a third, and it was the greatest. 'What do you think, Odd,' said Gudmund, 'causes this?' Odd said: 'I have heard tell that two winds will blow at the same time in the air and clash and from their collision will come a big crash. Now we should expect bad weather to come.'

And they built a bulwark across their ships and prepared other things, after Odd's instructions, and it was all done, they had made their arrangements, when weather struck so evil that it drove them away from land, and they ran out of control and had to keep bailing. So the weather became so bad that they thought that their vessels would founder under them. Then Gudmund called from his ship to Odd and said: 'What should be done now?'

'One thing should be done now,' said Odd. 'What is that?' said Gudmund. 'Take all Lappish plunder and throw it overboard,' said Odd. 'What will that achieve?' said Gudmund. 'Let them decide that for themselves,' said Odd. It was done, the Lappish plunder was all broken up. Then they saw that it was driven along one side of the ship, and back the other, so that it came up into one mass, and then it was driven rapidly against the wind, so that it was soon out of sight. Soon after this they saw land, but the wind kept up and drove them to ashore, and they were then most exhausted except Odd and his kin and Asmund.

They reached the land now. It is not told how long they had been at sea. They unloaded their ships. Odd then advised that they drag their ships up and build strong defences. Then they set about it, and built themselves a hut. And when they had finished this, they explored the land. Odd thought that it must be an island. They saw that there was no lack of animals, and they shot them, as they needed food.

It happened one day when Odd had gone to the forest, he saw a huge bear. He shot at it and did not miss, and when the animal was dead, he flayed off the whole skin. Then he put a spike in its mouth and right through it. He let it stand mid-path, and facing towards the mainland. Odd had a happy time on the island.

But one evening, they were out when they saw a number of people on the mainland, and that crowd gathered on the headland, people both big and small. 'What do you think, kinsman Odd,' said Gudmund, 'that this crowd is?'

'I don't know,' said Odd, 'but I will try to go ashore and listen to what they are talking about.'

Odd asked Asmund to go with him. They went

to the seaside, and stepped into the boat and rowed to the headland and put up oars and listened to the people talk. Now one who was a chief began to say, 'As you know, a few children have come to the island which we own, and done us great damage, and I come here to propose that we kill these squatters on our property. I have a bracelet on my arm. I will give it to those who will work their death.' A woman came forward to the assembly and said, 'We are fond of gewgaws, us women, so give me the ring.'

'Yes,' said the giant, 'you will do it well, the job which you carry out.'

Now to return to Odd, they went back home, and told them what had happened, what they had heard. But sooner than expected they saw that woman wading across the sound from the mainland to the island. She wore a leather robe, and was so large in size and evil-looking that they thought they had never seen such a creature. She went to the ships and took the two prows and shook them so that they thought the ships would all be broken. She walked up the path, but Odd put himself behind the bear. He had already put glowing embers in the mouth of the beast. He now took an arrow and shot it right through the beast. She saw the arrow that flew at her, and stopped it with the palm of her hand, and it bit no more than if it had hit stone. Then Odd took Gusir's Gifts and shot one like he had the first. She put up her other hand, and it went through it and into her eye and out the back of her head. She still came in their direction. Odd shot the third arrow. Then she put up her other hand and spat in it before, and it went as it had before, into her eye and out the back of the head. She now turned around and went back to the mainland and told them it had not gone smoothly. They stayed peacefully on the island for a while.

Chapter Six

One evening, when they were there present outside their hut, they saw that a group had gathered on the headland as they had before. Odd and Asmund rowed to land and rested their oars. Then the chief spoke up on the headland. 'It is a great surprise,' he said, 'that we cannot kill these children. I sent there the noblest woman, but they have a creature that blows arrows and fire out of its nostrils and mouth, and now it follows that I am so sleepy that I must go home.' And so did Asmund and Odd.

Yet a third evening, they saw the same thing happen on the main land, and Odd and Asmund rowed there and listened. The same man began to speak up on the headland. 'It is as you know, that we have condemned these children, and nothing has come about, but now a vision is given to me.'

'What do you see now happening?' asked his comrades. 'What I see,' he said, 'is that here are two children arrived by boat, and they listen to what we say, and I will send them a gift.'

'Now we must be getting away quickly,' said Odd. And immediately a stone flew from the headland and came down where their boat had been, and then they rowed back. Then the chief said, 'This is a great wonder! Their boat is still whole and so are they. I will throw another stone, and a third, but if they miss each time then I will leave them alone.' So great was the third stone that Odd's boat was flooded. Then they rowed away from the shore, and the giant began to speak: 'They are still safe and so is their boat, but now I am so sleepy that I cannot stay awake.' And then the giants went home. Odd said, 'Now it will make sense to pull the boat ashore.'

'What do you want do now?' said Asmund. 'Now I must know where this group lives.'

They went ashore and came to a cave, and a fire burned inside. They took up position and saw that trolls sat on both benches. An ogre sat on the throne. He was both big and evil-looking. He had long black hair like whalebone. He had a snotty nose and wicked eyes. His woman sat next to him. To describe one is to describe the other. Then the chief said, 'Now a vision is given to me, and I see the island, but now I know who they are who are there. They are kinsmen, the sons of Grim Hairycheek, Odd and Gudmund. I see that the Lapps have sent them here, and they believe that we shall kill them, but we cannot bring about that outcome, because I see that Odd is fated to live much longer than others. Now I will give them a wind to get away as fair as that the Lapps gave them to come here.' Odd said between his teeth: 'Of all men and trolls you give the worst gifts.'

'This I see, too, that Odd has the arrows called Gusir's Gifts, and so I will give him a name and call him Arrow-Odd.' Odd then took one of Gusir's Gifts and put it to the string, and intended to pay him back for his fair wind. When he heard the whine of the arrow that was upon him, he dodged it and collided with the rock, and the arrow came under one armpit of the woman and out the other, but she ran up and flew at the giant and scratched him. The trolls jumped up from both benches, and some helped him, but others his woman. Odd shot the second of Gusir's Gifts into the giant's eye and after that went to the ships, and the brothers were jubilant. 'How far did you go, Odd?' said Gudmund. Odd then recited a verse:

> *'I sought my goal*
>
> *With Gusir's Gifts*
>
> *Between the crags*
>
> *And burning fire.*
>
> *An ogre I hit*
>
> *In the eye,*
>
> *But in the ribs*
>
> *His rock-lady.'*

'We expected,' said Gudmund, 'that you would achieve much, seeing as you were so long away, or did something else happen during your journey?'

'A name was given to me,' said Odd and recited:

> *'I got my nickname,*
>
> *That I have wished for,*
>
> *Down from the crags*
>
> *Ogres called it,*
>
> *They said Arrow-*
>
> *Odd they would give*
>
> *A fine wind*
>
> *To cross the waves.'*

Wind was promised us to sail away from here, and I am told that the breeze will not be worse than that the Lapps gave us when we came here.'

They now readied themselves for the journey with as fine a show as before, and then went, and when they got some way from land the same gale as before struck them, so it swept them out to the sea, and often they had to bail, and they had no relief from the weather until they came to the same harbour as before, from which they had been driven, and then all the huts were derelict, and when they got a good wind they sailed to Hrafnista, arriving late in the winter. Grim was happy and invited them home with all his followers, and they accepted this offer. They put all their belongings into the hands of Grim and stayed with him for the winter.

Chapter Seven

Odd was so famous for this that no one thinks any other such thing has been achieved from Norway. There was great joy in the winter and much drinking. When spring came, Odd asked his kinsmen what they wished to do next. 'You can decide for us,' they said. 'Then I will go on Viking raids,' said Odd. He then told Grim that he wanted four ships to be readied to sail from the land. When Grim knew that, he took charge and told Odd when they were prepared. 'Now I want,' said Odd, 'you to direct us to some Viking you think worthy of us.' Grim said, 'Halfdan is the name of a Viking. He anchors in the east, off Elfar Skerries and has thirty ships.'

When they were ready, they sailed south round Norway, and when they came to the Elfar Skerries they found anchorage for their ships, but Halfdan was not far off. And when they had pitched their tents Odd went off with a few men to where the Vikings were moored. Odd saw a huge dragonship in the fleet. He called out to the ship and asked who the commander was. They lifted up the awnings, 'Halfdan is the name of this fleet's leader, but who asks?'

'He is called Odd.'

'Are the Odd who travelled to Bjarmaland?'

'I have been there,' said Odd. 'What is your errand here?' Halfdan said. 'I want to know which one of us is the greater man,' said Odd. 'How many ships have you?' Halfdan said. 'We have three vessels,' said Odd, 'all big ones with a hundred and twenty men aboard each, and we will be here tomorrow to meet with you.'

'We will sleep soundly despite that,' said Halfdan. Odd rowed away and came back to his people and told them what had happened. 'Now we will have a job,' said Odd, 'but I have now decided what we will do. We'll carry our cargo to land, put it ashore to make our ships lighter, but we will cut down some trees and put on each ship the largest and most leafy,' and so they did. And when they were ready, Odd said: 'I want you, Gudmund and Sigurd, to board the dragonship from the other side.' And so they did, and now quietly they rowed towards the ships which were anchored down the inlet. Odd rowed out to the dragonship, and when they were on both flanks, the vikings were taken by surprise, because the attackers swung trees against the dragonship with a man on every branch, and beat at the vikings through the tent awnings, and Odd and Asmund fought so fiercely that they had soon cleared the dragon up as far as the quarterdeck before Halfdan got to his feet, and they slew him there on the quarterdeck, and then Odd gave them two choices, if either they wanted to keep up the fight or give up, but they took the easier option and surrendered to Odd. He picked out all the men that he thought toughest. Odd took the dragonship into his possession and a second ship, but all other ships he gave to the Vikings. He took all the treasure himself. He gave the dragonship a name and called it Halfdan's Bequest.

They sailed home to Hrafnista having achieved a great victory, and stayed there over winter. But when spring came, Odd prepared to journey from the land. When they were ready, Odd asked his father, 'Where can we find a raider who is truly exceptional?' Grim said, 'Soti is the name of a Viking, and I will tell you how to get to him. He lies south of Skid. He has thirty ships and men.'

Chapter Eight

The kinsmen now moored in five ships south off Skida and sailed away from Hrafnista. But as the summer wore on Soti heard about Odd's movements and went to meet him and sailed day and night so that they might encounter each other. Then Soti ran into contrary winds, and he said, 'Let us lay our ships one alongside the other in a line, and I will put my boat in the middle, because I have heard that Odd is a daring man, and I think that he will sail his ships straight for us. But when they come and have reefed their sails, we will encircle their ships and let not one mother's son escape.'

Now to speak of the plans of Odd. 'I know what he and his men plan,' he said, 'They believe that we will sail straight at their vessels.'

'Will that not be rather unwise?' said Gudmund. 'Do not disappoint Soti,' said Odd, 'but we should take countermeasures. I think,' he said, 'I'll sail first in my dragonship to where Soti is. We'll clear the whole deck back to the mast.' And so they did, and the dragonship Halfdan's Bequest went fast. The ship was all covered with iron right round the prow, so it went with its keel just touching bottom. 'I intend to sail the dragonship straight for Soti,' said Odd, 'but you will sail in my wake. And I think that the ropes between their vessels will break.'

Odd sailed that dragonship as fast as it could go, but Soti learnt of his coming no earlier before he sailed straight up to him up and cut apart the links between the ships, and Odd and Asmund ran past the mast clad for war. They surprised him, rushed aboard the ship, and then they cleared the dragonship and killed him before Gudmund came to join them. Then Odd gave the Vikings the option whether they wanted to take peace from him or keep up the fight, but they decided on peace with Odd. Odd took the dragonship, but gave the other ships to the rest.

Then they sailed home to Hrafnista with great wealth, and Grim was happy to see them, and they stayed there over the winter in great respect. But when spring came, Odd readied the ships to sail, and he was now very choosy about the troop he picked to go along with him. Odd gave Gudmund and Sigurd the dragonship Soti's Bequest. He had the whole of the dragonship Halfdan's Bequest painted, and gilded both dragon heads and the weather vane. When the journey was prepared, Odd went to Grim, his father, and said, 'Now tell me where the best raider you know of is.'

'It is clear,' said Grim, 'that you are not satisfied with being great men, since it seems to you that no one could withstand you, but now I refer you to the best two Vikings I know of, and the best in everything. One is Hjalmar the Brave, and the other is called Thord Prow-Gleam.'

'Where are they,' said Odd, 'and how many ships do they have?'

'They have fifteen ships,' said Grim, 'and a hundred men aboard each.'

'Where is their homeland?' said Odd. 'Hlodver is the name of the King of Sweden. They stay with him in the winter, but stay aboard their warships in the summer.' And when they were ready, they went, and Grim went with them to the ships, and the father and son parted with much affection.

Chapter Nine

It is said of Odd that they sailed out from Hrafnista when they got wind, and nothing is told of their journey until they came to Sweden, at a place where one headland jutted out to sea from the mainland. They raised the awnings of their ships. Odd went ashore to see what was about, but there on the other side under the headland were fifteen ships and a camp on the land. He sees that there were games being played outside the tents. The leaders of these ships were Hjalmar and Thord.

Odd walked back to his ships, and told them the news. Gudmund asked what they should do. 'Now we will split our men in halves,' said Odd. 'You shall bring your ships around the headland and yell a war cry at the men on the shore, and I will walk overland with my half of the troop up into the forest, and we shall shout another battle cry at them, and it may be,' said he, 'that this will shake them. Come to think of it, they might flee into the woods and we won't need to do anything more.'

But it is said of Hjalmar and his men that when they heard the battle cry of Gudmund that they didn't heed it, but when they heard another battle cry from the land, they stood still a while. And when the time of the war-cry was past, they played as before. Now both groups turned back from the headland, and Odd and Gudmund met. 'I don't know,' said Odd, 'that these people that we have met here are so easily frightened.'

'What will you now do?' said Gudmund. 'Quickly now is my advice,' said Odd, 'We should not sneak up on these men. Here we shall lie tonight beside the headland and wait here for tomorrow.' Then they went ashore with their troop up to meet Hjalmar, but when his men saw the Vikings ashore, then they armoured themselves to meet them. Hjalmar asked, when they met, who led the troop. Odd answered: 'There are more chiefs than one.'

'What is your name?' said Hjalmar. 'My name is Odd, son of Grim Hairycheek out of Hrafnista.'

'Are you the Odd that went to Bjarmaland recently? What is your errand here?'

'I want to know,' said Odd, 'who is the greater man of us.'

'How many ships do you have?' said Hjalmar. 'I have five ships,' said Odd, 'and how many troops have you?'

'We have fifteen ships,' said Hjalmar. 'It is heavy odds,' said Odd. 'Ten of my ships' crews shall sit back,' said Hjalmar, 'and we'll fight it out man to man.'

Then both sides prepared for battle and the troops lined up and fought while day lasted. In the evening the peace shield was held up, and Hjalmar asked Odd how he thought the day had gone. But he was very pleased. 'Do you want to continue the game?' said Hjalmar. 'I will not consider any other option,' said Odd, 'for that I have met no better boys or hardier men, and we will continue the fight in daylight.' And everyone did as Odd suggested, and they bound their wounds and returned to camp for the evening. But the morning after both sides drew up their troops for battle and fought all that day. And as the day wore on, they drew up a truce. Then Odd asked what Hjalmar thought of the battle that day. But he was very pleased. 'Do you want,' said Hjalmar, 'to have this game on a third day?'

'In this case, it would settle things between us,' said Odd. Then Thord said, 'Is there plenty of treasure and money in your ships?'

'Far from it,' said Odd, 'we have got no plunder this summer.'

'I think,' said Thord, 'that never have such foolish men met, because we fight for nothing, only pride and ambition.'

'What do you suggest we do?' said Odd. 'Do you not think it good advice,' said Thord, 'that we combine our efforts?'

'It pleases me well,' said Odd, 'but I am not

sure what Hjalmar would think.'

'I want only the Viking laws,' said Hjalmar, 'which I have always had.'

'This I will know,' said Odd, 'when I hear them, how agreeable to me they are.'

Then Hjalmar: 'This is the first rule, that I will not eat raw meat, nor my troop, because it is many people's custom to squeeze flesh in cloth and call it cooked, but it seems to me that it's a custom more fit for wolves than humans. I will not rob merchants or farmers more than now and then to cover my immediate needs. I never rob women, even if we find them in the land alone with a lot of possessions, and no woman's to be taken to the ship to be raped, and if it may be that she is taken unwillingly, then he who does will lose his life whether he is rich or poor.' [69]

'Your laws seem good to me,' said Odd, 'and they will not stand in the way of our comradeship.' And then they joined forces, and it is said that now they had such a great troop that they had as many as Hjalmar had before they met.

Chapter Ten

After that Odd asked where they could expect to get loot. But Hjalmar said: 'On Zealand I know are five berserks, hardier than other men I have heard of, one called Brand, another Agnar, the third Asmund, fourth Ingjald, and fifth Alf. They are all

---

[69] Comparable Viking laws appear in *The Saga of Fridthjof,* while Robin Hood is similarly chivalrous for a medieval bandit in the Middle English poem *A Gest of Robyn Hode.*

brothers and have six vessels, all large. What do you say now, Odd, we do?'

'I want to sail,' said Odd, 'to where the berserk are.' They came to Zealand with their fifteen ships and heard the news that berserks were gone ashore to meet their mistresses. Then Odd went ashore alone to meet them. And when they met, a battle began, and it ended up that he killed them all, but was not wounded. When Odd went ashore, Asmund missed him and spoke to Hjalmar, 'Yes,' he said, 'There is no doubt that Odd has gone ashore, so we should not be idle meanwhile.' Hjalmar sailed with six ships to where the other Vikings were, and began a battle, and just as Odd came down from the land Hjalmar had taken the ship. And now they told each other their news, and both had amassed wealth and honours.

Now Hjalmar invited Odd to come with him to Sweden, and Odd accepted. But the Halogalanders, Gudmund and Sigurd, went north to Hrafnista with their troops, agreeing to meet again at the Gautelf. When Hjalmar and the rest reached Sweden, King Hlodver welcomed them with open arms, and they stayed there for the winter, and much honour was done to Odd, because the king thought he had no match. Odd had been there only a little while before the king gave him five farms. The king had an only daughter, named Ingibjorg. She was very attractive and skilled in womanly arts. Odd asked Hjalmar why he did not ask for Ingibjorg's hand, - 'because I see that both your hearts beat as one.'

'I have asked her,' he said, 'but the king will not give his daughter to anyone who doesn't have a king's rank.'

'Then we shall gather the army next summer,' said Odd, 'and give the king two choices, fight us and or give you his daughter.'

'I'm not sure about that,' said Hjalmar, 'because I have long had sanctuary here.' They stayed there quietly for the winter. But in the spring they went raiding when they were ready.

Chapter Eleven

Now nothing is told of their journey until they met at the Gautelf, and discussed where they should sail that summer. Odd said most of all he was for going west over the sea. Then they had twenty vessels and Odd skippered the dragonship Halfdan's Bequest. They came to Scotland, and made raids there, harrying and burning everywhere where they went, and there was no stopping them until they laid everywhere under tribute. From there they went to the Orkneys, and they put them under them and stayed there for the winter. But in the spring they went to Ireland and raided both along the sea and inland. Odd went nowhere without Asmund with him. But children and women and men fled away into the woods and forests, hiding their possessions and themselves.

There was a day when Odd and Asmund were together some way up-country. Odd had his quiver on his back, and a bow in his hand, and they wanted to see if they could find anyone. Now before Odd suspected, a bowstring hummed and an arrow flew from the wood and it hit Asmund, and he fell and died quickly. This seemed to Odd the worst news he had suffered in his lifetime. He went ashore, but left Asmund there, and Odd was in so evil a mind, he intended nothing else but give the Irish all the hurt he could, whatever came to mind. He came at once to a clearing where a large number of women and men stood. He saw a man in a very expensive tunic, and with a bow in his hand, but the arrows were in the ground before him. Odd was sure that he would find his revenge where the man was. He took out an arrow, one of Gusir's Gifts, and laid it to the bowstring, and aimed at this man. It struck him in the middle, and then he fell down dead. Now he shot at the others, so that he killed three more. And now the people fled into the forests. Odd was so evil in heart to the Irish that he meant to do them all that harm he was able. He now went up a great forest path. He tore up every shrub by the roots that was in his way. He pulled up one shrub, which was less firmly rooted than the others. Then he saw a door and pulled it up and went down into the ground. There he found four women in an earth-house[70], and one was far more attractive than the others. He seized her hand and tried to pull her out of the house. She spoke then and said: 'Let me loose, Odd,' she said.

'What troll are you,' he said, 'to know I am named Odd and not anything else?'

'I knew,' she said, 'when you came here, who you were, and I know that Hjalmar is with you, and I know to tell him if I am taken unwillingly to the ships.'

'Nevertheless, you'll come,' said Odd. Now the women took hold of her and wanted to keep her there, but she ordered them stop. 'I will bargain with

---

[70] Similar earth-houses appear in The Saga of the Volsungs; Chapter 17 of this saga; and the Old English poem *The Wife's Lament*.

you,' she said, 'you should let me go in peace, for I have no lack of treasure.'

'Far from it that I want your treasure,' said Odd, 'for I don't lack gold or silver.'

'Then I will make you a shirt,' she said. 'It is still the case,' said Odd, 'that I have enough of shirts and shirt-making.'

'You will never have,' she said, 'such a shirt as that I will make, because it shall be sewn with gold, and made out of silk. I will give the shirt qualities so you will not have had such great virtues before.'

'Let me hear them,' said Odd. 'You shall never be cold in it, neither by sea nor on land. You shall not be tired when swimming, and nor will fire hurt you, and never shall hunger grip you, and iron shall not bite you, and it will ward you from all things except one.'

'What's that?' said Odd. 'Iron will bite you,' she said, 'if you retreat, even if you're in the shirt.'

'I've better things to do in battle than to flee,' said Odd, 'and by when shall it be made?'

'By next summer,' she said, 'at the same time of day as now, and with the sun in the south. Then we will meet here in this same clearing.'

'What do you think,' said Odd, 'I will do to you Irish then, if you do not fulfil this, as I have much to pay back for what they did to Asmund?'

'Do you think you still have not avenged him,' she said, 'when you have killed my father and my three brothers?'

'It does not seem to me that I have avenged him at all,' said Odd. They settled their deal and went their ways.

Odd went to where Asmund was, took him up now and laid him on his back and so went down to the sea. Hjalmar had come ashore with all his men, and was looking for Odd. They met near the ship, and Hjalmar asked what had happened, and Odd told him. 'Did you avenge him?' said Hjalmar. Poetry sprang to Odd's lips:

I ran down that wide

Wagon trail road,

To the fierce arrows

I turned my face.

To have Asmund back

By my side

I would give

All my gold.'

'What shall we do now?' said Hjalmar. 'You'll now want to plunder here, and do evil everywhere.'

'Far from it,' said Odd, 'because I want now to be off quickly.' The Vikings were very surprised by this. But Hjalmar said it should be as Odd wished. They raised a howe over Asmund. The Vikings were angry about this, and they grumbled about Odd behind his back. But he acted as though he did not know it.

They sailed west until they came to Hlesey. An

earl, who is not named, was there and he had thirty ships. They met in battle, and there was a fierce fight. Odd then cleared himself of the coward's name that the Vikings gave him in Ireland. Odd and Hjalmar won the victory in this battle. From there, they sailed to Denmark where they heard the news that a troop had been mustered against them to avenge the five berserks who they had defeated before they went west to Ireland. Two earls led the troop, and it ended so when they met they killed them both, and took tribute from the land.

Chapter Twelve

Now they divided their forces, and Gudmund and Sigurd sailed north to Hrafnista, and they settled there quietly and decided to give up raiding. But Odd stayed in Denmark for the winter, while Hjalmar went to Sweden with his followers, and they agreed to meet east in Skane in the spring, and both stayed quietly at home over the winter. In the spring, Hjalmar and Thord Prow-gleam sailed from the east at the time agreed for them to meet. When they met, Hjalmar asked where Odd wanted to go that the summer. But he said that he wanted to go to Ireland. 'You didn't want to plunder there last summer,' said Hjalmar. 'However it might have then,' he said, 'I shall now go there in the summer.'

Now they sailed from the land, and they had a good wind until that they came to Ireland. Odd said: 'Let us camp here, but I will go up-country alone.'

'I will come with you,' said Hjalmar. 'I will go alone,' said Odd, 'because I am seeing here some women in the woods.' Odd went until he came to that same clearing where Olvor had agreed to meet him, and she had not come. He was already filled with great anger for the Irishmen and right away resolved to harry the land. But after he had gone thus for a while, he heard some carts coming towards him. He found it was Olvor, and she greeted him first, 'Now I hope you won't be angry with me, though I am later than I said.'

'Is the shirt done?' said Odd.

'I do not doubt it,' she said, 'and now you shall sit down with me, and I will see how well the shirt fits you.' And so he did, took it and unfolded it and put it on, and it fitted perfectly in all respects.

'Do all the qualities go with the shirt,' said Odd, 'that you spoke of?'

'They do,' she said.

'How so,' said Odd. 'Did you make this treasure yourself?' Then poetry came to her lips:

This shirt is sewn out of silk

From six lands:

An arm in Ireland,

The other with Lapps in the north,

Started by Saxon maidens,

But Sutherey women spun it,

Welsh wives wove it,

On the warp of Othjodan's mother.'

Then poetry came to Odd's lips:

'Not like the hauberk

Of blue rings

Ice cold about me

Upon my body,

When down my sides,

This silk shirt,

Gold embroidered,

Went close.'

'How do you find the shirt?' she said.

But he was well pleased. 'Now, choose your reward for the shirt,' said Odd.

'Here there has been little happiness,' she said, 'since my father was slain, and the land is running out of my control. Therefore I will choose the reward that you stay here three winters.'

'Then we must make another deal,' said Odd, 'and you can come with me and be my wife.'

'You must think me eager to get a husband,' she said, 'but I shall accept.' Then Odd looked around and saw nearby a group of warriors. He asked if this troop was sent to kill him. 'Far from it,' she said. 'These men shall accompany you down to your ships, and you will now leave with more honour than last summer.' He returned to his ship and these warriors with him, and they met Hjalmar at the tents.

Now Odd asked Hjalmar to stay with him for three winters, and so he agreed. Odd now married

Olvor. But in the summer they stayed aboard their warships and killed the Vikings attacking there. And when they had sat there for such a time as was decided, they had wiped out all the vikings, both near and far in Ireland, some were killed, while some fled. By then Odd was so tired of being there that nothing could discourage him from leaving.

Olvor and Odd had a girl called Ragnhild. They argued about it because Odd wanted to take her with him, but Olvor refused this. They asked Hjalmar about it, and he said that the girl should grow up with her mother.

When they were ready, they sailed away and came to England. They heard that there lay a Viking named Skolli, and he had forty ships. And when they dropped anchor, Odd went off in a boat and wanted to have words with Skolli. But when they met, he asked Odd what errand he had in that country. 'I mean do battle with you,' said Odd. 'Why do you want to do me harm?' said Skolli. 'Nothing,' said Odd, 'but I will have your treasure and life because you are making war on the king who is ruler here.' His name was Edmund. 'Are you the Odd,' said Skolli, 'who went to Bjarmaland a long time ago?'

'This is the same man,' said Odd. 'I am not so vain,' said Skolli, 'that I'm going to think myself your equal. Now you must learn why I fight King Edmund.'

'Well that I may,' said Odd. 'The king killed my father here in the country, and many of my kin, and then he settled in the realm. But I have sometimes seized half of the country, and sometimes a third. Now I think you would get greater glory if you combined your troop with mine, and we kill King

Edmund, and put the realm under us. I will seal this deal with witnesses.'

'Please,' said Odd, 'summon eight farmers off the land to swear oaths on your behalf.'

'So shall it be,' said Skolli. Now Odd went to their ships and found Hjalmar and told him that if it went as Skolli had said, they should fight alongside him. They now slept through the night. In the morning they went ashore with all their followers. Skolli had been busy that night, and he had come down from the land with the farmers, and they swore oaths of support. After that they joined their forces and went up-country and went to war, burning everything and destroying everything which they came to. But the people fled away and went to the king. However, in the south of the country they met, and the battle began between them, and they fought for three days. And it ended that King Edmund fell there. Odd laid the land under him and stayed there for the winter. In the spring Skolli offered to give him the land. Odd refused to accept, - 'but I can suggest you give it to Hjalmar.' But Hjalmar refused. 'In that case,' said Odd, 'we should give Skolli the land.' And he accepted it, and said that they could stay there at any time they wanted, whether it was winter or summer. They now equipped twenty ships to sail from the land, and nothing is told of their journey until they came south of Skida.

Chapter Thirteen

Two kings are mentioned. One was named Hlodver, the other Haki. They were there with thirty ships. When Odd and his men lay with their ships by the shore, ten ships came rowing at them. And when they met, no words were bandied, because at once a battle broke out between them. Odd had twenty ships. They attacked so hard that Odd had scarcely ever come to such a pass that he had been so sorely pressed. But in the end it worked out that they defeated the ten ships. Then Odd said, 'They were hardly the terrors they have been reported as.'

'Do you think that?' said Hjalmar. 'These were the scouts of the men who were sent out to meet us.' But they rested little time, then the twenty ships from offshore rowed towards them, and at once broke out a battle so hard and intense, that Odd had never met such great men, neither at sea, nor on land. And the fighting ended up with both kings dead and all with them. As it is told, Odd and Hjalmar had no greater force than they could sail away with in one boat, and they came to the islands that are called the Elfar Skerries. In the islands are creeks called Tronuvagar. They saw there were two ships, and with black awnings over them both. This was the beginning of the summer. 'Now I don't want them,' said Hjalmar, 'to notice us, for those vikings lie quiet under the awnings.'

'I cannot accept,' said Odd, 'that I have no words with men who I meet on my way.'

Now Odd called and asked who was in charge of the ships. A man lifted the hem of the awnings, and said, 'That man is called Ogmund.'

'Which Ogmund are you?' said Odd. 'Where have you been that you have not heard tell of Ogmund Eythjof's-Bane?' the shipman said. 'I have heard tell of you,' said Odd, 'and never have I seen such an evil-looking person as you.' It is said about this man that he was black of hair, and a tuft hung down over the face where the forelock should have been, but nothing was seen of his face except his teeth and eyes. He had eight men with him, much the same in looks. No iron bit them. They were more like giants than men in terms of stature and evil. Then Ogmund said, 'Who is the man finding fault with me so?'

'He's called Odd,' he said.

'Are you the Odd,' said Ogmund, 'that went to Bjarmaland a long time ago?'

'That is the man,' said Odd, 'who has come.'

'It is good,' said Ogmund, 'for I have sought you for most of my life.'

'What have you my mind?' said Odd. 'Where would you fight, at sea or on land?' Ogmund said. 'I will fight at sea,' said Odd. Then Ogmund and his men took down the awnings. Hjalmar and his crew made ready and loaded stones in his ship. And when they were ready on either side, they had some hard fighting, and lay their ships next to each other. They had a long and hard battle. And when it had gone on for a while, Ogmund raised a peace flag and asked Odd how he thought it went. He said that he thought it went ill. 'Why is that?' Ogmund said. 'Because I have always fought with men before, but now I should think I fight Hel,' said Odd. 'I hacked at your neck before, which I thought easy with the sword I hold, and it did not cut.' Ogmund answered: 'Each of us could say about the other, that he is more a troll than a man. I hacked at your neck, which I thought easy, and the sword I used has never wavered in the fight before, and it did not bite, and do you now wish that we fight anymore?' said

Ogmund, 'or do you wish that we part, because I can tell you how the battle will: here will die the sworn brothers, Hjalmar and Thord, and your troop too. Then will all my warriors die, and only we two will remain standing. But if we fight it out, I will fall to you,' said Ogmund. 'On with the game then,' said Odd, 'until all my troop is wiped out, and yours.' They thrust shields together a second time and fought until only three remained standing, Thord, Hjalmar and Odd. But Ogmund still stood, and eight with him. He spoke: 'Do you now, Odd, want to part, because I now call equal numbers of slain, because things will go as I told you, but you are meant to live much longer than others. You have a shirt that means you cannot be hurt.'

'It seems better to me,' said Odd, 'to part sooner than later as long as you put no name of coward on me.'

'Then we break off now,' Ogmund said, 'Because I call our numbers of slain equal.' Odd said he wanted to get away from the creeks, and they did so, and went to an island. Odd said that three things lay ahead: one was go to the forest and shoot animals, second, to guard the ship. 'I will light a fire,' said Hjalmar, 'and do the cooking.' Odd went to the forest, but Thord kept the ship. When they came back, Thord was gone. They went and looked for him. They found the boat in which he had been securely tied. They looked for Thord and found him in a rock crevice. He had sat there and died. 'This is an evil event,' said Odd, 'We have not had such a loss since Asmund died.' They now look for what caused his death, and found that a spear is under one arm, but the head came out the other. 'That villain Ogmund thought,' said Odd, 'that we weren't even. We shall put into the bays to search for them.' And so they did, but Ogmund had gone away. They sought him through all the skerries, forests, islands and headlands and did not find him, nor hear of him. They went back to Thord, and brought him to Sweden and raised a burial mound over him. Then they went home to Uppsala and told the king the news. The king received them with open arms, and they sat quietly, but when summer came again the king invited them to stay there - 'and I will give you both a ship and crew from the land, so that you may entertain yourselves.'

Chapter Fourteen[71]

It is now told of Odd that they fitted out two ships and he had forty men on each ship. They sailed from the land. Then they were exposed to bad weather, and they came to an island called Samsey. There are bays there called Munarvag. They anchored their ships and raised the awnings. But during the day the gable head on Odd's boat had broken. When morning came, Odd and Hjalmar went ashore to chop down a tree. Hjalmar was accustomed to walk wearing all his armour which he had while fighting. Odd had left his quiver down at his ship, but he wore his shirt day and night. The whole of their troop was asleep. Vikings attacked them by surprise, and their leader was named Angantyr. They were twelve in number, and were all brothers. By this time they had gone around the world and nowhere met resistance. Now they came to where the ships of Odd and Hjalmar were. They attacked the men aboard, and to make a long story short they killed every man on the ships. Then the

---

[71] The encounter with the berserks also appears in Saxo Grammaticus' *Gesta Danorum* and *The Saga of Hervor and Heidrek*.

brothers spoke and said thus: 'It is the case that Arngrim, our father, never said a bigger lie but when he told us these men were hard and mighty vikings, so that no one could stop them, but where we have gone no one has borne himself worse and shown less fight. Let's go home and kill that shit of a man as payback for his lies.'

'There is another question,' said some, 'either Odd and Hjalmar have been most over-praised, or else they have gone ashore, since the weather is good. Let us go ashore and look for them rather than go back untried.' Now the twelve brothers did so, and now came the berserk fit, and they went roaring. Then the berserk fit came upon Angantyr, but it had never happened to him before. Just then Odd and Hjalmar came down from the woods. Now Odd stopped and hesitated. Hjalmar asked what it was. Odd said, 'Something odd keeps happening to me. Sometimes I think that bulls or dogs are yelling, but sometimes it is like men somewhere screaming, and do you know whose nature it is to behave thus?'

'Yes,' said Hjalmar, 'I know the twelve brothers.'

'Do you know their names?' said Odd. Then a verse came to Hjalmar's lips:

Hervard, Hjorvard,

Hrani, Angantyr,

Bild and Bui,

Barri and Toki,

Tind and Tyrfing,

Two Haddings,

East in Bolm

They were bairns,

Sons of Arngrim

And of Eyfura.

I learned that these men

Are malevolent

And most dishonourable

In their acts.

They are berserks,

Bringers of evil,

Our two ships they swept

Of our loyal sailors.'

Then Odd saw the berserks legging towards them, and poetry came to his lips:

'I see men walking

War-hungry

From Munarvag

In grey mailcoats.

Vile the fight

These men have fought.

Broken our ships

On the beach.'

Odd said: 'It is no good,' he said, 'because I left my quiver and bow when we left the ships, but I have this axe in my hand.' Odd then recited a verse:

'I felt fear

Once,

When they bellowed,

Leaving the longships

(And screaming

Ascended the island)

Inglorious,

Twelve men together.'

Odd then went back to the forest and cut a club, but Hjalmar waited for his return. When he came back, then the berserks came legging up to them. Whereupon Hjalmar said:

'Mighty are the warriors

Leaving the warships,

Twelve men together

Inglorious;

I think this evening

I will be Odin's guest,

Two sworn brothers,

But the twelve will live.'

Then Odd followed with:

'To your word will I

Provide an answer:

They will this evening

Be Odin's guests,

Twelve berserks,

We two shall live.'

Then a verse came to Angantyr's lips:

'It has gone

Hard for you

All your fellows.

Have fallen

And you must follow,

And feast in the hall.'

Then Odd said:

'There are come

Trudging together,

Inglorious,

Those twelve.

One by one, the

Battle waging

Is the hero's way,

Unless his heart fails.'

'Who are these people,' said Odd, 'that we meet here?'

'There is a man named Angantyr,' said the other, 'who is the leader. We are twelve brothers, the sons of Earl Arngrim and of Eyfura from east Flanders[72]. And who asks?' Angantyr said. 'This one is called Odd, son of Grim Hairy-cheek, the other is called Hjalmar the Brave.'

'A warm welcome,' said Angantyr, 'for we have sought you widely.'

'Did you go to our vessels?' said Odd. 'We went there,' said Angantyr, 'and we've taken everything for ourselves.'

'How do you feel now,' said Hjalmar, 'about our meeting?'

'I think,' said Angantyr, 'we should do what you said earlier, fight this one to one, and I want to fight you, Odd, because you have a shirt that means that iron shall not bite you, but I have a sword that is called Tyrfing and dwarves forged it and promised that could bite through anything, even iron or stone. We shall divide our troop into halves, and have seven in one group, and I and four men in the other.

---

[72] In <u>The Saga of Hervor and Heidrek</u> Eyfura is a princess from Gardariki (Russia).

I am said to be equal to the two Haddings. Then there's one more against Tyrfing.' Then Hjalmar said, 'I will fight Angantyr, because I have armour which has kept me from acquiring wounds. It has fourfold rings.'

'It would be a bad idea,' said Odd, 'for we will do well if I fight with Angantyr, but it will be hopeless otherwise.'

'However it goes,' said Hjalmar, 'I shall prevail.' Then Angantyr: 'I want this,' said Angantyr, 'If anyone survives here, let no one rob the dead of weapons. I would have Tyrfing in the mound with me, if I die. And so Odd shall have his shirt and arrows, and Hjalmar his armour.' And so they agreed that they must raise a burial mound over the dead, if they live.

Now first approached the two Haddings, but Odd smote each with his club, and they did not need more. Then one came after the other to fight Odd, and so it ended up that he killed all who came against him. Now Odd took a rest. Then Hjalmar stood up and someone came against him in the contest. They closed their business when he fell. Then came a second, and a third and a fourth. Then came Angantyr, and they fought hard and long, and so it ended up that Angantyr fell before Hjalmar. Then Hjalmar went to a hillock and sat down and sank against it. Odd went to him and recited:

What worries you, Hjalmar?

Your colour is wan.

Wasting your strength

Are multiple wounds;

Your helmet is hacked,

And the hauberk on your chest,

Now I deem you have seen

The end of your days.'

'And have proved that which I told you, that you would not listen to, if you fought with Angantyr.'

'That doesn't matter,' said Hjalmar, 'everyone has their time to die,' and he said this:

'I have sixteen wounds; my byrnie is split,

My sight is darkened, I cannot see.

Angantyr's blade entered my heart:

That sharp sword was steeped in poison.'

'Now I have had a loss,' said Odd, 'that will never be made good as long as I live, and it has now gone badly because of your obstinacy, and we would have got here a great victory, if I had had my way.'

'Now, settle down,' said Hjalmar, 'and I will compose a poem and send it home to Sweden with you.' He said this:

'They'll never hear,

The women back home

That I ever cringed

From sword cuts.

They'll not tease me

About me retreating,

The sly girls

At Sigtuna.

I sailed away from the songs of women,

Eagerly voyaging eastwards with Soti;

Travelling swiftly after joining a troop,

Left at last my friends in the hall.

I went from the white cloaked woman,

To Agnafit on the edge of the sea;

It is true what she told me there,

That I would never be near her again.

I abandoned her, young Ingibjorg,

Hastily determined,

The day of destiny.

She will soon mourn me,

Bitter in her mind

But never again

Shall we meet each other.

Carry there to display,

From my combat,

Helmet and mailcoat

To the royal hall.

Tears will drop

King's daughter,

When she sees broken

The byrnie on my breast.

Five were the farms I had for my own,

But never have I known joy of them;

Now I must lie with my life taken,

Wounded by the sword on Samsey.

Slip the red-gold ring from my hand,

And bear it to young Ingibjorg;

Her misery will remain in her thoughts,

For I'll never be seen in Uppsala again.

Well I remember sitting

With the women persuading

Me not to set out

From there.

Hjalmar will never

Know joy in the king's hall,

Fine company or ale.

Now I wish, too, that you bear my greetings to all our bench companions, and I will mention them by name:

We drank and talked

Many a day,

Alf and Atli,

Eyvind, Trani,

Gizur, Glama,

Gudvard, Starri,

Steinkel, Stikill,

Storolf, Vifil.

Hrafn and Helgi,

Hlodver, Igull

Stein and Kari,

Styr and Ali,

Ossur, Agnar,

Orm and Trandill,

Gylfi and Gauti,

Gjafarr and Raknarr.

Fjolmund, Fjalar,

Frosti and Beinir,

Tindall and Tyrfing,

Two Haddings,

Valbjorn, Vikar,

Audbjorn, Flosi,

Geirbrand, Goti,

Guttorm, Sneril.

Styr and Ari,

Stein and Kari,

Vott, Vesela,

Audbjorn, Hnefi.

We all shared a single bench

Sat at ease;

As a result I am

Reluctant to flee.

Svarfandi, Sigvaldi,

Saebjorn and Kol,

Thrain and Thiostolf,

Thorolf and Sval,

Hrapp and Hadding,

Hunfast, Knui,

Ottar, Egil,

Ingvar and all.

'Now I would ask you,' said Hjalmar of Odd, 'that you do not lay me in a mound beside such evil fiends as these berserk are, for I deem myself much better than they were.'

'That I will give you,' said Odd, 'as you ask, because now it seems to me that you are rapidly going.'

'Now, pull the ring from my hand,' said Hjalmar, 'and bring it to Ingibjorg, and tell her that I sent it to her on my dying day.' Now poetry came to Hjalmar's lips:

The earls sit

All drinking

Ale heartily

In Uppsala.

Many warriors

Weaken at beer,

But alone with my wounds

On the island I suffer.

From the east the raven flies, abandons his bough,

After him the eagle flies as well:

I feed him with flesh for a final time,

Now he will guzzle my dripping gore.

And after that Hjalmar died. Odd dragged the berserks together in a heap and piled timber around them. It was not far from the sea. Here, he laid with them their weapons and clothes, and he robbed none of them. Then he covered them with turf and after that sand. Then he took Hjalmar and laid him on his back, and went down to the sea, and he set him down on the beach, but he went out to the ship, carried to the land every man who had fallen, and lay them in another mound, and it is said by those who have gone there since that you can still see signs today of what Odd did then.

Chapter Fifteen

After that Odd put Hjalmar aboard the ship and set out to sea. Then Odd used his magic, hoisted sail in calm weather and sailed back to Sweden with Hjalmar's corpse. He landed at a place he had chosen. He beached his ship, and put Hjalmar on his back and went to Uppsala with him and set him down in the entrance hall. He went into the hall and carried Hjalmar's armour in his hand and also his helmet and laid them down in the hall before the king and told him what had happened.

Then he went to where Ingibjorg was sitting on a chair. She was sewing a shirt for Hjalmar. 'Here is a ring,' said Odd, 'that Hjalmar sent you on his dying day and greets you with.' She took the ring and looked at it, but said nothing. She sank down then back against the chair posts and died. Odd then burst out laughing and said: 'It is not often that things have gone well recently, so I should be rejoicing. Now they shall enjoy each other dead, which they could not in life.' Odd took her up and carried her in his arms, and laid her in the arms of Hjalmar in the entrance hall, and sent men into the hall after the king and asked him to see how he had done this. After that the King welcomed him, and set Odd on the throne with him. But when he had taken a rest, the king told him that he wanted to hold a funeral ale for Hjalmar and Ingibjorg and raise a burial mound for them. So the king ordered everything to be done as Odd said. When the helmet and armour that Hjalmar had worn was displayed, it seemed he had been a great man worthy of his achievements and the spirit with which he had defended himself, and now they were lying both in one pile. So all the people came to see this remarkable work, for Odd had made it with great honour. Odd now sat quietly over winter with King Hlodver, but in the spring the king gave him men and ten ships, and then in the summer Odd went to look for Ogmund Eythjof's-Bane again but could not find him.

Chapter Sixteen

So it came to pass in the autumn that Odd came to Gautland. There he heard about a Viking named

Saemund. He was told that he was harder to deal with than others. He had fifty five ships. Odd came to him with ten ships, and when they met there was a battle long and hard, with no lack of deeds. And it ended up that evening that all vessels belonging to Odd had been cleared and he was the last of his side standing. Odd jumped overboard when it was near dark. A man saw this. He snatched up a throwing spear, and hurled it after him. It caught in Odd's calves so that it hit the bone. It came to his mind, the way things were at present, he could be said to be on the run. He swam back to the ships, but the Vikings saw Odd and pulled him into the boat. Saemund told them to fix shackles to his feet, and bind his hands with a bow string. It was done as he told them.

Now Odd sat in fetters, and twelve men were told to watch over him, but Saemund had himself taken to the shore and set up camp. Odd said to those who had been told to watch over him, 'Do you wish that I entertain you, or do you wish to entertain me, since it's so dull work?'

'We reckon,' said he who led them, 'that you may not give much entertainment while you are in chains, and meant to be killed tomorrow.'

'I am not afraid of that,' said Odd. 'Everyone has their time to die.'

'Then we choose that you entertain us,' they said. He began to sing and did not stop until they were all asleep. Then Odd crawled to where an axe was lying on the bulkheads. He also managed to twist it so that the edge faced up. Then he turns his shoulders, and rubbed his hands against until he was free. He untied the fetters and got them off his feet.

And when he was free, it seemed to him he had room to move. Now he went to where they slept, and prodded them with the axe handle and told them wake up, - 'because as you slept like fools, the prisoner has got free.' Then he killed them all, took his quiver and climbed into the boat and rowed ashore. Then he went to the woods and pulled the spearhead out his foot, and bound up his wound.

Now it is told of Saemund that he woke up in the tent, and sent men out to the ships where the guards were, and learnt that Odd was away and had killed all the guards, and they missed their friends and went to Saemund and told him what had happened, and now he searched everywhere in Gautland seeking Odd, but Odd was in a different place seeking Saemund.

It was early one morning that Odd came out from the wood. He saw Saemund's tents on the shore, but the ships out in the harbour. He turned back into the forest and cut a club, came down to the tent and felled it on top of Saemund and his men. He killed Saemund and then fourteen more. Then he gives them choices, those aboard, that they shall accept his guidance and make him their chief, and that they preferred. Odd now went home to Sweden and he had but a small troop, and he stayed there over the winter.

Chapter Seventeen

Then Odd sent messengers north to Hrafnista and asked his kin to join him, so Gudmund and Sigurd would come from the north in the spring. They were glad and went to Odd. And when they met, there was a joyful meeting.

Afterwards, they set sail from the land in their ships and keep south hugging the cost, and the water was much shallower, and Odd had never been there before. They now plundered southern Gaul, Frankland and Halsingjaland. Here they wreaked havoc.

Nothing is told of their journey until they wrecked their ships on a certain shore. Here they went ashore with their troops. As they went inland, they saw a house before them. It was built in some way they had never seen before. Up they went to the house. It was made of stone and the door was open. Odd said, 'What do you think, Sigurd, is this house that we have here?'

'I do not know,' he said. 'But what do you think, kinsman Odd?'

'I am not sure,' he said, 'but I expect that men live in the house and will come back here, and we shall not go in as things stand.' They settle down in a place outside the house, but after a while, they saw people hurrying to the house, and also they heard a noise which they had never heard before. 'I think,' said Odd, 'that these are very strange men in this country. We shall now wait here till they come from the house.' It went as Odd guessed, that the time drew near, and the men hurried from the house. One of the local people went where Odd sat, and said, 'Who are you?' Odd told him the truth, - 'and what country is this that we've come to?' The person said that this place was Aquitania. 'But what is this house where you have been standing for a while?'

'This we call either the minster or church.'

'But what kind of noise is it you have been

making?'

'That we call the Mass,' said the local man. 'But what about you, are you an utter heathen?' Odd said, 'We do not have any faith, we believe in our might and main, but we don't believe in Odin, but what religion you have?' the man said: 'We believe in him that created heaven and earth, the sea, the sun and moon.' Odd said: 'He who has built all that must be great, that I can understand.'

Now Odd and his men were shown to lodgings. They were there several weeks and had some meetings with the locals. They asked them and Odd, if they would take the faith, and in the end Gudmund and Sigurd converted. They asked Odd if he would take the faith. He said he would offer them a deal, 'I will take your faith, but I will act the same as before. I will sacrifice neither to Thor nor Odin or other idols, but I am no mood to be in this place. Therefore I will wander from land to land, and be sometimes with pagans, sometimes with Christians.' In the end, however, Odd was baptized. They stayed there for a while.

One time Odd asked Sigurd and Gudmund if they would go away. They say: 'We have liked being here more than elsewhere.'

'Then here is a disagreement,' said Odd, 'I have been so bored here because nothing has happened.' He did not ask leave from his brothers, stealing away alone, but they stayed along with all their people.

And as he came away from the city, he saw a large group of people coming towards him. One man rode while the others walked. These people were all clad elegantly, and no one carried weapons.

Odd stood by the street, but the people went past him, and did not speak to each other. Then Odd saw where four men ran. They all had long knives in their hands. They ran to the man who was riding, and cut off his head. Then they ran back past Odd the same way, and one had in his hand the head of the man who was killed. Odd thought he knew that they had done great evil. Now Odd ran after them and chased them, but they ran away to the forest, and went to ground in an earth-house there. Odd ran after them into the earth-house. Because they showed resistance, Odd attacked them. He gave them no relief until he had killed them all. Then he took their heads by the hair, and tied them together, then went out and carried their heads and the head that they had when they went there. Odd went back to the city. Then there were others come to church with the corpse of the man who was killed. Odd threw the heads into the minster and said: 'There is the head of the man who was killed, and I have avenged him.' They thought highly of this deed that Odd had done. Odd asked who it had been that he had avenged. They said that this man was the bishop. Odd said, 'Then it was better work than not doing it.' So now they kept an eye on Odd, because they did not in the least want him to go. But just as he had before been bored by being there, now things were worse since he found that they kept watch on him, and now he waited a chance to get away.

One night he got the chance and he ran away. He went from land to land, and came at last to the river Jordan. There he took off all his clothes including his shirt. Then he went into the river and washed himself as he pleased. Then he got out of the river and into his shirt, and it held all the magic as before. Now he went from there on out and he had his quiver on his back. Then he went still from land to land. Now he came to a wild forest and he had no other way to live but by shooting animals for food or birds, and so it went for a while.

Chapter Eighteen

It is said that one day Odd came to a crag, and some big ravines, where a river fell in streams with much noise. He wondered how anyone could get across, and he saw no way. He sat down, and he had not been there long when something caught him up and lifted him into the air. A vulture had come flying at Odd and snatched him with its claws so fast that he could not protect himself against it. This creature flew with Odd across many lands and seas. But eventually it flew with him to some cliffs and landed on a grassy ledge. Here its young waited. When it let Odd loose, he was whole and unharmed, as his shirt had shielded him from the claws of this vulture as from all else that has already been mentioned.

Now Odd was left with the vulture's young in the nest. There was a high cliff above, while a sheer drop was underneath. Odd could see no way to get away without risking his life and jumping into the sea. But there seemed to be no chance of getting ashore anywhere and he saw no end to the cliffs. The chicks were still unfledged. The vulture was rarely home in the lair, and it was always looking for prey. Odd bound up the beaks of the young, but concealed himself in a rock cleft behind the nest. The vulture carried there more fish and birds and human flesh, and of all sorts of animals and livestock. It came about at last that it carried cooked meat there. But when the vulture goes away, Odd took the food, but concealed himself in between.

One day Odd saw a great giant rowing in a stone boat towards the nest. He shouted and said: 'An evil bird is nesting there, as he is accustomed to, steal away my freshly boiled meat day after day. I shall now seek to avenge myself somewhat. When I took the oxen of the king, I did not mean that a bird that would have them.' Odd stood up and killed the chicks, and called to the giant: 'Here is all that you are looking for, and I have taken care of it.' The giant went into the nest and took his meat and bore it to the boat. The giant said, 'Where is the little bairn that I saw here? Don't be scared, come out and go with me.' Odd showed himself then, and the giant took him and put him in the boat. He said: 'How shall I kill this monster?' Odd said, 'Set fire to the nest, and when the vulture comes back, I feel it may be that he will fly so near that fire will catch its feathers, and then we can kill it.' It happened as Odd said, and they defeated the vulture. Odd cut off its beaks and claws, and took them with him and climbed into the boat, and the giant rowed away.

Odd asked him his name, and he said he was called Hildir and he was one of the giants of Giantland and he had a wife called Hildirid, and with her a daughter named Hildigunn. 'And I have a son called Godmund and he was born yesterday. I am one of three brothers. The name of one is Ulf, the other Ylfing. We have arranged a meeting next summer to elect the person to be king of Giantland, who is to be the one who does the most remarkable deeds and has the most savage dog in the dogfight in the meeting.' Odd said, 'Who do you think out of you will become king?' Hildir answered: 'It seems to me that one of them will receive it, because I have always been the least of us, and so it will still be.' Odd said, 'What would you choose that would be best in this case?' Hildir answered: 'I would choose to be king, but it is however mighty unlikely, because Ulf has a wolf that is so fierce that no dog can tolerate him. Ulf has killed that animal called the tiger, and he has the head of the beast to prove it. But Ylfing, my brother, is, however, even harder, since he has an unbeatable polar bear. Ylfing has killed an animal that is called the unicorn, but I have no deeds to compare with theirs and no dog to compare either.'

'Well, it seems to me,' said Odd, 'that there would be a solution if someone applied himself, if a man was sympathetic.' Hildir said, 'I have never met a child as little as you, nor as arrogant as you nor as crafty, because I think it may turn out that even though you're too clever by half, you are the greatest treasure, and I will bring you Hildigunn, my daughter, and she can have you to play with and foster you and bring you up with Godmund, my son.'

After that Hildir set to the oars and rowed home to Giantland and Odd thought the boat went very fast. When he got home, he showed them the child that he had found, and asked his daughter to take care of this child with their own. Hildigunn took Odd and when he was with her, he stood close to her thighs, but Hildir was taller than her, as a man would be. But Hildigunn picked Odd up and put him on her knees, then she turned him to look at him, and said:

This tiny pip

Has a tuft under his nose,

But Godmund is bigger,

Though born yesterday.'

She put him in a cradle with the giant baby and sang lullabies to the child and cuddled with them. But when he was restless in his cradle, she put him to bed with her and caressed him, and it came about that Odd played the games he wished and now things went well with them. Then Odd told her that he was not a child, though he was smaller than local men. But the people of Giantland are so much bigger and stronger than any other kind; friendly, they are handsome, but no wiser than most men.

Odd stayed there over the winter and in the spring he asked Hildir how generous he would be with a man who led him the dog that could beat his brothers'. Hildir answered 'I would oblige him. Can you get me something matching that description?' Odd said, 'Perhaps I can show you, but you should take it yourself.' Hildir answered, 'I will get him, but you show me it.' Odd said, 'An animal lies on Varg Island called a hibernating bear. Such is the nature of it that it lies asleep all winter, but in summer it gets up and then it is so greedy and cruel that nothing is safe, neither cattle nor men nor anything it meets. Now I think that this animal would beat your brothers' dogs.' Hildir said, 'Take me to this dog, and if it turns out as you say, then I will you pay well when I'm in power.' They got ready to go. Then Hildigunn spoke to Odd. 'Will you come back after this?' He said that he did not necessarily know. 'It would mean a lot to me,' she said, 'because I love you greatly, although you are small. We must not hide it from ourselves that I am with child, though it seems unlikely to think that you could do this, so small and feeble as you are. There is, however, no one except you who can be the father of the child that I carry. And though I love you very much, I do not mean to stop you going wherever you want, because I see that you do not have the character to be with us here any longer, but do not doubt it, you could not get away from here, unless I permit it. Now I will rather bear grief and sorrow and mourn here emptily, whatever happens, than you not be in the places that seem to you good. But what do you want me to do with our child?'

'You must,' said Odd, 'send him to me, if it's a boy, when he is ten years old, because I have hopes for him. But if it is a girl, then she should be brought up here, and look after her yourself, because I will not have anything to give her.'

'You shall have your own way in this as in everything else,' she said, 'between us, now farewell.' She cried bitterly, but Odd went to the ship.

Hildir rowed. To Odd it seemed he was too slow the oars, because the way was long. He resorted to the magic which Hrafnista men were given, and he hoisted the sails, and there came a fair wind, and they sailed out of the country and it was not long before Hildir got to his feet in the boat and went to Odd, seized him and knocked him down, and said: 'I will kill you if you don't stop this magic of yours, for the shore and mountains run past as if they are sheep, and the ship will sink under us.' Odd said, 'Do not think that, for you are dizzy because you're not accustomed to sailing; now let me stand up, and you will learn that I'm telling the truth.' He did as Odd asked. Odd reefed the sail; the shore and mountains were calm. Odd asked him not to wonder, however, if he saw this often when they sailed, and he said he could stop when he wished. Hildir was now calm after what Odd said, and he understood that this way was quicker than rowing;

Odd hoisted the sails and sailed away, and Hildir was quiet.

There is nothing told of their journey until they came to Varg Islands and went ashore. There was a large scree slope. Odd asked Hildir to stretch his hand down among the stones and see if he could get something. He did so, and his arm went into the stones up to the shoulder, and said, 'Oh, here's something odd inside, and I will get my rowing glove,' and so he did and then pulled out a bear by the ears. Odd said, 'Now, treat this dog just as I said; take it home with you and don't let it loose earlier than at the meeting when you fight with the dogs. Do not feed it until the summer and keep it alone in the house and tell no one that you should have got it. But first day of summer, match it with your brothers' dogs, but if it's not enough, then come to this grim place another summer; I will then give more advice if this does not work.' Hildir had got bites all over his hands. He said, 'This I wish you to do, Odd, that you come to this grim place next spring but one, at this time.' Odd agreed to it.

Hildir went home with the animal and did everything Odd had said, but Odd went other way, and we cannot speak of his actions or accomplishments until the second spring when he went to the place where they had agreed to meet. Odd came first and went into the woods a short way from there and would not let Hildir see him, because he did not want to meet him, thinking that he would want revenge if everything had not gone according to what that he had told him. And not much later he heard the sound of oars and saw Hild come ashore, and in one hand had a cauldron full of silver, and in the other two very heavy chests. And he came to the place where they had promised to meet, then he waited there for some time, and there was no sign of Odd. Then said the giant, 'It is a shame now, Odd, foster son, that you did not come, but I see no point in staying here long, because my domain's leaderless while I am away, then I leave here these boxes, which are full of gold, and a cauldron full of silver; please have this treasure, even if you come later. I will put on top of it this flat stone so no wind blows them away, but if you cannot see it, I'm putting down these treasures, a sword, helmet and shield. But if you're any closer, so that you can hear my words, then I tell you that I was chosen king out of my brothers and I had a great savage dog because he bit to death both the dogs of my brothers and many of the men would rescue the dogs. I produced the beak and claws of a vulture, and it seemed a greater deed than those my brothers had achieved; I am now the king of the land that we three brothers had formerly. Now I will go back to my kingdom. Come to me, I shall give you the best of everything. I can also tell you that Hildigunn, my daughter, has given birth to a boy named Vignir, and she said that you fathered him upon her; I shall bring him up to be a lord. I will teach him sports and do all for him as I would for my own son, and when he is ten years old he will be sent to you, according to what you told her to do.' Then he rowed off in his craft. And when he had gone, Odd stood up and went to where the treasure was under the slab, but it was so big a rock that a crowd of people could not have stirred it. Odd could only reach the goods that lay on top of the slab, and they were worth a great deal of wealth. Having taken this treasure, Odd went on his way into the forest.

Chapter Nineteen

One day Odd came to the edge of the forest.

He was very tired, and he sat down under an oak. Then he saw a man walking past. He wore a blue-flecked cloak, high shoes, had a reed in his hand, and he had gold emblazoned gloves, was an average man in stature and genteel in appearance; a lowered hood covered his face. He had a big moustache and long beard, both of them red. He turned to Odd, where he sat, and greeted him by name. Odd welcomed him and asked who he was. He said he was Grani, called Raudgrani. 'I know all about you, Arrow-Odd,' he said, 'it seems to me good to hear, since you are the greatest hero and an accomplished man, but you have few followers, and travel rather like a pauper, and it is bad that a man like you should be so reduced.'

'It has been long now, though,' said Odd, 'that I have not been a leader of men.'

'Will you now swear an oath of brotherhood with me?' Raudgrani said. 'It's hard to deny such an offer,' said Odd, 'and I will take it up.'

'You are not yet wholly luckless,' said Raudgrani. 'Now I will tell you that there are two champions in the east of this country and they have twelve ships. They are sworn brothers; one comes from out of Denmark and is called Gardar, and the other Sirnir and comes out of Gautland. I know of no other heroes on this side of the sea and they do well at most things, and there I will bring you into brotherhood with them, yet you'll have the most say of us all, although following my advice will be best. But where would you want to sail if this is arranged as I have now said?'

'It is always in my mind that I would find Ogmund Eythjof's-Bane, who is called by another name, Tussock.'

'Stop, stop,' said Raudgrani, 'and don't say that, because he is not a man of humankind, is Ogmund, and if you meet Ogmund another time you will get from him far worse than before, so put this idea to find him from your mind.' Odd answered: 'One thing I wish to do is to avenge Thord, my blood brother, and I shall never give up until I can find him, if that is my fate.'

'Do you want me to tell you,' said Raudgrani, 'how Ogmund was born? If I do, you will see there is no chance that he will be killed by mortal men, if you know of his origin.

'Now is it told first in the tale that Harek was the name of a king who ruled Bjarmaland when you made your Viking raid, you will remember what damage you did to the Bjarmians. When you had gone away, they thought they had got a bad deal and would gladly take revenge, if they could. This was how they did it, they got a giantess who lived under a large waterfall, filled her with magic and sorcery, and laid her in bed with the king, and with her he had a son; the boy was sprinkled with water and given a name and called Ogmund. He was unlike most mortal men from an early age, as you'd expect from his mother, but his father was the greatest of men for sacrifices. When Ogmund was three years old, he was sent to Finnmark, and he studied all kinds of magic and sorcery, and when he was fully trained he went home to Bjarmaland. He was then seven years old and as big as a full grown man, very powerful and bad to deal with. His looks had not improved while he was with the Lapps' sons, because he was both black and blue, with his hair long and black, and a tussock hanging down over the eyes where a forelock should be. He was called Ogmund Tussock. They meant to send him to meet you and slay you; although they knew that much would need to be prepared before they could bring you death. It was next that they strengthened Ogmund with witchcraft, so that no normal iron should bite him. Subsequently they sacrificed to him and altered him so that he was no longer a mortal man.

'Eythjof was the name of a Viking. He was the greatest of berserks and an unparalleled hero, so that there did not seem to be any hero greater than him, and he never had fewer ships than eighteen when raiding. He never spent time on land and lay out on the sea, winter and hot summer. Everyone was scared of him wherever he went. He conquered Bjarmaland and forced them to pay tribute. Then Ogmund got eight comrades. They were all dressed in thick woollen cloaks, and no iron bit them. They were named thus: Hak and Haki, Tindall and Toki, Finn and Fjosni, Tjosni and Torfi. Then Ogmund joined up with Eythjof, and they went to war together. Ogmund was ten years old. He was with Eythjof for five winters. Eythjof was so fond of him that he could not refuse him anything, and for his sake he freed Bjarmaland from tribute. Ogmund rewarded Eythjof no better than to kill him sleeping in his bed and conceal the murder. It was easy to do because Eythjof had put him in the same bed with him, and not done anything against him, and he planned to make him his adopted son. He left Eythjof's men, and they went where they pleased, but Ogmund had two ships fully crewed. He was then called Ogmund Eythjof's Bane. And that same summer you fought him at Tronuvagar, and was Ogmund then fifteen years old. He hated getting no vengeance against you, and so he murdered Thord

Prow-Gleam, your sworn brother. Then he went to meet the giantess, his mother, who was Grimhild when she was with humans. But then she was a *finngalkin*. She looks human as far as her head, but like an animal further down and has remarkably large claws and a tremendous tail, and with it she kills both humans and livestock, animals and dragons. Ogmund tried to get her to get you, and now she lives in the forests with animals and has reached the north of England and is looking at you. Now I have told you plainly of Ogmund.'

Odd said: 'It seems to me understandable why most men find him hard to fight, if he is as you say, but I still want to meet him.'

'Worse he is, though,' Raudgrani said, 'he is said to be more wraith than man, so I think that he will not be killed by any humans. But let us go down to the ships first,' - and so they did. And when they came to the sea, Odd saw where many ships floated. They went aboard. Odd saw two men who stood out from the rest. They stood up and greeted Raudgrani as their blood brother. He sat down between them and told Odd to sit. Raudgrani said, 'Here's a man who you sworn brothers will have heard told of, called Odd and Arrow-Odd. I wish that he be sworn our blood brother; he shall also be one to lead us, because he is most experienced in warfare.' Sirnir answered: 'Is he the Odd who went to Bjarmaland?'

'Yes,' said Raudgrani. 'We shall benefit,' said Sirnir, 'if he is sworn as our brother.'

'Full well I like it,' said Gardar. They bound this fast with promises. Then Raudgrani asked where Odd meant to go. 'Let us first,' said Odd, 'sail west to England.' So they did, that they sailed to the place, and when they came to the country they put up awnings over the ship, and lay there for a while.

Chapter Twenty

One day of good weather Sirnir and Gardar went ashore for entertainment and many with them, but Odd stayed on the ship. Raudgrani was nowhere to be seen. The weather was surprisingly warm, and the sworn brothers took off their clothes and went swimming in a lake. There was a forest nearby. Most of the people were at some game or other. But as the day wore on, they saw that an incredibly large animal come out of the woods. It had a human head and immense fangs. Its tail was both long and stout, its claws remarkably large. It had a sword in each claw: they were both gleaming and big. When this *finngalkin* came out to the men, she howled menacingly at them and killed five men in the first attack. Two of them she cut down with a sword, a third she bit with her teeth, two she struck with her tail, and both died. Within a little time she had killed sixty people. Gardar dressed and stole out against the *finngalkin* and struck her with his sword so hard that one sword was knocked from her claws and into the lake, but she hit him with the other sword, so that he fell to the ground. Then she jumped on top of him. In came Sirnir with a sword that never failed, named Snidil, best of all blades, which never wavered in the fight. He struck the beast, and knocked the second sword into the water. The *finngalkin* trampled him under her, so that he was knocked out. Men who escaped ran to the ships and told Odd that the foster-brothers, and many others, had been killed and said that none of them could withstand monsters, - 'and please, Odd,' they said, 'sail immediately from this country, and save us as quickly as possible.'

'It would be a great shame,' said Odd, 'if we went away and I did not avenge the foster-brothers, such valiant men were they, and I'll never do it.' He took his quiver and went ashore. And when he had gone only a short way, he heard a terrifying noise. A little later Odd saw where the *finngalkin* was. He puts one of Gusir's Gifts to the bowstring, and shot it into the eye of the beast, and out the back of the head. The *finngalkin* went at him so hard that Odd could not use the bow. It clawed at his chest so hard that he fell on his back, but the shirt protected him as ever, so that the claws did not harm Odd. Swiftly he drew the sword he was girded with, and cut off the animal's tail when it was going to strike him, but he kept one hand out so that it could not bite at him. And when he had cut off her tail she ran to the wood screaming. Odd then shot another of Gusir's Gifts. It got the animal in the back, right in the heart and through the breast; the *finngalkin* then fell to the ground. Many people ran up to the animal then and hacked and hewed, who had not dared to come close before. The animal was utterly dead. Then Odd burnt the animal, and took the sworn brothers to the ship to be healed.

They went away from there and stayed in Denmark over the winter. They spent the following summers in raiding and fought in Sweden, Saxony, Frankland and Flanders until Sirnir and Gardar grew tired of raiding and settled down in their respective countries. Raudgrani followed them, for he had come down to the shore when they were ready to sail, after Odd had killed the *finngalkin*. Rarely was Raudgrani there when there was danger for people, but he was a great adviser when it was needed, and he rarely tried to stop them from performing great deeds.

Chapter Twenty One

Odd went raiding and he had three ships well manned. He went again to seek Ogmund Eythjof's-Bane. Ten years had now passed since Odd left Giantland. One evening Odd lay off a headland and he had pitched a tent. He saw a man rowing in a boat. Whoever it was was rowing powerfully, and he was amazingly big to see. He rowed so hard up to Odd's ships that everything was broken before him. Then he went ashore, to where the tent was, and asked who was in charge. Odd said to him, - 'Who are you?' He said he was named Vignir - 'Odd, are you the one who went to Bjarmaland?'

'It is true, that,' said Odd. 'I am speechless,' said Vignir. 'Why so?' said Odd. 'Because,' said Vignir, 'I can barely believe that you're a father to me, so small and weak-looking as you seem to be.'

'Who is your mother?' Odd said, 'And how old are you?'

'My mother is called Hildigunn,' said Vignir; 'I was born in Giantland, and I was brought up there, but now I'm ten years old. My mother told me that Arrow-Odd was my father, and I was thinking he would be a real man, but now I see that you are the least of nobodies to look at, and so you will turn out to be.' Odd said: 'Do you think that you will do more or work greater feats than I have? But I will accept my kinship with you and you're welcome to remain with me.'

'That I will, and I accept it,' said Vignir, 'but it seems to me, however, very demeaning to be mixed with you and your men, because I think they more closely resemble mice than men, and it seems to me very likely that I will do bigger things than you, if I live long.' Odd asked him not to insult his men.

In the morning they got ready to sail. Then Vignir asked Odd where he would sail. He said he wanted to look for Ogmund Eythjof's-Bane. 'From him, you'll get no good, if you find him,' said Vignir, 'because he is the greatest troll and monster ever created in the northern part of the world.'

'It cannot be true,' said Odd, 'that when you mock my stature and my men, you are now so scared that you dare not seek or find Ogmund Tussock.'

'No need,' said Vignir, 'to taunt me with cowardice, but I will repay you for your words some time, so that it will seem to you no better than this does to me now. But I will tell you where Ogmund is. He's in the fjord named Skuggi, in Helluland's wastes[73], and his nine tussocked lads with him. He went there because he cannot be bothered finding you. Now, you may visit him, if you want, and see how it goes.' Odd said it should be so.

Then they sailed till they came to the Greenland Sea, then turned south and west along the coast. Then Vignir said: 'Now I shall sail in my boat today, but you can follow after.' Odd let him go his own way. Vignir was master of one ship. They saw that day where two rocks emerged from the sea. Odd wondered much at that. They sailed between the cliffs. But as the day wore on, they saw a huge island. Odd asked them to sail up to it. Vignir asked why. Odd asked five men to go ashore and seek

---

[73] Helluland was discovered by Leif Eiriksson at the same time as his voyage to Vinland (America). It is usually identified as Baffin Island.

water. Vignir said there was no need, and he said none of his ship were going. But when Odd's men came to the island, they had been there only a little while before the island sank and drowned them all. The island was covered with heather. They did not see it again. When they also looked at the rocks, they saw they had vanished. Odd was very surprised by this, and asked Vignir why this was. Vignir said: 'It seems to me that you have no more sense than stature. Now I will tell you that these are two sea monsters. One is named Hafgufa, the other Lyngbak. The latter is the greatest of all whales in the world, but Hafgufa is the biggest of monsters created in the ocean. It is her nature that she swallows both men and ships and whales and all that she can reach. She stays submerged day and night together, and then she lifts up her head and nostrils, then it is never less time than the tide that she stays up. Now that sound that we sailed through was the gap between her jaws, and her nose and lower jaw were the rocks you saw in the ocean, but Lyngbak was the island that sank[74]. Ogmund Tussock has sent these creatures to you with his enchantments to work the death of you and all your men. He thought that this would have killed more men than those that drowned, and he meant that Hafgufa would swallow us whole. Therefore I sailed through her mouth because I knew that she had just risen to the surface. Now we have seen through these contrivances of Ogmund, but it is my thinking that we will suffer from him worse than any other men.'

---

[74] Known in Greek as the *aspidochelone*, a creature identical to Lyngbak appears in other stories, including those of Sinbad, St Brendan, and Pinnochio. Hafgufa later developed into the legendary Kraken, tentatively classified by Linnaeus as a cephalopod.

'That's a risk we're going to have to take,' said Odd.

Chapter Twenty Two

Now they sailed until they came to Helluland and into the fjord called Skuggi. But when they had moored, father and son went ashore and to a spot they saw where a fortress stood, and it seemed that it was a well-defended place. Ogmund went out on one of the walls with his companions. He greeted Odd blithely and asked them their errand. 'You do not need to ask,' Odd said, 'because I want your life.'

'The other idea is better,' said Ogmund, 'that we accept full settlement.'

'No,' said Odd, 'that will not be, because the first idea has been in my mind since you had Thord Prow-Gleam, my blood brother, so shamefully killed.'

'I only did that,' said Ogmund, 'because we did not have equal numbers of slain, but now if you've caught up with me, you will never defeat me while I am in the fort, but now I offer you, that either you two fight me and my companions, or we stay in the fort.'

'It must be,' said Odd, 'and I will fight with you Ogmund, and Vignir will fight your companions.'

'That shall not be,' said Vignir, 'I will now reward you for your taunting words that you said to me the first time that we first met, that I would not dare encounter Ogmund.'

'We'll regret this arrangement later,' said Odd, 'though now you get your own way.'

Then they started fighting. It was a close thing. It was some hard fighting that Ogmund and Vignir underwent, because both their strength and power was the same as was their weapon skill. And Vignir pressed Ogmund so hard he ran northwards along the sea cliff, but Vignir ran after him until Ogmund ran down over the rocks onto a grassy ledge, but after him came Vignir; they were forty fathoms above sea level. Then they met and were faced with a great struggle and bitter, because they tore up the earth and stones like loose snow. Now we go back to Odd. He had a big club in his hand, because iron bit none of the Tussock boys. He hit about him hard with a club so that in a moment he had killed them all. He was weary, but he was unhurt; this was caused by his shirt. Odd decided he should look after Vignir, and learn from him what had happened. He went along the cliff edge until he came up to that place above where Vignir and Ogmund had been fighting. And at that point Ogmund surprised Vignir so that he fell, and as soon as he did he bent down over him and bit out his throat. Vignir was dead. Odd said that sight was the worst he had ever seen, and most saddening. Ogmund said: 'Now, I think, Odd, it would have been better that we had settled as I asked, because now you have got a loss from me that you'll never recover from, as your son Vignir is dead, a man that I think would have been the most valiant and strongest of all in the northern lands, for he was now ten years old, and he would have gained victory if I was an ordinary man, but now I more a wraith than a man. And he violently crushed my body and he has near enough broken everything in me, every bone, so that they all scrape within the skin, so that I would be dead if it was in my nature to do so, but I am afraid of no one in this world except you, and from you I will get my own ill fortune,

411

sooner or later, because now you have more reason for revenge.' Odd then became wildly angry, and then he jumped down the cliff, and landed down on the ledge. Ogmund moved himself quickly and threw himself down the rocks into the sea head first, so that sea spray surged up the cliff. There was no sign of Ogmund again so far as Odd could see. Then they parted this time, and Odd felt the worst of it, and then he went to the ships and sailed away. He went to Denmark and found Gardar, his foster-brother, and he gave Odd a warm welcome.

Chapter Twenty Three

Odd stayed in Denmark that winter, but when spring came he and Gardar went to war and they sent word to Sirnir in Gautland. He went to meet them, and with him went Raudgrani. Raudgrani asked Odd where he wanted to go. He said he wanted to seek Ogmund Eythjof's-Bane and continue the search for him. 'It seems to me that you seek sorrow,' said Raudgrani, 'you keep looking after Ogmund, but every time that you meet, you get from him both shame and wretchedness, and there's no need to think that Ogmund has changed since you parted. But I can tell you where he's gone, if you are interested. He went east to the giant Geirrod[75] in Geirrodargard and he has married Geirrid, his daughter, and both are the worst of trolls, and I wouldn't advise you to go there.' Odd said he would go anyway.

Then they all made ready, the sworn brothers, to go east, and when they came to Geirrodargard,

---

[75] Geirrod also appears in the Edda, where he comes into conflict with the god Thor, and in *Gesta Danorum* and various other legendary sagas.

they saw where a man was sitting in a boat to fish. It was Ogmund Eythjof's Bane indeed, and he had on a shaggy cape. When he had separated with Odd, he had gone away to the east and become son-in-law of Geirrod the giant, and he took tribute from all the kings of the Baltic in such a way that they would send him every twelve months their beards and moustaches. Ogmund had made of them the same coat that he wore. Odd and his men headed towards the boat, but Ogmund retreated; he rowed rather strongly. The sworn brothers all jumped into a boat and rowed after him furiously, but Tussock rowed so mightily that they kept the same distance until that they came to land. Then Ogmund ran ashore leaving his boat on the strand. Odd was the fastest of the men to get ashore and he was followed by Sirnir, and both ran after Ogmund. But Ogmund when saw that they would catch up, he spoke, and recited:

'I pray to Geirrod

For the gods' favour,

Greatest of warriors,

Grant me assistance

And my wife

Quickly to others,

I need now all

The aid they can give.'

Then the old saying was proved true, that if you speak of the devil, he's sure to appear. Geirrod came there with all his people, and there were fifty of them in all. Then came Gardar and Odd's men. They entered into the hardest battle. Geirrod hit rather hard, so in a little time he had killed fifteen men of Odd's. Odd then looked for Gusir's Gifts. He took Hremsu and laid it on the bowstring and shot. It hit Geirrod in the breast and came out at the shoulders. Geirrod still came on even after taking the arrow, and he killed three men before he fell dead to the ground. Geirrid was also a threat because she killed eighteen men in a small time. Gardar turned to her and they traded blows, but it ended that Gardar was beaten dead to the ground. When Odd saw that, he was tremendously angry. So he put one of Gusir's Gifts to the string and shot it into the right armpit of Geirrid and it came out of the left. As far as anyone could tell it did nothing to her. Then she rushed into the battle, and killed five people. Odd then shot another of Gusir's Gifts. It came into her small intestine and out of her thighs; she died soon after.

Ogmund also did not waste time in battle, since he had killed thirty men in a short while before Sirnir turned towards him, and they had a hard fight, and Sirnir was quickly wounded. A little later, Odd saw that Sirnir retreated from Ogmund. He turned that way, but when Ogmund saw that, he turned and fled and ran in disorder rather foolishly, but Sirnir and Odd went after him. Both of them were running very fast. Ogmund wore his fine coat well, but when they were almost level with him, Ogmund threw down the cloak and recited:

Now must I cast

Away my cloak,

Which was made

Of kings' moustaches,

Embroidered with them

On both sides,

I am very grieved

To give it up.

They pursue me

At full pelt,

Odd and Sirnir,

From the encounter.'

But now that Ogmund was lighter clad, he pulled away. Odd hardened himself then, and he ran quicker than Sirnir. And when Ogmund saw that, he turned towards him, and they got to grips. They were wrestling and fighting both hard and long, since Odd was not as powerful as Ogmund, but Ogmund could not knock him off his feet. Then Sirnir came up with a drawn sword, Snidil, intending to strike at Ogmund, but when Ogmund saw that he turned and thrust Odd between himself and the blow. Then Sirnir held back. So it went, that Ogmund used Odd a shield and Sirnir could do nothing, but even when Odd was hit, he was not wounded because of his good shirt. And at one point, Odd braced both feet against a solid stone sunk in the earth so hard that Ogmund was brought to his knees. Sirnir hacked at Ogmund. Then he had no opportunity to parry the blow with Odd. It hit him in the buttocks, and took a slice. Sirnir cut so great a piece out of Ogmund's backside that no horse could carry more. This worried Ogmund so that he sank down into the earth where he was. Odd grabbed his beard with both hands, with so much force that he tore it from him and beard and skin down to the bone, and all the face with both cheeks, and so it went on up the forehead and the middle of the crown, and they went their ways as the ground opened, but Odd kept what he held. The earth closed above the head of Ogmund, and so they parted.

Odd and Sirnir returned to their ships, and they had experienced considerable loss of life. Odd thought it was the greatest sorrow that he had lost Gardar, his foster-brother. Raudgrani was also gone, and Odd and Sirnir never learnt what became of him after they found Ogmund in the boat. It was true that he himself seldom faced danger, but he gave the toughest advice. The sworn brothers never Raudgrani again, it is told. Men think he may have actually been Odin. The sworn brothers went away, and it seemed to people that Odd had still not got the better of Ogmund, having lost Gardar, his foster-brother, a high-spirited man who had helped Odd and achieved a lot by killing those monsters who were with Ogmund. Geirrid had a son by Ogmund Eythjof's-Bane, named Svart. He was three years old when he came into the story. He was tall and it looked likely that he would turn into an evil man.

Chapter Twenty Four

Odd returned to Gautland with his blood brother, Sirnir, who invited him to stay for the winter. Odd accepted. And as the winter wore on, he became very depressed. To his mind came the miseries he had got from Ogmund Tussock. He did not ever want to risk his blood brother's life in the fight with Ogmund, because he thought he had suffered losses enough already. It then became his plan to steal away alone at night. He then got transport where he needed, but he travelled through wildernesses, and forests, and ran along long mountain paths. He had the quiver on his back. He went now through many countries, and it came about at last that he had to shoot birds for his food. He folded birch bark round his body and feet. Then he made a big hat with the bark. He was not like other men, far bigger than any other, and he was all covered in bark.

Now nothing is told about him before he came out from the forest, and he saw settlements before him. He saw that a great farm stood there, but there was another farm close by. It came into his mind that he would try the smaller farm; though he had never previously tried anything like that. He went up to the door. There was a man at the door chopping wood. The man was small in size and white-haired. He welcomed him, and asked the man his name. 'My name is Barkman,' he said, 'but what is your name?' He was called Jolf. 'You would like to stay the night,' said the man. 'That I would,' said Barkman. Now he followed the man into his living room, where his wife sat alone on a chair. 'Here is a visitor,' said the old man, 'you shall entertain him, I have many things to do.' The old woman grumbled a lot, and said that he often offered people accommodation, - 'but there is nothing to give him.' Now the man went away, but the woman sat with Odd. And at evening, when Jolf came in, there was a table set for them with one dish, but on the side Barkman sat, he put down a good knife. Two rings were on the knife, one of gold, the other of silver. When Jolf saw it, he reached for his knife and examined it. 'You have a good knife, mate,' said the man, 'how did you come by this treasure?'

Barkman said: 'When I was at a young age, we made salt together and one day a ship was wrecked near where we were. The ship was broken to pieces, and the men were washed ashore, and were very weak, and we quickly finished them off, and I got a knife in my share of the plunder, but if you, man, have any use for it, then I will give you the knife.'

'Best of luck to you,' said the man and he showed the woman his knife. 'This is good,' he said, 'and see this knife is nothing worse than the one I had before.' After that they had their food, and then what followed was Barkman went to sleep, and slept through the night, and he did not wake until Jolf was away, and his bed was cold. Then he said, 'Will it not be best for me to get up and go out and look for breakfast elsewhere?' The old woman said that the old man wanted him to stay in his home.

It was near the middle of the day when the man came, and the Barkman was on his feet. Then the table was laid. There was a dish on the board, the old man put down beside him three arrows with stone heads. These were large arrows and fair, so Barkman thought he had never seen that kind of arrow. He took one up and looked at it. 'This arrow is well made,' he said. 'If you think,' said the old man, 'you like them, then I will give them to you.' Barkman smiled at him and said, 'I am not sure there's any reason for me to carry these stone arrows along with me.'

'That you'll never know, Odd,' said the man, 'when you might need them. I know that you are called Arrow-Odd and are the son of Grim Hairycheek from north in Hrafnista. I know, too, that you have three arrows called Gusir's Gifts, and you will think it strange, when you come to a time when Gusir's Gifts fail you and these arrows save you.'

'Since you know that my name is Odd, and also that I have the arrows named Gusir's Gifts, it could be,' said Odd, 'that you are right, what you said before. I shall certainly accept the arrows,' and he put them in his quiver. 'What do you say, man,' said Odd, 'about this land? Is there a king?'

'Yes,' said the man, 'and he is called Herraud.'

'Who is the noblest men with him?' said Odd. 'There are two men,' said the man, 'one called Sigurd, and the other Sjolf. They are the chief men of the king, and the best of all fighters.'

'Who are the king's children?' said Odd. 'He has one beautiful daughter called Silkisif.'

'She's a beautiful woman?' said Odd. 'Yes,' said the man, 'there is none other as beautiful in Gardariki and elsewhere.'

'Tell me, man,' said Odd, 'how they'll receive me, if I go there? And do not tell them who I am.'

'I can hold my tongue,' said the man.

Then they went to the royal hall. Then the old man put his foot down and refused to go further. 'Why do you stop?' said Odd. 'Because,' said the man, 'I will be put in shackles if I go in here, and I will be happier when I get off.'

'No,' said Barkman, 'we shall both go in together, and I cannot settle for anything but that you go,' and clutched him. Then they entered the hall. When the king's retainers saw the old man, they mobbed him, but Barkman supported him, so that they bounced off. Now they went along the hall, so that they came to the king. The old man greeted the king politely. The king took it well. Then the king asked whom he brought along with him. 'It may be that I can't say,' said the man, 'and so he must tell you that himself.'

'My name is Barkman,' he said. 'Who are you, mate?' said the king. 'This I know,' he said, 'I am older than anything you know, but there is neither wit nor memory in my skull, and I have lived outside in the forest of almost all my life. Beggars always want to be choosers, O king, and I ask you for winter lodgings.' The king replied, 'Are you at all skilled?'

'No,' he said, 'Because I am clumsier than other men.'

'Will you work a little?' said the king. 'I do not work, since I can't be bothered to work,' said Barkman. 'Then it looks unpromising,' said the king, 'for I have made a vow to take only men who are at all skilled.'

'Nothing I ever do,' said Barkman, 'will benefit anyone.'

'You must know how to collect game, when they go shooting,' said the king. 'It may be that I will go hunting sometime.'

'Where do you want me to sit?' Barkman said. 'You should sit farther out on the lower bench, between slaves and freedmen.' Now Barkman saw the old man out and after that went to the seat he had been offered. There were two brothers. One was named Ottar, the other Ingjald. 'Come here, mate,' they said, 'and you shall sit between us,' and that he did. They sat close at his knees on either side, and asked him about other lands that came to mind, but no one else knew what they were talking about. He hung up his quiver on a peg above him, but the club under his feet. They always asked him to take away the quiver, and it seemed to be a great nuisance, but he said he would never let it be taken away from him, and he went nowhere but he would he have it with him. They offered him bribes to take off the bark, 'and we will give you good clothes,' they said. 'That may not be so,' he said, 'because I have never worn anything else, and while I live I never will.'

Chapter Twenty Five

Now Barkman sat there and generally he drank a little in early evening and then lay down to sleep. So it went on, till the men began to go hunting. It was autumn. Now Ingjald said one evening, - 'we must get up early in the morning.'

'Why is that?' Barkman said. Ingjald said they were going hunting. Then they lay down to sleep that evening, but in the morning the brothers rose and called to Barkman and they could not wake him, he was fast asleep, and he did not wake up until every man who would go hunting was gone. Barkman spoke and said: 'What is happening now, are they all ready?' Ingjald answered, 'Ready,' he said, 'but all the men are away, and we tried to wake you all morning, and we will never shoot any animals today.' Then Barkman 'Are they very great sportsmen, Sjolf and Sigurd?'

'We would know that,' said Ingjald, 'if ever anyone competed against them.' They came to the

421

mountain, and a herd of deer ran past them, and the brothers drew their bows, and they tried shooting the deer, but missed each time. Then Barkman 'I have never seen,' he said, 'anyone do as badly as you do, and why do you made such a poor try at it?' They said: 'We have already told you that we are clumsier than others, but we were late getting ready in the morning and now the animals we meet are those others have already stirred up.' Barkman said: 'I do not believe that I could be worse than you, now give the bow here, and I will try.' Now they did so. He drew the bow, and they told him not to break it, but he pulled the arrow to the tip and the bow snapped into two pieces. 'Now you have done badly,' they said, 'and it has done us much damage. It is now unlikely that we will shoot any deer today.'

'Things have not gone well,' he said, 'but do you think my stick will work as a bow, and do you not both feel some curiosity to know what's in my bag?'

'Yes,' they said, 'we are pretty curious.'

'Then you spread your thick cloaks, and I will empty out what is in it.' So they did, and he threw down the bag's contents on the cloaks. Then he drew his bow and put an arrow to the string, and shot it over the heads of all the men that were at the hunt. So he did all day, shooting at the deer that Sigurd and Sjolf were going for. He shot all his arrows except six, the stone arrows he got from the old man, and Gusir's Gifts. He did not miss a deer that day, and the brothers ran with him, and great was their joy to see his shooting.

But in the evening, when the men came home, all people's arrows were brought to the king, and each man had marked his arrow, and the king saw how many deer each man had killed during the day. Now the brothers said, 'Go there, Barkman, after your arrows, on the table before the king.'

'You go,' he said, 'and say you both own the arrows.'

'They will not believe us,' they said, 'the king knows that as sportsmen we can hardly shoot like other men.'

'Then we shall all go together,' he said. Now they went before the king. Then Barkman said, 'Here are the arrows which we fellows claim.' The king looked at him and said: 'You are a great archer.'

'Yes, sire,' he said, 'because I am used to shooting animals and birds to eat.' And after that they went to their seats. Now time passed.

Chapter Twenty Six

One evening, when the king had gone to bed, Sigurd and Sjolf rose up and went with a horn to offer drink to the brothers, Ottar and Ingjald, and asked them to take it and drink from it. And when they had drunk, they came with another two, and they took them and drank. Then Sjolf, 'Does he always lie down, your associate?'

'Yes,' they said, 'he thinks it better than drinking himself senseless like we do.' Then Sjolf: 'Is he a good archer?'

'Yes,' they said, 'it is his gift as well as many other things.'

'Do you think he can shoot as well as both of

us?' Sjolf said. 'As we see it,' said they, 'he will shoot much farther and straighter.'

'We must bet on it,' said Sjolf, 'and we will make the stake a bracelet worth half a mark, but you shall stake two rings of equal weight.' So it was agreed that the king should be there, and his daughter, would see their shooting, and they should take the bracelets before and give them to whoever the winner was, and then they laid their wager. They slept through the night. But the next morning, when the brothers woke up, it came to their minds that they had made fools of themselves over the bet, and they told Barkman. 'The bet seems to me to be unpromising,' he said, 'because even though I can shoot deer, it is but little compared with competing with such great archers, but I will try all the same since you have staked all your wealth.'

Now the men had drinks, and after drinks people went out, and now the king wanted to see the shooting. Now Sigurd went out and shot as far as he could, and a pole was placed in the ground, and Sjolf went up to it. A spear was put haft down and placed on top of it was a gold chessman, and Sjolf hit the chessman, and it seems to everyone that this was excellent shooting and he said that Barkman need not bother trying to compete. 'Good luck often alters bad,' said Barkman, 'and I'm going to try.' Now Barkman shot a single arrow, and stood where Sigurd had stood. He shot up in the air, so that the arrow remained out of sight for a long time, but when it came down, it went straight through the middle of the chessman, and into the spear shaft so that it did not move. 'As good as the shot was last time,' said the king, 'the shooting is now much better, and I can say that I have never seen such shooting.' Now Barkman took another arrow and shot so far that no one could see where it came down, and it was now agreed that he had won the game. After that, they went home, and the brothers were given the bracelet. They offered it to Barkman. He said he wanted their treasure to remain as things stand.

Now, some days later, another evening, the king had gone, and Sigurd and Sjolf went with a horn each which they offered to Ottar and Ingjald. They drank from them. Then they brought them another two. Then Sjolf, 'Still Barkman lies there and doesn't drink.'

'He is still better mannered than you in everything,' said Ingjald. 'I think there's more to it,' said Sjolf, 'that he will have rarely ever mixed with noble men, and he will have lain often out in the woods like a poor man, but does he swim well?'

'We expect he is good at most sports,' they say, 'and we think he's a very good swimmer.'

'Would he swim better than both of us?'

'We think that he is a better swimmer,' said Ottar. 'Here we will lay a bet on it,' said Sjolf, 'and we will stake a bracelet worth a mark, but you shall stake two rings, each a mark in weight.' Now it was so agreed that the king and his daughter should see their swimming contest, and it was all ordered as it was the first time. They slept through the night. In the morning, when they woke up, news of their bet had gone round the benches. 'What's this they're saying?' Barkman said. 'That you accepted another bet last night?'

'Yes,' they said, and then they told him all about

425

the bet. 'Now I think it looks unpromising,' said Barkman, 'for I am not a swimmer, and I cannot stay afloat when I try, and it's a long time since I came into contact with cold water, and have you wagered much money?'

'Yes,' they said, 'but you don't have to try, unless you wish. It would be right if we had to pay for our foolishness.'

'That shall never be,' said Barkman, 'that I should not try, since you treat me with great honour, and the king and Silkisif will see that I will certainly go for a swim.'

Now the king was told, and his daughter, and now people went to the water, and it was a big lake and close by. When they came to the water the king and his retinue sat down and the competitors went swimming in their clothes, but Barkman wore the guise that he was accustomed to. They swam to him when they came from the shore, and tried to push him under and held him down for a long time. Then they let him come up, and took a rest. They ganged up on him a second time. He reached for them and took them in each hand, and forced them down and held them down so long that it seemed unlikely that they would come up again. He gave them a short rest and took them a second time and held them under, and for a third time and held them down so long that no one thought that they would arise alive. But they still came up, and then out of the nostrils came blood from both these excellencies of the stock of kings, and they needed to be helped back on land. Then Barkman took them and cast them ashore. Then he went swimming and played a lot of games, and the troop was glad to play at swimming. But in the evening he went ashore to meet the king. And then the king asked: 'Are you not a better sportsman than the rest, both at shooting and swimming?'

'You have now seen all my skill that I have,' said Barkman, 'my name is Odd, if you want to know that, but I will not tell you anything about my family.' Now Silkisif gave him the bracelets. Then they went home. Then the brothers said that Odd should have all the rings, but he refused it, - 'and you shall have them for yourselves.' Then time passed, but not long. The king was very anxious about who the man who was there with him might be.

Chapter Twenty Seven

A man named Harek was there with the king. He had great respect from him. He was an old man and he had fostered the king's daughter. The king would talk to him about this issue, but he said he did not know and said he thought it likely that the man would came from a noble family. It happened one evening, when the king had gone to bed, that Sjolf and Sigurd went up to the brothers and they brought two horns, and they drank from them. Then Sjolf said, 'Does the great Odd sleep?'

'Yes,' they say, 'it is more sensible than drinking yourself witless like we do.'

'That could be because he is more used to lying out in the forest or lakes than to drinking well with people, or is he a great drinker?'

'Yes,' they say. 'Would he be a better drinker than us both?' Sjolf said. 'It seems to us,' said Ottar, 'he drinks a lot more.'

'We must bet on it,' said Sjolf, 'and we'll stake this bracelet, which stands at twelve ounces, but you shall stake your own heads.' They bound this agreement with them as they had in the past. Now that morning Odd asked what was said. They told him. 'Now you've really made a dumb bet,' said Odd, 'that what you have now increases the stakes from what they were formerly, since now you risk your heads, but it is not certain that I shall be the greater drinker though I am bigger than the others, but I will take them on when I go to the drinking match.' Then the king was told that he wanted to compete as a drinker, and the king's daughter was to sit in and watch, and Harek, her foster father. Now Sigurd and Sjolf went up to Odd. 'Here is a horn,' said Sigurd, and poetry came to his lips:

'Odd, you've never

Been in the fight

When helmeted troops fled,

Burst mail shirts;

Battle raged,

Fire blazed in the town,

When our king won,

Victorious, against the Wends.'

Sjolf brought him another horn, and told him to drink it and recited:

'Odd, we didn't see you

At the sword clash,

We dealt the king's forces

Death on a plate;

I took sword cuts,

Six and eight,

But you were begging

Your food from boors.'

Then they went to their seats, but Odd got up
and went before Sigurd, and brought him a horn,
another to Sjolf and recited a verse to each of them
before he went away:

'I shall serve to

You my song

Sigurd and Sjolf,

Seat companions,

You both need payback

For such ornate poetry

A couple of pansies,

Are the pair of you.

You were, Sjolf,

On the kitchen floor

Deeds lacking,

Undaring cowards

And out in

Aquitania

Four people

Had I felled.'

They drank from the horns, but Odd went to sit down. Then they went over to Odd, and Sjolf gave him his horn and recited:

'You, Odd, have been

With beggars

And received titbits

From the table,

And I alone

From Ulfsfell

My hacked shield

Held in my hand.'

Sigurd brought him another horn and said this:

'Odd, we glimpsed you not

Out with the Greeks,

Fighting the Saracens

We reddened our swords;

We made the hard

Sound of harrying,

Felled the fighters,

The folk in red.'

Odd now drank from the horns, but they went
to sit down. Then Odd rose and went with his horn
to each of them and said this:

'You were giggling, Sjolf,

With the girlies,

While keen flames

Played through the fort;

We killed the hard

Hadding there,

And Olvir later his

Life we took.

You, Sigurd, lay

In the lady's bower,

While we battled

The Bjarmians twice;

Warlike heroes

With hawk like minds,

While you slumbered in the hall,

Slept under a sheet.'

Now Odd went to sit down, but they drank
from the horn, and men thought it a great
entertainment, and had given a good hearing so far.
After that they went before Odd and brought him
two horns. Whereupon Sjolf:

'Odd, we saw you not

On Atalsfjalli,

When the fen-fire

We had gathered;

We the berserks

Bound up there,

Of the king's troop many

A warrior was killed.'

Odd now drank from the horns, but they sat
down. Odd brought them a horn and said this:

'Sjolf, you weren't seen,

Where you could see

Men's byrnies

Washed in blood;

Spear tips dug

In ring-sarks,

But in the king's hall

You'd rather cavort.

Sigurd, you weren't seen,

When we cleared six

High-pooped ships

Of Hauksnes;

You weren't seen

West of England,

When Skolli and I

Shortened the king's stay.'

Odd sat down now, but they brought him the horn and with no poetry. He drank of it, but they settle down. And now Odd brought them horns and said this:

'Sjolf, you weren't seen,

When we reddened our swords

Sharp on the Earl

Off Laeso island;

But you bunked down there

At home, torn between

The cuddlesome

Calf and the slave girl.

Sigurd, you weren't seen,

When on Zealand I slew

The battle-hard brothers,

Brand and Agnar,

Asmund, Ingjald,

Alf was the fifth;

But you were couched

In the hall of the king

Teller of tall tales,

A comic turn.'

Now he went to sit down, they stood up and brought him two horns. Odd drank them both. Then he brought them horns and said this:

'Sjolf, we saw you not

South at Skida,

Where noble kings

Knocked helmets;

Rapidly with blood,

We became ankle deep;

I was slaying men,

We saw you not there.

Sigurd, we saw you not

At Svia Skerries,

When we paid Halfdan

For his hospitality;

Our swords hacked

Battle-hewn shields,

Swords sliced,

He died himself.'

Now Odd sat down, but they brought him the horns and he drank them off, but they went to sit down. Odd then brought them the horns and said:

We sailed our ash-ship

Through Elfar Sound,

Content and happy,

At Tronuvagar;

There was Ogmund

Eythjof's Bane,

Tardy to flee,

With two ships.

Then we showered

Linden shields

With hard stones

And sharp swords;

Three of us survived

But nine of them.

Captive rogue,

Why so quiet now?'

Odd then went to his seat, but they brought him two horns. He drank from them and offered them two more and said this:

'Sigurd, we saw you not

On Samsey island,

When we received

Strokes from Hjorvard;

Two of us,

But twelve of them;

I seized victory,

You sat quietly.

I went over Gautland

Grim in mind

Seven days I went,

Until I met Saemund;

I took then,

Before I travelled,

Eighteen people's

Lives away,

But you took – you

Pitiful wretch,

Late at the sunset –

A slave girl to bed.'

Then there was a great cheer in the hall at what Odd had sung, and they drank from their horns, but Odd sat down. The king's men enjoyed their entertainment. Once they brought Odd two horns, and he finished quickly both of them. After that Odd stood up and went to them and he thought that now that the drink and all had defeated them. He gave them the horns and said this:

'You will never

Be thought worthy,

Sigurd and Sjolf,

Company for a king;

Of Hjalmar I think,

The brave,

Who briskly swung

His sharp sword.

Thord was sharper

Who broke shields,

When we were in conflict

The heroic king;

He laid Halfdan

Upon the earth,

And all of his

Fellows and allies.

We were together, Asmund,

Often in childhood

Sworn brothers together

Many a time;

I often bore

In battle a spear,

Where kings

Clashed in the fray.

We smote the Saxons

And raided the Swedes,

Ireland and England

And once Scotland

Frisians and Franks

And to say anything;

Smote them all

I was like a pestilence.

Now I'll list

All of them;

Those fierce warriors

Who followed me there;

Will never again

Will then never

See in battle

The brave people.

Now I've listed

All the deeds,

That long ago we

Had done;

We returned,

Pride of place,

To sit in our high seats;

Let Sjolf speak.'

After that Odd sat in his seat, but the brothers fell down and now there was no more of them in the drinking, but Odd drank for a long time, and after that they lay down and slept the night.

In the morning when the king came to the throne, Odd and his comrades were already up outside. He went at once to the water to wash. The brothers saw that the bark cuff was torn on one of his hands, and there was a red arm and gold rings on the arm, and they were not narrow. And then they ripped off all his bark. He did not try to stop this, but underneath he was clad in a scarlet robe of costly stuff, but his hair lay down to the shoulders. He had a golden band on his forehead and he was the most handsome of all men. They took his hands and led him into the house to the throne of the king, and said: 'It seems that we did not fully appreciate whom we have had here in our care.'

'It may be,' said the king, 'and who is this man who has so hidden his identity from us?'

'I am named Odd, which I told you months ago, son of Grim Hairycheek from northern Norway.'

'Are you not the Odd who travelled to Bjarmaland a long time ago?'

'He is the man who has come here.'

'It is not strange that my nobles did badly with

you in sports.' The king now stood up and welcomed Odd well and invited him to sit on the throne with him. 'I will not take it like that, unless I go with my comrades.' It is said that they now changed their seats and Odd sat next to the king, but Harek moved from his place to a stool before the king. The king showed much respect to Odd, and he valued no man more than him.

Chapter Twenty Eight

Odd and Harek often discussed things with each other. Odd inquired if men had not ask to marry the king's daughter. 'It is a fact,' he said, 'Both leading men have asked her for wife.'

'How did he answer this matter?' said Odd. 'He has said there is a chance,' he said. 'Let me hear about it,' said Odd. 'The king wants to collect tribute from a land named Bjalka. It is ruled by the king who is called Alf and nicknamed Bjalki. He is married. His wife is called Gydja. He is a great man for sacrifices and both are the same. They have a son together, called Vidgrip. They are such magicians that they could hitch a horse to a star. The king has tribute to collect from there, and it has long been unpaid. The king said that he would marry his daughter to the man who could collect the tribute from that land but it amounted to nothing, because they asked to go with so large a force to the country, the king thought he wouldn't have enough warriors to defend his realm.'

'So it seems to me,' said Odd, 'that either the tribute won't be gathered, or else that it must be gathered with a smaller force, but do you think the king will want to give me such a chance as the others, if I can retrieve the tribute?' said Odd. 'A wise man is the king,' said Harek, 'and I guess that he'll see the difference between you and the other suitors.' And now this issue was mentioned before the king, and not to make a long story of it, it was concluded that Odd would go on this expedition and collect the tribute, and if he completed his mission and got the tribute, he should marry the king's daughter, and he promised the woman with many people as witnesses.

Now Odd got ready to go, and gathered together such a troop as he wanted, and when he was ready the king saw him off. They were going by land. 'There is a costly treasure,' said the king, 'that I will give to you.'

'What is it?' said Odd. 'It's a shieldmaiden who long has followed me,' said the king, 'and has been a shield for me in every battle.' Odd smiled and said: 'It has never come to pass that women have been a shield for me, but I'll take all that you think good to offer.' The King and Odd parted now, and Odd went on until he reached a great swamp, and he crossed it with a running jump. The shield-maiden was next after him, and she became frightened when she came to the swamps. Odd asked, 'Why did you not jump after me?'

'Because I was not prepared,' she said. 'Yes,' he said, 'prepare yourself.' She hiked up her skirt and ran at the swamp a second time, and it went as before, and so the third time. Odd then jumped back over the swamps and grabbed her hand and flung her out into the swamp and said: 'Go there now, and all the trolls take you,' then jumped back over the swamps for the third time now, and awaited his men. They were all went to the end of the bog, because it was wide and hard to get across. Odd then went with his troop and sent spies before him, and they brought him news that Vidgrip had amassed a large army, and against them he marched. They met each other on a plain, and it was evening by then.

They both encamped there, and Odd kept a lookout that the evening for where Vidgrip pitched his tent. When the men had fallen asleep and all was calm and quiet, Odd stood up and walked out. He was so equipped that he had a sword in his hand and no other weapon. Soon was he there, at the tent where Vidgrip slept, and he stood there some time, and waited to see if any man would come out of the tent. It happened that a man walked out, but it was very dark. He began to speak and said, 'Why are you hiding here?' he said, 'Come into the tent or go away.'

'Yes,' he said, 'I have got myself lost. I can't find my bedroll, where I lay down early in the evening.'

'Do you know whereabouts it was in the tent?'

'I am sure that I was lying in Vidgrip's tent and one man lay in between me and him, but as it goes now, I can't find my way, but I will be every man's laughing-stock if you will not help.'

'Yes,' said the other, 'I will lead you to the bedroll that Vidgrip lies on,' and so did he. 'Yes,' said Odd, 'let's now be quiet, and all is well now, because now I see my space clearly.' Now he walked away, but Odd stood there looking after him to where he's going, until he was asleep. Then Odd stuck a peg through the tent wall where Vidgrip lay. After that he went out and went behind the tent, where that peg was. Then he lifted the tent flap and pulled Vidgrip out and cut off his head on a log. He closed the tent and let the body fall back, then he went to his tent and lay down and acted as if nothing had happened.

Chapter Twenty Nine

And the next morning, when the Vikings woke up, they found Vidgrip dead and his head gone. It seemed to them such a marvel that all wondered. They now talked together, and it was decided that they take another one as leader, and call him by Vidgrip's name and have him bear the banner during the day. And now Odd woke and armoured himself. He arranged things there so that they had a standard pole erected and he set Vidgrip's head on the top of the pole. Now the two armies drew up. Odd went out before his troop and he had a much smaller force. Odd started speaking and called on the native force, and asked if they recognised the head that was borne before him. Then the people of the land thought they recognised Vidgrip's head and marvelled greatly that it could be so. Odd now gave them two choices, whether they wanted to fight against him or give up. But it seemed to them that their outlook was bleak whatever they tried, and it was advised that they yield to Odd. He took them and all these followers and went to where Odd encountered Alf Bjalki. Both had a great troop, and yet Odd had fewer than Alf. At once battle broke out between them. It was so fierce that Odd was amazed at the slaughter that happened, because he thought he saw a lot of losses from his troop. 'It follows, too,' said Odd, 'I can cut my way up to the banner of Alf, but I see him nowhere.' Then one countryman spoke, who had been with Vidgrip before: 'I am not sure,' he said, 'what's wrong with you, since you do not see him, for he goes just behind his banner and never leaves it, and this is a sign of it, that he shoots an arrow from each finger and kills a man with each one.'

'I still cannot see him,' said Odd. Then the man raised his hand above Odd's head and said: 'Look from here under my hand.'[76] And then Odd saw Alf and everything else the man had said. 'Hold it there for a while,' said Odd, and he did so. Now Odd felt for Gusir's Gifts and took one of them and put it to the string and shot at Alf Bjalki; he put up the palm of his hand, and the arrow did not want to bite. 'Now you shall all go,' said Odd, 'though none of you will suffice.' He shot all of them, but none of them bit, and then all Gusir's Gifts dropped down in the grass. 'I am not sure,' said Odd, 'but maybe it has now come to pass, what old man Jolf said, that they are now gone, Gusir's Gifts, and I will try the man's stone arrows,' and he took one of them and laid it on a string, and shot at Alf Bjalki. When he heard the whine of the arrow that flew at him, he still raised his palm, but the arrow flew through it and out of the back of his head. Odd took another and laid it to the string, and shot at Alf. He put up the other palm and meant now to protect his remaining eye, but the arrow came through that eye, into the brain, and out of the back of his head. Alf did not fall any more than before. Then Odd shot the third, and hit Alf in the waist, and now he fell dead. Now all the old man's stone arrows vanished, as he had said that they could be shot once and then they would not be found.

Now the fight was quickly over, because the enemy was routed and retreated to the city. Gydja stood there in the gate and she shot arrows from all

---

[76] A similar method of detecting someone under a spell of invisibility is used in the *Gesta Danorum* (Book 2).

her fingers. Now the battle died away, and everywhere the enemy troop surrendered to Odd. Near the city were shrines and temples, and Odd had them set on fire and burnt everything near the town, and then poetry came to Gydja's lips:

'Who is causing this blaze,

This battle;

Who on the other side

Uses spears?

Shrines are blazing,

Temples burn,

Who has reddened the sword edge

On Yngvi's troop?'

Now Odd answered and said this:

'Odd burns shrines

And breaks temples

And destroys

Your idols of wood;

They did no

Good in the world,

From out of the fire

They could not save themselves.'

Then she said:

'I laugh at that,

Learning what you've done

To earn Frey's anger,

His great fury,

Help me gods

And goddesses,

Aid me, Powers,

Your own Gydja.'

Then Odd said:

'I don't care

If you curse me,

Filthy woman,

With Frey's anger;

I saw your gods burn

In the blaze,

Trolls take you,

I trust God alone.'

Then she said:

'Who fostered you

To be so foolish,

That you do not want

To worship Odin?'

Then Odd said:

'Ingjald raised me

In childhood,

Who ruled Eikund

And lived in Jaederen.'

Then she said:

'I would feel rich,

I'd have enough,

If I could see

My Alf again;

I'd give sacrifices

And four estates;

And I'd fling you

Into the fire.'

Then Odd said this:

'Odd bent his bow,

Arrows flew from strings,

Jolf's work pierced

Alf right through;

I don't think he

Will accept your offer

Ravens feast

On his carcass's flesh.'

Then she said:

'Who encouraged you,

East-faring here,

A terrible journey

And treacherous?

You must have wanted

A war badly,

When you sent Alf

The fatal arrow.'

Then Odd said:

'My arrows aided me

And Jolf's work

Mighty arrows

And powerful bow;

But lastly because I

Never befriended,

Those gods you worship

I give my word.

I gave Frey

And then Odin,

Blinded both,

Thrust them in the blaze,

Off ran the gods

Away out of sight,

Anywhere a gaggle of them

Had been found.'

And again he said:

'I harried the gods

Fainthearted two,

Like goats from a fox

They ran afar;

Evil is Odin

As a close friend;

It must not continue,

Their devilish curse.'

Odd now attacked Gydja with a huge oak club. She ran away into the city with the army following her. Odd chased the fugitives, and killed everyone that he could lay hands on, but Gydja fled to the chief temple in the city, and ran inside and said this:

'Help me gods

And goddesses,

Aid me, Powers,

Your own Gydja.'

Odd came to the temple and would not go in after her. He went up the roof and saw where she was lying through the window. Then he took up a large stone and threw it through the window. It hit her on her spine and smashed the giantess against the stalls, and she died there. But Odd fought a battle throughout the city. He came to where Alf was; he was not yet dead. Odd then beat him with a club till he was dead. Now he gathered tribute all across the land and established the chiefs and governors. But as he says in his poem, it was in Antioch that he killed Alf and his son. And when he was done, he went away from there with great wealth and immense riches, so that no one could calculate its worth, and nothing is told of his journey until he come back to the Greek kingdom. Meanwhile it had happened in the country that King Herraud was dead, and he had been laid to rest with a mound over him. Odd at once ordered a funeral ale for him when he returned to the land, and it was prepared, then Harek betrothed to Odd his foster child Silkisif, and now at the same time the men drank the marriage ale and the funeral ale of King Herraud. And at that feast Odd was given the name of king, and he now he ruled his kingdom.

Chapter Thirty

It had come to pass seven winters before that the king who ruled in Holmgard had been snatched by death, but an unknown man called Kvillanus seized the realm, and he became king there. He was somewhat strange looking because he had a mask over his face, so that no one ever saw his bare face. Men thought this strange. No one knew his family and ancestry nor land, nor where he was from. The men debated this a great deal. The news spread, and it came to Odd's ears in Greece, and it seemed to him very strange about this man, that he should never have heard about this man during all his travels. Then Odd got up in public and made a solemn vow that he should surely learn who ruled the kingdom in Holmgard in the east, and a little later he collected his forces and left home. He sent word to Sirnir, his blood-brother, and he came to meet him east of Wendland, and had thirty ships, but Odd fifty. They were all well equipped with weapons and men. They sailed eastwards to Holmgard.

Gardariki is so large a land that it contains many kingdoms. Marron was the name of one king. He ruled Moramar; this land is in Gardariki. Rodstaff was the name of a king. Radstofa was the name of where he ruled. Eddval was the name of a king. He ruled the realm that is named Sursdal. Holmgeir was the name of the king who ruled Holmgard before Kvillanus. Paltes was the name of a king. He ruled Palteskjuborg. Kaenmarr was the name of a king. He ruled Kaenugard, where the first settler was Magog son of Noah's son Japheth. All these kings now named were tributaries under King Kvillanus.

And before Odd entered Holmgard, Kvillanus had mustered troops for the previous three winters. Men thought that he had known of Odd's coming. All kings mentioned formerly were with him. Svart Geirridson was there. He was so-called after Ogmund Eythjof's Bane had disappeared. There was also a great host of Kirjalalandi and Rafestalandi, Refaland, Virlandi, Estland, Livland, Vitland, Courland, Lanland, Ermlandi and Pulinalandi. It was so great an army that no one could count it in hundreds. Men marvelled much at where this immense army should be gathered from. When Odd came ashore, he sent messengers to the king Kvillanus and challenged him to a tournament, and Kvillanus responded quickly and went to meet him with his army. He wore a mask on his face, as he was accustomed to do. But when they met, they got ready for the tournament. They had strong lances and long. They broke four lances, and they tourneyed for three days, and did not achieve anything more. Then Kvillanus said, 'It seems to me now that we've tested each other, and I think we are equal.'

'I suppose that's right,' said Odd. 'It seems to me that we understand,' said Kvillanus, 'and should fight no longer, and I will invite you to a banquet.'

'There's just one thing,' said Odd. 'What is that?' Kvillanus said. 'That,' said Odd, 'I do not know who you are, but I have made a solemn vow to learn who is king in Holmgard.' Then Kvillanus took the mask from his face and said: 'Do you know who owns this ugly head?' Odd realised that this man was Ogmund Eythjof's-Bane, because he could see all the marks he'd given him when he had torn off his beard, his face and head back to the middle of his crown. It was all healed over the bones but no hair grew. Odd said. 'No, Ogmund,' he said, 'I will never come to terms with you. You have done much harm to me, and I challenge you to fight tomorrow.' Ogmund accepted, and the day after they met in battle. It was both violent and brutal, and it there were the greatest casualties with men killed on both sides. Sirnir fought well as usual and killed many men, because Snidil bit all that was before him. Svart Geirridson turned against him, and there was a fierce battle, but Snidil failed to bite although Svart had no armour. Svart lacked neither strength nor malice, but at the end of their duel Sirnir fell dead although with much honour. Odd killed all the tributary kings under Kvillanus, some he shot, and some he hewed down. But when he saw the fall of Sirnir, it angered him strongly, and it seemed it was happening all over again, a loss of life at the hands of Ogmund and his men. He put an arrow to the string and shot at Svart, but he put up the palm of his hand, and it would not bite. Thus went another, and the third. Then it passed through his mind that he had experienced a great loss now Gusir's Gifts were gone. He turned away from the fight and into the forest and cut himself a big club and went back into battle. But when he met Svart, they started fighting. Odd struck him with a club, not turning away till he had broken every bone in Svart and left him there dead. Kvillanus had not been idling away his time, for it is said that arrows shot out of his fingers and a man was killed by each, and with the aid of his men he had killed every man with Odd. Many had also fallen on Kvillanus' side, so that he could hardly count the dead. Odd was still up and fighting valiantly. He was neither tired nor wounded because of his shirt. Night fell upon them, and it became too dark to fight. Kvillanus then went to the city with his men who had survived. He had no more than six hundred men, all tired and wounded. He was then called Kvillanus Blaze. He ruled long in Holmgard.[77]

---

[77] These days known as Novgorod. According to the poem at the end, it was at this point that Arrow-Odd participated in the Bravic War on the side of King [Sigurd] Hring, as described

Odd walked off through the wilderness and woods until he came to Gaul. At that time two kings ruled, but there had been twelve realms[78]. One king was named Hjorolf, the other Hroar. They were the sons of two brothers. Hroar had killed Hjorolf's father to get the throne and he ruled the whole realm, except that Hjorolf ruled one county. Odd had come to his coast. The king was young and amused himself by shooting at targets, but it went poorly. Odd said that the shooters were bad shots. 'Could you shoot better?' said the king. 'It does not seem much to me,' said Odd, but now he shot, and always hit. Then the king made much of this man and formed a high opinion of him. The king told him how he was treated by King Hroar. Odd said he ought to request an equal division of the realms. They sent twelve men with letters to the king, and when he had read them he answered and said that it was not modest to beg such things, and that he would send them back so that no one would wish to beg such again. And then both collected men, and Odd and Hjorolf had less than a twelfth of Hroar's forces. Odd asked people to point out King Hroar. Then he took an arrow and shot at him, and hit him in the waist, and King Hroar fell there, and there was no battle. Hjorolf offered the realm to Odd, but he was not happy there long and he sneaked away overnight. Then he wandered through the woods until he came to his kingdom, and he settled there in peace. Somewhat later Kvillanus sent Odd gifts rich both in gold and silver and many precious objects and with them a message of friendship and

---

in the *Gesta Danorum* (Book 8) and *Fragment of a Saga of Some Kings of the North* Chapter 8.

[78] Gaul also has twelve realms in Geoffrey of Monmouth's *Historia Regum Britanniae*.

reconciliation. Odd accepted these gifts because he was wise enough to see that Ogmund Eythjof's Bane, then called Kvillanus, was unbeatable, since he was no less a man than a wraith. And it is not written that they had further connections, and this was the end of their conflict.

Chapter Thirty One

Odd now stayed in his country, and he had a long life there and had two sons with his wife. Asmund was named after his foster-brother, and the other was named Herraud after his mother's father, and they were both promising. One evening time when the king and queen came to bed Odd began to speak: 'There is one land where I'm going to go.'

'Where are you going?' Silkisif said. 'I'm going north to Hrafnista,' he said, 'and I want to know who holds the island, because I own it and my family.'

'I think,' she said, 'you have enough property here, you have won all Gardariki, and can take other goods and countries that you want, and I think you should not covet a small island which is useless.'

'Yes,' he said, 'it may be that the island is worth little, but I will choose the ruler it shall have, and you will not discourage me because I have decided to go, and I will only briefly be off.'

Then he sailed two ships from the land and forty people aboard each, and there is no story of his journey until he came north to Hrafnista in Norway. But the men welcomed Odd when he got there, and prepared a banquet to greet him, and they gave him a fortnight of feasting. They invited him to take over the island and all the property that belonged there. He gave back all the property and would not stay there. Then he prepared for his journey, and the people brought him fine gifts.

Odd now sailed out from Hrafnista until they came to Berurjod, which they think lay in Jaederen. Then he told his men to reef sails. Odd went ashore with his troop and came to where Ingjald's farm had been, and it was now only ruins grown over with turf. He looked over the place and then said: 'This is terrible to see, that the farm should be in ruins, instead of what was here earlier.' He then went to where he and Asmund had practiced shooting, and commented on how different the foster-brothers had been. He took them where they had gone swimming in the water, and named them every landmark. And when they had seen this, he said, 'Let us go on our way, and it won't help now to stand looking at the land, no matter what we feel about it.' Now they went down, and everywhere the ground had eroded, while it had bloomed when Odd was there before. When they went down, Odd said: 'I think now that hopes are fading that the prediction will be fulfilled, as the seeress predicted for me long ago. But what is there?' Odd said, 'what lies there, is that not a horse's skull?'

'Yes,' they said, 'and extremely old and bleached, very big and all grey outside.'

'Do you think it will be the skull of Faxi?' Odd prodded the skull with his spear shaft. The skull shifted somewhat, but then an adder slithered out and struck at Odd[79]. The snake bit his foot above the

---

[79] A similar prophecy and conclusion appears concerning Oleg in the *Russian Primary Chronicle*.

ankle, so that the venom worked at once, and the whole leg swelled up. So it took Odd so fast that they had to lead him down to the sea. And when Odd was there, he sat down and said, 'Now, split my troop in half, and forty men shall sit with me, and I will write a poem about my life, while the other forty shall make me a coffin and gather firewood. Light a fire there and burn everything up when I am dead.'

Chapter Thirty Two

Now he began the poem, while one group made the coffin and collected the wood. But those who had been chosen memorised the poem. Now Odd said this:

1st

Listen to me warriors,

To what I will say

I give form to, speak

Now of my friends;

Too late to hide it,

Or fool yourself

No self-delusion

When fate is ruling.

2nd

I was brought up

By my father's wishes,

Fostered I was,

At Berurjod;

I was not

Unaccustomed to bliss,

Of all Ingjald

Could offer me.

3rd

We both

Spent our boyhood,

Asmund and I,

In childhood;

Shaped shafts,

Ships built,

Fletched arrows

A happy time.

4th

The seeress spoke

True runes,

But I lacked the

Wisdom to obey;

I told the young

Son of Ingjald,

That I would the fields

Of my father visit.

5th

Asmund said

He would always be eager,

As long as he lived,

To follow my lead;

I said to his father,

That I would come

Back never;

Now I've broken my word.

6th

Keen to cruise

Our craft in the surf,

Was not needed

A hand to navigate;

We arrived at the island

Steep with cliffs,

There Grim owned

Great garths.

7th

They greeted me blithely,

When I came to the farm,

His men favoured me

Celebrated my coming;

I guess I might

With my friends

Exchange gold

And fair speech.

8th

It was in spring

That I learnt Sigurd

And Gudmund were going

To raid the Bjarmians;

Then I told them

Sigurd, and Gudmund,

I wished to wander

With these valiant warriors.

9th

They commanded

Warships

My two kin had them

At their behest;

Rowers wanted

To conquer,

To take the treasure

Of the Tyrfi-Finns.

10th

We approached the Bjarmian

People's bothies

Sailing in safety

Our merchant ship;

Attacked with fire

Their families;

Took as captive

The Tyrfi-Finn's serving man.

11th

He could show us,

So he said,

Where much plunder

Was to be found;

He told us to walk

Further up the way,

If we wished treasure

More to win.

12th

Bjarmian folk

Soon came to defend

Their great mound

And mustered their forces;

But they died then,

Before we left,

A number of them

Lost their lives.

13th

We left hastily

For our vessels below

Then the flight took us

Over the fen;

We found we'd lost both

Boat and sails,

Wealth and riches,

When we arrived.

14th

I quickly kindled

In thick forest

Burning fire

Upon the land,

So the flames

Keenly played

Touching the sky;

Flame burnt the timber.

15th

We saw splendid vessels,

Hasten to land

Rich-clad rowers

Racing to the shore

Glad they were,

They showed it clearly,

My kinsmen,

To greet us.

16th

Forced to leave

Our lives to fortune

Brave bold boys

In driving weather:

Seemed to carry

Sand on deck,

Our men looked for land,

Saw it not there.

17th

We arrived at an island

Beyond steep cliffs

In late summer,

Then reefed our sails;

Made haste

Most of all

To set ships on rollers

Briskly on the strand.

18th

We raised tents,

While some were

Hunting bear,

Who knew to bend bows?

On the island

We lit a good fire

Before the blaze,

Set a bear's carcass.

19th

The mountain folk claimed

They would fling us

Out of the island;

Into the waves;

We did not consider

It encouraging, hearing

The promise of

The lava people.

20th

We feared them not

When we settled the islands

We weren't afraid

Of anything;

Some of us built

On the cliff above

A mighty wall;

I was one of them.

21st

I went looking

With Gusir's Gifts

Between the cliffs

And kindling flame;

I hit in the eye

One of the ettins

But in the breast

The berg-lady.

22nd

Then I got a name,

Just what I needed,

Out of the mountains

Monsters called it,

Rewarded Odd

Of the Arrows

With a fair wind

To sail away.

23rd

So we were soon ready

To sail away

From the island,

When the wind we got;

Whole we returned

Sailed back home,

So celebrated

Our family, greeting us.

24th

All warriors together

That same winter,

Glad of our gold

And good conversation;

In the spring

When the ice split

Our well-adorned vessels

We dragged to the water.

25th

We sailed off

South along the coast

All on watch

Twenty and one;

Expecting plunder,

There is for men,

If we the Elfar Skerries

Should lay waste.

26th

Found at last

Off the coast

Those two heroes,

Thord and Hjalmar;

They inquired

Which we'd rather,

Whether we wanted friendship

Or to begin the fight.

27th

Talked of treaties

Counselled together,

We thought it seemed a poor

Chance of wealth;

The band of Halogalanders

We thought best,

To join together

Seemed the better choice.

28th

We sailed our ships all

To any shore

That presented the best

Chance of booty;

Not terrified by

Any chieftains

We fought

In our warships.

29th

Raging angry

We ran into

The heroes we met

Off Holmanes;

We took

All the equipment

From those pretty boys

Of six ships.

30th

All stood

West with Skolli,

In the land where he ruled,

The people's lord;

By his enemies

We were blood-soaked,

Cut with swords,

But we seized victory.

31st

The earl's warriors

Wasted the headland,

Warriors fled, pursued,

Like foxes by hounds;

Hjalmar won the fight,

Setting on fire,

With swords and damage,

Destroyed ships.

32nd

Gudmund asked

If I wished to go

Home in the autumn

And accompany him;

But I said to him,

That I would see

The north no more

Or my kinsfolk.

33rd

All agreed

To meet next summer

Eastwards at the Gautelf

And go plundering;

Hjalmar the brave

Wanted to harry

With my troops

Terrorise the southlands.

34th

They divided

Into two groups

Hardy heroes,

When the wind was good;

We sailed our ships

To the Swedish kingdom,

To visit Ingvi

At Uppsala.

35th

To me gave Hjalmar

The brave

Five estates

For my own;

In my prosperity,

I took pleasure

When people offered me

Rings and peace.

36th

It was for all of us

Happy days

When Swedish warriors

And Sigurd of the north;

Plundered all

The islanders

Of their wealth,

While they felt the flame.

37th

We sailed to the west

In speeding ships

To Ireland, across

The crashing waves;

When we went there,

Women and men,

Hurried away

From out of their houses.

38th

I ran down a wide

Wagon trail,

Till I set my face

Towards the arrows;

To have back Asmund

All my wealth

I would give;

All my gold.

39th

I glimpsed at last,

Where they gathered together,

Stout men

And their wives;

Where I aided four

Of Olvor's family,

Helped them lose

Their valuable lives.

40th

Called to me out of the wagon,

The elf-woman, said goodbye,

And she made me

Promise her;

Asked me to return

In the next summer,

To receive the reward

That awaited me.

41st

Unlike a byrnie

The blue rings,

Ice cold about me

Above my sides;

On my flesh

A silk shirt

Sewn with gold

Was woven close.

42nd

We left the west

Looking for plunder,

So that my men

Called me coward

Until at Skida

We encountered

Evil brothers

And their death ensued.

43rd

Soti and Halfdan

At Svia Skerries

Many men

Had they murdered;

They seized,

Before we split,

Six hundred ships

Cleared stem to stern.

44th

Next we met

In our wanderings

Cunning sly fellows

At Tronuvagar;

Undoomed was Ogmund;

Of our men,

Three remained there,

But nine of his.

45th

News of killing

Could I make my boast

When we got back

To our boats;

Hjalmar and I were

Greatly dismayed

When we found Prow-Gleam

Run through.

46th

We went home from there,

Heroic boys,

The barrow of Thord

We built high;

No man dared

To go against us,

We had our way

In everything.

47th

Hjalmar and I

Each day were glad

While our warships

We did steer,

Until on Samsey

We met the fighters

Who knew well

How to wield weapons.

48th

We forced them

Under eagles' feet

Gloriless

Twelve berserks;

I suffered the death,

On that day of destiny,

The terrible loss

Of my friend.

49th

Never have I known

In all my life

A nobler man

Braver-hearted;

I bore him on my shoulders,

Hero cruel to helmets

And to Sigtuna

I took him back.

50th

I did not allow

A long wait

Before I sought Saemund

Who was at sea;

His men cleared

My ship quickly,

But myself there

I saved by swimming.

51st

I went through Gautland

Grim in mind

Six half-days passed,

Before I found Saemund;

I confronted him and his men,

Forced them to stand;

Six and eight

Faced my sword.

52nd

I went southwards over the sea

A long journey,

Till to the shallow

Creeks I went;

I walked alone,

But other

Men took

The road to Hel.

53rd

Still I came there

To Aquitania

Strong men

Ruled over cities;

Where I left four

Fallen lie,

Courageous boys;

Not where I am now come.

54th

It was in former days,

That I despatched

Messages to the north

My own folk;

I was as glad

To greet them

As the hungry

Hawk to feed.

55th

With many a mark

Of high esteem

All us three

Were honoured;

But I continued

Despite their kindness;

My brothers both

Remained back there.

56th

I travelled in haste

Away from the host,

Until I reached the spacious

City of Jerusalem;

I raced down

Into the river

And then I was clear

How Christ should be served.

57th

I recalled that

They cascaded, the waters

Of Jordan over me

Beyond the Greek empire;

Still held, however,

As I had known,

My magic shirt

All its merits.

58th

I met the vulture

Near the valley,

It flew with me

Across far countries,

Until it came

To the high crag

And let me rest

In its nest.

59th

To me Hildir

Hurried then

Glorious-framed giant,

In a rowing boat;

Let me stay

This strong fighter

Twelve months

For a rest.

60th

I help Hildir's daughter,

Huge and large,

Handsome girl,

Giant's daughter

And with her

Rather mightily,

A fine brave

Son I had

And unique among

The native people.

61st

Ogmund killed him,

Eythjof's Bane

In Helluland's

Lava desert,

His nine companions,

I crushed their flesh;

Never was a Viking

Worse thought of.

62nd

Moreover he also

Slew my sworn brothers,

Sirnir and Gardar,

I snatched off his beard;

He looked unlike

Anyone at table

And was then called

Kvillanus Blaze.

63rd

Men thought me great-hearted

A gallant warrior,

When we battled

At Bravellir;

When Hroar called

For the wedge formation[80]

Odd the Wanderer

Led it into the fray.

64th

I came across two

Resolute kings

A little later,

---

[80] Elsewhere Odd is said to have fought on Sigurd Hring's side, against Harald Wartooth, who was taught the wedge formation, or swine-array, by the god Odin, and used it to conquer a wide empire. When Harald saw that Sigurd Hring's men had adopted the same tactics, he saw it as evidence that Odin had now betrayed him, and doom was at hand.

Controlling the country;

I chose to aid

One against the other,

The young ruler

Regained his heritage.

65th

I came at last,

Where were so cocky

Sigurd and Sjolf

In that king's country;

The other noblemen

Begged me to test

My skills with theirs

In sport and shooting.

66th

I shot fewer

Than those fellows,

A subtler shaft

Was the spear in my hand;

Soon I competed

With them in swimming;

I gave them both

Bloody noses.

67th

I was set

Beside the shieldmaiden,

When to war

We went marching;

I knew that far-away

In Antioch

Men were falling,

But we grew wealthy.

68th

Felled with my sword

Many folk

And I

Whacked away;

I beat the beams

At the gate

I knocked down Bjalki,

With an oaken club.

69th

Then to me Harek

Offered comradeship,

Betrothed to me

His foster daughter;

I married Silkisif

Hilmar's daughter

Together we ruled

Righteously our realm.

70th

I wasn't allotted

Lasting bliss

For very long

As I would wish;

I could teach you

From my travels

Many lessons;

But this is the last.

71st

You must hasten

Down to the haven

We must say goodbye,

Here we part;

To Silkisif

And our sons

I send my greetings,

I'll go not there.'

And when the poem was complete, weakness quickly seized Odd, and they led him to where the coffin had been made. Odd said: 'Now all this is true, what she told me, the seeress. I will lie down in the coffin and die there. Then you shall set fire to the outside and burn everything up.' Then he lay down in the coffin, and said: 'Now you shall carry my greetings home to Silkisif and my sons and to our friends.' After that Odd died. They set fire to the wood and burnt everything up, and did not go until it was all burned. Most people say that Odd was twelve ells high, because that was the size of the coffin inside. Now Odd's comrades got ready for the journey and they travelled back east. They had a good wind until they came home. They told Silkisif the news, what had happened on their journey, and they carried her his greeting. It seemed this was sad news for her and her people, and she ruled over the kingdom after this and Harek, her foster father, with her, and held the land until Odd's sons were able to take over. Now the family line of Odd's grew up in Gardariki. But the maiden Odd had left behind in Ireland, who was named Ragnhild, had left the west along with her mother and went northwards to Hrafnista and had since married, and many people are descended from her, and her family line grew up there. And now the history of Arrow-Odd finishes, as you have now heard told.

THE SAGA OF AN BOW-BENDER

The Saga of An Bow-bender is about another member of the Hrafnista family that includes Ketil Trout, Grim Hairy-cheek and Arrow-Odd. Chiefly set in Norway, it features almost no forays into the supernatural (although a dwarf provides An with his bow and arrows), unlike the other Sagas of the Men of Hrafnista.

An is an outlaw and archer, much like Robin Hood or William Tell, and most of his saga concerns itself with his struggle to survive in the wilds while feuding with the corrupt king Ingjald of Namdalen. Like his maternal great grandfather Ketil Trout (not to mention other legendary or semi-legendary figures such as Beowulf, Offa, and Prince Hal), An is an idle youth who goes on to prove his worth in later life. And like his kinsman Arrow-Odd, the great feud of his life ends ultimately in an uneasy truce, rather than outright victory or defeat.

An the Bow-bender appears to be identical to Ano Sagittarius (Ano the Archer) in Book Six of

Gavin Chappell

Saxo Grammaticus' *Gesta Danorum*, although in the latter story he is no longer an outlaw feuding with a king, but a king's retainer loyal unto the death – although he remains a superlative bowman.

The Hrafnista men were claimed as ancestors by some of the more powerful families in medieval Iceland, and their supposed descendants included the troublesome Egil Skallagrimsson, a Viking *par excellence* of the Viking Age, and even that violent, treacherous literary figure of medieval Iceland, Snorri Sturluson, author of the *Prose Edda*. A later version of the saga even noted the presence of men in mid-seventeenth century Iceland who were not ashamed to claim descent from the men of Hrafnista.

Here begins the saga of An, who was descended from Ketil Trout

Chapter One

This saga begins in the days when the petty kings were in Norway. A father and a son ruled over one district. The father was named Olaf and the son was Ingjald, but Ingjald was an adult at the beginning of this saga. The two grew up very differently from each other. King Olaf was popular, but Ingjald was the most guileful of men. Their retainers were named Bjorn and Ketil: he was called Bjorn the Strong. They were of like temper to King Ingjald, overbearing and ready for anything. King Olaf had a daughter named Asa, most beautiful and talented of

496

women. The father and son ruled over Namdalen district[81]. King Olaf was old when the saga begins. He had taken two queens to wife, and had outlived both. The second one he married was named Dis; she had previously been married to Anund the Denier, who was king in Fjordane, and had borne him two sons, both called Ulf. They now ruled over Fjordane, and Ingjald meant to claim that half of the kingdom with his brothers as an inheritance from his mother. He fought two battles with them and in both met defeat.

There was a farmer named Bjorn. He lived in Hrafnista, which lies off the Namdalen coast. Bjorn had much influence over the farmers in the north. His wife was named Thorgerd. She was the daughter of Bodmod Framarsson and Hrafnhild, daughter of Ketil Trout. This Bjorn had a daughter named Thordis. She married Gaut of Hamar, who was a worthy man. They had a son named Grim. He was soon both tall and strong. Bjorn and Thorgerd had more children. Thorir was the name of the elder son, a promising man, courteous and talented in all respects. He was a retainer of King Olaf and was greatly esteemed by him, and to show this King Olaf gave Thorir a sword that his ancestors had in the family for a long time and was regarded as a great heirloom. It was named Thane[82]; it was both long and broad and was the sharpest of all swords; it was thrice polished. For a long while, Thorir stayed one winter with the king and another with his father. The younger son of Bjorn was named An. He soon grew tall but was unpromising and rather slow, although

---

[81] In central Norway.
[82] Old Norse *þegn*, 'thane, franklin, freeman, man', related to similar Old English *þegn,* 'servant, attendant, retainer.'

497

his strength was not known by men, not having been tested at that age, and instead he was considered foolish. He had little love from his father, but his mother loved him a great deal. Men thought that he was unlike his former kinsmen, such as Ketil Trout and other men of Hrafnista, except in size. An did not lie in the kitchen[83], but some men called him a simpleton. He did no work. Because of this, he was disliked when he was nine years old. By then he was no smaller than Thorir, his brother. He was a shocking sight, meagrely and poorly clad, with holes at both the knees and elbows. But when he was twelve, he ran away for three nights, so that no one knew what had happened to him. An entered a forest clearing. He saw there a stone that stood tall and a man near a stream. He had heard about those people named dwarves, that they were more skilful than other men. Then An went between the stone and the dwarf and with a spell blocked his entrance into the stone and said he should never return to his home, unless he made An a great and strong bow and with it five arrows[84]. It should have the property that he would hit everything he shot at, on the first shot, as he wished. Within three nights it should be done, and An waited in the meanwhile. The dwarf did so without cursing the weapons[85], and that dwarf was named Lit. An gave him some silver coins that his mother had given him. The dwarf gave An a fine chair. After that he went home, carrying the chair on

---

[83] i. e., he was not that stereotype of saga literature, the 'coal-biter', who lazes in the warmth of the kitchen rather than heroically seeking glory.

[84] Under similar circumstances, King Svafrlami suborns two dwarfs into forging the sword Tyrfing in The Saga of Hervor and Heidrek

[85] Unlike in the saga mentioned above.

his back. Men laughed at him a great deal. An gave his mother the chair and said that he had to give her the best reward.[86]

Chapter Two

When An was eighteen years old, he was bigger than other men in the north, but he had not yet grown in intelligence or courtesy. That winter Thorir had stayed in Hrafnista and had taken his sword's name as a nickname, and he was called Thorir Thane. And in the spring Thorir prepared to travel to meet with the king. An asked to go with him, but Thorir flatly refused. But when he went out to his ship, An followed him there. Thorir asked what he wanted now. An said that he would go with him whether he gave him any leave to or not. Thorir said he would not go, - 'you know nothing about how to act among noblemen,' he said, 'since your usual custom is barely good enough to stay here at home.' Then he took An and bound him very fast to an oak. An didn't struggle. Then Thorir went but it was not long before he saw that An was following and he was dragging the tree after him. He had pulled it up by the roots. Then Thorir said: 'You are a prodigy, kinsman, as strength goes, but I still do not advise that you go to meet the king with such a disposition as you have.' Then Thorir cut off his bonds and said, 'You value my word little.' He lifted the sword Thane and threatened him with it: 'This sword will teach you the manners that you do not have already, and it won't respect you and it will block your path.'

An spoke: 'You must not intimidate me like a

---

[86] A similar episode, though less explicit, appears in The Saga of Ketil Trout.

chastised child but so you know what I can do to you, you shall find out now.' An took hold of Thorir and lifted him in the air and shook him like a child, and said: 'See now, how much you have me under you, if we don't see things the same way.' Then he let him loose, and then Thorir saw what the stuff this man was made of.

Then they went out to the ship, and An wondered where he could put himself that would be the most inconvenient. The merchants asked each other who this man could be. An spoke: 'Why don't you ask me about this? I know what to tell you. I am called An and I'm of the Hrafnista family; my brother is Thorir Thane,' but they said they could not believe him. He said it was true. They said they would make him welcome. An was poorly clad. Thorir asked the crew to cut him up some clothes from the cargo, so that he would not be so odd-looking, and so it was done. It was little use to him, because he fastened them clumsily to himself, and it was no improvement in his dress at all. The crew were well-disposed to An. He knew nothing but to be friendly in return.

Chapter Three

Thorir came to Namdalen and there they heard the news that King Olaf was dead, and Ingjald was the king of the country which they had both ruled. Thorir said: 'He died, the better man, and I would not have come from the north if I had known about this.' Thorir now went to the king's farm. An took with him his bow, and when they arrived at the hall, he strung it, and it was extremely strong. Thorir asked why he did that. An said it would soon become clear. He had the string run before his breast, and the bow across his shoulders, and he had his arrows in his hand. And when they came to the hall door, doorkeepers gave space for Thorir, but when An arrived there was a great tumult because he had not change his costume. Then he went right to the doors, but the bow stuck out beyond his shoulders, and it did not have enough space for the door, and had to either break or bend strongly, because the doorway blocked the way. Then An came into the hall; the bow bent but did not break. An settled down near the entrance, and Thorir went to the king and spoke to him. The king welcomed him and told him to sit on the high seat opposite. 'You shall be welcome here with us, but who is that with you, and why did that man so quickly split from you?'

Thorir said, 'That man is my brother, and he hardly knows the manners of a commoner.'

The king said, 'He shall be welcome here, and let him sit next to you. Let us do it for your sake, and we have heard tell of him, and he is a remarkable man in many respects.'

Thorir met An and told him the king's words, - 'and turn this to your advantage, brother.'

An answered, 'We will not share a seat. It is more important to me that I get winter lodgings.' Thorir said he thought that it would be readily available.

Nonetheless Thorir went to the king and said, 'I wish to beg winter lodgings for my brother at his request, even though he will stay in his seat.'

The king said, 'Readily available to him are winter lodgings, but what seat is better for him than with you?'

Thorir said he could not do anything with him

- 'it suits him best to get his own way, and so I was reluctant to have him come with me, because I knew that his nature is odd.'

Thorir told An the King's word. An said, 'It has turned out well. Now go, brother, to your seat.' Thorir did so.

An was aloof and refused to socialise; he stayed the longest in his seat, except when he went to the privy. The retainers laughed at him a lot, and chief in this was Ketil[87]. An turned a deaf ear to that, and so it went until Yule. Then the king proclaimed that he would give Yule presents, as his father had done, and said that he wished his men to pay him tribute like this. And on Yule Eve all people accepted their gifts except An. The king asked why An refused his gifts, 'will he not accept gifts like others?' This was repeated to An.

He rose to his feet and said: 'I think it good to have gold.' He did not resemble a glorious warrior when he went up to the King. He was quite incredible to look at.

The king said: 'What twanged so loud, An, when you walked in through the doors for the first time?'

'My bow,' said An, 'because your hall doors were so small, O king, that the tips bent all the way back when I had it on my shoulders before I came in, and it made a loud noise when it sprang back.'

'You must,' said the king, 'be called An the Bow-bender.'

'What will you give to me as a naming gift?' said An.

---

[87] Previously mentioned as one of Ingjald's retainers.

'You shall have a gold ring,' said the king, 'as both a naming gift and a Yule gift, because I heard what you said earlier. You must be a very strong man, as big as you are.'

'I think,' said An, 'that I am very strong, but I don't know.' An took the gift and did not thank him. He played with the ring, and put it on his mailcoat. He tossed it from hand to hand, and once the ring shot away. He went to look in the antechamber, but when he came back, he looked like he had bathed in shit. His bench-companions asked him why he looked so terrible. He spoke hardly at all, but later he told one, - 'I'll tell you, if you can keep a secret.'

He said he would keep quiet.

An said, 'It is true what is said, 'Wealth that provokes jealousy is soon gone. Now the ring is lost.'

His bench-companion said, 'Let's keep quiet about it.'

An said, 'So shall it be, but this ring is not meant for me, and I will give it to the man who finds it.' This was told to the household, and everyone mentioned it to each other, but Ketil laughed and said that it had gone as it should be expected if you give gold to a fool. He went and looked for the ring with the men. They squeezed together into the antechamber.

An said, 'Why is it that the men crawl on hands and knees and toil in shit? Has there been a fight?' He was told that they wanted to make good his loss and find the ring. An said, 'I am so forgetful. Here is the ring in my hand, but now I've paid you all back for frequently mocking me.' The retainers said they had been made to look foolish. An agreed that it was how it was. The mockery halted a while, but it soon began again the same as ever, and Ketil was the worst.

Chapter Four

One day it happened that the two brothers were outside the hall. Then the retainers came out and said: 'You must be a strong man, An.'

He said: 'Perhaps that is so, but I have not been tested.'

They said: 'Will you wrestle with Bjorn[88]?'

He said: 'On the condition that you serve me, and make a fire big for me.' They did so, and they invited him to warm himself. He said he would have more need for that when he came from the wrestling match. Then they got ready for wrestling in the hall. An had come wearing a shaggy cape that his mother had given him. He did not have a belt on, and the cape was so long it dragged behind him more than an ell's length; the sleeves fell down over his hands. Bjorn ran at An, but An stood fast. Bjorn was the strongest of all men. He took An up and threw him outside and on the fire, so that his shoulders were in the flames, but his legs struck farther out on the fence. Then there was great laughter. An stood. The fire had not hurt him because of his shaggy cape.

The king said: 'It seems to me, An, that you are not as strong as you claimed.'

An said, 'He seems to me stronger, O king, who falls first.'

---

[88] Like Ketil, mentioned in the first chapter as a retainer of Ingjald.

The king laughed at him. An then put on a harness and shortened his cloak and rolled up the sleeves. They ran at each other a second time. An dragged Bjorn to him and shook him like a child and then threw him farther out onto the fire and so let him loose. The retainers ran to him and pulled him out of the fire, but Bjorn was badly burned. They said this man was strong enough. An was pleased at this, that he was called strong, and he said now it could be seen that he wanted Bjorn to warm himself at the fire, and said Bjorn needed it more than him. An recited this verse:

'Sneering fellow, he should not

have flung me at the fence;

I wasn't at all able

to endure him; curse that man;

when I caught him in my clutches,

I flung fuel on the fire

I denied him honour, rather;

damn that man forever.'

Now the winter wore on, and one day the brothers were once again standing outside together. Then Thorir said: 'Are you not unhappy coming here, when you have found mockery and reproach?'

An said he wasn't unhappy, - 'I have received gold here and good winter lodging, but I do not care who reproaches me.'

Thorir said: 'I will try something that occurs to me. I will give you the sword Thane, so you can kill the two king's men, and settle the score yourself.'

An said, 'I want to see the sword, and I will accept it, but I will not promise to pay them back.'

And another day, when it was time for drinking An stood up and faced him who sat next to him, and looked at him, and so he did with everyone in the hall; he stood before the king the longest. Then he went to Thorir and laid his sword on the table before him and said he did not want to have it. There was much laughter at this, but Thorir was very annoyed.

Another time found the two brothers together, and Thorir asked: 'Why did you act so outrageously, brother, and other than I had planned?'

An said, 'I did wonder whether I wanted revenge on the king's men, and it seemed to me I didn't. But I stared most at the king, because that was when my mind wavered the most, whether I should do it or not.'

Thorir said, 'You're too stupid, the king is sympathetic to you.'

An said, 'We do not need to discuss him, because I think that no worse man will grow up in Norway but the king.'

Then they left off speaking, and then came spring. Then King Ingjald called a gathering. He stood up in the assembly and said: 'Men know that my father is dead and I have succeeded to his realm, and I wish to declare that I will pay compensation to all I have dealt with unjustly, and give them and all of you good laws. But I ask you, O my thanes, to attend a meeting with my brothers, and we may peaceably negotiate our claims to the realm, and I will provide my men food and beer.' Here was much applause.

Then An said, 'You will think the king's words good, brother.'

Thorir said that remained to be seen.

An said, 'I may tell you that he is now the worst disposed to his brothers and thinks in this way to bring about the most evil for them.'

Thorir said he had not turned his mind away from the king. After that they prepared themselves. An asked Thorir whether he wanted him to go with the retainers, - 'and you and the king. It's a small thing if I go on this journey as I am, and it's quite unclear how I would manage for food in the meantime. So I am more willing to go with you, it will last longest and turn out worst.'

Thorir said he wanted him to, and they went north with the king and anchored off some islands. Then said the king that they should make a harbour mark. An then recited a verse:

'Good for you, sallow,

you stand near the water

very well leafed;

a man shakes from you

morning dewdrops,

but I, on a thane,

think night and day.'

Thorir said, 'Do not do that, because I will give you the sword Thane.'

An said: 'I am not thinking of that thane.'

Ketil said: 'I believe that you think of some man[89] or other, and you would bugger him,' and at this they made much sport and mockery.

'Not so,' said An, 'I am not thinking on such a thane, I'm thinking of Thorir Thane, my brother, because he is so shallow-minded that he trusts this king, but I know that he will be the death of him.'

Then they come to Fjordane. King Ingjald said: 'I think that we are now in the realm of my brothers, and I have heard that they will not make peace with us. It seems to me the best choice that we should fight, and deliver ourselves from their opposition.'

Many would then rather have sat at home than gone there. But when the brothers heard this, they gathered an army to go against King Ingjald. King Ingjald gave his men drink, so that they would be the more daring. Then a big ox horn came to An. He recited:

Better it seems to me,

if bodies shall fall

that faster we force

our feet to the spears' meeting;

drink freely from the ox's

forehead spear-flincher,

sharply will the swords

swing, if I prevail.'

The king said, 'This is well composed, and he is not shieldless when you go at his side.'

---

[89] One meaning of the word 'thane', (see note 2).

An said, 'I don't think that it will be so useful today, although I am able to offer aid.'

The king said he did not know what sort of thane he would be. An said two possibilities would show themselves. He lay down on the ship when the others went up to fight.

Thorir said, 'Your behaviour has been very bad since you first came here, and now to lie aboard this ship when your help is needed; I thought you would have courage.' An said he did not care about his words.

The king went ashore, and the army came against them. They met near some woods and fought. An stood up and went to the woods and sat on a tree stump. He looked out across both armies and he saw two standards carried before the brothers of King Ingjald. An spoke to himself, 'Why would it not be good to offer help to King Ingjald, though that it is least needed, and yet he desires it himself? I will shoot, and it's more likely that I will hit my target, because it was said by the one who gave me the bow and arrows that I would be a good shot, and that was the dwarf who I met once in the woods of Hrafnista, but they thought me lost, when the dwarf and I made this deal, and I will now try out the work with which he redeemed himself and his head when I enchanted him out of the stone. He said I would shoot three famous shots, one with each arrow.'

He shot and aimed at one of the Ulfs[90], and the arrow flew through him and into the brush behind him. Then the standard fell. An recovered the arrow and ran to the ships. And when the people

---

[90] i.e. one of the two sons of King Anund the Denier and Dis, now kings of Fjordane, half-brothers of Ingjald.

saw it, they told the king that he must have been laid low by a throwing-spear or bow-shot.

In the evening they came to the ships. Everyone was discussing the shot. An heard that and said they should press the attack, - 'if it is half-completed.'

In the morning the king urged people to go ashore, and said he expected victory. An stayed behind, and no one told him to go ashore. He thought that King Ingjald might need help. He shot another arrow. It hit Ulf's chest, and it was not as hard as the previous shot, so the arrow stuck there. People recognised the shot and thought that the same man must have loosed both shots, though no one had been seen. The king said, 'For a long time I was certain that An would be a man of prowess.' The king sent for him, and said that he would reward him for his acts. The messengers saw that An had got into the boat and was not very near. They told him the king's message, and said that he would be respected for his conduct. An said, 'I will not go to the king, for he will give me a gallows for my work.'

The men went back and told the king. He said: 'He was not far wrong, and I do not want him to kill any more important men secretly, and I intended my brothers to live and for me to hold their domain under their name.'

Thorir said: 'It goes ill for you, you would rather have done it yourself. There was not any time when you did not want them dead.'

The king replied, 'If he had gone ashore with us, he would be worthy of honour, but for secret killing[91] he must be executed.'

510

Thorir said he expected that he would have an equal reward for him. Ingjald claimed his brothers' lands and appointed men to govern it. A mound was raised for his brothers, which was called Ulfahaug. The king was on board and ready to go out. Ketil said he wanted to meet his friend, who lived a short way away.

The king replied, 'Do not delay, because we sail soon.'

Ketil had An's arrow in his hand. He came to the farm of a farmer close to the ships. He did not know him. The farmer greeted him and asked his name.

He said, 'My name is An the Bow-bender, who you'll now have heard tell of because of my shots.'

The farmer replied, 'An-wanted[92] were your arrows here, because our chiefs were trustworthy men. But stay with us tonight.'

He said he would accept. There was no one else there except his wife and daughter. She was called Drifa.

Now to speak of An, he went into a hidden bay and came to the same farm, and hid himself to listen to the men speaking. The guest spoke up and said: 'Is that your daughter, farmer?'

'It is true,' he said.

'I'm going to get into bed with her tonight,

---

[91] In Norse society a distinction was made between killing in fair fight and 'secret killing.'

[92] The dialogue in this sequence includes several puns on An's name.

and you shall not get a better offer.'

The farmer did not say much about that. Ketil said he had done greater things than to get into her bed. And when An heard this, he went to the door and knocked. A servant came to the door and went out a long way before he saw the man. He asked his name. The man said An was his name.

The slave said: 'What's going An? That's the name of the man inside.'

An said that might be so, and he entered and sat down opposite Ketil. The farmer asked him his name. He said he was called An. The farmer said, 'Are you Another one, and will you be with us?'

He said he would accept, 'but I will have to wait a while before I eat, or has Ketil named himself An?'

He said: 'I did it as a joke.'

An said, 'I have endured this since we met. We lodged together, you asked about some aspects of my abilities, and did not think to look into it, but rather, thought me a fool, but I am however a skilful man, and I know a remedy that will end your womanising. Earlier I heard that you were looking to make the daughter of the farmer your mistress.' He now snatched his forelock, sent him tumbling outside and recited:

> *You will understand,*
>
> *when you're shovelling shit,*
>
> *that you will never be*
>
> *An the Bow-bender;*
>
> *a bread bender*

> *not a Bow-bender,*
>
> *a cheese bender*
>
> *not an elm bender.'*

He bound him and shaved off his hair and covered him with tar, and said that he should fly as should anything feathered. He put out one of his eyes, then he castrated him. After that he turned him loose and gave him two staffs, - 'but I will take my arrow back.'

An said, 'It is called a king's treasure, if there is something unequalled. You are now altered somewhat, and so I send you now to King Ingjald, and I give you to him in compensation for one of his brothers, whenever one of them is compensated for.'

Ketil went to the ships and told the king, and his staffs bore witness to his disablement, but the sight of him was more evidence, for his eye and testicles were both missing. 'You are unfit for me,' said the king, and he drove him away.

Chapter Five

Now to tell of An, he said to the farmer, 'You welcomed me, and you should not suffer on my behalf. We must leave the farm and go to the forest, because the king's men will soon be here,' and they did that. An guessed rightly; the king sent men by night, who burned the farm and then went back.

The king said to his men: 'If An has escaped, then I will offer three marks of silver for his head, and I will make him an outlaw through all Norway.' This was heard widely. The king returned to his kingdom. An stayed with the farmer, and rebuilt his farm that summer.

In daily life An was dressed so that he had a white fur coat; it was so long that it went right to his heels. He wore over it a grey fur coat that came down to his mid-calf. Over that he had a red robe, and it came down to his knees. Over that, he had a homespun shirt that came down to his thighs. He had a hat on his head and a wood-axe in his hand. He was quite large and manly but not good-looking.

It happened one day that An met outside Drifa, the farmer's daughter. Three women went with her. She was the fairest and well dressed. She was in a red robe, long-sleeved and not wide below, and long in the body and tight at the waist. She had a lace ribbon round her forehead and was the best-haired of women. They laughed at him a lot, and mocked his get-up.

Drifa said: 'Where are you coming from now, fool?'

'From smithing,' said An. Up came the farmer and asked them not to mock him. An recited this verse:

The maidens asked me

when they met me,

fair-haired ones:

'Where do you come from, fool?'

But I say to

the silk-valkyrie

mocking her back:

'Where does mild weather come from?'

'It seems to me,' said An, 'your tunic suits you

no better than my shirt, because it hangs below the bottom of your cloak.' Then they parted. When the farm was rebuilt, the farmer told An in the autumn that he could stay there for the winter, - 'and you have worked well.'

An said he would accept. He liked the farmer's daughter, though she had made fun of his clothes, and he excused that. But in the spring he declared that he would go away and set himself another task. 'And if it turns out as I think that your daughter is pregnant, well, there are few men here, and I will admit to fathering the child. If it is a boy, then send him to me when you learn of my permanent home, and give him this ring as proof, but you may look after her yourself if it is a girl.'

And then he went away, east into the forest. There lay a footpad called Garan. And that day, as An went down the forest road, he saw that a man followed him in hiding. He had a black shield and a helmet on his head, a bow in hand, and a quiver on his back. He saw the newcomer and shot a broad arrow at his shield and it hardly went through it. An took aim at him and shot an arrow through the shield, and it went into his upper arm, so that he was wounded. The footpad said he thought that this was hard shooting so he laid down his weapon and went to meet this man and asked him his name. He said An was his name. Garan said he had heard his name, - 'and you're famous.'

An said, 'I have heard tell of you, always to your discredit.'

Garan said, 'I will be good to you. I want to offer to you to stay with me and be my comrade, and we will achieve much.'

An said, 'There'll be enough to do, if we want

to do evil.'

They came to a shack which stood in the forest, and the door was closed. They went in, and found no lack of treasure, weapons or armour. An saw two stones, one higher than the other. An asked what they could be.

Garan said: 'There I have tried the back strength of men who have visited me.'

An said, 'Cruelly have you dealt with your guests, but which stone would it be suitable to bend you over?'

He said he had not thought much about that, although the higher stone was better suited for reason of its height. The day drew on.

Garan said: 'Now we should prepare our supper. Which would you prefer, to get the water or make a fire?'

An said he would make the fire, because he said he was used to that work. When he was crouched down he threw his sword which he had as a weapon on his back. He heard a whine over him and the robber struck him, and he hit the sword, and that saved him. Then he jumped up and said, 'Now you are not faithful, and now you want to break our fellowship hastily, and I have done little to deserve this. Perhaps you will now stay on the high stone this evening.'

There was a hard struggle, and each wished to avoid the stones. It happened that Garan came near the stone. An stood on his instep, put his hands on his chest, bent him over the stone; and his spine broke apart. An left him dead. He cut off his head and dragged him outside and stuck his nose in his crotch so he would not walk after death[93]. The night went on. An was there over the summer, did no harm to anyone and did not let anyone see him. But with autumn approaching, he locked up the hall and went off and wanted to have other winter lodging.

In the evening of the day he came to a wealthy widow named Jorunn. He was there that night and hid his identity. When the lady came into the hall, she asked the guest his name. He said whatever he thought suitable. She walked away and turned back and said: 'Why did you come here? It is my hunch that you are An the Bow-bender.'

He said it was true.

'Why did you come here?' she said. 'You will find no protection from the king.'

An said he did not expect it would be needed any more, - 'I will risk being here, if you give permission.'

She said, 'I will not withhold food from you.'

He was there for a while and was busy running her estate, and that was a good arrangement.

An said: 'I would like to stay over winter with you but I'll not altogether commit myself to being your own man.'

She said it was not good for him to be there, - 'the king is searching for you; we can do little for you.'

He said that he believed King Ingjald would not harm him. 'I will not withhold food from you,' but he himself would manage his own affairs. He

[93] The approved remedy against the restless dead in the sagas.

became a very active man. Later a conversation occurred between them. He said that he had it in mind to propose marriage to her. She said it would have to be done with her relatives' consent and it was close to her thoughts, but no one tried to stop them, and they got married. An was the greatest of stewards and very adept. He had a boat-house in the forest not far from the farm, where he built a ship. Soon their stock of wealth and honour increased. He had four large farms, and with him thirty fighting men in each household. The men of the region took him as leader. He was popular and unstinting. King Ingjald heard this and searched for him. Thorir his brother often went eastward with offers of terms, and things were friendly between the brothers. By then their father Bjorn, in Hrafnista, was dead, and their brother-in-law Gaut kept the farm, and Thordis, their sister. Grim, their son, was tall, handsome and strong, and none of his relatives were as close to him in temperament as An. He went to him. An welcomed him, and he stayed there a long time. He was popular. Thorir often asked An to yield to the king, - 'and do not hesitate, brother, because I can see clearly he is cruelly disposed towards you.'

'Fate will settle things between the king and I,' said An, 'You trust him too much. I would rather you looked after our farm.' But it did not happen.

Chapter Six

There was a man named Ivar, of Upplander stock and noble lineage. He came to the court of King Ingjald, and he welcomed him well but he had not been there when An was with the king. Ivar was a skilful man. He had really set his heart on Asa and had asked to marry her. The king was slow to grant this. They talked over the matter among themselves. The king said, 'You are trying hard for this, and I will give you a chance. You should go to find An and bring me his head, and when you come back, you may expect this marriage that you request, because then you will be called a great man and suitable in-law for the king.'

Ivar said this was not easy to do, - 'but do you, the king's sister, consent to this plan?'

She answered, 'I'm going to submit to the decision of my brother, if you succeed on this errand.'

With this he went east inland to find An and to ask him for winter lodgings. An asked who he was, and said he could hardly know what sort of man at heart any man might be, but he wasn't prone to refusing men food, 'I do not expect recompense in return for food until I know how it is accepted or valued.' Ivar was keen to help him in building and other work.

One evening when they were going home Ivar thought about what he had to do. He ran at An and struck at him. An went quicker than Ivar thought and was taking big strides, and Ivar's stroke sank into the earth and all the way into a tree's roots. An noticed his attack and turned back and said that feeding him was not paying off. An bound him with a bow string, and drove him home before him. He kept Ivar chained for the night. But when people knew of this, they asked to kill him and they would tell him when they had done so. An said they should not. 'Then it would be said that I made myself the king's enemy, if people do not know the true story. I will call a big gathering and let the king's man tell his story and make clear to everyone the trouble he has made,' - and so it was done.

An came to the gathering and led Ivar after

him. An said, 'Tell us now about your errand.'

Ivar did so. Then all said that he had sentenced himself to death. An spoke, 'No,' he said, 'that will not be. I know who he had to visit at home, as you have heard.' He had his legs broken all the way to his knees and let them heal and twisted his feet in the opposite direction to before; then his toes pointed backwards[94]. An said, 'Stand now before me,' and so he does. An said, 'Now you're a king's treasure, because you are quite unlike other men.' Then he mangled his face somewhat and said, 'Now you will stand out from other men at both ends, your face is memorable and your feet are unlike other men's. Now go to King Ingjald. With you I will pay for his other brother, and now he has no reason to visit.'

Ivar met the king and said it had not gone smoothly. The king said, 'I know that men have fought and killed each other, but I barely knew that such injury could be done, and to call it a king's treasure, but it seems to me there is no treasure to be found in you, so go to your lands.'

The king's sister said, 'Do you not want to agree to him marrying me now?'

The king said that it was not the same, and Ivar had been overconfident that he would be successful, - 'and therefore no flat refusals were brought against you.'

Thorir had not long been at home.

After this, the king sent twelve men to bring back An's head and spoke thus: 'I will send you with

---

[94] A similar grisly punishment features in *The Saga of Halfdan, Foster Son of Brana.*

the intention of meeting An, to ask winter quarters from him, but he is generous and will ask, why do so many people travel together. Say that you pooled all your earnings together, and you trust no one to split them but him. If he takes you in, you should bring an equal number of men over to your side with gifts of treasure, and I say then it will be easy for you to stop him from getting away.'

Then they went to meet An, and their speech went as the king had expected. He took them in, and they stayed there until after Yule.

One evening Jorunn was talking with An. 'What do you think of the guests who have visited us?'

He said: 'I think that they are good men, and we may expect good from them.'

She said she did not believe that they would prove trustworthy, - 'and I suspect that either they have done wicked deeds or they are going to, because every time you go from your seat, they follow you, and afterwards change colour.'

He said he did not believe it.

'I am taking more trouble for you than I expected,' she said, 'I want you to leave the house in the morning, and if they do nothing suspicious, then what I say is not true. Say that you will be home in the evening and that you want to go alone, and if they bring any suspicion on themselves, then you will know what kind they are.' An agreed that he would do this.

The next morning An left the house, and when the winter guests saw it, they thought they had an opportunity to capture him, and they went away in two groups, six in each, but six spies stayed home

521

with six house-carles, who had taken treasure for An's head. There were six of them in ambush. They waited beside An's path. Jorunn met Grim and said that their movement seemed suspicious, - 'and go and get information.'

He said he was ready and went to the forest with many men, so that the others did not know, and they saw nothing. When the evening came, they thought it most needful to go home and wait for the right moment, so nothing would go wrong with their plot. They came home. An was already in the high seat and he was frowning. Grim had also come home. An said, 'It is now fitting for our winter guests to tell us their errand, and how they intended to see me dead today. I now know your plot, and for a long time I suspected your guile against me, but I do not have trusty servants.'

They had to admit it.

An said, 'I will not kill my household, let them go. But I give the king's men into the power of Grim, my uncle, and he may be entertained with them today.' Grim said this was well said. He went to the forest with them and hanged them all together on one gallows.

King Ingjald heard of this and took it very badly. Thorir had come to the court. He was silent and seemed very angry about something. The king asked why he was so silent, - 'we want to treat you well, as before.'

Thorir said: 'I do not question that, but it is hardly comfortable.'

The king asked: 'What is lacking about this, beside what my father did?'

'I do not complain about this,' said Thorir,

'but your father gave me greater gifts, such as this sword.'

The king said, 'Is it a great treasure?'

'See,' said Thorir.

The king took it and drew the sword, and said, 'Not the possession of a man dishonoured.'

Thorir said: 'Take it, sir.'

The king said: 'I do not want it: you shall have it and it will be yours longest.' He went up to Thorir on the throne, and thrust him through, and left the sword in the wound. He said, 'Many will be the gifts we exchange, An and I.' Then he went to his ship, and there were sixty men crewing it, and told them to go and find An and lay anchor by him and lure him onto the ship, - 'and say that Thorir has come here, his brother, and he wants to arrange peace. If he comes into your grip, kill him, and then some compensation will be paid for my brothers. Go to An early in the day.'

This deed was spoken of in much disapproval, and he was now called Ingjald the Ill by men.

They went their way. But the night before they came ashore, An had a dream and told Jorunn: 'It seemed to me Thorir came here looking mournful, but he has always come to me when he appears in a dream. But I don't want those who bring him here to come in vain, my mind tells me, as he seemed to me all covered in blood, and there was a sword through him.'

She said that it might be true, that would explain his dream. An jumped up and said that men would come. He had prepared four vessels, and two were anchored off an outlying isle, the other two in a secret creek by the harbour near the farm. An sent men to the settlement to tell people to prepare a joyous ale to welcome Thorir if he came happy and whole, otherwise to ready their weapons. An remained at the farm, but his men on the ships, and he waited for whatever would be at hand. After that, they saw a ship sailing into the harbour by the farm with red shields on. The crew sent An a message to come down and meet Thorir his brother who had come to seek a reconciliation. An said, 'Often he has thought it a small thing to walk up to the house, but now he falls short.'

They said that he was sleepy. An said he would go down to the ship, but no further. They dared not to go with him and pushed Thorir out of the ship and asked An to accept King Ingjald's present. An picked Thorir up and said: 'You have paid for your credulity, you trusted the king, but there is something more important to do than rebuke you.'

He put him in the cave whose mouth jutted out, and jumped up onto the ship and lifted a red shield. He was now upon them, and they fought, and men of King Ingjald fell wounded. One man fought on his knees. Grim attacked him, but the man struck the back of his knees and cut off his calf to his heel bone and he was stiff-legged before he was healed. They killed every mother's son. An had a mound built and had the ship set inside with Thorir on the afterdeck, but the king's men on either side, so that it seemed that all served him. Grim was healed. The king now heard the news, although his honour and dignity had not grown much.

Chapter Seven

One morning when An was at the home at his farm he said, 'I think this,' he said, 'that there are very many men in the woods, and maybe, when it comes down to it, a king's might is great and a king's luck is great.' Then An woke up his retainers and said, 'Often it is evident that I married well. Jorunn has often warned me that I should not sit here to meet the king's hatred, but I wanted to meet him face-to-face, however it will be turn out.' Then he took a pole and cut it in two and carved a hand grip on the two pieces. An said, 'When we come out, we will be surrounded, but I think it wrong to flee. But Grim and I will not come to weapons,' and he told him to take the other wooden club, and so he did.

They now turned to the sea. There the king came with a large host. An cleared the path before him, and swung his club on either hand. The king's men thought that it was no good to put up with that, but An's men came after them, and many were killed, but the women fled for protection from Jorunn. An and Grim went aboard a rowing boat and saw the king's fleet around him, but a scout ship was in the middle of the sound. An said that he thought it would be good if they did them some mean trick, - 'since they are set to do harm to us.'

An flung a forked boathook of iron under the gunwale of the boat, and it happened that the blue sea entered at this place, and men called to the king's ship that they must help them. An escaped out between them. An said that Grim would be more useful at rowing if both his legs were equal. He said nothing should be lost because of this. An noticed no earlier than when the oar handles struck him between the shoulders, that Grim had died from exhaustion from rowing. An went overboard, and now wanted least of all the king's men to lay their hands on him. They saw that a man had stepped overboard, and the other lay dead in the bilge water. They told the king this.

He said: 'It was my expectation that An would begrudge us laying hands on him, but it shall all come to the same thing, and we shall set guards all along the coast so he shall not land.'

This had come to An's mind, and he turned and swam to an outlying island, and went ashore there and was utterly exhausted. A man called Erp lived there with his wife. There were no other people. Erp was checking the beaches and had taken a wagon and he saw that a big man lay on the beach. The farmer thought him dead and that things had gone poorly for him. An told him to tread boldly. Erp said: 'You would have a better blanket beside Jorunn at home.'

He drove him home now, and his feet stuck out of the cart. His wife asked him not to bring home dead men. Erp said it was not that way and he explained things to her. She said that they would have much treasure if a good warrior was about. Then An regained much strength. King Ingjald thought An dead, and he went home. An was with the old man, and when he was healed, Erp ferried him to the mainland. An said that they had done well and he gave the woman gold, but he gave Erp the island and said their reward would be much more in time. Then An came home. Jorunn had kept things up efficiently meanwhile, but she lacked much that appearances could be maintained. The men warmly welcomed An, but he said to his wife, 'I have not always been fair about money with you until now.'

She said she could not grumble if he remained with her. It came to his mind that it would not be a bad idea to check the money in Garan's hut, because he thought now there was a need for it. He brought it home now and said to Jorunn, 'Here you may see my belongings,' and told everyone about his good fortune. It seemed he wasn't poor, as people had thought. Their wealth returned to normal as before or more.

Then An sent out scouts on all sides. King Ingjald heard this, and he had guards surround him and slept in a hut with his retinue. An went on with his smithing, as before. And one evening, as he walked from the smithy, he saw a fire burning on an island. He had thought that the king must be visiting or vagabonds were after his treasure. He was curious and went to sea by himself, and took a boat and rowed to the island. He saw a man sitting by the fire, youthful and big. He wore a shirt and linen breeches. He was eating. A silver dish stood before him. He had an ivory handled knife and he stabbed pieces of food up from the kettle and ate whatever came up, but threw it back when it cooled, and took up another. An thought he was not being cautious. He shot at him, and the arrow hit the piece of meat he was taking up from the kettle, and it fell into the ashes. He put the arrow down beside him and kept eating as before. An shot a second arrow, and it hit the dish in front of him, which broke into two pieces. The man sat still and paid no attention to this. Then An shot a third arrow, and it hit the knife handle that stuck out from his hand, and the handle flew apart into two pieces. Then the young man said: 'This man did me harm, but to little avail did he ruin my knife.'

He snatched up his bow, but An thought it

was not certain where a badly shot arrow would fly. He walked to the other side of an oak, and kept it between them. The young man shot the first arrow so that An thought it would have hit him in the middle, if he had waited; another looked like it would have hit his ribs, the third his eye, and all stuck in the oak where An had been standing. Then the young man said, 'It would be best for the man who shoots at me to show himself now, and we should meet, if he has a claim against me.'

An went out, and they began wrestling, and their struggle was very mighty. An tired soon, because the other was strong-legged and tough. An asked for a rest, but the young man said he was ready for either rest or fighting, and An got his own way. He asked: 'What is your name?'

He said he was called Thorir, and said his father was called An, - 'Who are you?'

'My name is An,' he said.

The young man said: 'That must be true since many of your belongings are now An-available, and you are now An-aware of this wether, which I stole.'

An said, 'Let's not resort to hateful words, and this sheep was of little worth, but what tokens have you, if you find your father?'

'I think I have a sign of the truth of my story, but I am not obliged to show you it,' said Thorir. An said it would be better all the same to show the signs of his fatherhood. Thorir showed him the ring. An said, 'True are these signs that you have met your father here, now we'll go home and get better lodgings.'

Then they did so and went home, and his men sat and waited for him with fear and apprehension, because they did not know what had befallen him. An sat in his seat and Thorir with him. Jorunn asked who this young man was. An asked him to introduce himself. He said: 'My name is Thorir, and I am the son of An.'

She said, 'It has come to this, as it is said, that everyone is richer than he thinks. You did not tell me that you had this son, but I think this is not unimportant. Pull off his wet shoes and socks. How old you are?'

'Eighteen years,' said Thorir.

She said: 'I think that I shall call you High-leg, because I have seen no one taller at the knees.'

He said: 'I like this name, and you will give me a naming gift, so that they call me that.'

She said this was true and gave him much gold.

An asked Thorir about growing up with the old man. He said that the word had gone out that a daughter had been born, 'because King Ingjald wanted to kill me, and I fled to the north when I could.'

Thorir stayed there for the winter.

An said one day: 'I do not intend to feed you sitting here any longer if you do not prove yourself.'

He said he had no valuables except the ring.

An said it would be better to have a mission, - 'it seems to me that you are obliged to avenge your namesake on King Ingjald. I suppose that it is your destiny, rather than others of our kindred, because it is proven that the king and I will never lay hands on each other, and you didn't need to visit here except if you were to take revenge, whether you owe me or not. You shall have the sword Thane, and if you succeed in this work, the king's sister is there. Take her with you and give her a son in compensation for her brother.'

Thorir said it would be done and he sailed the ship fully prepared to war, and in the autumn he had five ships, well equipped. He was a very bold man and strong, and the greatest Viking warrior. He came to King Ingjald's farm by night and set fire to the hall. At the smoke, men awoke. King Ingjald asked who had started the fire. He said it was Thorir High-leg there.

The king said: 'It may be that these sparks have flown from Drifa, the old man's daughter, which I have long suspected, and it may be that our goose is cooked.'

Thorir said that he wanted his crimes to end. King Ingjald had the wall beams broken up and carried to the door, and said he did not want to burn. Then they ran out. Thorir was standing nearby when the king came out, and he struck him his death blow. He carried off Asa, and took with him much of the wealth and sent both to his father. An welcomed Asa and Thorir went out raiding and did many brave deeds. He was an outstanding man and much like his father. Thorir visited An when he became wealthy, and was well received. He stayed there for the winter.

But that spring, An said that he wanted to go off - 'and I give you all my lands, but don't covet the possessions that King Ingjald had, for it is not long before the petty kings will be no more[95]. It is better

---

[95] This is a prophecy of the conquests of Harald Finehair, first king of all Norway, in whose day Iceland and other countries

to consider your own honour than sit in a higher place only to be cast down. But I will go north to my estate on Hrafnista. Take care of Erp and your foster-father and mother.'

Then An went north and Thorir became a great man. An came north to an island, and he had a daughter there, named Mjoll, mother of Thorstein, son of Ketil Raum, father of Ingimund the Old in Vatnsdal[96]. An had often to fight skin-clad people in the north there, and he was considered the greatest of men. The son of Thorir was Ogmund Field-destroyer, father of Sigurd Table-Bald, a noble man in Norway.

And here ends the saga of An the Bow-bender.

---

were settled by refugees from what they perceived as his tyranny.
[96] In Iceland.

ABOUT THE TRANSLATOR

Gavin Chappell was born in northern England and lives near Liverpool. After studying English at the University of Wales, he has since worked variously as a business analyst, a college lecturer and an editor. He is the author of numerous short stories, articles, poems and several books.